Praise for
the Merry Widows Series

Just One of Those Flings

"It might be just one of those flings, but it's a grand reading experience in Hern's capable hands. She brings the Regency to life with her endearing characters, whose steamy passion only serves to heighten the powerful emotions and leave you begging for more."
—*Romantic Times* (4½ stars, top pick)

"Effervescent, unconventional, and brimming with honest sensuality, Hern's second installment in her clever, well-conceived Merry Widows series about five wealthy widows bent on avoiding marriage but experimenting with affairs is a lively, thoroughly delightful tale that is sure to please."
—*Library Journal* (starred review)

"Brilliant characterization, steamy love scenes, and witty dialogue make *Just One of Those Flings* one of the most engaging books I have read this year."
—Historical Romance Writers

continued . . .

"Candice Hern writes as an artist paints—with beautiful lines and special attention to details. The final piece of work is something to treasure. The May/December romance between Beatrice and Gabriel only made their love affair even more special. . . . The final declaration of their love is unforgettable . . . a beautifully written romance. It absolutely gets a Top Pick from me!"   —Romance Readers at Heart

"Hern writes the best kind of romances—ones with the love story front and center and told with solid writing, a strong sense of purpose, and unapologetic eroticism. She envelopes the reader in the depth, the sensuality, and the fantasy of the story so that before one is aware, the last page has turned with nothing having jarred one from the romantic reading experience."
—Romance by the Book

In the Thrill of the Night

"Shimmers with humor and sexual tension that only someone with Hern's sensibilities about the era and women's fantasies could write. Here is the idle night's guilty pleasure."
—*Romantic Times* (4½ stars, top pick)

"Outrageously sexy fun as only Candice can deliver. . . . Every page is pure satisfaction."
—Lisa Kleypas

Lady Be Bad

The Merry Widows Series

Candice Hern

A SIGNET ECLIPSE BOOK

SIGNET ECLIPSE
Published by New American Library, a division of
Penguin Group (USA) Inc., 375 Hudson Street,
New York, New York 10014, USA
Penguin Group (Canada), 90 Eglinton Avenue East, Suite 700, Toronto,
Ontario M4P 2Y3, Canada (a division of Pearson Penguin Canada Inc.)
Penguin Books Ltd., 80 Strand, London WC2R 0RL, England
Penguin Ireland, 25 St. Stephen's Green, Dublin 2,
Ireland (a division of Penguin Books Ltd.)
Penguin Group (Australia), 250 Camberwell Road, Camberwell, Victoria 3124,
Australia (a division of Pearson Australia Group Pty. Ltd.)
Penguin Books India Pvt. Ltd., 11 Community Centre, Panchsheel Park,
New Delhi - 110 017, India
Penguin Group (NZ), 67 Apollo Drive, Rosedale, North Shore 0745,
Auckland, New Zealand (a division of Pearson New Zealand Ltd.)
Penguin Books (South Africa) (Pty.) Ltd., 24 Sturdee Avenue,
Rosebank, Johannesburg 2196, South Africa

Penguin Books Ltd., Registered Offices:
80 Strand, London WC2R 0RL, England

First published by Signet Eclipse, an imprint of New American Library,
a division of Penguin Group (USA) Inc.

First Printing, August 2007
10 9 8 7 6 5 4 3 2 1

Copyright © Candice Hern, 2007
All rights reserved

SIGNET ECLIPSE and logo are trademarks of Penguin Group (USA) Inc.

Printed in the United States of America

PUBLISHER'S NOTE
This is a work of fiction. Names, characters, places, and incidents either are
the product of the author's imagination or are used fictitiously, and any resemblance to actual persons, living or dead, business establishments, events, or
locales is entirely coincidental.
    The publisher does not have any control over and does not assume any
responsibility for author or third-party Web sites or their content.

Dedicated with love
to Betsy Berger

ACKNOWLEDGMENTS

As always, a big shout-out to my blog partners, the Fog City Divas (www.fogcitydivas.com), many of whom are also brainstorming partners. Thanks also to Diana Dempsey and Lynn Hanna for additional brainstorming help. Special thanks to my editor, Ellen Edwards, for her extraordinary patience, and for introducing me to a fabulous little Greek restaurant in Greenwich Village; to my agent, Annelise Robey, who is always there with support and encouragement, even when I don't derserve it; and to the New American Library art department for another beautiful cover.

I'd also like to send out big, sloppy kisses to all the Bluestockings (and a Shroom or two) at the Candice Hern Discussion Board (www.candicehern.com/board). You guys are the best! Your kind words of enthusiasm about my books keep me motivated. I hope Rochdale lives up to your expectations!

$\mathcal{P}rologue$

"There is not a woman in London whose bed I could not seduce my way into with very little effort."

John Grayston, seventh Viscount Rochdale, was a bit the worse for drink, having spent the last hour and a half in the card room at Oscott House, where obliging footmen kept his glass filled. But his statement was no idle boast fueled by too much claret. It was a fact, pure and simple.

His companion, Lord Sheane, had commented that some women would never allow themselves to be enticed into a love affair, and Rochdale could not allow the remark to stand unchallenged. Women, all women, were hungry for seduction—some openly, others unwittingly. It was no great accomplishment to get any one of them between the sheets. All it took was a quick assessment of the game, to determine whether she wanted the Great Lover or the Notorious Libertine. In his considerable experience, he'd found that most women of the *ton* were intrigued by the wicked nature of his reputation, by the unsavory tales associated with him, most of which were true. Even the highest-ranking ladies of the aristocracy enjoyed the notion of flirting with danger.

There were a few, though, who simply wanted him for his lovemaking skills. Their indifferent or bungling husbands sent them in search of sexual satisfaction elsewhere, and Rochdale was pleased to accommodate them.

Then there were the ones who didn't know they desired him, who generally believed they wanted nothing to do with him. The ones who loathed his love affairs and his scandals and did their best to avoid him. Those were the real challenges. But he'd never failed to successfully seduce one of those supposedly virtuous women once he'd set out to do so.

No, it had been no idle boast. He knew precisely how to make any woman desire him.

Lord Sheane narrowed his eyes at Rochdale over the rim of his wineglass. "Is that so?" He had to raise his voice to be heard over the music in the adjacent ballroom and the general hubbub of voices and laughter in the card room. "No woman in London can resist you?"

Rochdale shrugged his shoulders. It was not a subject that required debate. Of course, a man like Sheane, who'd gone a bit soft in the belly and jowly around the mouth, would label Rochdale arrogant rather than admit to his own envy.

"Shall we put it to the test, old boy?"

Rochdale arched an eyebrow. "I beg your pardon?"

"You said you could seduce any woman in London." Lord Sheane's mouth twisted into a sneer. "Are you willing to prove it?"

A familiar prickle of anticipation settled in the base of Rochdale's spine. He braced himself for the irresistible siren call of a wager. Donning an air of supreme indifference, he said, "What did you have in mind?"

"I'll stake Albion that I can name a woman you cannot seduce."

Albion? Damnation. Sheane, the blackguard, knew Rochdale had coveted that particular horse ever since he'd won the second class at Oatlands last year. He'd twice offered to buy the bay gelding, but Sheane had refused. Albion was a winner and the star of Sheane's stables. And yet here he was now, offering the horse as stakes in a wager he was bound to lose. It was almost too good to be true. Was the fellow so drunk he did not realize what he was doing?

"Has Albion suffered an injury?" Rochdale asked. "You seem anxious to be rid of him."

Sheane threw back his head and laughed. "Damn me, but you are an arrogant bastard. So much so that I am sure you would have no qualms in offering Serenity as your stakes in our little wager."

"You think to win Serenity off me?" Rochdale chuckled. "I don't think so." Serenity was his best horse, his favorite horse. The little chestnut mare had won more races than any other horse in Rochdale's stables, including the king's plate at Nottingham and two cups at Newmarket. He would as soon cut off his arm as give Serenity to Lord Sheane.

But, of course, if he accepted the wager, he would have to do no such thing, for he could not lose.

"If you are so confident," Sheane said, "then you will have no qualms about offering her as stakes. My Albion against your Serenity that you cannot seduce a woman of my choosing. What do you say?"

It was too easy. Rochdale studied the man closely, wondering what trick he must have up his sleeve. He had lost a fair amount of money to Rochdale that evening, but for an inveterate gambler like Sheane, it meant nothing. And he would no doubt win it all back, and more, tomorrow night, or the night after that. Such was the life of a gambler.

But a gambler never bet against a sure thing. What was Sheane up to?

Rochdale held out his glass while a footman refilled it, then took a swallow of claret. "You have a particular woman in mind, I suppose."

"One or two, actually."

Rochdale gave a crack of laughter, and several heads turned in his direction. He lowered his voice and said, "One or two? You believe there is more than one woman immune to my charms?"

"Your arrogance will be your undoing, Rochdale. I am certain there are several women at this very ball whom even you could not seduce."

"Then let us be more specific in the wager. You must name a woman in attendance here tonight." Not that he had any doubts about the matter, but at least that would limit the field to women of his own class. Rochdale could not imagine a single woman among those in the ballroom whom he could not coax into bed. It might prove to be unpleasant if the chosen woman was a gnarled and wizened antique, or had a face that would curdle cream. Or was, God forbid, the wife of a friend. But he could do it. For the chance to add Albion to his stables, he could do it.

"All right," Sheane said. "One of the guests at this ball. Excellent. So, here is the wager: I shall name a woman and charge you with seducing her. If you fail, I get Serenity. If you succeed, you get Albion."

"How long do I have? These things can take time, you know. It is to be a seduction, after all, not a ravishment."

"Until the end of the Season?"

"Hmm. That is less than two months. It may not be enough time."

Sheane scowled. "Good God, you astonish me. I thought you were a master at wooing women into your bed. And yet, two months is not long enough?"

"A master knows that a true seduction can take two minutes or two years, depending on the woman. Certain delicate creatures require more seducing than others. Since I do not yet know the identity of the woman, how can I say how long it will take?"

Lord Sheane snorted. "There must be a time frame. Where is the sport in an open-ended wager?"

"Indeed. Then let us name a date."

"It cannot be years, Rochdale. The horses will not be worth winning if we drag this thing out too long. Suppose we use the Goodwood Races as a deadline? You are planning to run Serenity for the Cup, are you not? If it takes longer than three months to bed a woman, then you are not the man you claim to be."

"All right, then. Goodwood it is. I will seduce the woman you name by then or forfeit Serenity. But if I succeed before Goodwood, I win Albion. Agreed?"

"Agreed."

Rochdale offered his hand and Sheane shook it with a level of enthusiasm that boded ill. Rochdale did not trust him. What harpy was the man going to inflict upon him?

"Let us survey the ballroom," Sheane said, "shall we?"

Lord Sheane placed his empty glass on a side table and made his way through the maze of card tables. Rochdale upended his own glass and finished the last of his claret. He followed Sheane and saw that he spoke to several gentlemen on his way, each of them laughing and turning to gaze at Rochdale.

Damnation. He was making their wager known. Rochdale had had enough public scandal in his life. He had no desire to play out another seduction under the eyes of every gambler and club man in London. They would all be laying in bets for or against him. How was he to seduce a woman if it was public knowledge that a wager was involved? No woman in her right mind would succumb to him under such circumstances.

He caught up with Sheane as he was laughing with Sir Giles Clitheroe. "A word with you, Sheane." He caught the man by the sleeve and led him out of the room.

When they were in the main corridor, Rochdale turned to him and said, "I will not have this wager made public, Sheane."

"Since when have you developed such fine sensibilities?"

"Since I wagered my best horse. I will not have you jeopardize my chances by trumpeting the wager to the world." He lowered his voice as a couple in conversation walked past. "If the woman got wind of it, you cannot imagine she would welcome my advances."

"Ah, but you said *any* woman in London. Correction: You amended your boast to encompass only those women in attendance tonight. But you said nothing about what they may or may not know of the wager."

Rochdale put his face so close to Sheane's that their noses almost touched. "Let us say that I would not consider it sporting if you were to make the wager public. Do you take my meaning, sir?"

Sheane raised his eyes to the ceiling and stepped back. "Dammit, Rochdale, there is no need to threaten me. All right, then. I promise to keep the wager in confidence."

"How many men in the card room already know?"

Sheane heaved a sigh. "Clitheroe, Dewesbury, and Haltwhistle."

"Confound it. Do they know which woman you will name?"

"No."

"Good. Let's keep it that way. Do we understand each other?"

"Yes, yes. What a fusspot of an old woman you've become, Rochdale. But I suppose that business last year with Serena Underwood took a bit of the wind out of your sails, eh?"

Rochdale would not be baited by reminders of his most notorious indiscretion. "Name your woman, Sheane. Let me see how easy this is going to be."

"All right, then."

He made a show of surveying the room, which was filled with pretty young girls in white dresses smiling at the men who partnered them in the country dance. Sheane would not choose one of them. There were just as many older women, mothers and chaperones of the pretty dancing girls. Some of them handsome. Some of them gone to seed. Would he choose one of them? There were the dowagers, too, the grandmotherly types in plumed turbans, gathered in gossipy groups along the walls. God help him if Sheane chose one of those. And there were the wallflowers—spinsters growing a bit long in the tooth after too many Seasons, or younger women too unattractive to entice a dance partner.

Rochdale eyed every one of them, judging how he might woo her into his bed, regardless of how distasteful an exercise it would be.

"Her," Sheane announced. "I name her."

Rochdale followed the man's gaze and groaned aloud. "Mrs. Marlowe? The bishop's widow?"

"The very one. There's your challenge, Rochdale. And what a challenge she will be." He cackled in glee as they watched Mrs. Grace Marlowe walk past, chatting with Lady Gosforth. She glanced in his direction and caught him staring at her, pursed her lips in disapproval, and turned away.

Rochdale shook his head in disgust. He ought to have known Sheane would pick the most prim and proper woman in the room. As straitlaced a prude as ever lived. The widow of that old windbag Bishop Marlowe, for God's sake.

Grace Marlowe was young and attractive, to be sure. If he did not know who she was, Rochdale would no doubt find her desirable, with all that honey blond hair, those smoky gray eyes, and that perfectly sculpted profile. But he did know her, and no amount of beauty could change the fact that she was the

Widow Marlowe, hailed by one and all as a Good Woman. A God-fearing woman. A do-gooder. The sort of woman who despised men like him.

But in his long career he had broken down the defenses of more than one so-called virtuous woman. He knew how to get around their fine scruples and tenacious morality. Mrs. Marlowe might be a more difficult case, but he had no doubts about his success.

"A challenge, indeed," he said. "I shall find no joy in it, but seduce her I will."

Sheane raised his eyebrows. "You think so, do you?"

"I know so. I have no intention of handing my best horse over to you. And I covet that bay gelding of yours. I shall alert my head groom to make room for him in the stables."

"I would not get your hopes up, Rochdale. That woman will not be seduced. I guarantee it."

"Yes, she will." He watched her walk away and detected the merest hint of a sway in the hips beneath the silk of her skirts. "She will be one of those delicate cases that will take a bit longer than others. But I shall have her before Goodwood. *I* guarantee it."

Chapter 1

She would not panic. Grace Marlowe never panicked. She prided herself on her stalwart composure in any situation. Even as she watched her friends'
carriage disappear down the drive, leaving her alone
at night in a small tucked-away villa two hours from
London with the worst libertine in all of England, she
refused to panic.

Grace stood in the open doorway and did not move.
The night air had grown chilly and the carriage was
long out of sight, but she did not turn around. *He*
stood behind her. Lord Rochdale. She could feel his
presence like an ill wind at her back, could feel his
eyes on her, assessing, judging, mocking.

Those heavy-lidded blue eyes had been plaguing her
for weeks. At balls and concerts and routs, they
seemed to seek her out, to follow her, to compel her
to return his gaze. She never did, of course. He was
a horrid man with a horrid reputation. He'd seduced
countless women and utterly ruined at least one.
Grace could not imagine what possible interest he
could have in a woman like her, a woman of high
morals and impeccable propriety, but his unsettling
gaze seemed to follow her everywhere. She had no

intention, however, of giving him the satisfaction of seeing even a hint of discomposure.

At first she had assumed he was simply leering at her the way he did every woman under the age of ninety, and she'd ignored him. But he had not been rebuffed, and his continued attentions had begun to seriously annoy her, even to frighten her a little. At a public gathering she could turn away and pretend not to notice him. But here . . .

"Well, now." His voice was low and tinged with mockery. "This is an interesting development, is it not, Mrs. Marlowe? Your friends have sadly deserted you, leaving you all alone here. With me. They must have great faith in your resourcefulness. Or my restraint. And so here we are, you and I, with this house all to ourselves. Whatever shall we do?"

Grace turned and was brought up short to find him closer than she'd expected. His proximity caused her almost to lose her balance, and she instinctively put up her hands to steady herself, only to find them pressed against the buttons of Lord Rochdale's waistcoat. He chuckled softly as she quickly removed them and stepped back.

He was half a head taller than she was, and was still close enough to seem to loom over her, so she took another step back and set about collecting herself. She brushed at her skirts to give her hands something else to do, and said, "This entire evening has been a series of interesting developments, sir, from the moment we heard that poor Emily had been prevailed upon to run off with you, until her young gallant knocked you flat."

Rochdale smiled and fingered the darkening bruise beneath one eye. "Your tender ministrations helped to soothe my wounded pride. But in my defense, ma'am, allow me to say that it was I who was prevailed upon, not Miss Thirkill. The whole thing was that little vixen's idea."

"And I daresay you did not think to dissuade her, even knowing she likely had no idea what she was doing."

"She's a beautiful young lady. What man could have resisted such a tempting offer, to be the instrument of her ruin?"

"Not you, certainly."

Emily Thirkill, a headstrong girl of seventeen, was the niece of Grace's friend Beatrice, Lady Somerfield, who was acting as Emily's chaperone for the Season. When it was discovered that the wretched girl had run off with the notoriously wicked Lord Rochdale, Grace had accompanied Beatrice in her pursuit of the runaway. Mr. Jeremy Burnett, who was in love with Emily, had also insisted on coming with them, and he had brought along Lord Thayne to be his second, in the event of a duel. Thank heaven it had not come to that, as it appeared they had arrived before the girl's seduction and ruin were complete, and Lord Thayne had persuaded his young friend to forgo the scandal of a duel. Grace was pleased, however, that Mr. Burnett had not allowed Rochdale to escape entirely unscathed.

She had, though, felt awkward and uncomfortable when prevailed upon to help Beatrice tend to the cuts and bruises inflicted on Lord Rochdale by Mr. Burnett.

"Certainly not," he said. "When a pretty girl asks me to take her away and make love to her, I am generally happy to oblige. But since the lot of you arrived in the nick of time, so to speak, no harm has been done." He lowered his voice and quirked a flirtatious smile. "Not yet, anyway."

Grace lifted her eyes heavenward and sent up a silent prayer. How was she to deal with this loathsome man? He was precisely the sort of gentleman—if such a term could be used to describe him—who rendered her most uncomfortable. His blue eyes, which her friend Beatrice had called "bedroom eyes," were too knowing, his black hair too long and deliberately rakish, his tall form too languid in its grace. She could observe him from afar, flirting and flattering and dallying, bringing laughter and blushes and yearning glances from other women. But whenever he turned that roguish, assessing gaze on her, which was rather too frequently of late, she always had the cowardly inclination to run and hide.

Outward composure, however, was second nature to Grace. Her late husband, the great Bishop Marlowe, had trained her well in presenting a serene, unflappable face to the world. One odious man was not going to break her.

"I can only rejoice," she said, stepping back and putting more distance between them, "that we were able to remove that poor girl from your clutches, Lord Rochdale. And for her sake, I trust that no unseemly gossip about her will make its way through the clubs."

"No need to give me that fish-eye glare, my dear Mrs. Marlowe. Thayne already extracted an oath from me in that regard, though he needn't have been so deuced high-handed about it. Say what you will about me, I am not one to spread tales. I am, in fact, the very soul of discretion."

Grace gave a derisive little snort. "Indeed? And here I thought you were famous for debauching young ladies and publicly abandoning them."

He arched an eyebrow. "You presume a great deal of knowledge about my private business, madam."

"Even respectable women hear tales of your . . . amorous adventures, my lord."

"For shame, Mrs. Marlowe. I would have expected an upstanding churchgoing woman like yourself to be above such gossip."

The truth of his words brought a brief flush of heat to her cheeks. "I do not spread gossip, sir. But one cannot help hearing the tales. I am sure every vigilant mother in London has heard them and warned her daughters about you."

"Do you have daughters, Mrs. Marlowe?"

"No."

"Then why do you care?"

Grace opened her mouth to speak and found she had no honest response. Instead, she clamped her lips tightly together and said nothing.

His lip curled into a mocking smile. "It is neither here nor there to me what tales are spread about town, Mrs. Marlowe. People may say whatever they want about me. And frequently do."

"And the ladies? Do you have no concern for involving their names in public speculation or scandal?"

His blue eyes regarded her with amused contempt. "I always allow the lady to decide how public or private a love affair should be, as it really doesn't matter to me in the least. As Miss Thirkill's family—and Thayne, for some reason—wish tonight's little episode to remain a secret, I have promised not to speak of it, and I will not. In fact, for you, my dear Mrs. Marlowe, I shall go a step further, just to prove what a . . . er . . . gentleman I can be. If gossip about tonight does arise somehow, I promise to put a halt to it by stating emphatically that the girl was never here. I trust that will eliminate any apprehension on your part."

Grace was a bit taken aback by this unexpected pledge. She was not entirely prepared to trust him, but for now would have to take him at his word. "Thank you, Lord Rochdale."

He reached out and touched her forehead, just above the bridge of her nose, causing her to flinch. "Do not look so puzzled, my dear. It creases your lovely brow, which is much too fine a thing to mar."

She took another step backward, instinctively shrinking from his touch and the unwelcome tingle on her skin it left behind.

He grinned at her retreat. "I am not a complete ogre, you know. Not all of the time, anyway. I actually have a scruple or two. At least, I think I must have one somewhere, otherwise tonight would have turned out quite differently."

"I am glad to hear it, my lord," she said in a clear voice that betrayed nothing of how unsettling his touch had been. "In fact, I shall call upon those scruples right now, if I may. I should like to request the use of your carriage to take me back to town."

His dark brows lifted in mock surprise. "What? So soon? When we're alone at last? Surely you are not in that big a hurry. Do come back inside, Mrs. Marlowe, and relax for a while. You must allow me to offer you a brandy, or sherry, if you prefer, to calm your nerves after such a trying evening. I could have a cold supper prepared, if you like. A cozy table by the fire, just the two of us."

She regarded him with a practiced arrogance that generally discouraged unwelcome attentions. Not that she expected it would work on Rochdale. "No, thank you, my lord." She kept her tone excruciatingly polite, even though she knew that what he was suggesting was anything *but* polite. He was deliberately trying to provoke her outrage, which seemed to amuse him, but she would not give him the satisfaction. "All I require is your carriage. At once, if you please."

"Well, as it happens, I do *not* please. I was hoping to stretch out in front of the fire for a while with a beefsteak on my eye, a brandy in my hand, and you by my side to keep me amused." He heaved a sigh. "But as I can see you are determined to be off, I shall forgo the beefsteak and bring a flask along with me. Happily, I shall still have you by my side to amuse me."

Grace's famous reserve almost slipped. "I . . . I beg your pardon? I did not mean that you should—"

"My dear Mrs. Marlowe, surely you do not believe

I would allow you to travel all the way to London alone? So late at night?" He shook his head and tried to appear serious, though his eyes twinkled wickedly. "I would never forgive myself if some harm came to you on the road. I shall certainly accompany you."

"That will not be necessary, my lord, I assure you."

"Of course it is."

Grace's head began to buzz with unsettling visions of two hours with this beastly man in the close confines of a carriage. It was not to be borne. "I do not wish to be rude, Lord Rochdale, but I would prefer to travel alone."

"I am sure you would. But that is not how it will be. I must return to town myself in any case, so it will be more convenient for us to travel together."

"Please, my lord, I—"

"If you wish to return to London, Mrs. Marlowe, it will be with me beside you. Now, come inside and make yourself comfortable while I instruct the coachman to prepare the carriage. I daresay there will be time for a glass of sherry while you wait."

Grace Marlowe, who seldom allowed spirits to pass her lips, hoped the glass would be a very large one.

It was almost too good to be true.

Rochdale had been doing his subtle best to get under her skin for quite some time now. She was a difficult case, to be sure. A delicious challenge. He'd been studying her for weeks, circling like a predator planning his attack. Her outward reserve, that cool self-restraint, lay over her as smooth as the features of an elegant bird, tightly and neatly arranged, not even a wisp of down out of place. The perfect image of unruffled calm. Yet if one looked closely, as he so often did, miniscule hints of disarray, almost invisible, could be discerned beneath the pristine plumage. It was those tiny disorderly feathers he intended to keep tweaking, in hopes of ultimately dislodging all the rest.

Contrary to popular belief, Rochdale had little experience seducing virtuous women. In point of fact, he'd spent most of his adult life avoiding them. When it came right down to it, though, he supposed they were no different from the rest. Manipulative. Grasping. Shrewish. The primary difference with a woman like Grace Marlowe was that her sexual nature would be tightly repressed or closely guarded. It would take some finesse to coax it into the open, but who better to do so than the Great Libertine?

He had watched her everywhere, and made sure she knew he was watching. She'd pretended to ignore him, but he could read her uneasiness in the way she held her body, in the tight tone of her voice, in the too-obvious manner in which she avoided eye contact. And especially in the secret looks she'd cast in his direction when she thought he wasn't looking.

Fixing his gaze on Grace Marlowe had been no hardship. The longer he looked the more her beauty was revealed to him. She may be the sort of sanctimonious prig he despised, but she was easy to look at, with her thick, golden hair and gray eyes. Under the right circumstances—in a moonlit garden or a candlelit bedroom—he could imagine those refined, aristocratic features softening, and he suspected she would be quite breathtaking.

And here was his first real chance to begin steering her toward that ultimate surrender.

He'd been almost knocked off his pins when she'd shown up at his doorstep tonight with the rest of the erstwhile rescue party. When that hotheaded puppy had flattened him and then Thayne had rung a peal over his throbbing head, Rochdale had assumed the presence of Grace Marlowe in his country villa was to be a lost opportunity. Then the Fates had smiled upon him when she was obliged to give up her seat in Thayne's carriage to the Thirkill chit, leaving her behind with him. Alone.

Sheane's Albion, that lively prize-winning bay gelding, would be housed in Rochdale's stables before the month was out.

The coachman was not pleased to be roused from his sleep to drive all the way to London, but neither did he seem entirely surprised. He was accustomed to his employer's unpredictable ways.

"Oh, and Jenkins," Rochdale said, "take your time harnessing the cattle. No need to rush, if you take my meaning."

Jenkins caught the coin Rochdale flipped him, pocketed it, and grinned. "Right you are, milord. I'll check everything over twice. Wouldn't want nothing to go amiss at this time o' night."

Rochdale could not wipe the smile off his face as he walked back to the house. He had known Grace—he always thought of her as Grace and not Mrs. Marlowe, because in his thoughts he was always seducing her—would insist on leaving at once, and he had only teased her about staying with him at his villa so that a carriage ride would seem the lesser of two evils.

In truth, it had all worked out exactly as he'd hoped, for he knew he could make better progress in the intimate atmosphere of a carriage. Fortunately, he'd brought his small traveling chariot to Twickenham, which meant they would have to sit side by side, as there was no seat opposite. And the movement of the carriage would no doubt cause their bodies to brush against each other. In fact, he would make sure of it. He might even have to hold on to her if they hit a bad patch of road or bounced into a rut.

Yes indeed, the seduction Rochdale had been quietly setting in motion for weeks would begin in earnest tonight.

He found Grace in the sitting room perched on a chair near the fire, stiff-backed and formal, the very picture of rigid propriety. It still seemed incongruous to him to see such a prim and respectable lady in this room, where many less than respectable women had cavorted over the years at the parties that had become rather infamous for their level of debauchery. If Grace Marlowe had even an inkling of the sort of activities that had taken place in this room, in this house, she would have run screaming out the front door.

She had donned her bonnet and buttoned her pelisse almost to her chin, armed for travel with a notorious scoundrel. She regarded him with a practiced cool arrogance that was surely meant to discourage unwelcome attentions. But he was far from discouraged.

Rochdale studied her for a long moment before approaching her. His intent regard disconcerted her, though she tried not to show it. He could melt most women with a single look. Grace Marlowe would melt soon enough. Her discomfort would turn to acquiescence, then to pleasure, and finally to surrender. His lips twitched in anticipation of the latter as he continued his close appraisal.

If she weren't so damned tight-laced, he'd have been attracted to her. He'd always been partial to blondes. All that honey gold hair and creamy skin, though, was not what defined her beauty. It was more a perfection of structure and proportion that set her apart. She had the sort of face that did not have a single bad angle. It might have been carved in marble by Praxiteles, so exquisitely formed were the bones of her cheeks, the well-defined jaw, the straight line of nose. It was a face to be memorialized in profile on a coin or a shell cameo. Noble. Elegant. Almost too perfect.

All comparisons to lifeless marble or shell, however, were shattered utterly by her eyes. Her best feature, as far as Rochdale was concerned. They were a deep, smoky gray, ringed with midnight blue along the outer edges of the iris. Intelligent eyes, but very private. Locked. If they were a window to her soul, the shutters were drawn tight. What gave them added interest, though, were the darker brown lashes and eyebrows, an intriguing contrast to the gold of her hair. The striking coloring lent an intensity to her face, giving it more depth and character than was usual, in his experience, of beautiful women.

Rochdale was certain there was more to Grace Marlowe than what one would expect of a prim, righteous, upstanding bishop's widow. Yes, this was going to be one of his more interesting conquests.

The glass of sherry stood empty on the candlestand beside her. That was a surprise. He'd only been gone a few minutes. Was she perhaps a secret tippler, or simply fortifying herself for battle? It was to Rochdale's advantage in any case.

He almost laughed aloud with pure glee at how everything was falling so beautifully into place. He schooled his features as he approached her.

"Jenkins is making the carriage ready," he said and walked to the sideboard. "Allow me to pour you another sherry while we wait."

"No, thank you, I do not—"

He had refilled her glass before she could stop him.

"Oh." She looked at the sherry as though unsure what to do with it.

"For myself," he said, "I prefer a good brandy. A bit for now"—he poured himself a glass—"and a bit for later." He used a small funnel to pour brandy into a flat sterling flask. After securing the top, he placed it in a pocket inside his coat. Taking the glass with him, he walked to stand before Grace.

"Here's to a pleasant journey." He smiled and lifted his glass in salute. When she did not return the toast, he clicked his tongue and said, "My dear Mrs. Marlowe, another small glass of sherry will do you no harm, and in fact may help to make the drive to London less disagreeable for you."

"How? By getting me foxed?"

He laughed. "It is only one glass. I doubt it will

cause you to lose control. But if by some chance it did, I confess I would love nothing more than to be a witness."

"And yet you never will be."

"A man can hope, Mrs. Marlowe."

"You are incorrigible, my lord."

"So they tell me." Not wishing to appear to hover, he moved away and stood before the fire, resting one arm on the mantel. "But you mustn't worry. I promise to be on my best behavior throughout the journey. We shall engage in polite conversation, and by the time we reach London, I daresay we shall be the best of friends."

She gave a quick burst of laughter, a rich, throaty sound that took him so completely by surprise that he almost choked on his brandy. Good God, how did such a prim, prudish lady come by such a laugh? Sultry and provocative, it was the sound one associated with dark nights and tangled sheets, not with a tight-laced bishop's widow.

"I sincerely doubt you and I could ever be friends, Lord Rochdale. I have no interest in gamblers or libertines, and you can certainly have no interest in a good Christian woman like me."

"You underestimate your charms, Mrs. Marlowe. You're a beautiful woman."

She furrowed her brow as though puzzled, then reached for the sherry glass and took a sip. After a moment, she turned those smoky eyes on him and said, "You confound me, my lord. I do not know what to say to you. I find it difficult to understand a man of your reputation."

"And I find it difficult to understand a woman of *your* reputation. So you see? We have something in common after all. Perhaps we can build a temporary bridge between us during the long drive to London. You can tell me all about your Benevolent Widows Fund and your other charitable work, and I can tell you"—he lowered his voice and leaned toward her—"anything you like."

She uttered a soft groan and took another sip of sherry.

It was all rather more encouraging than he'd hoped. She had not swooned at the thought of being alone in a carriage with him. She had not fallen into a fit of the vapors. She had not closed up like a clam and refused to speak to him. No, she had drunk sherry and butted heads with him. All in all, a good start.

Rochdale smiled.

Chapter 2

The man was insufferable. He sat too close, making sure that his thigh was in almost constant contact with her own, taking advantage of every bounce and sway of the carriage to press himself against her. And he frequently touched her as he spoke. Just a quick brush of her arm or her shoulder. Very nonchalant, though Grace suspected it was a well-practiced strategy, every small move specifically planned to unnerve her.

It was working.

She almost jumped out of her skin when he placed his gloved hand over hers. She'd been turned away from him, looking out the side window, and her hand had been resting on her thigh. She gave an involuntary squeak.

He chuckled. More like a subdued rumble deep in his chest. The soft shaking of his body transmitted through her own from where he touched her. "If you are thinking I will ravish you, Mrs. Marlowe, you need not worry. I do not ravish women." He leaned closer and pitched his voice low. "It has never been necessary."

She did not know what was worse: his arrogance or the warmth that flushed her cheeks. Though no lantern was lit inside the carriage, bright moonlight bathed the interior from the broad, uncovered front

window and the unshuttered side windows. He would
see her blush. No doubt the blackguard was amused
by what he would consider her prudishness. But she
did not care. As long as he did not believe her to be
frightened, which was surely what he wanted, Grace
did not care how much he scorned her moral integrity.
Let him laugh at her blushes.

"Given my reputation, however," he said, "I am not
surprised that you fear I might take advantage of you.
Let us make a small bargain, shall we? You allow me
free use of your hand—just to touch it and hold it,
nothing more—and I promise not to seduce you."

"As if you could."

"Oh, I could, Mrs. Marlowe. Never doubt it. And
nothing would give me greater pleasure, I assure you.
But for now, I shall be satisfied with your hand. Then
you may astonish your friends by reporting that Rochdale, that notorious scoundrel, did nothing more than
touch your dainty fingers."

Her friends? Dear heaven, he could not possibly
know about the Merry Widows and their foolish pact
to take lovers and share all the intimate details with
one another, could he? No, he could not know about
that. Nor could he know how their frank discussions
about lovemaking had made her feel. He was merely
speaking in generalities.

Wasn't he?

"I will take your silence as consent." He took her
hand and began a gentle caress. "Now, tell me more
about your charity fund. All those formal balls must
be a great deal of work."

Grace took several slow breaths before speaking.
Rochdale set up a leisurely stroking of her fingers
while she told him about the Benevolent Widows
Fund that she headed, and about the almshouses in
Chelsea they had purchased and converted into temporary housing for war widows and orphans who had
no other resources. She had hoped to bore him with

details, but the more she talked, the more intently he watched her. Even when she wasn't looking, she could feel that unwavering blue gaze upon her.

And he continued to stroke her fingers.

No doubt she ought to have squashed herself against the back corner, as far away from him as she could get in such a small space, crossed her arms across her chest, and tucked her hands tightly beneath her armpits, out of his reach. She ought to have at least uttered an objection to his impertinence. But, by heaven, she was determined that he never know how much he'd rattled her. Rochdale was the sort of man who delighted in discomposing a lady. It was very likely his favorite form of amusement, and Grace was to be his evening's entertainment.

Or so he thought. Grace was not going to make it easy on him.

"I have plans for a new wing at Marlowe House." She was speaking a bit too fast and took a moment to control the twitchy nervousness brought on by that soft fingertip running up and down the length of her forefinger. "If we can raise enough funds at our final ball of the Season, then I hope to hire a builder to begin work during the summer. We cannot accommodate all the families who—Oh!"

She could have bitten her tongue off for allowing that single syllable to confirm her uneasiness. But the wretched man had taken complete possession of her hand and had inserted his thumb under the wrist of her glove.

"Do not be alarmed. I merely hoped we could dispense with the formality of gloves during our journey, just as I have already dispensed with my hat. And besides, I am finding it rather warm inside the carriage. Don't you agree?"

Before she could respond—and what would she have said? *Yes, my skin is indeed flushed from head to toe and if you don't lower a window soon I might swoon?*—he had yanked off one of his own gloves with his teeth, then transferred her hand to his bare hand while he pulled off the second glove.

"Ah, much better," he said. "But I can feel the warmth of *your* skin even through the fine leather of your gloves."

She had no doubt of it. The yellow kid was as thin as chicken skin. Grace had been rather proud of this particular pair of gloves with tiny flowers embroidered along the edge. She was not a slave to fashion, but she liked to look her best. Just now, though, she wished she had worn thick, scratchy, unattractive woolen gloves. With Rochdale, however, it would have made no difference.

"You must allow me to make you more comfortable." His voice was pitched low—it almost always was, probably so that one would have to lean in close to hear him properly—with a slight roughness that saved it from being unctuous. It was a voice of seduction, and he knew it. Worse, Grace feared that despite all her stiff-necked propriety, she might not be entirely immune to its allure. It was deep and velvety soft, a voice to charm a man out of his fortune or a respectable woman out of her clothing.

Truly, the man was a devil.

He began carefully to peel off her glove, tugged it just below the wrist, and stopped. He ran his thumb, his bare thumb, over the skin of her wrist. Dear God. It was the first time she had been skin to skin with any man, even in the most innocent way, since the bishop had died. That simple touch, that naked caress, sent a sharp, prickling warmth through her body, from her toes to the very roots of her hair.

He looked at her with those bedroom eyes and said, "May I?"

She heard his words, but only barely, beneath the furious rumbling of her own confused thoughts. When she did not immediately reply, he lifted his black eyebrows in question. He wanted to remove her glove, but completely disarmed her by asking permission. She should refuse. She should pull her hand away and tell him to leave the glove right there on her hand where it belonged, ineffective armor though it was. She should tell him to stop deliberately confusing her.

Grace nodded.

Rochdale cocked his head at a slight angle, as though evaluating and confirming her foolishly unspoken agreement, blue eyes gazing at her with an intensity that set off another pricking of heat dancing all over her skin.

What was wrong with her?

He smiled and then bent to the business of removing first one glove and then the other, teasing the soft leather over her palm and fingers, stroking each new inch of bare skin with his knuckles. He placed the gloves neatly beside him on the tufted velvet bench—he'd tossed his own on the floor—then took one of her hands and covered it with both of his.

She could barely breathe.

He smiled again, white teeth flashing in the moonlight, bright against the darker olive of his skin. The carriage took a sudden bounce, causing a lock of black hair to fall over one eye. All that was needed was an earring and an eye patch and he'd have made the perfect pirate. Which was precisely the look he strove for, no doubt. Grace supposed certain women liked that hint of danger, the suggestion of uncivilized roughness and raw masculinity. She did not.

"There," he said as he turned her hand palm-up and began to caress the base of her thumb. "Isn't that better?"

No, it was much worse. She called upon long practice and forced her face and body to remain calm and composed, seemingly indifferent to his touch. She would die before she let him see how he affected her. Or to sense the confusion she felt over being affected at all. Grace was a good Christian woman who did not allow emotion or passion, especially physical passion, to rule her. The bishop had taught her the importance of self-control. He had sometimes preached about the evils of the flesh, and Grace had listened well, knowing in her heart that the admonition was directed at her.

"Tell me more about the improvements you plan for Marlowe House." The words were innocuous, even formal, but Rochdale's tone was intimate and he began doing things with her hand that were anything but innocuous.

Grace steeled herself against the unbidden reaction to his touch and began to relate all the details of the planned addition to the halfway house in Chelsea. The dry recital helped to distract her attention from the way he caressed her hand. Somewhat.

"You are a remarkable woman, Mrs. Marlowe, to give so much of your time and resources to those less fortunate. I confess I had no idea the charity balls you and your friends host had such tangible results."

He referred to the other trustees of the Benevolent Widows Fund. The four other women on the board, who privately called themselves the Merry Widows because of that silly pact, had become her closest friends. She wished they were here right now, sitting behind her, telling her how to cope with this awkward situation and this dangerous man.

"What did you think we did with the money?" she asked. "Kept it for ourselves?"

He smiled. "No, I knew you helped people with it. I just did not know how. To be perfectly honest, I never gave it a thought. I suppose I assumed you simply handed it out to the poor."

"That would be only a temporary solution," she said. "The wretched war is creating more widows every day, many of them with large families, left with nothing to live on when the meager funds from their soldier husbands stop coming in. At Marlowe House, we give them a temporary shelter until they can find employment or other means to survive. We even have an agency in house that helps to find positions for most of the women, in service or in trade, whatever is appropriate. If we did not help them, these poor women and their children would likely end up on the streets."

She pretended to ignore what he was doing with her hand, stroking each finger from base to tip, and drawing soft circles on her palm.

"Remarkable," he said. "I salute you, Mrs. Marlowe, for all the good you do."

He lifted her hand and his lips grazed ever so softly against the knuckles, then brushed butterfly kisses on each fingertip. Dear God. Every nerve in her body thrummed. This was the last straw. She jerked her hand away.

He gave a deep-throated chuckle, and Grace chided herself for allowing him to believe he had flustered her. She was *not* flustered. She was simply unaccustomed to having a man touch her like that, kiss her like that. She might be forgiven for the involuntary tingling deep in her belly, and lower, brought on by the sensation of his unexpectedly soft lips. This was something altogether new and she'd been unprepared, that was all. But it was surely wicked, so she made a greater effort to regain composure, for she'd be damned before allowing him to know what she felt. She would no doubt be damned in any case for having such wayward feelings.

No one had a more powerful resolve, however, than Grace Marlowe, and this horrid man would never get past it.

"You promised me your hand," he said in that velvety voice.

"I promised no such thing."

"But you did not refuse it to me when I gave you

the chance, so I take that as sufficient approval." He reached over and took her hand again, easily accomplished since she had not tucked it out of sight, as she ought to have done. "There, you see? Nothing to be so anxious about. It is merely a hand, not your virtue. And I promise not to bite it off. I may take leave to kiss it now and then, however." And he did so.

Grace bit down on her back teeth so hard she felt the muscles of her neck grow rigid. At least she wasn't trembling. "I wish you would not," she murmured.

He lifted his head and arched an eyebrow, a decided twinkle in his scoundrel eyes. "Why? You like it. I can tell."

"I do *not* like it."

"Yes, you do. Oh, please do not give me that face, Mrs. Marlowe. All that frowning mars your perfect brow. And do not deny that you like to have your hand kissed. Of course you do. And why shouldn't you? It is not sinful, after all."

Yes, it was. It made her *feel* sinful—all that tingling, her skin prickling into gooseflesh—and he knew it. It was not at all proper. But what could one expect from such a man?

Grace hated being so aware of him. She certainly did not wish for the physical response he so expertly drew from her with the practiced skill of a seducer. She disliked him. Loathed him, even.

She must do something to divert his attention. Bore him. Disgust him. Anything to distract him from her hand, where he was once again drawing little circles on her palm. She ripped her attention from his wicked touch and concentrated on the sounds around her, allowing the ordinary chorus of travel to soothe her nearly shattered nerves. The steady rhythmic hoofbeats of the team of horses. The jangle and clank of the harnesses. Bits of dirt and gravel thrown up from the wheels and pinging against the window glass. The outside lamps swinging back and forth with a continual two-note screech. The rattle of the raised shades against the side windows. The occasional shout of Jenkins, who rode postilion on the lead horse. The constant creak and grind as the carriage swayed and bounced along the road.

Carriage travel was a noisy business, but it somehow quieted her busy brain and allowed her to think more clearly. And all at once, she was struck by an idea that was bound to send Lord Rochdale scooting as far away from her as possible.

"I have another project that occupies a great deal of my time," she said.

"Oh? And what is that?"

"I am editing the bishop's sermons."

That did it. Or almost. He did not scoot away, but he ceased drawing circles, those strangely intimate caresses, and stared at her.

"The bishop's sermons?"

"Yes. Not his parliamentary addresses, which are well documented, but his church sermons. They are most instructive."

Grace's late husband, Bishop Ignatius Marlowe, had been an important man and a great orator. As Bishop of London, he'd sat in the House of Lords as one of the Lords Spiritual, where he had famously addressed the issue of Catholic emancipation, and from his pulpit at St. Paul's he'd given spectacular and stirring sermons on the plight of the poor and the need for social reform. In fact, he'd often been called upon to speak at less official gatherings, where the general populace could benefit from his views. Grace had been so proud of him. But he'd also preached from the pulpits at several of the royal chapels, and those sermons were more personal. He had written them out before delivering them, and it was from those notes that Grace was putting together a collection of his work for publication.

It had so far been a project of immense personal

satisfaction for Grace, something of value she could do for the bishop, in appreciation of all he'd done for her. The only negative aspect had been the reaction of his daughter, Margaret, who'd never liked Grace and made it clear she did not approve of her rummaging through the bishop's papers. Margaret was very protective of her father's memory, and Grace did her best to convince her stepdaughter of her good intentions. She feared, however, that she would never win the woman over, but did not allow that to deter her efforts in editing the sermons.

"I am sure they are full to bursting with useful instruction," Rochdale said in a sarcastic tone, and Grace could swear his eyes rolled to the ceiling briefly.

She smiled. "They are truly wonderful sermons that teach how to live one's life in the best possible way through selfless acts and the avoidance of sin. But I don't suppose such instruction would be of interest to you, my lord."

He uttered a disdainful snort. "You suppose correctly. Besides, the last thing any of us needs is another book of sermons from some old . . . I beg your pardon, Mrs. Marlowe, but it should come as no surprise that I found your late husband to be a pompous old windbag."

"Lord Rochdale! I will not have you speak of the bishop in such terms to me."

He waved away her objection . . . with the hand that was no longer holding hers. She had won that battle, at least.

"I am certain he was a good man and a saintly husband," he said, "but his views on reform were naïve and impractical and altogether too self-righteous."

"What do you m—"

"He loved to talk about helping the poor, but he had a very narrow definition of the *deserving* poor. His implication was always that most of them were lazy and stupid."

"No, he—"

"If I had to hear one more harangue on how gin was the cause of all misery in London and the manufacture of it should be outlawed, I swear I would have to run screaming through the streets."

"But you have to admit that—"

"If only he'd put more of his persuasive powers into relieving some of the miserable conditions that drive those poor souls to gin, then I'd have had more respect for him. As it was . . . Oh, confound it all. I beg your pardon. He was your husband, and I should keep my opinions to myself."

"Yes, perhaps you should," Grace said sharply. She had never heard anyone speak of the bishop with anything other than admiration and respect. It shocked her to hear Lord Rochdale, of all people, take him to task. And she was certain it had not been said to deliberately upset her, as all his other actions had been. He'd really meant it. To think that anyone could have such an opinion of Bishop Marlowe shook her totally off balance.

"I do apologize." He took her hand again and his voice returned to the more usual deep timbre, spilling over her as thick as honey. "That was rude of me. And quite spoiled my mood. Let us have no more talk of the bishop and his reforms." He began to softly caress her fingers again.

"But I never mentioned his ideas of reform," Grace said, determined to hang on to the one subject that seemed to take his mind off seduction. "I am working on his church sermons, which are quite different. He liked to take a verse from Proverbs, for example, and build a whole sermon around its lesson. Why, just yesterday I found his notes for a sermon based on the proverb 'Pride goeth before a fall.' It is most enlightening."

"And wrong, if that's how he quoted it."

Grace furrowed her brow. "What do you mean,

wrong? Proverbs sixteen, verse eighteen. 'Pride goeth before a fall.' "

Rochdale smiled as he realized he'd found the opening he needed. "I say you are wrong."

She gave a little chortle of laughter. That unexpectedly dark, husky laugh again that made him want to lay her down on the bench and make mad love to her. He would have to be careful of that laugh. It was a sound that could get under a man's skin and melt it right off. Pure seduction, and she did not even know it.

"As if a man like you," she said, "would have even a passing acquaintance with the Bible."

"I am willing to wager that you have the verse wrong."

"And I am willing to wager that it is correct."

He smiled. "Excellent. We shall have a proper wager, then."

She eyed him warily. "I have heard about men like you, chronic gamblers who will wager on anything and everything."

He shrugged. "I will not deny that I enjoy a good game. And a wager will always make a horse race or a cockfight or a mill all the more enjoyable. A bit of risk now and then adds a hint of piquancy to the everyday humdrum of life. You should do it more often. Taking risks. Stepping outside the strict boundaries of what you think is expected of you. This will be a good start for you. A small wager over a Bible verse."

"But there is little risk when I know I am right."

Better and better. This would be as easy as the turn of a card. "Since you are so confident, then you will have no objection if I set the stakes."

"This is one wager you will not win, sir. I am a churchwoman. A vicar's daughter and a bishop's widow. I know my Bible. In fact, set the stakes high, for when I win I shall use the money to help build my new wing at Marlowe House."

"You agree that I may set the stakes?"

"So I have just said. Name any amount."

"All right, then. But I wasn't thinking of money. I was thinking of . . . a kiss."

Her smoky eyes widened and her cheeks flushed a deep shade of pink. Lord, she was trying so hard to pretend not to be affected by him, and had no idea how delightfully she failed.

She bristled into speech. "You have already kissed my hand, Lord Rochdale. That was quite enough."

"Was it? Not for me, I assure you." He brought her hand to his mouth again and slowly drew his lips across her knuckles. He inhaled a deep breath through his nose, taking in the incredible fragrance she must have dabbed at her wrist. It was not the sort of soft, flowery scent he would have expected from her, but something slightly heavier and more intoxicating—jasmine, perhaps?—and as incongruous as her laugh. Rochdale added a quick flick of the tongue across her knuckles before lifting his head.

She sucked in a sharp breath and drew her hand away. "You have not won the wager yet, my lord."

"Ah, but that was not a true kiss. Certainly not worthy of a wager. But I can tell you liked it."

"No, I d—"

"In fact, I am quite sure you would like to be kissed. By me."

"That's not tr—"

"You are simply dying to know what it would be like to be kissed by the oh-so-wicked man with the oh-so-dangerous reputation." He moved closer to her, pressing his hip firmly against hers, until she had no recourse but to flatten herself into the corner, with no place left to go.

"You, sir, are impertinent. And remarkably arrogant. I have no wish to be kissed by you."

"Of course you do. The need is radiating off your body like heat waves. I can almost taste it. But you are all tied up in your Bishop's Widow's propriety and afraid to let yourself be simply a woman. A woman with a woman's needs and desires. It is nothing to be ashamed of. In fact, it is infinitely more shameful to keep yourself all tied up in self-imposed knots."

He leaned in close, and her whole body strained to put some distance between them. It seemed to him that her spine must be fused to the side wall panel. But he had not lied. He could feel her desire in the touch of her hand, which he still clasped. When he let go, she gave a shuddery breath, then held it again when he began to loosen the ribbons of her bonnet.

"All tied up," he said, "just like this bonnet. It is unhealthy to be so tight-laced all the time, you know. One has to breathe." The satin ribbon slipped loose and he gently lifted the straw bonnet off her head and placed in on the small shelf beneath the front window, beside the high-crowned beaver hat he'd discarded earlier. Her blond hair was coiled in a plaited crown high on her head, more silvery than gold in the moonlight streaming in the front window. She had not cut and teased short curls at her cheeks and temples like so many ladies of fashion did. All was sleek and simple, giving attention to her elegant cheeks and long white neck. Her beauty was cruelly serene.

As he studied her again—gray eyes huge with anxiety, full lips slightly pursed, skin so finely textured it might have been unglazed porcelain—Grace did not struggle. She did not try to throw him off or strike him. She might not have believed it, but he would have stopped if she had done any of those things. But she did none of them. It was as though she had so thoroughly trained herself to keep all emotion under control that she became rigid as a statue, unable to speak or move.

Rochdale wondered if she'd always been such an ice princess, or if it was the bishop's doing. And what would happen to her once he'd chipped away that cool, polished marble façade and let out the warm-blooded woman beneath? Would she loosen her tight laces forever and open herself up to life?

Perhaps she would thank him as he rode off on Sheane's Albion.

"I spoke before of taking risks. Isn't it time you took a small risk, my dear Mrs. Marlowe?"

Her breathing became slightly ragged, a nervous agitation. She was out of her depth, even a little frightened. Yet she did not drop her unbending composure. Was it courage? Or simply pure mule-headedness?

"I am taking a risk," she said, "merely by being in this carriage with you, am I not? Is that not enough?"

"But what are you risking? Your virtue is safe with me, as I have already assured you. And sharing my carriage was no risk for you since you had no choice in the matter. No, I think you require more of a risk than that."

"Of course you do. You are a gambler. Taking risks is your way of life. It is not mine."

"Not yet." He brushed a knuckle down the edge of her cheek and along her jaw. She blinked rapidly a few times but did not flinch. "But as you say, I live to take risks. And do you know what? I find I am all agog to win this wager with you."

"You won't win."

"And yet I have every intention of doing so. But I think it only fair that we both appreciate what the stakes are. Let us see exactly what we are playing for."

He slid an arm around her shoulder, pulled her toward him, and kissed her.

Chapter 3

Grace steeled herself against an assault, but his lips were unexpectedly gentle. And mobile. This was not a static kiss, the only type of kiss she'd ever known. His lips moved over her own, testing and tasting, tempting and confusing her.

Her palms were pressed flat against his chest. He held one arm around her shoulders, lightly caressing her, just as he'd done with her hands. His other hand cradled her chin while he continued his slow exploration of her mouth. She flinched at the touch of his tongue tracing the seam of her lips. So thoroughly shaken at the very notion of tongues being involved in a kiss, and lost in the odd wet sensation of it, she did not at first realize what he wanted. When it came to her at last that his tongue was trying to coax open her lips, and his hand was trying to relax her jaw, she sucked in a startled breath—and in so doing, inadvertently parted her lips. In the next instant, his tongue was inside, *inside* her mouth.

Grace had never experienced anything like this in all her life. Her entire body tingled and trembled, every inch of her heated and flushed. She ought to be disgusted, but she was not. She ought to push him away. But dear God in heaven, she did not want him to stop.

A yearning that was both pleasure and pain spread

through her body, coalescing in the most private part of her, setting off a warm throbbing between her legs. Her breasts tightened beneath her stays. Hardened nipples strained against the whalebone.

She should not be feeling like this. She should impose more control over her body. But she couldn't stop the sensations flowing through her and over her. It was wrong. It was frightening.

It was exciting.

Her body seemed to have come alive in a whole new way, a way so unrecognizable that for an instant she felt like a stranger in someone else's skin. Someone loose and carnal, sensual and unbridled. So, *this* was passion. This was the exhilaration the bishop had warned her against.

Remembering her husband's words caused her to be a little frightened at what was happening to her. Fear wound its way around tentative passion, intensifying it, adding more danger to the moment. Rochdale was infamous for using and discarding women. Publicly so. She should not allow him, of all people, to do this. Yet she could not seem to muster the will to put a stop to it. Instead, she simply allowed herself to experience it. For once in her life.

And before she realized it, fear had been transformed into need and wanton desire.

Grace kissed him back.

Her tongue hesitantly touched his, and he responded by clasping her tighter against his chest, and setting up a dance where their tongues circled each other and retreated, circled and retreated. Heat and longing spread through her like a fever. She was lost in pure sensation.

Her hand had somehow crept up over his shoulder and into his hair. Silky black hair between her fingers. Lord Rochdale's black hair. *Lord Rochdale*. His name and all it represented brought her back to earth with a thud.

Dear God, the man was a devil. A black-hearted spellbinder. *What had he done to her*?

She pushed him away with such force he became unbalanced and almost slid to the floor. Grace pressed a hand to her mouth, horrified at what she'd allowed to happen. "How dare you," she said in a voice so strangled she hardly recognized it.

Rochdale righted himself, straightened his neck-cloth, and stared at her. "I beg your pardon?"

"You have no right to kiss me like that. I cannot believe you are so lacking in decency that you would accost an unwilling woman, trapped in a carriage with nowhere to run."

"Ah, but I am the man who debauches young ladies and publicly abandons them, am I not? You cannot expect decency from such a blackguard."

"Ooh, you are loathsome!"

He smiled and his teeth caught the moonlight, giving him a diabolical look. "Claws in, cat." He reached inside his coat and brought out the silver flask, unscrewed the top, and held it out to her. "Perhaps a sip of brandy will calm you down. You are unsettled, to be sure. But you were not unwilling. Certainly not uninvolved. In fact, you were quite charmingly responsive."

"I was not!" she snapped, and knocked the flask out of his hand, furious and resentful because he was right. She was angry with him because he'd coaxed her into dropping her guard for the first time in more than a dozen years, since the early days of her marriage. Angry at herself for allowing it. Angry at the world for placing her in this untenable limbo of confusion.

"Don't worry." His voice was full of laughter as he retrieved the flask from the carriage floor. "You could not help it. It was a perfectly normal reaction."

"Not for me." She realized she had all but admitted to her wanton response and bent her head in shame and embarrassment.

"No, I daresay it was not normal for you, Mrs. Marlowe. And what a pity, for you are rather good at it. In fact, I look forward to collecting my winnings when we prove that I have won our little wager."

"You will not win." And thank heaven for it. Grace did not know if she could withstand another kiss like that.

"I do not suppose you have a Bible in your reticule so we can resolve the wager right now? I am anxious for another kiss, my passionate prude."

That label sent a rush of heat to her cheeks, for she feared it was altogether too close to the truth. "No, I do not have a Bible with me. I wish I did, for I would spend the rest of the journey reading it to you."

He gave a theatrical shudder. "Thank *God* I shall not have to endure that penance. We shall simply have to settle the wager tomorrow. I shall call upon you to collect my winnings."

"No, please." The thought of Rochdale in her home was too much to bear.

His black eyebrows lifted. "You wish to come to my house instead?"

"No!"

He grinned. "I thought not. Then you may expect me tomorrow. And I do not know if you happened to notice, but we are almost at your front door."

"Oh." She had not, in fact, noticed. All at once, she was gripped by a rush of anxiety. What if she was seen at this hour of the night with Lord Rochdale? She reached for her bonnet and quickly set it in place. "My gloves, please," she said as she tied the ribbon beneath her chin. He handed her the yellow kid gloves and she struggled into them awkwardly.

The carriage slowed and Grace saw the familiar brick façade of her Portland Place town house. A faint light shone in the glass above the front door, but all else was dark. It must be almost two o'clock in the

morning. And she was arriving home at this late hour
with an infamous libertine.

When the carriage stopped, she rose from the
bench—rather awkwardly, bent from the waist, her bonnet knocking against the carriage roof—and reached for
the handle to open the door.

Rochdale touched her arm. "Wait. Allow me." He
made a move to descend before her, but she held up
a hand.

"Don't you dare step out of this carriage." In a
clumsy tangle of skirts and booted legs, she made her
way down the lowered step. "I do not wish to be seen
coming home with you at this hour."

He chuckled and moved back into the darkness of
the carriage. "A wise decision. We must have a care
for your reputation. It has been a most enjoyable journey, my dear Mrs. Marlowe. I shall wait here until
you are safely inside. Then I will do myself the honor
of calling upon you tomorrow. Good night, ma'am."

She thought to tell him not to call on her, but
turned away instead. It would do no good to tell him
anything. He would do as he pleased, and she could
not stop him. But tomorrow, she would ask him to
stay away from her. She never wanted to see him
again.

Grace reached for the house key in her reticule, but
the door opened before she could retrieve it.

"Good evening, madam." Her butler stood aside to
allow her to enter.

"Thank you, Spurling. You really need not have
waited up so late. I do have a key, you know."

He smiled, and there was a look in his eye she could
have predicted, a look that said he knew his duty and
would do no less, regardless of what she had to say
about it. "May I ask, madam . . . Is the young
lady . . . ?"

Grace had sent round a note when she had gone

off with Beatrice that afternoon, alerting Spurling of the situation. She had not known how long she would be gone or even if she would return tonight at all, and she hated for her household staff to worry about her.

"She is safely returned to her home, I am happy to say, and no harm was done." Not to young Emily, perhaps. Grace could not say the same for herself. She was still shaken by what had happened in the carriage. In fact, she was making a supreme effort not to fall apart in front of poor Spurling.

"Excellent news, madam."

"Yes. But I am quite exhausted. Is Kitty awake?"

"I will send her upstairs right away. Shall I have Cook prepare a tray? A light supper or a pot of tea?"

"No, thank you, Spurling. I could not eat a bite. But if you would be so good as to ask Kitty to bring me a glass of warm milk, I'd be grateful. It has been a trying evening and perhaps it would help me to sleep."

Grace continued to cling tightly to her self-control while her maid assisted her with the complicated ritual of undressing, deftly managing the various tapes and laces, buttons and pins. The poor young woman had obviously been roused from her bed to see to Grace. Sleepy-eyed and silent, she removed each garment and carefully stored it or put it aside for the laundry. When Kitty finally left the room, taking the garments to be laundered with her, Grace sank down on the edge of the bed and sighed aloud. Her body shivered as she released the tension she'd been holding in for hours.

And that only served to remind her of a different kind of shiver she'd felt that evening. Before she could stop herself, she was reliving every moment of Rochdale's kiss. It was wicked to have such thoughts. She ought to erase the whole experience from her memory and forget it ever happened.

As if such a thing were possible.

How her friends, the Merry Widows, would laugh if they could read her thoughts just now. For weeks they had been sharing intimate details of their love affairs. It had begun with Penelope, Lady Gosforth, who announced she had taken a lover during the winter she had spent in the country. Then Marianne Nesbitt had begun a quest to find a lover, and ended up having an affair with her late husband's closest friend. And then Beatrice, Lady Somerfield, had embarked on a clandestine affair with Lord Thayne that had blown up into a public scandal and precipitated tonight's messy little episode with her niece Emily. And Penelope had a new lover, as did Wilhelmina, the dowager Duchess of Hertford.

They all had lovers and talked about them in ways that made Grace blush to listen. And even though she made no secret of her disapproval, she *had* listened. She'd been shocked and embarrassed by most of it—all of it, actually—but deep in the most secret, private corner of her heart, she had wondered. Wondered what it would be like to experience what they described.

It was not as though Grace had no understanding of relations between a man and a woman. She had been a wife to Bishop Marlowe in every way, though the physical aspect of marriage had been difficult for her.

The bishop had been older than Grace by more than thirty years, but he had been a handsome man, tall and robust. Although she'd married him because her parents had demanded it, she had still been young and romantic enough to want a real marriage. She'd wanted to love and be loved, to touch and be touched.

Her young body had sought physical intimacy with his, and he gave it to her, but only insofar as he thought proper. In that first week of marriage when she was still dazzled by the fact that he'd chosen her, out of all the women he knew, to be his wife, she'd been overeager. The bishop had rebuffed her when she kissed him too warmly. He'd been shocked when

Grace had attempted to initiate lovemaking, or eagerly opened her legs to him, or arched her body up to his, seeking release. He gently chided her for giving in to such wanton behavior, so unseemly in a good Christian wife.

Mortified, Grace had stopped responding at all and laid still and quiet whenever he came to her bedchamber. He did his business quickly, in the dark, lifting her nightgown and nudging her decorously closed legs apart with his knee. He'd always given her a quick kiss afterward and apologized for troubling her, then returned to his own bedchamber. Under his kindly tutelage, Grace had learned the proper way for a wife to behave.

The bishop taught her to embrace modesty. He taught her that, because of their weak nature, women must constantly strive to keep under control those passions which, if unrestrained, would drive them into sensuality and licentiousness. "True feminine delicacy," he had said, "should recoil at anything that arouses the passions."

Grace had been a good student. She had become the perfect bishop's wife—modest, chaste, and reserved.

But when Rochdale's lips had touched hers tonight, something long dormant had been awakened. He had made her feel sensations she had once eagerly sought but now knew to be wrong. He had coaxed forth some of those warm sensations the bishop had taught her were anathema to the frail nature of female virtue.

It would have been the easiest thing in the world to have pushed him away. But Grace had been transfixed by what was happening, by the novelty of the experience. When she should have screamed *No!* a tiny part of her brain had whispered *Yes!*

Guilt warred with fascination, tying her stomach into knots. Dear God, she was surely wicked, but she could not stop thinking about his kiss, about every

movement of his lips and tongue and hands, about the
taste of him, about the smell of him, about the pressure of his body against hers, and about how it all had
made her feel. A good, virtuous woman did not dwell
on such things. She felt sinful and soiled.

And unwittingly entranced by the memory.

She did not know how she was to face him again.
How could she look him in the eye in the light of
day as though nothing had happened? She could not
pretend to have been unaffected by his kiss. He'd felt
her response. She'd kissed him back, after all. He
would look at her with mockery in his eyes and know
her for a fraud. He alone knew her darkest secret:
She was not a virtuous woman, not in her heart.

Tears fell down her cheeks as Grace crawled under
the covers and buried her face in the pillow. She wept
for all the wickedness in her that even the bishop had
never been able to fully eradicate. She wept for her
treacherous body, which had betrayed her so thoroughly. She wept for briefly wanting a man she
detested.

Finally, Grace thought of her friends and about all
that they had said to make her wonder. She no
longer wondered.

She knew.

Rochdale was thoroughly pleased with himself as
he rode toward Portland Place. After last night, the
seduction of Grace Marlowe could proceed according
to plan. That kiss had told him all he needed to know:
She wanted him. She might not like the idea and
would certainly deny it, but she wanted him.

Having taken her measure, he knew he must tread
lightly with her if he was to win the wager. He could
not simply pounce. Grace Marlowe would require
wooing. And so, when he kissed her, he had tried to
keep it simple, slow and gentle, to keep her calm and
relaxed. She had not closed her lips tight, as he'd half

expected, but had tentatively accepted his mouth, allowing it to move over hers, to nibble and nip, to taste and explore. When he'd finally breached the inside of her mouth, he'd been pleasantly surprised by her response. Her tongue had been real and warm and shy as a bird's. And surprisingly arousing.

For a brief moment before she'd come to her senses, pushing at him like an avenging fury, Rochdale had discovered the passionate woman beneath the prim exterior. Even if there had been no wager, he'd be eager to unleash that passion. He doubted the old bishop had provided her with an outlet. The poor woman probably had years of untapped passion bottled up inside and ready to explode. And, by God, he would be there when it happened.

Afterward, he would collect his fine new gelding from Sheane and be on his way.

In the meantime, though, he would take things slowly. She was skittish. This business of seduction was too new to her. She had to become accustomed to the idea, so he would not rush her. He would take his time, and he would enjoy every minute of it.

Rochdale dismounted in front of Grace's house. Portland Place was a broad boulevard, the broadest in London, and not conducive to an army of street urchins ready to hold one's horse for a coin. Fortunately, the entire length was lined with an ironwork fence, so he simply secured the reins to it. He crooned in the horse's ear to assure her he would not be long, and opened the gate.

Rochdale had done his research and knew that Bishop Marlowe had left his widow a tidy fortune. Marlowe had come from a wealthy family, and had made more money in a year as Bishop of London than many people would earn in a lifetime. The children from his first marriage had inherited a great deal of property. His widow had been left this grand house

on Portland Place as well as enough cash and invest-
ments to keep her comfortable for the rest of her life.
Grace Marlowe was a rich woman, and her home reflected her wealth.

He straightened his coat, tugged down his waistcoat,
and rang the bell. A pretty red-haired maid in
starched apron and cap opened the door. He flashed
the smile that had won the trust of many a housemaid
and said, "Lord Rochdale to see Mrs. Marlowe." He
handed her his card.

"My lord," she said, and bobbed a curtsy. Her eyes
had grown wide and she looked flustered. No doubt
she knew his name. His reputation would be well
known even among the servant class, who were generally bigger gossips than their employers.

Since she seemed reluctant to let him in, he said,
"She is expecting me," and stepped past her into the
entry hall.

Rochdale glanced about him with approval. Most of
the homes on Portland Place had been built by Robert
Adam in the last century, and this house appeared to
have been decorated by him as well. Or at least in his
style. All was classical coolness in pale blues, mint
greens, and soft grays with cream-colored ornament.
The plasterwork ceiling was magnificent. The room
might have been designed with Grace in mind, the
coloring and refinement of decoration were so perfectly
suited to her. Like a delicate Sèvres bonbonnière to hold
Grace, the sweetmeat, inside. Through a screen of col-
umns at the far end of the hall he could see a staircase,
but the housemaid indicated a different direction.

"If you will wait in here, my lord, I will see if
Madam is in."

She led him into a small anteroom off the hall,
clearly meant for uninvited visitors or tradesmen.
Rochdale didn't mind the slight. He was in Grace's
house, prepared to collect his kiss and further chip

away at her resolve—one more step toward winning Sheane's gelding, and that was all that mattered. The maid bobbed another curtsy and left him alone.

Afternoon sunlight poured in from the two windows facing Portland Place, picking out bits of gilt in the ceiling and over-door decoration and in the moldings. A fine landscape—a Ruisdael, if he was not mistaken—was given pride of place over a marble fireplace, and several smaller paintings were hung on the wall opposite the windows. It was an elegant room. Even the few pieces of furniture were of good quality. If such care was given to a small anteroom that was probably seldom used, he could only imagine what the rest of the house was like.

Rochdale removed his hat and placed it on a table, then dragged his fingers through his hair to give it the disheveled look he preferred. He was going to kiss Grace, and he might as well make himself attractive for her. The too-long hair that fell in waves over his brow and ears gave him a slightly disreputable look that most women found irresistible. They might pretend to prefer the perfectly groomed and polished gentleman of the *ton*, but what they really wanted was the uncivilized rogue. And Rochdale aimed to please.

There was also the added unruly appeal of a purple bruise under his left eye, a souvenir from last night's farce, along with a cut over his eyebrow. Damn that puppy Burnett. He had a surprisingly powerful right. The young fool had knocked Rochdale clean off his feet. It had been worth it, though, for the staggering good fortune that had brought Grace Marlowe with him. What was a bruise or two if it meant expediting the resolution of the wager with Sheane, bringing Albion into his stable?

He had begun to study the paintings, figuring he was in for a long wait, when he heard footsteps on the marble floor of the hall. He turned just as Grace reached the anteroom door, wearing a simple pink dress with long sleeves and a ruff of lace at the neck. Her hair was pulled into a twisted arrangement at the back of her head, held together with a large comb. She paused in the doorway, gray eyes flashing, and lifted her head so that she seemed to look down upon him, even though he stood taller.

"Lord Rochdale."

He swept her a bow. "My dear Mrs. Marlowe, you look surprised to see me. I told you I would call on you this afternoon, did I not?"

"I had rather hoped you'd forgotten about that."

He flashed a smile. "On the contrary, I have thought of little else." He'd been holding a small bouquet of pink carnations and ivy, and he held it out to her now. "Will you accept these as a token of my appreciation for the pleasure of your company last evening?"

Grace stepped into the room but kept her hands at her sides and did not take the flowers. A flicker of uncertainty gathered briefly in her eyes, as though she wanted to reject the flowers but knew it would be rude to do so. For a long, silent moment her indignation almost visibly faded in and out while she stood still as a statue. Good manners won the day at last, however, and she reached out and took the bouquet. "Thank you. They're very pretty."

"And match your dress. What a clever fellow I am, eh?"

She lifted her elegant eyebrows as if to challenge that statement, but did not. "I appreciate the gesture, my lord, but I am afraid I have guests and must return to them. Thank you for—"

"Ah, but there is something else. Surely you have not forgotten why I have come?"

She glared at him without comment. She had not, of course, forgotten. The way she maintained her distance, he was certain she remembered exactly what to expect.

"I have brought something else for you." He reached into an inside pocket of his coat and brought out a tiny book, no bigger than a deck of playing cards, bound in white leather. "Please, take it."

She hesitated a moment, then placed the flowers on a nearby table and took the small volume he offered. Her fingers touched the gold embossed lettering on the cover. *Holy Bible*. She stiffened slightly, then looked up, her face set into a stern mask. "It's lovely."

"Open it to the page marked by the ribbon."

Clearly she did not wish to do so, and she continued to stare at him owlishly. Perhaps she already knew what she would find. In fact, he would be astonished if she had not pulled out the family Bible the instant she'd returned home last night.

"Go ahead," he said. "Read it. I believe you will agree it is most interesting."

She stared at him so long he thought she might refuse, but she finally opened the volume to the marked page. Her eyes scanned it, then closed, as though unable to face the truth. Her face paled, and he realized she had not in fact checked her own Bible. She had not known the truth. Had she been so confident? Poor self-righteous little prig. She was in for a set-down.

"Read it," he repeated. "Proverbs sixteen, verse eighteen."

"I have done so." She did not look up or open her eyes.

"Aloud, if you please."

She took a deep breath, opened her eyes, and read: " 'Pride goeth before destruction, and an haughty spirit before a fall.' "

He grinned broadly. "I believe I have won our wager, Mrs. Marlowe. Wouldn't you agree? I have come to collect my winnings."

He stepped toward her, and she backed away, putting both hands in front of her, palms out, in a halting gesture. "No!"

Rochdale arched an eyebrow. "You will not honor your bargain, ma'am? A good Christian woman like you, defaulting on a promise? *Tsk, tsk*, Mrs. Marlowe. You shock me."

She waved her hands at him, still backing away toward the door. "No, no. I . . . I will honor my promise. You were right about the verse."

She muttered something under her breath that sounded suspiciously like *Damn you*. He chuckled. The Bishop's Widow was piqued into blasphemy. He reached for her again. "Then you must allow me to have my prize."

"No, not now." She was trying her damnedest to remain cool and aloof, but Rochdale saw the agitation beneath the calm. "I have guests. I cannot . . . cannot be kissing you now and return to them looking . . ."

"Like you'd been kissed?"

"Yes! You unnerve me, Lord Rochdale, as I'm sure you know. I will settle our wager, since I am honor-bound to do so, but not now, please. It is a meeting of the trustees of the Benevolent Widows Fund and I must get back to them. We have much to do to prepare for our ball next week. It is the final charity ball of the Season, our most important event. You must excuse me, my lord. I must go."

Aha. The other charity widows were there. Rochdale had learned, quite by accident, about a little pact among those ladies. His friend Cazenove had been in his cups one night, furious with Marianne Nesbitt for refusing his initial marriage proposal. The fellow became so foxed he probably had no idea he had let so many secrets drop. The most intriguing one involved a conversation he'd overheard at Ossing Park that indicated the charity widows had more on their minds than fund-raising. It seemed the ladies were determined not to remarry, and instead had set out to find the best lovers in town, and then to share every private detail with one another.

Cazenove had been livid that he was to be a pleasure toy and not a husband. Eventually, however, Marianne had relented and they were now married. Lady Somerfield had singled out Thayne, who had not been thrilled to learn the truth from Rochdale, to discover he'd been used and his sexual technique discussed with the other widows. Lady Gosforth was toying with Eustace Tolliver, and Rochdale had no inclination to warn the man, whom he did not like. And Wilhelmina, who used to toss around her favors with abandon before she became a duchess, had grown more circumspect, and more selective, and seemed to be angling after Ingleby.

And then there was Grace Marlowe. Rochdale was certain she had not taken a lover—yet—but her association with the other women meant she'd at least listened to tales of their sexual games. Perhaps she was even titillated by them. Enough so that when an opportunity to have a lover for her own presented itself, she just might be open to the idea.

Had she already told them about last night, and that blistering kiss in the carriage?

"I will not keep you from your friends," he said. "But before I go, I should like to know when I can expect to get my kiss. When shall it be?"

Her brow furrowed even as a blush rose in her cheeks. Lord, she was marvelous. So deliciously flustered and yet so proud. Rochdale hadn't had this much fun in years.

She shook her head. "I don't know."

"I do."

Still frowning, she lifted her eyes to his. "You do?"

"I believe I will collect my winnings at your ball next week. That is, if I am invited. I promise a hefty contribution if I am."

"Yes, yes, of course you will receive an invitation. And your contribution will be most welcome."

"And so will your kiss."

She heaved an exasperated sigh. "Lord Rochdale, please. I am a respectable woman. I lost my head last night when you took me by surprise, which was wicked of you. But I ought to have been stronger, and I deeply regret what happened. I have promised one more kiss. One, and no more. But, by heaven, sir, you will not make a public spectacle of me at my own charity ball."

His eyes widened in mock outrage. "My dear Mrs. Marlowe, you wound me. I give you my word that no one will see it or even know of it, unless *you* tell them. As I have told you before, I am the soul of discretion. I would not dream of importuning you in public."

"Thank you."

He had not lied. For once, Rochdale truly did intend to maintain discretion. He would lose the wager for sure, would lose his beloved Serenity, if even a hint of public scandal touched the Bishop's Widow. She would thoroughly and irrevocably cast him out before he so much as removed her garter.

"But I *will* collect my kiss," he said. "You may be sure of it."

She rolled her eyes. "I have no doubt you will, my lord."

"It is to be a masquerade ball, is it not?"

"Yes. At Doncaster House."

"I trust you will not be so disguised that I won't recognize you."

"That is unlikely."

"What costume will you wear? Or is that a secret?"

"I haven't decided yet."

He grinned. "No doubt it will be dreadfully proper, tight-laced, and buttoned up to your chin, not at all provocative or revealing. Well, I don't care because I know the woman beneath the mask. And I can't wait to have her in my arms again."

Chapter 4

Grace stood to one side of the drawing room doors, so that no one inside could see her, and took several slow, deep breaths, blowing each breath out through her lips. At the same time, she recited the Lord's Prayer in her head. The breathing exercise always helped her collect her composure whenever it threatened to slip; the prayer helped to refocus her thoughts away from whatever agitated her at the moment. It was a trick the bishop had taught her, one he often practiced before addressing Parliament.

Both actions eventually brought a small measure of peace to Grace, whose nerves had once again been frazzled by that dreadful man. She almost wished she had let him kiss her and get it over with. At least that way she would not have to see him again. He would be out of her life.

Instead, he had given her a week to fret over it, to imagine it, to lose sleep over it, to punish herself for anticipating it. Lord Rochdale was altogether too clever. He'd known exactly how it would be for her during the next week—the agony of delay, the dread of anticipation. And he would kiss her at an event for which she was a patroness and where she was obliged to remain for the entire evening. She could not make a scene. She could not escape to her own home. She would be trapped there, forced to deal with the pre-kiss anxiety as well as the post-kiss trauma. It would be an unbearable evening from start to finish. And he knew it. Too clever by half. And she had played right into his hand.

How he must be laughing at her.

She gave herself a mental shake. If she did not get such thoughts out of her head, she would have to recite another prayer or two. Grace would be ashamed for her friends to see that she was disturbed and perhaps guess the cause.

It was not actually a meeting of the trustees, as she had told Rochdale. Not a business meeting, anyway. That had occurred the day before. Today it was simply a gathering of friends. Wilhelmina and Marianne and Penelope had come to learn the outcome of yesterday's pursuit of Emily. They were concerned for Beatrice and her niece. The friends met here at Grace's Portland Place home for regular business meetings of the Benevolent Widows Fund trustees. More often than not, however, the serious meetings descended into a gathering of the Merry Widows, in which all manner of intimate secrets were shared. And so Portland Place also became the first place they gathered when one of them was in trouble.

Grace had not been surprised to see her friends, had even expected them, and had tea and cakes brought in while she related the events of the evening. Most of them, anyway. She had not yet reached the end of the tale when a maid had brought Rochdale's card. Grace had pocketed the card without mentioning his name and excused herself. And so now the ladies would want to hear more details of last night's adventure, which would place Grace at the center of attention. If she appeared the least bit unsettled, they would notice and question her. So she breathed and prayed until she was the embodiment of serenity.

Head held high, she entered the drawing room. It was her favorite room in the house, and its elegant beauty was soothing to both the eye and the soul. The walls were covered in butter yellow damask. Picture niches and door cases were carved with neoclassical ornaments picked out in pale pinks and cool blues, echoing the same color scheme of the elaborate plasterwork ceiling. Robert Adam's style was not so much in favor at the moment—he was considered old-fashioned—but Grace loved his work, and was pleased that the original owner, from whom the bishop had bought the house, had passed along all of Adam's watercolor designs for the ceilings and carpets. Those watercolors were now framed and hung along an upstairs corridor.

Marianne and Wilhelmina sat together on a French sofa speaking quietly. They both looked up at Grace's entrance. Penelope stood gazing out one of the tall windows overlooking the street. Short of stature but big of personality, Lady Gosforth was the most outspoken of the group, always airing her opinions without artifice or restraint. She was a curvaceous woman with a heart-shaped face framed in glossy chestnut curls that caught the glint of sunlight slanting through the windows. She turned and was the first to speak.

"Was that Rochdale? A man who looked suspiciously like him just left your house, Grace."

Oh, dear.

"Rochdale?" Marianne stared at Grace in puzzlement. "Here?"

Three pairs of eyes pinned her to the spot. But Grace was calm and collected. She could handle this.

"Yes, that was Lord Rochdale."

"Grace Marlowe! You cheeky wee devil." Penelope's clear blue eyes flashed with astonished amusement. "What was the worst rake in London doing *here*?"

"I suspect there is more to last night's episode than Grace has yet told us." Wilhelmina, a beautiful

golden-haired woman who would never reveal her
true age, which Grace guessed to be in the early for-
ties, was the most even-tempered and unflappable of
the Merry Widows. She had more experience of the
world than the rest of them. She'd made her way up
from the humblest beginnings, as a blacksmith's daughter, to become the lover of a series of high-ranking
noblemen said to include the Prince of Wales himself.
Her last protector, the Duke of Hertford, had truly
loved her, and when his wife had died, he'd shocked
Society by marrying Wilhelmina. She was now a
widow, the dowager Duchess of Hertford, exceedingly
rich but only marginally acceptable. Grace adored her,
as did all the Merry Widows. She was everything they
were not, and wise in the ways of love.

And she had a keen eye for seeing what others
sometimes missed.

Grace sighed. She had debated over how much, if
anything, she should tell her friends. She had been
tempted to remain as mum as an oyster, revealing
nothing. That was impossible now that Rochdale had
been seen. She would have to offer some explanation.
But she was not prepared to confess everything.

"Yes, there is more to tell." She busied herself with
adding fresh hot water to the teapot from a silver urn
perched on an elegant stand. She could certainly do
with a restorative cup of tea. "When everyone was
ready to leave, I gave up my seat in the carriage to
Emily, who could not be pried from Mr. Burnett's
arm. We shall be hearing the banns read for those two
any day now, I believe."

"That is wonderful news!" Marianne, a recent bride
herself, was very romantic of late. There was such happiness in her brown eyes that one could hardly blame
her for becoming sentimental now and then. "Mr.
Burnett was so clearly in love with Emily. I am glad
to hear he was able to win the attention of the silly

girl at long last. That will certainly go far toward eras-
ing the scandal her wretched mother created over
Thayne. Bravo, Mr. Burnett!"

Penelope groaned. "Pull your head out of the clouds
for a moment, Marianne. The more important piece
of information is that Grace gave up her seat in the
carriage."

Marianne looked puzzled for a moment; then understanding dawned. "Oh!"

Penelope frowned. "You were left alone with that
man, weren't you, Grace?"

"Tell us what happened," Wilhelmina said.

"Did he importune you?" Penelope asked.

"No, of course not." A blush heated her cheeks and
Grace hoped her friends would think it was because
of the nature of the question and not because the
answer was a lie. It was not entirely a lie. Grace had
allowed that kiss, after all. She had to take some of the
blame, if only for being a naïve pawn to Rochdale's
deliberate manipulation. "He simply brought me
home in his carriage. That is why he called just now.
To ensure that I was all right, considering all that
had happened."

"And are you?" Wilhelmina asked, no doubt reading more into those flushed cheeks than Grace was
willing to admit.

"Yes, I am fine."

"After two or more hours alone in a carriage with
Rochdale?" Penelope shook her head in disbelief,
causing the curls about her face to bounce. "You are
a stronger woman than I, Grace. He is one of those
exasperating men who makes one want to either throttle him or make love to him. Well, most women, anyway. Not you, Grace. I know you do not approve of
such things. Although I would not be surprised if you
throttled him. You are certain he behaved himself?"

"Yes, Penelope. Nothing untoward happened."
More lies. A few hours with Rochdale and Grace had

fallen into every sort of wickedness. She poured fresh tea for Marianne and Wilhelmina. Penelope declined another cup. Grace poured herself a cup, sat down, and took a long, calming swallow.

"It had to have been an awkward situation for you," Marianne said. "I remember at our wedding he seemed to make you uneasy."

Grace and Rochdale had been the only witnesses to Marianne and Adam's wedding. He had leered and grinned and generally made what ought to have been a joyful day a misery for her. Marianne had been beaming with such happiness, Grace had assumed she was oblivious to Rochdale's behavior. But that day paled beside what had occurred last night.

"It was not a comfortable journey, to be sure. He is a rather . . . unsettling person." A greater understatement had never been uttered.

Penelope laughed. "That he is. And devilish handsome, of course. Too bad he's a terrible scoundrel. You know how much I'd love to see you let down your hair, so to speak. To truly be a *merry* widow. But he's not the man for you, Grace. He would chew you up and spit you out without a backward glance. *And* he wouldn't care who knew of it. You are fortunate that he did not try to seduce you in that carriage. It would be just the sort of thing he would do."

"I believe Lord Rochdale can be a gentleman when he wants to be," Marianne said. "Or so Adam keeps telling me." Her husband, Adam Cazenove, was one of Lord Rochdale's closest friends. It had been through Adam's help that they'd been able to track down Emily to Rochdale's Twickenham villa. "And it sounds as though he did not touch poor Emily after all, so perhaps he is not always the blackguard everyone believes him to be."

"Oh, he is a blackguard, all right," Penelope said. "I was there at the Littleworth ball when he turned his back on poor Serena Underwood and walked away."

"So was I," Grace said. It was a troublesome memory that had haunted her for the last two days.

Penelope shuddered. "It was horrid, Marianne. You would not be so willing to give him the benefit of the doubt if you'd been there. Serena was hysterical, pleading with him to marry her because he'd ruined her. I will never forget it. The room was silent as a tomb. No one spoke, of course, not wanting to miss a single moment of such a juicy scandal. The music stopped. Everyone was watching. And Rochdale, calm as you please, peeled her arms from around his neck and said, 'Never.' Poor Serena sank into a collapse while he simply turned and walked out of the room. Dreadful man!"

"Serena went into seclusion the next day," Grace said, "and I cannot blame her. I certainly do not condone her behavior in allowing him to seduce her and then letting everyone know of it. But he was the worse villain for abandoning her in so ungentlemanly, and so publicly, a manner. Her reputation was destroyed utterly. I do not believe she has been seen in town since that night."

"She went into seclusion to have his child," Penelope said.

"I had heard that rumor," Grace said.

"I am somewhat acquainted with Lord Rochdale." Wilhelmina cast them each a look that said she would not be questioned on that topic. "He is not a monster. I daresay he has a side to this story that we will never know. He should not be so severely judged without us knowing the facts." Her soft voice held a note of reproof. She hated gossip, and for good reason. For much of her life, she'd been the subject of it.

"Quite so," Marianne said. "Adam believes Rochdale enjoys the villainous stories about himself and so does nothing to contradict them. His bad reputation amuses him. Even Adam is never sure what is true and what is apocryphal."

"Many woman are drawn to danger," Wilhelmina said, "and Rochdale knows it, which is why he cultivates the rakish image. A man who cares for nothing but his own pleasure, who is liable to do something frightfully bad at any moment, is exciting to certain women. They enjoy the risk he brings to a liaison."

Grace remembered his words to her: *A bit of risk now and then adds a hint of piquancy to the everyday humdrum of life. You should do it more often.*

Not likely. Look what happened to Serena Underwood for taking a risk. Not to mention the unnaturally wicked direction of her own thoughts after risking one carriage ride with him.

"Where there is smoke, there is fire," Penelope said. "Rochdale may enjoy being bad because he *is* bad. In any case, I am sorry, Grace, that you were forced to sit beside him in a cramped vehicle for two whole hours."

"I am, too, my dear," Wilhelmina said. "Rochdale may not be the ogre Penelope paints him to be, but you must be careful. He is certainly warm-blooded where women are concerned, but he can be coldhearted, too. I don't think he likes women very much."

Grace uttered a very unladylike snort. "I rather thought he liked them too much." Even prim and prudish bishops' widows.

"He likes to take his pleasure from women, but that's as far as it goes with Rochdale. He has a kind of disdain for women, I think. He cares for no one but himself, so take care—"

Just then a housemaid entered with Rochdale's carnations arranged in a crystal vase. "Where would you like me to place the gentleman's flowers, ma'am?"

Grace's teacup rattled in its saucer. Damn the man. She rose quickly and took the vase from the maid. "I'll take care of it, Millie. You may go."

The girl bobbed a curtsy and left. Grace turned her back to her friends for fear they would see the embarrassment in her face and misunderstand it. Or worse, understand it completely. She walked to a table on the far side of the room and placed the flowers upon it.

"Good heavens," Penelope said, a hint of amusement in her voice. "Are those from Rochdale?"

Grace did not turn around, but nodded her head in silence as she pretended to rearrange the ivy around the carnations.

"Well, well, well. Isn't this interesting?" Wilhelmina began to chuckle softly, then added, "Pink carnations. *And* ivy. A fascinating message."

Grace whirled around. "What message?"

"My dear Grace," Penelope said, "did your mother never teach you about the language of flowers?"

Grace shook her head. She had no idea what they were talking about, but was very afraid she was not going to like it.

Wilhelmina flashed a broad smile. "Pink carnations mean 'I'll never forget you.' And ivy means the sender is anxious to please you. I do believe you have made an impression on that coldhearted, self-absorbed libertine, my dear."

"What do you think of that little dappled gray mare?"

Rochdale tore his gaze from an impressive chestnut gelding to watch the horse Adam Cazenove indicated as she was being put through her paces in the circular nclosure at Tattersall's. He wasn't fond of dappled grays, as a rule. Too showy and not enough performance, and by the time they developed their highly decorative coloring, many of them were past their prime.

This one appeared relatively youthful, however, maybe five or six years old, a nice little Arab with a lot more life in her yet. She had the small head, dished face, and thin muzzle typical of her breed, and moved with elegance and spirit.

"She has a decent gait," he said. "Good trotting

action. Her quarters are well muscled and nicely rounded. Hard, clean legs. A bit too low-bodied for speed, though."

Cazenove laughed. "I'm not thinking of racing her. I'm looking for a mount for Marianne. A belated wedding present."

The rider dismounted and began walking the gray toward the main enclosure with its famous cupola, where the horse would be auctioned. He stopped along the way so potential buyers could examine her more closely. When she stopped beside Cazenove, she shook herself all over and blew through her nostrils. She had not liked all the poking and prodding and lifting of her feet and checking of her teeth. She thought herself above such indignities, poor girl. While Cazenove made his own inspection, Rochdale scratched her behind the ears, causing her to snort with pleasure.

"I think she's a beauty," his friend said. "Head light and lean and well set on, withers high and long. Seems good-tempered. I'm inclined to believe she will do very nicely."

"Looking to bid on her, Rochdale?" A familiar voice interrupted their conversation.

Rochdale looked over the mare's nose to see Lord Sheane approaching, as cocky and smug as ever in a black-and-yellow-striped waistcoat that made him look like a bumblebee. "Not me. Too decorative for my tastes. Cazenove here wants her for his wife. Besides, I'm holding my last empty stall for Albion."

Sheane gave a bark of laughter. "Making progress in that arena, then, are you?"

Rochdale was fairly certain he was. Grace had agreed to pony up that kiss he'd won off her. He would not have been surprised if she'd turned welsher on him, but now he knew she had a core of honor that would not bend. A potentially valuable bit of knowledge. That streak of integrity might come in handy again during the course of his seduction.

It had been a stroke of pure spontaneous brilliance that had made him set the masquerade ball as the date for collecting his winnings. She had no doubt been tying herself into knots all week, just thinking about it. And he would take pleasure in untying each and every one of them while he kissed her into oblivion.

Rochdale did not believe he was being arrogant to think that winning the wager with Sheane would be as easy as shooting fish in a barrel. Others might be of the opinion that he was taking too long. But some women required more foreplay than others. And he'd be willing to bet Grace Marlowe never had any foreplay in her life. She had a wealth of passion beneath that cool reserve, though, and Rochdale was just the man to unleash it.

It would be fun while it lasted. He loved nothing more than a good challenge, whether on the racetrack or in the bedroom. But once he'd taken his pleasure from Grace and won the gelding, he would move on to something, or someone, requiring less effort.

"Yes, Sheane," he said, "things are moving along quite nicely. I'll be ready to take Albion by the end of the month, if not sooner."

Sheane gave another loud crack of laughter, causing heads to turn in his direction. The fellow had no social graces whatsoever. "It won't happen, Rochdale, believe me. I'll be taking Serenity off your hands before you know it. A nice fresh stall is ready and waiting for her. Ha! Oh, and Cazenove . . . Haltwhistle has an eye on that gray. He's been lucky at the tables of late and may have a lot of blunt to throw around."

"Blast!" Adam took another look at the horse as she was led down the colonnaded path toward the auctioneer. There were several horses ahead of her on the lists, but she caught a lot of interest from the rows of gentlemen lining the path. "The bidding's bound to go high if Haltwhistle gets involved. The animal could be a blind and lame packhorse, for all he cares."

"Very true," Sheane said. "He simply likes to own things, anything, that someone else covets. Quit staring at that dappled posterior, Cazenove, and he might not realize you're interested."

"Right you are, Sheane. I appreciate the warning. By the way, I understand you have a new painting on display." Cazenove's brows lifted in question while his eyes twinkled in amusement.

Sheane, who was a veritable font of vulgar laughter today, cackled once again so that his striped belly shook. He was an amateur painter whose subjects were not the sort one could display in public. Instead, he had a private "gallery" in his town house where he showed his works to gentlemen by special invitation. And then there were the parties, often hosted at Rochdale's Twickenham villa, where Sheane would bring along his latest model and paint her on the spot, so to speak. As the evenings progressed, other women who'd been brought to the parties would sometimes get into the spirit and bare all in order to be painted by Sheane. By the time dawn rolled around, more flesh than clothing would be on view. Rochdale had more than one of Sheane's paintings hanging at the villa, mementos of particularly lively evenings.

Cazenove was something of an art connoisseur and thought Sheane actually had some talent. He'd often teased the man about painting proper subjects that might be displayed at the British Institution, where Cazenove was one of the governors, but Sheane had no interest in it. He preferred a nice, plump female's ass, or other ripe parts, to a landscape or classical study.

"As it happens," Sheane said, grinning like a fool, "I do have a new painting. You must come by and view it, Cazenove. I think it will amuse you. You might recognize the face, if nothing else, as belonging to that new little dancer at Drury Lane, Delilah Munro."

"The redhead with the big . . ." Cazenove made a curving motion in front of his chest.

"The very one," Sheane said. "She was an extremely . . . compliant model, and I was able to capture a most interesting pose. I look forward to your opinion. Now, if you both will excuse me, I want to see how the bidding goes for the black filly."

He turned and walked down the colonnade, disappearing into a sea of top hats and frock coats.

"There's something devilish unsavory about that fellow," Rochdale said.

"An interesting assessment, coming from you."

"Even so."

"But what is this about Serenity and Albion?" Cazenove asked. "Do not tell me you have staked your best horse on some wager with him."

"I have indeed."

Cazenove's eyebrows disappeared beneath his hat brim and his mouth hung open for an astonished moment. Then: "I can't believe it. I did not think you would ever give up that horse."

"I do not intend to give her up."

"Ah. A sure thing, then?"

Rochdale smiled. "Yes. The surest thing that ever was."

Chapter 5

Grace had sent an astonished Kitty away and stood alone in her dressing room, gazing at her reflection in the pier glass. She could hardly believe she'd done it. A week ago she would never have had the nerve to wear such a costume. But a week ago, everything had changed.

Ever since Rochdale had insinuated himself into her life, his bad influence had pushed her into doing one wicked thing after the other. It was as though he had rubbed some kind of ungodly invisible ink into her hands while he'd caressed them, and no matter how hard she tried, she couldn't wash it off. And now, whatever she touched, a little stain of sin was left behind.

Lies—white ones, little ones—had been falling from her lips all week. Sinful thoughts—dark ones, big ones—had swirled dizzily in her head. And it was all his fault. The provoking man was some sort of evil magician. He had changed everything. He had changed . . . her.

The bishop had been right. Without him around to guide her, the frail nature of her virtue had indeed been compromised. The first man to show an interest in her, however insincere or opportune, had broken down defenses that had been over ten years in the building. Grace had shown herself to be precisely the weak-willed female her husband had warned her against.

And yet . . .

She felt alive. Rochdale was going to kiss her tonight, and she was not entirely averse to the idea. All week long, her head had been spinning with memories of his kiss in the carriage. The very fact of remembering was surely a sin, but she couldn't help it. She recalled every detail.

Her body had shimmered to life in a way it had never done before—never been allowed to before—and the recollection of it had consumed her. Grace had always suspected there was more to what men and women, husbands and wives, shared together physically. She had instinctively reached out for it in the first days of her marriage, before she'd learned it was wrong and had to be suppressed.

For all of her adult life, she'd known the sort of feelings Rochdale's kiss had provoked were sinful. But then her friends had begun to speak candidly about lovers and lovemaking and intimacies she'd never imagined. As much as their confidences embarrassed her, Grace knew they were not depraved, evil women. Even Wilhelmina, with her colorful history, was not immoral. When they spoke so openly and joyously of physical passion, it had not sounded wicked. It sounded . . . exciting.

Grace had never, of course, admitted to them any of her perverse thoughts. She allowed them to believe in her prudish disapproval. But she had listened and silently pondered all they said.

Now, she knew in her heart that they'd been right, and she was shamefully anxious to taste once again a little bit of what they'd described. Just a little bit. One kiss, that was all, and then she'd toss the rogue out of her life for good. She would not give him the chance to take it any further.

It still made no sense that Rochdale was interested

in her at all. The bishop had warned Grace that men would be drawn to her beauty and would make illicit overtures. Perhaps that was all it was with Rochdale. He was attracted by her looks. Grace was not a vain woman, but she knew the face she saw in the mirror was a pretty one. Her husband had commented on it often enough, and she was sure that he'd enjoyed having a pretty woman at his side. Under his tutelage, though, she had learned never to flaunt her looks, to use them to draw attention to herself, or to become too prideful about what God had given her. For years she had given little or no thought to the way she looked, and while the bishop was alive, no man would have dared to cast her an admiring glance.

Since his death, her public persona was still so tied to the bishop that no men indicated any sort of interest in her. Or if they had, Grace had not been aware of it. Perhaps because she hadn't looked for it, had not really wanted it. Not until her friends began discussing their interest in various gentlemen had Grace even considered that a man might look at her in that way. Just her luck that the moment she became aware of such things, the one man who'd made his interest loud and clear was the most lechcrous cad in London.

Despite Rochdale's unsavory reputation, Grace could not help being flattered that he found her beautiful. She was only human, after all. She would have to be careful, however, not to allow flattery to persuade her to take things too far. One kiss, and no more. She had a feeling Rochdale would not be satisfied with one kiss, but that was where it would end. In the long run, she could never truly be a Merry Widow. She could never take a lover. Grace was a respectable churchwoman who lived a life of impeccable propriety. She was the Bishop's Widow. And always would be.

Except that it was not the Bishop's Widow who looked back at her from the mirror.

He had done this to her. *He* had teased her about being tight-laced and unbending. *He* had talked about taking risks, about stepping outside of everyone's expectations. *He* had forced her to show him that he was wrong about her.

The costume she wore would certainly do that. It was neither tight-laced nor buttoned up. It was light and loose and free. Grace felt like a . . . well, like a fairy queen. She felt beautiful, and for the first time in years, feeling beautiful did not seem so very wrong.

The rest of her costume lay on the bed. She reached for the pretty mask made all of pink silk rose petals and put it on, tying the ribbons underneath her hair. She picked up the matching gossamer silk shawl, if one could call such a wisp of fabric a shawl, and headed out the door.

The instant she left the safety of her rooms, her skin prickled with anxiety. Was she making a huge mistake? She was a patroness of the ball, after all. Perhaps the costume was too immodest. But it was too late to change now. There wasn't time. She dashed back into the dressing room, rummaged around a drawer, and pulled out an enormous paisley shawl. Standing before the mirror, she wrapped it around herself. Perfect. It was so big that almost none of the costume beneath was visible. It looked a bit odd, but she could claim to be chilled.

There was no time to do anything about her hair, though.

She tossed the gossamer shawl toward the bed. It floated gracefully, buoyed by a tiny current of air made by the mere movement of her arm in throwing it. She watched it flutter and billow in delicate waves until it landed in an elegant drift of pink silk upon the counterpane.

That was how she had felt only a moment ago. Lighter than air. Fairylike.

Grace took one more look at herself in the mirror

and frowned. God help her, for once in her life, she wanted to float. She wanted to take one small risk, just to show him, and herself, that she could.

She let the heavy shawl drop to the floor, picked up the gossamer silk, and left the room.

Rochdale arrived late to the ball, as he generally did. He disliked the ceremony of a receiving line, where the host and hostess pretended to be happy that he had graced their humble gathering with his presence. It was always an awkward affair. Either he was friendly with the husband, perhaps a fellow game-ster, and the wife made no secret of her disapproval of him, or he'd bedded the wife and had to look her oblivious husband in the face.

Tonight's receiving line would have included not only the Duke and Duchess of Doncaster— fortunately, he had only a nodding acquaintance with each of them—but all the patronesses of the Benevo-lent Widows Fund who sponsored the event and re-quired hefty donations to the charity from each attendee.

Grace Marlowe, who chaired the board of trustees, would likely be at the top of the line, but Rochdale did not want to face her in that formal atmosphere with all her friends looking on. He preferred a more private meeting, which meant he needed to study the lay of the land, searching for the perfect secluded spot.

So he'd arrived late, but well before the unmasking at midnight, and wove his way through the crowd, trying to be unobtrusive. Not an easy task at a mas-querade, where everyone openly stared at everyone else, hoping to discover the identities beneath the masks. Rochdale imagined that most people recog-nized him fairly easily, as he had not gone to great lengths to disguise himself. He was dressed as a high-wayman of the last century, complete with powdered bag wig, black tricorne, black mask, black skirted coat, and long top boots. The polished butts of two pistols tucked into the top of his breeches twinkled in the candlelight, as did a large ruby stickpin in the white lace at his throat. Truth be told, he felt rather dashing. It was the perfect guise in which to abduct his prim heroine for a passionate kiss in the dark.

Doncaster House was huge and brightly lit—three enormous chandeliers in the ballroom held hundreds of candles; standing torchères, candelabra, and sconces lit every other room and corridor—and required a bit of reconnoitering. Finally, Rochdale found a secluded anteroom that would serve his purpose.

But he had yet to find Grace. Since he had no idea what costume to look for, he studied every female form that looked to be the right height and age. There were noblewomen of every century: toga-clad Roman empresses, thirteenth- and fourteenth-century ladies in tall pointed hats and long-waisted gowns, sixteenth-century ladies in farthingales with enormous ruffs at their necks, and eighteenth-century ladies in towering wigs and wide skirts. There were princesses from every region of the globe, Arabia to China to Russia, and one young dark-haired woman in beaded buckskin wearing feathers in her hair. Queens from France and Egypt and England—more than one Queen Elizabeth, in fact. There were goddesses and milkmaids and shepherdesses. Birds, cats, and one elegant tigress.

But no Bishop's Widow.

Other widows and willing matrons caught his eye, though, and recognized him. Two blatantly proclaimed their availability for assignations later that evening, but Rochdale declined both invitations. He had only one woman on his mind tonight. As he continued to search for her, it occurred to him that a kiss was a far thing from a sexual assignation, and there was no reason to have declined those two offers. He chuckled at his own foolishness. Once upon a time, he'd have entertained both women and still sought out a third.

He must be getting old that he could concentrate on only one woman at a time. And one who would not even warm his bed tonight.

Where was she? He wondered if she had grown craven and stayed away. But no, this was *her* charity ball, and regardless of how much she might want to avoid kissing him, she would not fail in her obligations. Nor did he imagine she would go back on her promise to him. Rochdale had won their wager legitimately, without guile or trickery, and he believed she had a core of honor that would not allow her to break her word. No, she was here somewhere in this vast mansion, and he would find her.

He caught a glimpse of a nun and smiled to think that Grace might have found such a costume appropriate, but when the nun turned toward him, he saw it was the Duchess of Doncaster, his hostess. His gaze continued to sweep the room until it landed on a woman in a loose white robe, belted at the waist, wearing a long red wig and carrying a shield. She was either Boadicea or perhaps Athena—he could not be sure. But he had no doubt of her identity. It was Wilhelmina, the dowager Duchess of Hertford. She was smiling and talking with a Harlequin, a cavalier, and a woman with her back to him dressed in the palest pink with a long blond wig hanging past her waist and threaded with tiny pink flowers. Two transparent pink wings jutted from her shoulders. A fairy princess, he supposed. Or the Faerie Queen.

He decided he would approach the duchess and see if he could cajole her into revealing the costumes of her fellow patronesses. It would save him a great deal of time if only he knew what Grace Marlowe was wearing.

The closer Rochdale got, the more interested he became in the blond fairy. So much so that he momentarily forgot all about Grace Marlowe. She was a beautiful fairy, at least from the rear. The silky pink fabric of her dress clung to her curves rather nicely. But it was the hair that attracted him most. He'd always had a weakness for long hair, especially long blond hair, and even though this fairy's hair was surely a wig, it was nevertheless alluring: a thick golden mass hanging straight and heavy, its weight swaying slightly as she moved. Perhaps Wilhelmina would introduce him.

But no. Introductions were not necessary at a masquerade, where identities were allowed to be kept secret. He could simply stroll up and invite the pink fairy to dance. Assuming she wasn't hatchet-faced when she turned around.

The orchestra members were tuning up their instruments for the next dance, and the lines were beginning to form. Even without music, the din of a hundred conversations filled the air. But somehow, above the noise, a sound reached him that brought him to a halt. He almost collided with a turbaned Turk, and mumbled an apology. And there it was again. That luscious sound. One he recognized well. The rich, deep-throated, incongruously voluptuous laughter of Grace Marlowe.

And the damnedest thing was that it seemed to be coming from the pink fairy. It couldn't be Grace. Could it?

He moved closer until he was standing only a few feet away, when she happened to glance over her shoulder as though looking for someone. And her gaze collided with his.

Grace Marlowe. Even though she was masked, he knew her at once. Her eyes widened behind a mask of pink flower petals when she seemed to realize who he was, but she turned toward him and acknowledged his presence with a cool nod.

Well, well. She had surprised him yet again. Grace Marlowe, the fairy queen, was nothing short of breathtaking. Rochdale had to admit that even had there been no wager, he'd have been drawn to her tonight. He'd be willing to bet his second best horse, however, that she'd never have come dressed as she was had there been no wager. For without it, he would never have kissed her. No question about it, the kiss had changed her somehow. The costume was for his benefit. He was sure of it. And it amused him that she had dressed so provocatively for him, just to prove that she wasn't as predictably prim as he'd suggested.

Her pink dress was so silky and light that it floated like a cloud when she moved, falling against the curve of her hip, swaying softly, then clinging to her thigh. Thousands of tiny silver stars were sewn into the silk, catching the candlelight as the fabric swayed and swirled. Pink ribbons embroidered with flowers fell from beneath her bosom all the way to the floor.

And what a lovely bosom it was. The dress was not as revealing as many others, but it showed more of Grace Marlowe's charms than he'd ever beheld before. Even the sight of those pale rounded breasts, pushed up high by her corset, could not distract Rochdale from her hair. It shone gleaming gold in the candlelight—glossy as old silver, thick and straight—with sections here and there braided with small flowers. He ought to have known it was not a wig. This was Grace's hair. And it was magnificent.

He had an almost uncontrollable urge to lift its weight in his hands and comb his fingers through it.

"May I have this dance, Faerie Queen?"

A flicker of wariness passed over her eyes for an instant, but she nodded and took his proffered hand. She wore gloves of pink silk so diaphanous they were nearly transparent, hardly worth wearing, for he could feel the warmth of her skin as though she wore nothing at all. He brought the silky hand to his lips and kissed her fingers. They trembled slightly, which made him smile.

He placed her hand on his arm and led her to the dance floor, where the lines had formed for the next dance. "You know who I am, do you not, madam?"

"Yes, of course. Dick Turpin, is it not? Or perhaps Tom King?"

He grinned. "For tonight I am simply an unnamed highwayman. And you are . . ."

"Titania."

"Of course. You look beautiful, my queen. Did you do this for me? Because you knew what was to happen between us this night? Did you dress like this to entice me? If so, you have succeeded. In fact, we could skip the dance and—"

"Are those real?" She indicated the pistols at his waist.

"They are. Is this real?" The question gave him an excuse to touch her hair, which he did. Soft. Silken. It even smelled sweet, as if all those tiny flowers were real and not made of silk. "My God, it is. You are positively brazen tonight, Titania. It suits you."

They took their places at the bottom of the line just as the music began. They did not speak as they moved through the steps, but Rochdale took every opportunity to touch her, rubbing clandestine little circles on her palm with his thumb whenever he held her hand, giving her waist a quick squeeze when he twirled her. And he took great pleasure simply in watching her move. She was well named, a light and graceful dancer. Not one of those boisterous and energetic dancers, like so many others tonight, she was elegance personified, every move lithe and supple, almost sensuous. The remarkable dress floated and swirled about her in the most tantalizing manner as she moved. He could not take his eyes off her, all the time imagining her slender white limbs tangled with his, that long, loose hair tumbled upon a pillow.

Whoever thought he'd be eager for a prim, do-good, sermon-quoting prude to warm his bed?

And what a jumble of contradictions she was. Dressed to entice, yet wary and reserved, almost unapproachable. She allowed the costume to reveal her body, yet she was still wrapped up in her mantle of fierce propriety. But the costume was an important step. Perhaps during the past week her anxiety over the kiss had changed to anticipation. Perhaps she had decided she'd liked kissing him after all, and looked forward to doing so again. Whatever the reason, Grace Marlowe was a changed woman. And might be even more so before the night was over.

Other men were equally captivated by the fairy queen. More than one cast a hungry glance in her direction, though she seemed not to notice. Rochdale experienced a stab of annoyance that her revealing costume, surely meant for him alone, nevertheless allowed every slavering fool in the room to ogle her. He'd hoped to see all that golden hair falling loose around her shoulders in private. Now, every man in the room enjoyed the glory of it.

The pang of jealousy passed in an instant, and Rochdale laughed at his own foolishness. He did not deny his desire for Grace Marlowe, but she was the project of a wager, not the object of a romantic pursuit. Once he'd had her and won Sheane's horse, he'd go back to the lusty, accommodating women he was accustomed to.

In the meantime, he enjoyed what he saw and couldn't wait to see more of her. All those other ogling idiots could undress her with their eyes all night long. It was of no concern to Rochdale, for he was the only one who was going to undress her with his hands, the only one who would taste every inch of her porcelain skin, the only one who would wrap himself up in her golden hair. Maybe not this night, but soon.

His thoughts must have been written clearly on his face, for after once intercepting his hungry gaze, she never again lifted her eyes to his.

When the dance ended, Rochdale took her hand and pulled her away from the line. "Come. Let us forgo the rest of the set. I have something to show you."

"What?"

"You'll see." He placed her arm on his and they threaded their way through the dancers and finally through the main doors to the ballroom. A man dressed as Caesar made a suggestive remark and leered at Grace as they passed. Rochdale stopped, placed his hand on the butt of a pistol, and glared at the blackguard. Caesar backed away and disappeared into the crowd.

The corridors and other salons, including one set aside for cards, were almost as crowded as the ballroom, with masked revelers laughing and drinking and generally behaving in a more uninhibited manner than would have been typical had they been dressed in normal evening clothes. Costumes did that to a person, gave them license to do and say things they might not otherwise. Would Grace's ethereal costume have a similar effect on her? Lord, he hoped so.

He took her through a series of rooms until he finally came upon the door he sought. He opened it and gestured for Grace to enter. She shot him an anxious look, but went inside. He followed her and closed the door behind him.

It was a small anteroom with only a table in the center and a few chairs against the walls. The fire was lit and a tray holding a decanter of wine and two glasses sat on the table. The latter had been the result of a few coins slipped to an accommodating footman. But the fire had been lit earlier, so the room was meant to be used by guests. Probably for just such an assignation as this one.

"Is this what you wanted to show me?" she asked.

"Yes. Not so much to show you as to bring you

here. I thought it the perfect private place for collecting on our wager. May I pour you some wine?"

"Please, let's just get on with it."

"*Tsk, tsk*, Titania. Why the hurry? Let's enjoy ourselves." He passed her a glass of claret, and she took it.

He circled the table, placing it between them, and watched her as she took a swallow. And then another. Dutch courage, he presumed. Despite the alluring costume, she was as tense as a thoroughbred before a race. He hoped to hell she was not planning to toss back the entire decanter. He wanted her conscious, by God.

"You never answered my question earlier," he said.

"What question?"

"About whether you wore that dress just for me."

She emptied the glass and placed it on the table, but did not answer.

Rochdale flashed a smile. "So you did wear it for me. I am honored. And delighted to have nudged you out of your tight-laced gentility. You look marvelous, you know. Beautiful. Extremely desirable."

A nearly transparent pink shawl, soft as thistledown, hung from the crooks of her arms, and she tugged it up to wrap across her décolletage.

"No, don't cover yourself, Titania. Don't have second thoughts about your costume. It was the right choice. The perfect choice."

"It wasn't just for you. I simply wanted to wear something different for a change."

"Or perhaps you wanted to be yourself, your true self, for a change. Is this the real Grace Marlowe—this ethereal, brazen creature—and the Bishop's Widow the guise?"

She shook her head vehemently, then lifted her chin at an imperious angle in an obvious effort to claim her identity as Bishop Marlowe's widow.

"Whatever the reason, I like this change." He removed his mask, then walked around the table to where she stood. "I like it very much." He reached up and carefully removed her mask. Then he took both her hands to pull her toward him, slid his hands up to the bare flesh above her elbows, and drew her closer. "Very much, indeed. You look positively delicious. Come, let me taste you."

He brought his mouth to hers and kissed her.

She stood stiff and unmoving, thoroughly uninvolved in the kiss. Was she punishing him for his impertinence? Or punishing herself for responding to him in the carriage?

Come on, Grace, old girl. You know you want it.

He went to work on her lips, using all his skill and seductive powers to relax her, entice her, unlock her. He slid one arm gently around her waist, while the other crept up her arm and around her shoulder right into the golden depths of her hair. He pressed her closer, tighter, then nipped her lip with his teeth until her mouth parted open ever so slightly. He took advantage at once and teased his tongue inside.

He knew the instant her restraint changed into something else entirely, something hot and sweet at the same time. God, he could almost smell her arousal through the fine pores of her perfect skin as her tongue answered his. He deepened the kiss and she followed. Her arms were now around his neck, clinging, pulling him down to her. Dear Lord, she was amazing, taking as much as she gave, setting him on fire.

And suddenly, she was gone. She'd pulled away so fast he hadn't been able to react, and now she skittered around to the other side of the table, out of his reach.

"Enough," she said. "You have got what was owed you. No more, please."

He smiled at her discomposure. By God, he had

rattled her good and proper. No, she had rattled herself, which was even better.

Progress!

"All right," he said. "No more. For now. But you cannot deny that you enjoyed it."

"You are a practiced seducer, Lord Rochdale, and know exactly how to make a respectable woman let down her guard. But you have had your fun and won your wager. We're finished." She picked up her mask and began tying it on.

"Allow me to hope that we are not. You are a beautiful and fascinating woman, Grace."

"I did not give you leave to use my Christian name, sir."

"No, you did not. I'm sorry. I simply thought that after such a passionate interlude we could be less formal. But it shall be as you wish, Mrs. Marlowe."

"Thank you. Now, I must get back to our guests. And I . . . I have to go over the contributions to see what was brought in."

"Enough for the new wing at Marlowe House, perhaps?"

"That would be wonderful. We could help so many more families, but it is unlikely we will raise so large an amount tonight." Her voice was tight, clipped, giving nothing away. "Now I must go."

She walked to the door, but he reached it before her. "Let me check first to ensure no one is about. It would not do for you to be seen coming out of a closed room with me."

She sucked in a sharp breath. "No, no, it would not. Thank you."

Rochdale opened the door a crack and peeked out. A friar and a gypsy girl strolled past, heads bent together in intimate conversation, oblivious to Rochdale and everything else. Once they had rounded a corner out of sight, he opened the door. "It's all right. You may leave safely now."

Grace hurried past him, but Rochdale placed a hand on her arm. She turned to look at him, her smoky eyes haunted and confused.

"May I call upon you again?"

She frowned and shook her head. "No. I'm very busy. Please excuse me."

And she was gone.

Rochdale went back inside and poured himself another glass of wine. He tossed it back and congratulated himself on the progress made tonight. That kiss had unnerved her—hell, it had very nearly unnerved *him*—and she was confused. He needed to make the next move before her head cleared. He had devised a plan, too. He knew her weak spot, and his plan would play right into it.

Chapter 6

Grace made her way back to the ballroom, outwardly collected—a forced attitude that was as natural to her as breathing—but thoroughly shaken inside. Perplexed. Bewildered. Utterly ashamed of her reaction to Rochdale's kiss. For the second time now, she had allowed him to coax an unnaturally wanton response from her.

When she had first seen him, dashing and dangerous in his highwayman gear and looking at her as though she were a ripe fig he wanted to bite into, all secret thoughts anticipating his kiss crumbled away, and suddenly she was afraid. She had hoped he would notice her costume. She had wanted to show him that she was something more than prim and proper. She had wanted him to look at her with admiration.

Now, that look of much more than uncomplicated admiration frightened her. Grace felt foolish for thinking to let Rochdale, of all people, see a glimpse of the girl she had once been before learning the potential evil of her feminine nature. His open desire made her afraid of what he might do to her. Grace would never, of course, allow him to know of her anxiety, so she held tight to her composure and had been determined to remain stiff and uninvolved, to give him what she owed him, her lips and no more.

A shiver had danced down her spine when he

leaned in to kiss her. Her first instinct had been to turn away and not allow it, but she had given her word and so she had not pulled back. Instead, she had come face-to-face with what she now realized she'd been most afraid of—her own unbridled reaction to his lips and tongue and hands.

She let him take her mouth and rip away her common sense. Before she'd become completely lost, however, there had been an instant of candid acceptance that she wanted to feel those wild sensations again. Even with this horrid man, whom she disliked and disdained. After a moment, after her part of the bargain had been honored, she had known she should end it. Instead, heaven help her, she'd found herself delaying the end, promising herself she would stop him soon. In a moment. Just one more moment.

It had taken a supreme act of will and a rush of pure disgust at her wanton behavior to finally push him away.

But it was too late. All those feminine frailties the bishop had taught her to keep in check had been let loose. She had never felt more sinful. All because she had enjoyed Rochdale's mouth on hers, the touch of his tongue to hers. He'd kissed her ravenously, and more thoroughly than she would ever have dreamed, using his tongue to acquaint himself with parts of her mouth she could never have imagined a man might want to know. Surely *that* was sinful, for it ought to have disgusted her, yet she'd loved it and, if she was perfectly honest with herself, she would love to experience it again. And again.

Lord, she was lost to wickedness. To immorality. He'd done this to her. She could have stayed in that cozy room with him for hours, letting him make her body tingle, setting off a heat in her blood like a deadly fever. She could have stayed. She'd *wanted* to stay. And that was what made her leave. The wanting. The novelty of unleashed cravings.

And all this for a man she could barely tolerate as a human being. A man whose life was marked with dissipation and debauchery and scandal. A man she would normally cross the street to avoid. And yet she had felt a glimmering of desire for him. More than a glimmer. Much more. How was that possible when she disliked him so? Was she so superficial that she could ignore his character because he was handsome?

Perhaps it was not really her fault. Perhaps that was why he was such a notorious rake—women could not resist him. Grace certainly could not, God help her.

As she leaned back against a pillar in the ballroom, wielding her fan against the warmth that still flushed her skin, she thought she might actually collapse from dizziness—not so much of the head, though her brain roiled in confusion, but of the soul. She no longer knew who she was. She wanted, but did not want. She felt lost, but also found. Grace had never been so confused in all her life. Even if her inner turmoil made her doubt everything about herself, outwardly she knew her role. Grace Marlowe did not collapse or swoon. She held her head high and faced the world with confidence. She would do so now and for the rest of the evening. It was what was expected of her.

She pushed away from the pillar and almost collided with a court jester. She recognized him as Lord Dewesbury and allowed him to sweep her into the country dance already in progress.

Grace danced with two other gentlemen, both known to her, both respectable, and both effusive in their compliments on her costume. Discounting the encounter with Rochdale, she found she rather enjoyed being the object of gentlemen's admiration, and decided the costume was not a complete mistake. It did no harm, she supposed, for Society to be reminded that she was a woman and not a fragile porcelain doll.

As much as she tried to put what had happened in the anteroom behind her, she was constantly distracted by the sight of that roguish highwayman, who seemed to be everywhere. Her eyes were reluctantly drawn to him. She wanted to ignore him, tried to ignore him, but she could not even pretend disinterest.

She silently scolded herself for a fool as she watched him with other women, dancing and laughing and flirting. It was ridiculous to think he truly had a special interest in *her*. He was interested in anything in skirts. There was nothing more between him and Grace than an accidental encounter that had placed them in a carriage together, and a silly wager that took advantage of the moment.

Once, though, his gaze landed upon hers with an intensity that made her feel like the only woman in the room. Then he smiled, and his face took on a look of open desire as he caressed her with his eyes.

Dear God, she was truly wicked. Otherwise she'd be able to control the rapid beat of her heart, the gooseflesh on her arms, the fluttering low in her belly merely at the sight of his smile.

She stumbled in the dance—while Rochdale was still looking, damn him.

"Steady on," her partner said as he tightened his grip on her arm.

Rochdale appeared to laugh, and a feverish flush of embarrassment warmed every inch of her. Grace hated the sensation, which she'd only rarely experienced until recently, and silently cursed her fair skin and the ease with which it could grow pink. Just as she had learned to maintain her composure at all times in public, she had long ago mastered the heat that could color her skin. The bishop had gently chided her for harboring thoughts so shameful they made her blush. If she felt shame or embarrassment or horror, she was to keep such feelings in check and only give into them within the privacy of prayer. Though he'd never said so directly, he'd made it clear that a red-faced wife reflected badly on a man in his position.

Grace had schooled herself well and it was now second nature to her to curb any untoward emotions from coloring her face. But this spring, when her friends had begun speaking so openly about the intimate details of their private lives, Grace had been unprepared for such talk and her fair skin reacted before she could control it.

That had been in private with female friends, however. Blushing in public like a giddy schoolgirl was mortifying. And she seemed to have lost the ability to master it. It was Rochdale's fault. He'd made her blush more times than she could count. Just looking at him made her think of his kisses, which sent heat spreading over her face and down her neck and across her bosom and shoulders, a rampant flush of warmth pinking her skin in its wake. There was no stopping it.

Everyone in the room would be able to see the telltale flush, announcing her wickedness to all the world. Just as the bishop had warned her.

She turned away and deliberately avoided Rochdale, and the blushes he caused, for the rest of the evening.

After a particularly lively reel, Grace curtsied to her partner, turned, and found Wilhelmina at her side. "It is almost midnight," the duchess said as she tossed a ridiculously long red curl over her shoulder. The wig fell about her like a cape. "Time for the unmasking. I don't suppose you will be surprised to learn the identity of a certain highwayman who swept you away earlier."

Grace felt her cheeks flame. Again. It seemed the mere mention of the man could set her off. "No, I knew him at once."

"And still danced with him."

"It would have been rude to refuse. Especially as a patroness."

"I suppose so." Wilhelmina's head cocked to one side and Grace could feel the intensity of her gaze even behind the black mask she wore. "He is showing an uncommon interest in you, my dear. I confess, I am rather astonished."

"No more than I, believe me."

"I hope you will not mind a word of advice." Wilhelmina switched Boadicea's shield to her other hand and pulled Grace close so she could be heard above the general noise without being overheard. "Be careful with him. He has the skill and experience to turn a woman's head before she knows what hit her. Take your pleasure from him, if that is what you desire, but guard your heart and soul. He will thrill you between the sheets, but he gets bored easily and can be callous when he deems an affair is over."

"Good heavens, Wilhelmina, I am not having an affair with Lord Rochdale!"

"Not yet. But clearly he is wooing you, something I've never known him to do. He's never had to woo anyone, after all, when there are always women throwing themselves in his path. But you interest him, Grace, and I will not be surprised if you succumb to his seduction."

"No, no, I could *never*—"

Wilhelmina held up a hand. "Never say 'never,' my dear. It saves a great deal of embarrassing explanation later. I am not warning you against an affair with Rochdale. Quite the opposite. There is no one better to teach you the joys of sexual pleasure, to teach you not to be afraid of that part of your nature. I just don't want you to get hurt. So, in time, if you decide it is something you want to do, go into it with both eyes open, knowing that it will be no more than a charming interlude. Do not expect constancy or exclusivity. Take what he offers and ask for no more."

Grace frowned. "It sounds as though you speak from experience. Were you and Lord Rochdale . . ."

"I have known many men like him. Libertines, pleasure seekers, immoral cads."

The noncommittal response gave Grace an odd twinge of distaste that she might have been kissing a man who had been intimate with her friend.

"All I am saying is to be careful," Wilhelmina continued. "This is new territory for you, Grace. An exciting adventure. Just . . . be prepared. Do not jump in feetfirst without knowing what to expect."

"Thank you, Wilhelmina, but I doubt it will go that far. Rochdale is just flirting. Teasing. Nothing more."

Wilhelmina took her hand and squeezed it. "If it threatens to become something more and you need someone to talk to, promise you will come to me."

Grace smiled. Despite her low birth, Wilhelmina was one of the finest women she knew. A true and loyal friend. She returned the squeeze. "I promise. But I—"

"Hey ho, my queens." Penelope approached, looking deceptively demure in her dairymaid costume. "It's been a grand success, has it not? I believe everyone we invited has made an appearance. And this ballroom . . . my stars, isn't it splendid? What a coup that Beatrice was able to secure it for us. It's a shame she isn't here to see it. Speaking of looking splendid, I still cannot get over your costume, Grace. You are positively gorgeous tonight. And I'm not the only one who noticed. I saw Rochdale dancing with you earlier. The man could not take his eyes off you! First flowers and now this? What a cunning little vixen—"

"It's time for the unmasking." The fourth Widows Fund trustee, Marianne, joined the group. She was dressed as a gypsy dancer, which suited her dark coloring. Blazing candlelight from the famous chandeliers picked up the gold of her long earrings and dozens of bracelets clinking at her wrists. "Our last ball of the Season. A success, to be sure. But my heart aches for poor Beatrice. I wish she had decided to join us."

"It is about to begin," Penelope said. "There are Doncaster and the duchess."

Grace watched their host, dressed as Cardinal Wolsey and looking especially jolly, and their hostess, beaming in a full nun's habit, approach the dais where the orchestra sat. They were followed by a maharaja whom Grace recognized as their son, the Marquess of Thayne, and a yellow-clad Artemis. "Is that . . . is that Beatrice?"

"My God, it is," Wilhelmina said. "Thayne has her arm. You do not suppose—"

"May I have your attention, please." The duke held up his hand until all conversation came to a halt. "Before we unmask, the duchess and I would like to make an announcement. I invite you to take a glass of champagne before we proceed."

Grace became aware that a small army of liveried footmen had entered the ballroom carrying trays of champagne glasses and were now circulating throughout. She and her friends each took a glass and shared speculative glances and smiles of anticipation. All of them were surely thinking, hoping the same thing: Their friend had found happiness out of scandal.

After a few minutes, the duke called for quiet again and raised his glass. In a booming voice, he said, "The duchess and I are pleased to have this festive occasion to announce the betrothal of our son, Lord Thayne, to Lady Somerfield. Please lift your glasses with me in a toast to their happiness."

The four trustees burst into huge smiles and clinked their glasses together.

"Well done," Wilhelmina said.

"Oh, isn't it wonderful?" Marianne's voice grew wobbly and her eyes glistened with tears.

"Yes, yes, yes!" Grace lifted her glass high in salute. She had been sure that the scandal caused by the public and very ugly manner in which their secret love affair had been revealed, and all that had happened since that dreadful night, would have ruined any hope

of happiness for Beatrice. She was so very glad to
have been wrong.

But she suddenly became aware that the room was
rather quiet, that the reaction to the announcement
had been subdued and overly polite. She glanced at
Wilhelmina, who seemed to have the same thought as
she looked about the room and frowned.

"What is wrong with everyone?" Marianne whispered. "This is almost worse than the night of the
scandal."

"That's the problem," Wilhelmina said, still frowning. "They think it is a patched-up betrothal meant to
salvage Beatrice's reputation. Not a happy occasion,
but merely a necessary and rather embarrassing one.
The idiots. The duke wouldn't make such a public fuss
if it was a marriage of convenience. Can't they see . . .
Aha! Good for Thayne. Ha!"

Lord Thayne had taken Beatrice in his arms and
was kissing her quite thoroughly. There were a few
gasps of shock, but the room remained awkwardly silent, the guests seeming not to know what to make of
this brazen display.

Wilhelmina uttered a derisive snort, placed her
champagne glass on the tray of a nearby footman,
then looped her shield over her shoulder. She moved
to the center of the room and began to clap her hands.
Loudly. Grace, Penelope, and Marianne looked at
each other, handed their glasses to the same footman,
and went to stand beside Wilhelmina. All four of them
applauded and cheered the happy couple, who were
still in each other's arms as they turned their heads
and smiled in acknowledgment of the applause.

That was all it took. The room erupted in more
applause and cheering and shouting and whistling. The
betrothed couple kissed again, and the ruckus grew
louder and more bawdy. It became a truly joyful
moment.

The mood of the crowd changed, lightened, brightened—perfect for the unmasking that followed. The duke then called for a dance and led his duchess to the dance floor, followed by Thayne and Beatrice. Couples quickly formed to join in the celebratory reel. Adam Cazenove, dressed as a pirate, appeared out of nowhere to claim a beaming Marianne for the dance. Eustace Tolliver, garbed as Pierrot and never far from Penelope's side, came for his favorite partner, with Lord Ingleby, in centurion gear, close behind to offer his arm to Wilhelmina. Grace smiled and guessed that their little joke was surely deliberate: the Roman soldier and the warrior queen who fought against him.

"May I have this dance?"

The familiar voice behind her brought Grace out of her euphoric mood, and a completely different brand of excitement sent a tremor across her shoulders. Her friends, who'd all begun to move away, each turned, almost in unison, and witnessed Grace's momentary discomposure and telltale blush. She collected herself at once and calmly pivoted to find the highwayman, unmasked and smiling, holding out a hand to her.

"I hope I am fortunate enough to find you free for this set," he said.

Grace sensed that her friends had halted their progress to the dance floor and were still watching, in varying degrees of astonishment, behind her. The pairing of the Libertine and the Bishop's Widow was as laughable as Boadicea and the centurion, as unimaginable to them as it still was for her. She could not refuse him, of course, as she was not engaged for this set. What she kept to herself, however, folded and sealed in a tight little secret, was the fact that she did not wish to refuse him.

What a wicked little fool I have become.

"Yes, of course." Her voice was cool, aloof, dripping with politeness. No one would guess her inner turmoil at the sight of him. She took his hand, and he tucked hers into the crook of his arm and led her away.

"I confess, Mrs. Marlowe, that I was hoping I might have a word with you. If you prefer to dance, it shall be as you wish. But if you will allow it, I have something I'd like to discuss with you."

"Oh. Yes, all right."

Her thoughts must have been written clear on her face, as he chuckled and said, "No, I am not stealing you away for another kiss, much as I'd like to. You made it very clear we were finished with that, unfortunately. No, it is a much more prosaic discussion I have in mind. A matter of business. Will you walk onto the terrace with me?"

Grace nodded and allowed him to lead her through one of several doorways leading from the ballroom onto a terrace. When they had danced together earlier and wandered off to the empty anteroom, Grace had held on to the hope that their identities were not obvious to everyone. Now that they were unmasked, however, it was clear that it was Mrs. Marlowe and Lord Rochdale walking together, and Grace intercepted more than a few interested glances.

Rochdale led her to the balustrade overlooking the courtyard below. They were not alone, as several other couples strolled about, so she knew he would not make any advances. At least she hoped he was gentleman enough not to do so.

"I daresay you must wish me to the devil," he said. "And that you believe I have unfairly taken advantage of you, first in the carriage, then with the surefire wager—"

"I never expected you to win that wager."

"I know you didn't. Who would ever expect the Infamous Libertine to know his Bible better than the Bishop's Widow? And so I did indeed take advantage of you, of the situation. I couldn't resist the opportunity to best you. Or to kiss you. It's the way I am,

Mrs. Marlowe. A rogue and a gambler." He lifted his shoulders in a shrug that seemed to say: *Take me or leave me; that's the way it is.* "However, never having importuned a good lady such as yourself, I find myself having the merest pang of conscience. And so I would like to make it up to you, if I may."

"Make it up to me? What do you mean?"

"In the carriage the other night, you told me about the work of the Benevolent Widows Fund and about Marlowe House. I confess I was impressed. You also mentioned the dream of building a new wing. How much do you need to raise in order to achieve that dream?"

Grace took a step back and studied him. Perhaps it was the powdered wig, or it could have been the moonlight that softened his normally hard-edged features. In any case, he did not look as predatory as usual. He looked almost . . . sincere. Was he truly going to offer her a large sum of money to help expand Marlowe House? As restitution for having kissed her?

Truth be told, he did owe her *something* for turning her life upside down. For the sake of the charity, she was more than willing to accept it.

"There is a lot involved," she said. "We must pay the architect and the builders and workmen. Then we have the materials and fittings and furnishings. We had hoped to use part of a new wing for training the women in various industrial jobs to make it easier for them to find employment, so there would be equipment to buy and instructors to pay. It amounts to quite a lot, actually." She named a large sum, prepared to see him flinch.

He did not. "Consider it done. I shall have my bank transfer the funds to you within the week."

Grace had to clench her back teeth to keep her jaw from dropping open. "You mean to . . . to provide us with the full amount?"

"Yes, of course. I may be a gambler, Mrs. Marlowe,

but I am a very successful one. I suppose it is high time I used some of my fortune for something besides racehorses and . . . other things."

Grace stared at him in complete astonishment. In return for a few kisses, some momentary discomposure, she was to have all this? She shook her head in disbelief. "You have taken me quite by surprise, my lord. I never expected such generosity."

"You never expected me to know my Bible, either. I live to confound people, Mrs. Marlowe. But yes, I am prepared to provide whatever you need for your new wing. On one condition."

Grace sighed. She ought to have known there was a catch. But if misquoting a Bible verse cost her a kiss, what on earth would he ask for in return for such a large sum of money? Surely not further intimacies. Dear God, surely not—

"I wish to see Marlowe House," he said. "I'd like to see exactly how the money will be used."

She let out a breath. "That's all? You ask only to see Marlowe House?"

Rochdale grinned, baring white teeth that caught the moonlight. "Good heavens, Mrs. Marlowe, what did you expect?"

"I never know what to expect from you, my lord."

He laughed. "That is a blatant lie, and you know it. You always expect the worst from me. And in most cases, you will be correct. This time, I merely want to see where my money will go."

"Of course. I shall give you the direction to Marlowe House and you should feel free to examine it at your convenience. Mrs. Chalk is the house supervisor. I shall let her know to expect you and she can show you about."

"No, my dear Mrs. Marlowe, you shall not get off as easily as that. I require that *you* be my guide. It is your vision, your dream. I want to see it through your eyes. How does tomorrow afternoon sound?"

"Oh." Another afternoon spent in his company. Could she bear it? For the sake of the charity, she would have to. "All right. I will show you Marlowe House and all that we hope to accomplish with your generous donation. Thank you, Lord Rochdale."

"Excellent. I shall call on you at two o'clock." He flashed another smile. "In an open carriage this time."

He reached for her hand and placed a fulsome kiss upon it. As he peered up at her through his thick lashes, a glint of triumph in those blue eyes made her realize how thoroughly he had manipulated her. He'd taken advantage again by pretending a sincere interest in her charity work and tossing buckets of money at her feet. He'd found a way for her to allow him to call on her again, even after she'd told him not to do so. The wretch!

She snatched her hand away before he could coax her into something else she did not want. Or did want, but hated herself for wanting.

"Tomorrow, then." She moved away from him and started walking backward toward the ballroom doors. "Thank you again for your generosity." Tearing her gaze from those intense blue eyes, she spun on her heel and hurried back into the ballroom.

And was immediately grabbed roughly by the arm and tugged to one side.

"What has got into you, Grace? Have you lost your mind?"

Lady Margaret Bumfries, the bishop's daughter, was dressed as a ginger cat, with pointy orange ears poking out of her halo of frizzed auburn hair, and black whiskers painted on her cheeks. The sight of her step-daughter's disapproving frown reminded Grace of all the wicked thoughts that had run wild in her head throughout the evening, and her traitorous skin prickled with new heat.

"Do you realize people are beginning to talk?" Margaret's grasp was so tight on Grace's arm she was sure there would be bruising. "What am I supposed to say when I am asked why my sainted father's widow is seen fraternizing with a debauched scoundrel like Rochdale?"

Margaret was two years older than Grace and had never approved of her marriage to the bishop. Like many others, Margaret had been shocked, even appalled, that her father had married a woman so much younger than himself. She idolized her father, though, believing he could do no wrong, and finally admitted that he would not have made a foolish match. Over time, she came to accept that Grace was a good wife to him.

It had naturally been a bit awkward at first for Grace to have stepchildren older than herself, but with the help of their father, she had forged a cordial relationship with both Margaret and her brother, Peter. She had never, however, enjoyed a warm relationship with either of her stepchildren. Margaret, in particular, could be very irksome at times. Especially when she was right.

"I am sorry that my speaking with Lord Rochdale has upset you, but I must tell you that he has offered a very generous donation to the Fund."

"You should have your man of business take care of such things so you do not have to be in the company of a blackguard like that. You know what is said about him. I cannot imagine Father would have approved of an association with that man."

No, he would not have approved. And if he'd seen what had happened earlier in the anteroom, he'd have been spinning in his grave.

"I could hardly dismiss Lord Rochdale when he made such a magnanimous offer," Grace said. "I chair the board of trustees, after all. It is not only my duty to raise funds but also to pay my respects to anyone who offers such a large gift."

"Is it also your duty to follow him into the night and allow him to kiss your hand? A man like that?"

Another uncontrollable burst of heat warmed her face. Grace snapped her fan open and attempted to cool her cheeks. As she pondered what on earth she could say in her own defense, Margaret continued.

"And that costume. I really cannot think what possessed you to wear such a scandalous dress. It is positively indecent. And with your hair hanging loose like a strumpet's. I can only imagine it is the company you keep that has exerted a bad influence on you. The dowager Duchess of Hertford, for example."

Grace could not allow her stepdaughter to disparage Wilhelmina, but before she could sputter a syllable of protest, Margaret was wrapping a long Norwich shawl about Grace's shoulders.

"You must cover yourself, Grace. My gown is respectable enough that I do not need the shawl. Heavens, I wish I had not arrived so late, but I had promised to attend the Raymond ball as well and went there first. To think of you wandering about in such dishabille for hours . . . Well, I can only remind you that you are still Mrs. Marlowe and have an obligation to the bishop's memory to behave with strict propriety at all times. Please, cover your bosom. I pray that you will not make a mistake in judgment like this again. Remember who you are!"

Grace pulled the shawl tight around her, ashamed that Margaret had to be the one to make her face the truth. It *was* an improper dress and her behavior tonight with Rochdale had been beyond wicked. Margaret would no doubt have fallen into an apoplexy if she knew that Rochdale had been kissing more than her hand this evening. But how provoking that her stepdaughter had to remind her of her position in Society, of her obligations to the bishop. Grace had never needed reminding before. She did not know what had got into her to behave in so uncharacteristic a manner.

No, that was not true at all. Grace knew exactly what had got into her and when it had happened. A kiss in the dark of a carriage and another in a private room here at Doncaster House had changed her. All the wicked, sinful, even lustful thoughts she'd had lately were not the thoughts of the widow of the great Bishop Marlowe. She wasn't sure who she was, but she was not the same woman she'd been a week ago. If she was to return to herself, she had to put Rochdale out of her thoughts and out of her life.

There was still, however, tomorrow and the tour of Marlowe House to get through and, if she guessed correctly, there would be more. What if he wanted to become more actively involved in the charity? Or in the design and building of a new wing? How was she to rightfully keep him out of her life?

And if she was perfectly honest about it—deep in the most private corner of her heart—why would she want to keep out of her life a man who made her weak in the knees when he kissed her?

Margaret would, naturally, tell her she was going straight to hell. Which was likely true.

Grace Marlowe, that pattern card of Christian propriety, was fast becoming a wicked woman.

Chapter 7

"Turn right on the next street. It's just beyond the square, on the left."

Rochdale made the turn, hoping Grace was suitably impressed with his driving skills as he negotiated the curricle between two large drays heading in the opposite direction. Most women he knew admired a man who could take a turn on one wheel without spilling over, or clear a passing vehicle with mere inches to spare, both feats having been demonstrated with ease during the long drive to Chelsea.

Grace Marlowe, however, was not most women. Or at least not like most of the women who'd flitted in and out of Rochdale's life. The sort of women who enjoyed taking risks, who'd find a spot of fast driving akin to foreplay. The sort of women whose invitations he'd rejected the night before. Lady Drake and Cicely Erskine had each been lively bed partners in the past. He still puzzled over his rejection of them in favor of one kiss from a prim bishop's widow.

The virtuous Mrs. Marlowe would never be as "fast" as Lady Drake or Cicely Erskine or a hundred other women he'd known, but she had not complained of the curricle's pace, as he might have expected. He'd been prepared to rein in the team and creep along like a spinster in a dog cart if Grace had complained or appeared to be alarmed. Instead, at the first hint of speed, she'd grabbed the strap with one hand and her bonnet with the other. He took that to mean she was ready for anything—whether ready to enjoy it or endure it, he could not say. He hoped the same attitude would hold true for all the other things he wanted to do with her. It was encouraging, or so he chose to believe, that she spoke nary a word of complaint as he drove the sleek sporting vehicle as it was meant to be driven.

When they'd been forced to slow down at the Knightsbridge turnpike, he had asked her if he was driving too fast for her.

"Not at all." The breathlessness of her voice spoke otherwise. He might toss them in a ditch and the stubborn woman would keep her bonnet on straight and never give him the satisfaction of having frightened her. "It is surprisingly comfortable," she continued, "and the ride is really quite smooth. I suppose it is one of those racing vehicles, is it not?"

Rochdale was so bloody proud of his curricle that he'd been hard pressed not to get too puffed up with his own consequence. Fast horses and fast vehicles were high on his list of the greatest pleasures in life, and this little beauty had been built to his own design.

"Yes, I had it made especially for racing," he said, "and I have won more than a few with it. The team, of course, is equally important. These two are my best carriage horses."

"I confess I was surprised that such a dashing vehicle was not pulled by a matched pair," she said. "But they seem to work well together."

"I pick my teams for speed and endurance, not for how well they look together." He leaned closer and lowered his voice to a more seductive tone. "But perhaps I ought to have brought a pair of matched grays today. To go with your eyes."

She smiled and made a soft *tut-tut* sound with her tongue, mocking his flattery.

Rochdale thought he had the prim widow figured out, but she kept throwing little surprises at him. He'd expected a snort, a *hrrmph*, an eye-rolling groan. Instead, he got a smile.

Progress!

"You should smile more often," he said. "You look even prettier when you smile." Which was as big an understatement as was ever spoken. Grace Marlowe was a stunner, pure and simple. He would never forget how she'd looked at the masquerade ball, with her hair down—Lord, such hair!—and her bosom on display.

But even today, with a short blue spencer jacket buttoned up to her chin and her hair hidden beneath a straw bonnet, Grace still looked as tasty as a ripe peach, just waiting for him to take a bite out of her.

Keeping his hands on the reins meant he hadn't been able to touch her the way he liked, teasing her hands until he felt them grow warm or tremble. But he'd made sure his thigh was in almost constant contact with hers. It was sufficient to keep her aware of him, physically. Wooing her through the charity was not enough. The most important business was the slow awakening of physical passion. He never wanted her to forget that he was a man who'd kissed her and desired her. Or that she had responded with desire of her own.

Two kisses had taught him a great deal about the Widow Marlowe. She had a wellspring of passion so deeply buried that it must either have lain dormant or under tight control for years. Rochdale had wondered about her marriage. It was not surprising that the bishop had been compelled to marry her. She must have been dazzling as a young girl. The old driveler had probably taken one look at her and been knocked right off his pins. And all that fine young flesh, wasted on an old fool more than twice her age.

One never knew about those pompous men of the

cloth who preached against the sin of fornication. In private, they might be perfunctory lovers full of self-loathing for giving in to animal urges, or they might be sexually brutal to the women they saw as the embodiment of temptation. Old Marlowe had been a robust man who'd chosen a beautiful young girl for his bride. He'd already had grown children, including a son, so what other reason to take a young bride than to warm his bed?

As much as he'd despised the fellow, Rochdale doubted that the priggish old blowhard had been a brutal husband. Grace would have exhibited a different type of skittishness in that case, based on fear. He had not seen that kind of fear in her eyes—only shock and confusion, and he'd be willing to bet that shock was based on her own physical response and not simple outrage at the actions of a notorious rake. So, either she was appalled to feel sexual stirrings for a man not her husband or simply appalled to feel them at all.

A bit of both, most likely. He'd wager his entire stable that Marlowe had never allowed her any passion. He probably kept his nightshirt on and made her lie perfectly still and silent beneath him. One good grunt and he'd be done, rolling off her with no concern for her pleasure. Afterward, he probably patted her on the head and thanked her for indulging his base nature.

He could be wrong about Marlowe, of course. But Grace was obviously not accustomed to having sexual desire set loose. It had taken very little to turn on that untapped wellspring of passion, hardly any skill at all, in fact. And that was what scared her, Rochdale was sure of it.

To win the wager, he had to rid her of that fear, to teach her to accept her sexual nature as something that was not improper or sinful. He had made progress with those two kisses. But she still did not trust him, and that was essential to a final capitulation. Today's venture into Chelsea would, he hoped, serve two purposes: that Grace would not only begin to trust him, but would also begin to trust herself.

Her grip on the strap as they careened through the streets of London, and the hint of a smile on her face as they did so, told Rochdale that he was making headway, however small, with both objectives.

Whenever they were forced by traffic to slow down, it was only natural to engage in conversation. Rochdale had kept her talking about the charity and her plans for its future. He never mentioned kisses or Bible verses or wagers. He never asked her if old Marlowe had ever made proper love to her. To keep her at ease, he let her do most of the talking, while he peppered her with questions about the work done at Marlowe House. By the time the building came in sight, Rochdale already knew more about the blasted place than he ever cared to know.

"Here it is," she said, indicating a long L-shaped building of old brick. Only the central portion of the long side of the L had a second story, where the main entrance seemed to be. The rest of the building sat low and heavy to the ground in a single story, as though it had settled there centuries before. But it did not appear neglected or run-down. It was neat and clean, with well-tended plantings along the walls and one large oak tree towering over the building at the junction of the two wings.

"It used to be an almshouse," she said as the curricle came to a stop at the main entrance. "We think it was built around 1630, but it had long been abandoned when we acquired it."

"You must have done a lot of work, then, to bring it back to life." He jumped down from the seat and tossed the reins to his tiger.

"It was a labor of love." She eyed the building with

a fond smile, then looked down to see Rochdale waiting to hand her down. The smile faded.

The curricle was not a particularly high vehicle, but it was high enough to make it awkward for ladies in skirts. Grace stood and quickly adjusted her balance, holding on to the edge of the folded-back bonnet as she stepped onto the first foothold. She ignored the hand he reached out to her—she was too busy making sure her white muslin skirts did not give the wicked libertine a view of her trim ankles or, God forbid, her legs—as she negotiated the second foothold. Since she did not take his hand, Rochdale reached up, grabbed her by the waist with both hands, and lifted her down.

He got more than a glimpse of her ankles. He got her soft, slender body sliding down his as he slowly brought her feet to the ground.

She had sucked in a breath the instant he'd placed his hands on her, and she let it out shakily as she took a step back and away from him. He flashed her one of his best smiles and added a wink for good measure. Her cheeks flushed that delightful shade of pink he was beginning to adore, and she quickly turned to walk toward the entrance.

The next hour passed in a blur as Grace gave him an excruciatingly thorough tour of Marlowe House. He'd seen the rabbit warren of living quarters, the dining facilities, the kitchens, the schoolrooms, the chapel, the stillroom, the sickroom, and a dozen other rooms with purposes he'd already forgotten. It was a very large and very busy operation, much more extensive than he'd expected.

He met Alice Chalk, the square, stocky matron who supervised all the operations. She had a twinkle in her eye and he liked her at once. He met several other members of the staff, most of whom were residents.

"All the adult residents are required to contribute in whatever small way they can to help keep the place running smoothly," Grace said. She'd removed her bonnet and now looked every inch the prim, respectable widow, with her gold hair pulled back into a thick knot at the base of her neck, with nary a loose tendril in disarray. There was almost no hint of last night's Faerie Queen. But every time he looked at her, he would remember Titania, with her loose, flowing hair and her soft, white bosom. She could not hide from him anymore, no matter how hard she tried.

"Depending on their skills and preferences," she continued, not realizing that the interest in his eyes had nothing to do with Marlowe House, "they can work in the kitchen or the garden or the sickroom. We do have a nurse on staff now. Mrs. Birch helped with the sick and wounded on the battlefields of Spain, and was so helpful when she came here as a widow that we gave her a permanent position."

"Do many others stay on like that?" he asked.

"No, there is only a handful of permanent staff. Everyone is here on a temporary basis. At least that is our hope. They stay here with their children because they have no place else to go. We do our best to find them work, or new homes, anything to keep them surviving and off the streets."

As they wandered through the halls, Grace had a kind word for each woman and child she met. She introduced each of them by name to Rochdale, who was astounded that she could remember them all. The living quarters were crowded, each room generally housing more than one family.

"You see why we want to expand," Grace said. "There is simply not enough room. And there are so many more families desperate for our help."

"You shall have your building fund, I promise you. I am humbled by what you have accomplished here. My contribution is nothing compared to the time and effort you have given."

She smiled, and he realized she'd been smiling almost since their arrival. This was her passion. This place and its work were what made her happy. One day very soon, he would see her direct that passion, that radiant smile, at him. And for a very different reason.

"I do not do it alone," she said. "My name happens to be on the building, or more rightly the bishop's name, but all of the trustees give time to Marlowe House. And we each have our favorite areas. Lady Somerfield takes care of the schoolroom. The Duchess of Hertford manages the stillroom, and Mrs. Cazenove the kitchens. And Lady Gosforth oversees the gardens. Which you haven't seen yet. Shall we?"

She led him through a double doorway opposite the main entry and into a sprawling and very healthy garden.

"We have a kitchen garden over there, a fragrance garden just beyond, and the section here is purely ornamental."

She went on to explain how each garden was laid out and how the residents tended them with care. Several women were at work, pulling weeds, pruning dead heads, and turning soil. When they approached the kitchen herb garden, a thin, dark-haired woman was bent over a low-lying shrub, cutting off pieces and tossing them into a basket held by an angular young girl with the same dark hair. A towheaded boy of about eight or nine sat on the ground building what appeared to be a pyramid of dirt.

"Ah, this is Mrs. Fletcher," Grace said, "and her two stalwart helpers who keep our kitchen garden flourishing."

The woman looked up and smiled, and Rochdale was almost knocked off his feet. Dear God, he knew that face, though he had not seen it for more than a dozen years. A phantom of days long past. A thousand memories flooded his brain all at once, with so dizzying a speed that he thought his legs might buckle.

He stared at the woman, momentarily struck dumb by this face from another time, another life. A life he'd left behind long ago and had no desire to revisit.

Her eyes grew wide in recognition. Hell and damnation. He'd hoped he had changed enough that she wouldn't know him, or that she'd forgotten him, so he could bank those unwelcome memories for now and bury them again once he'd left her and this place. But she knew him, and he'd have to face her. Damn, damn, damn.

"John? John Grayston? Good heavens, is it really you? Oh, but it's Lord Rochdale, is it not? How wonderful to see you again after all these years."

Her familiar voice, high-pitched and musical, took him back to a time and place he'd spent half a lifetime forgetting. He supposed there was no use in pretending he didn't know her. His start of surprise had betrayed him.

"Jane. Forgive me. I am beyond astonished to see you again." He ought to have reached for her hands, to greet her as an old friend, but he kept his hands clasped behind his back instead. In truth, he wanted to turn and walk away, but he supposed that was too cowardly, or too cruel, even for a gazetted scoundrel.

She wiped her hands on the soiled apron she wore over a well-worn dress that might once have been blue. Or perhaps brown. It had grown colorless from too many washings. In a self-consciously feminine gesture, she tucked a few stray wisps of hair behind her ears. She was younger than Rochdale by about two years, if he recalled correctly, but she looked older. Every feature of her face was as he remembered— large brown eyes, wide mouth, the nose slightly square at the tip. But the familiar eyes and mouth were bracketed with lines, the once charmingly freckled skin was sun-worn and brown, and there were strands of gray in the dark hair. And she was much too thin.

Even so, she still retained some of the prettiness he remembered.

She instinctively lifted a hand, no doubt hoping he would extend his own. He did not. She awkwardly brought her hand back, clasping it to the other at her waist.

"It is good to see you, John. Lord Rochdale, I should say. My goodness, how many years has it been? You haven't changed much at all. Still as handsome as ever."

Lord, did she have to be so damned cheerful? And did her smile have to be so familiar?

"You haven't changed either, Jane. Still the pretty girl who chased after Martin and me all over the fens." The words were flippant, but he did not smile or lighten his expression.

She laughed, undaunted by his aloofness. "Flatterer. I wear all my years on my face, you cannot deny it. But there is nothing to be done about it. Every line and gray hair was well earned. Oh, but you must meet the children who gave me all these gray hairs." She placed an arm around the girl at her side. "This is Sally, my oldest. Make your curtsy to Lord Rochdale, my girl."

Sally did so, looking at him warily through long lashes. She appeared to be about eleven or twelve and was not as pretty as her mother had been as a girl, though the fine bones of her face would serve her well through the years.

Rochdale acknowledged her with a curt nod. He did not want this awkward reunion. He would allow Jane to introduce her children, then he'd get the bloody hell out of there.

"And this is Toby." The fair-haired boy had been hiding behind his mother. Rochdale had been so stunned by the sight of Jane, he'd barely noticed him. Jane pushed the boy forward now, and Rochdale almost gasped aloud. He was the very image of Martin Fletcher, the man who was surely his father, the man who had once been Rochdale's closest friend. As a young boy, Martin had looked exactly like the child staring up at him now.

Rochdale glanced at Jane, who smiled and said, "He's very like him, is he not?"

"The spit and image. Hullo, Toby. I am pleased to meet you."

"Yes, sir. Me, too, sir."

As Rochdale gazed at the boy with the face of Martin Fletcher, it suddenly dawned on him why Jane and her children must be here at Marlowe House. A knot of pain lodged itself in the area of his heart. He looked at Jane. "Martin is . . . ?"

Sadness gathered in her dark eyes. "Yes. He died at Albuerra, two years ago now."

Rochdale closed his eyes briefly and fought back a lump that had lodged itself in the back of his throat. God, he did not want to hear this. Finally, he said, "I'm so sorry, Jane. I wish I'd known. I wish I'd kept in touch. I wish . . ." He wished he'd never learned of what became of Martin. And he wished he did not feel so damned responsible for his death. True, it was likely a French bullet or blade that had taken the life of his old friend, but if the tenant farms at home had not been allowed to fall into near ruin, Martin would never have felt obliged to join the army. He was a farmer, not a soldier. He ought to have died in his bed many years from now, with his grandchildren at his side and his cows grazing in the pasture.

"There was nothing you could have done, John."

He shook his head, rejecting that notion. But what could he say? *Forgive me for living a life of dissipation while Martin marched across Spain and his family was forced to come to a charity house?*

"Toby? Sally? Would you show me the new plant-

ings you have been working on this week?" Grace
stepped forward and placed a hand on the shoulder
of each child, steering them toward a patch of garden
several yards away. Funny, he had almost forgotten
about her. She must have assumed that he and Jane
had things to say in private, things that might be painful for the children to hear. She could not know that
there was nothing he wanted less than to hear of Jane
and Martin's life after Bettisfont. "I can see the hyssop
from here," Grace said, "And smell it, too. Let's go
have a look, shall we?"

"She is a very kind lady, Mrs. Marlowe is," Jane
said as she watched Grace herd her children away. "A
great lady. This place is all her doing, you know. I
cannot imagine what would have become of us without her help."

There was a long moment of silence during which
Jane watched him with a glint of expectation in her
brown eyes, surely hoping he would ask about all
those lost years. Dear God, how he wanted to bolt.
But he supposed he should simply get it over with.
Besides, if he did not ask about her life, she'd very
likely ask about his.

"What happened, Jane? The last I recall, you were
with Martin and his regiment."

"Yes, I followed the drum for several years. It was
a good life, an interesting one. His regiment took him
all over the world, you know. Sally, she was born in
Ireland, and Toby in Germany. But when things got
rough in Portugal, Martin insisted that I take the children back to England, to keep them safe. He had a
small amount of prize money and used it to secure us
a one-room cottage in Kensington. It was odd being
in town instead of the country, but the landlord was
a cousin to one of the other soldiers, and so we were
able to get the cottage for a reasonable price. And he
sent what he could every few months, Martin did, for

food and shoes for the children. But when he died, almost two years later, there was no more money coming in, and it was up to me to support the three of us."

She sent him a look full of apology and regret, as though it had somehow been her fault that she was left alone. Rochdale said nothing—what could he say?—but the despair in her voice twisted like a knife in his gut.

"I took in laundry and sewing," she said, "but it was hard, real hard, to make do for three. The landlord turned us out when I could no longer pay the rent. I found another, smaller place for us, but work was hard to come by. Finally, we were reduced to sharing a tiny room in St. Giles, and I collected rags and unpicked clothing, but I never made enough to feed us regularly. I was worried that the children would get caught up in that world, on the streets, victim to God knows what. I became desperate, I did. Ready to . . . to do anything to support my children."

Rochdale closed his eyes again and choked back a groan. She had been ready to prostitute herself for her children. Perhaps had done so. That sweet freckle-faced girl he'd once known, selling her body on the streets. Bile rose in his throat.

"And then someone told me about this place," she continued, "and how, as a war widow, I would be welcome. I thank the good Lord every day for Marlowe House, I do. I hate to think what would have become of us if we had not come here."

So did he. God. Now he really understood what Grace was doing here. She was quite literally saving lives.

Rochdale decided in that moment to double the amount he had planned to give her. But he would not come back again to see how she spent it.

"We try not to think about those bad times, or what might have been. They teach us here to look forward to a better future, and bless me, they make it seem like it could be true."

"Do you have someplace to go when you leave here?" he asked. "Have they found potential employment for you? Something? Anything?"

"Not yet, but there are possibilities. They don't let a family leave Marlowe House until they are confident that a safe situation is settled. I've seen many families leave with excellent prospects. Our time will come."

"I . . . I will find a place for you and the children, Jane." The words were out before he could stop them. What was he thinking? He had no wish to become entangled with someone from the old days. Someone to remind him of how far he'd fallen from the life he'd once known. But there were ways of doing things without getting personally involved. He could hand over the project to his man of affairs and stay out of it.

"Bettisfont is gone," he said, "but I have other interests. I will find something. I promise you."

She reached out and tentatively laid her hand upon his sleeve, then pulled it back. "John, you do not have to do that. You are not responsible for us."

"Let me do this, Jane. I owe it to Martin. To you and the children." His gaze followed the boy as he stood by Grace, obviously bored with the garden and fidgety with contained energy. He kept sneaking looks at Rochdale over his shoulder, but turned away, embarrassed, when Rochdale caught his eye. "God, looking at Toby is like seeing Martin again."

She smiled. "I know. And I'm grateful for that. I will never forget Martin's face, for I see it every day in Toby's."

"I will send him to school. And Sally, too." Again, the words were out before he knew he was going to say them. It seemed he'd been so stunned by seeing Jane again, and Martin in the face of his son, that all rational thought had deserted him. He had no desire to get involved with the Fletcher family. But Rochdale was a man of means, even if most of his fortune came from gambling, and it seemed wrong not to help these people, this woman he'd known as a girl and who'd been married to his friend.

"I would like to see that Martin's children are taken care of," he said. "With a proper education, they will be able to find work and support themselves. Let me do this, Jane. I will make up to all of you what my father's irresponsibility put you through. Damn it all, I wish I could send you back to Bettisfont, but I never rebuilt the house or the home farms. Just the stables."

"I know."

He lifted his eyebrows in surprise. "You do?"

"Yes, of course. We kept in touch with some of the other families for a while. And since we've been back, one cannot help but hear of the exploits of the famous Lord Rochdale."

He winced. "Infamous, I should say."

"Perhaps. But seeing you here today, with Mrs. Marlowe . . . does that mean you are mending your ways?" She glanced over at Grace, who was laughing with the children. "She is an angel from heaven, as far as I'm concerned. And she is very beautiful, is she not?"

"Yes, she is, but do not get the wrong impression. I have agreed to fund a new wing here, but that is the extent of it. And whatever I can do for you, of course. I am no do-gooder, Jane. Far from it. And I am afraid it is much too late for me to change my stripes. I am too deeply sunk in dissipation to crawl my way out at this stage of my life."

She frowned. "It's not at all the life I expected from you, John. When I first heard your name associated with . . . a certain scandal . . ."

"Serena Underwood."

"Yes. When I heard that, and then other tales, I did not believe it could be the same John Grayston I once knew. I thought you would be—"

"Yes, well, things change."

She blinked at the brittle, sharp tone of his voice, and a wary expression gathered in her dark eyes.

"People change," he continued in the same tone, hoping that look in her eye meant she understood that he wanted distance between them and not renewed friendship. "I'm no longer an idealistic young fool. But I do have money now. Quite a lot of it. And I will help you, Jane. I promise. It is the least I can do."

"Bless you, John. I cannot thank you enough."

"As soon as I have arranged something, I will send word to Mrs. Marlowe or Mrs. Chalk."

"Oh. All right. But will we see you ag—"

"Sir?" Young Toby had come running to stand beside his mother. Grace and Sally were approaching at a more ladylike pace.

Rochdale scowled at the boy, even though he was relieved at the interruption. "Yes?"

Toby swallowed hard but held his ground against Rochdale's fierce glare. His eyes were wide and wary, but with a glint of Fletcher stubbornness that was all too familiar. There was a hint of something more, too, a certain toughness of spirit that must have been forged in these last few years of hard times. Had he, too, been forced into a life on the streets before coming to Marlowe House? While his mother had picked the stitches out of old bits of clothing in order to sell the fabric, had Toby taken to picking pockets, or worse?

"Is it true you knew my papa?"

The question, and the keen anticipation in its tone, dispelled any notion of an artful street urchin. He may have lifted a watch or two in his time, but at the moment he was simply a little boy who missed his father. Rochdale's expression involuntarily softened, and though he would not realize it until much later, a tiny corner of his heart softened as well. The boy was so like Martin Fletcher that it was almost unbearable, but it was the look in his eyes that did Rochdale in.

He knelt down on his haunches in order to be at eye level with the boy. "I did indeed. I knew him when he was your age and even younger. He could be quite the little devil. Always into mischief." He reached out and tousled the boy's hair. "Just like you, I'll wager. His hair used to fall over his eyes, just like yours, too."

The boy shrugged. "I don't remember him much. I was only four when we came to England."

"Ah, but I remember him very well. He was fun and funny, full of laughter. But he was strong, too, and brave. I remember one time when one of the other children on the estate fell into a well. Your father pulled her to safety all by himself. He was a good man, your father."

Toby's eyes lit with excitement. "He pulled the girl out all by hisself?"

"He did indeed." Rochdale didn't think it worth mentioning that he and another boy held tight on to Martin's feet as they lowered him into the well. It was, after all, Martin who'd reached the girl and pulled her free.

"I figured he musta been brave," Toby said, "to go and fight old Boney and all. Do you have other stories about him, sir? Mama's told me a lot, but . . . well, she's a female and you know how they are. Please, sir, could you tell me more about my papa?"

In that moment, Rochdale knew he'd been reeled in like a trout to face a past he'd sooner forget, helpless against this boy with the familiar face and devilishly plaintive eyes. "Of course, Toby. What would you like to know?"

Chapter 8

"Would you look at that?" Jane's hand was splayed against her breast as she watched Toby and Rochdale seated side by side on a stone bench, heads together, the occasional burst of laughter splitting the silence of the garden. "I haven't seen him so animated since we moved from Kensington. How fortunate to have run into John . . . Lord Rochdale, that is. Toby has had so few men in his life since we left the army."

Grace was confounded by what had taken place between the Fletcher family and Rochdale. He was the last person she'd have expected to be acquainted with Jane, and certainly not the type to have ever been friends with her. Jane had told her she'd grown up in the country before following the drum, and Grace's first thought when she saw that Jane knew Rochdale was that she had been one of his early conquests. It was a common enough situation—a village girl who'd been seduced by the lord of the manor's son. But it seemed Rochdale had been a friend to Jane's husband, so perhaps Grace was wrong about a seduction.

"You do know who he is, don't you, Jane? What he is, I should say, since you obviously know him. I'm not sure he's the sort of man you want in Toby's life. He has something of a reputation, you know."

Jane lifted her brows. "I do know. But he is here with you. He told me it was because of a large donation, but you wouldn't allow him here if he was so bad."

Grace shrugged. "It was difficult to deny him when he asked to see where his money will be spent. But I would hate to see your boy come under the influence of a notorious libertine and gambler."

"I doubt John would do any harm to Toby. Despite what he may have become, I knew him as an intelligent boy and an honorable young man. That core of goodness is still there inside him, I'll wager."

A core of goodness? At the center of the worst rake in London? It was difficult to believe. And yet, he'd shown a remarkable interest in Marlowe House. Though it had seemed genuine at times, Grace had suspected it was merely an act, an excuse to get near her. Could she have been wrong about him? But no, this was the man who'd publicly ruined at least one young woman. No man of honor would have done such a thing.

"Besides," Jane continued, "Toby needs to know about Martin. He and John were close friends . . . a long time ago." She smiled as she watched her daughter edge closer to the bench. "Sally has more vivid memories of her father, but see how she listens while pretending to pull weeds. She is too wary of men to get closer, but she wants to hear the stories, too."

Grace experienced a pang of tender concern as she considered what might have made Sally wary of men.

Yet certain aspects of Jane Fletcher's past intrigued her, especially the parts that involved Rochdale. She glanced at the bench again to find him in animated conversation with the boy, who stared up at him with worshipful eyes. Grace knew the seductive power of the wretched man. Was he charming Toby, too?

"You trust him, then?" Grace tilted her head toward the pair on the bench, though Jane would surely know whom she meant.

"Of course."

Grace smiled. "You must be the only woman in London who does."

"Ah, but see, I don't know the London milord. It's the bright-eyed boy from Suffolk I remember, and he's the one I'll trust."

It was hard to imagine Rochdale as a bright-eyed boy, but Grace supposed that even a hardened libertine began life as an innocent. "You were childhood friends?" It was none of her business, but Grace was bursting with curiosity. Jane gave her an understanding smile, and Grace felt her cheeks flame.

"He was more Martin's friend than mine," Jane said. "They were both horse mad, and spent lots of time in the stables or riding about. I was just a tagalong girl, a few years younger and always underfoot. My father, he was gamekeeper at Bettisfont, the Rochdale estate, and Martin's father was one of the tenant farmers. I thought nothing of it at the time, but I expect it was a bit unusual for his lordship's son to find his playmates among our class. He was an only child, though, so I suppose he was lonely."

Jane bent to pick up the pruning sheers in the basket at her feet, then began fingering the borage plant she'd been pruning earlier. She located a fine, tall stalk and snipped it off, then tossed it in the basket. "We had grand times together at Bettisfont, the three of us did," she said as she worked. "We knew every rock and tree on the estate and beyond. Sometimes we'd play at knights and dragons, and sometimes we'd just lie in the tall grasses and watch the clouds or talk. John was the most serious of us, what with his book learning and all. He's the only boy I ever knew what loved schooling so much. He used to tell us about books he'd read, and I'll tell you plain that I didn't always understand him, not being much interested in books myself. Lord, but he did love his books. Always talking about some Greek or Roman fellows and their lofty ideas." She laughed. "Martin would look at me and roll his eyes. He didn't understand it any more than I did, but we were fond enough of John to let him go on and on."

Grace began to think they were talking of someone else. It seemed unlikely that a bookish child would grow up to be a rake and a gambler. "Rochdale was a studious child?"

"That he was. Idolized that tutor of his. Phelps, I think his name was. He wasn't all that keen on going away to school when he got older, but after his lordship married again, John was anxious to go away. He didn't much like his new stepmama or her daughter, I think, though he never said so outright. He loved school, though, Eton first, then Oxford. He came home as often as he could and told us of his studies. Became quite a scholar, our John did. I truly believe if he hadn't been his lordship's only son and heir, he'd have gone into the church."

"The *church*?" Grace almost sputtered in astonishment. Surely she had misheard.

"That's what Martin and me thought, sometimes. John would go on and on about Man and God and the meaning of life, ideas well above our understanding. He quoted the Bible a lot, too. We used to think it was sad he didn't have an older brother to inherit the title so he could have taken orders. Old Lord Rochdale would never have allowed it, though."

Grace was beyond astonished. She watched Rochdale as he spoke with the boy, a slightly wicked grin on his face. It could not be true. The very idea of Rochdale as a man of the cloth was not only laughable, it was . . . blasphemous.

Jane chuckled. "I expect it seems odd, seeing as what he's like now. But if you'd known him back then, you'd understand."

Grace shook her head. "I confess I'm finding it difficult to do so." She looked over at him as he and Toby laughed together. Rochdale and the church. It was unimaginable. It was no fluke, then, that he knew his Bible well enough to realize she'd misquoted it.

The bishop always said you could find good in everyone if you looked hard enough. Perhaps she hadn't looked hard enough at Lord Rochdale. "How could a person change so drastically?" she mused aloud.

"I think it must have been the fire that finally broke him."

Grace turned back to Jane, who had moved on to collect sprigs of thyme. "Fire?"

"It all started long before the fire, though. Things were never quite the same after his lordship remarried. We were all happy for him at first, glad to see he'd found someone else. His first wife, John's mother, left him, you know. Ran off with some foreign fellow when John was a boy. But the new Lady Rochdale . . . well, if you ask me, she married his lordship for money, and pissed it away like water. Didn't much like the country, either. They spent more and more time in London, and he began to let things go untended at home. Repairs weren't made to the main house or estate cottages. Fields were allowed to go fallow. Drains weren't cleared. After a few years, his lordship cut back on the staff. My pa was one of the first to be let go. He found new work up in Lincolnshire. Died a few years later, poor soul. He'd spent his whole life at Bettisfont and it near broke his heart to leave. And I made it worse, not wanting to go with him. Martin and me, we were crazy in love by then."

She paused and gave a wistful smile. She must have been remembering those days with Martin, so Grace did not prompt her to continue, though she was anxious to hear about the fire. After a moment, Jane gave a sheepish laugh and went on with her story.

"Martin and me, we got married, and so I stayed behind with him at Bettisfont to tend our own patch of tenant land. But there was no support coming from the estate, and we all began to suffer hardship. Lots of folk just up and left, taking off in hopes of finding a bit of land to work on some other estate. My Martin, though, he was stubborn, so we stayed on. John came home from Oxford as often as he could—he was courting the daughter of a local squire—and he always visited with us and brought provisions. He had great rows with his father over money and the condition of the estate. They almost came to blows over his stepsister's marriage portion. Thinking back, he started to change a bit then. He was still good-hearted as ever to us, but he was becoming more cynical, and angry all the time. Then there was the fire."

"What happened?"

"Bettisfont, that beautiful old pile, burnt clean to the ground, and his lordship with it. He'd run back in to find his wife. Poor man didn't know she'd already got to safety. He never made it out."

Grace shuddered. "Dear heaven, how awful. Were you there when it happened?"

"We were. Martin had finally given up on the farm and signed up to soldier for King George. We were just packing up our things to follow his regiment when the fire happened. It was heartbreaking, John losing his papa like that. And the house was gone—nothing remaining but the stables and a few outbuildings. Martin and I left a few days later. Thirteen years ago. It was the last time I saw John—Lord Rochdale, that is—until today."

So, he'd lost a beloved father and his family home at the same time. What a dreadful situation for a young man to face alone. Grace supposed that sort of tragedy would change anyone. Rochdale was certainly changed from the scholarly young man who might have been destined, by temperament if not position, for the church. Perhaps that cynicism Jane mentioned had taken root inside him, then spread and clung like lichen. She wondered if Jane was right about that core of goodness still being a part of him.

Grace feared she could never look at him again without searching for signs of that bright-eyed, bookish, good-hearted boy he'd once been.

She was staring at him. His eyes were on the team and the road ahead, but he could feel Grace's gaze upon him like a bare hand, could see out of the corner of his eye that the poke of her bonnet was turned in his direction. At any other time, Rochdale would have been pleased, knowing he'd in some way intrigued her. But he doubted it was his handsome person that captured her interest just now. She'd had too long a conversation with Jane Fletcher, and he suspected much of it was about him.

It was bad enough that he'd had to face Jane and her children, though the boy Toby was an engaging child. He did not want Grace or anyone else probing into his past. Instead, he would do his best to keep conversation on topics related to Grace and her charity work, which he hoped would distract her from other, less desirable topics.

"You must know," he said, "how impressed I was at what you've accomplished at Marlowe House. It's much more than I expected. In fact, I have decided to substantially increase the amount of my contribution."

The traffic had slowed enough that he was able to divert his attention from the road to look in her direction. Her eyes grew large and her mouth opened into a perfect O, then broadened into a full smile. "Your generosity overwhelms me, Lord Rochdale. I hardly know what to say. A simple 'thank you' seems inadequate."

"I am pleased to do whatever I can. It's an extraordinary operation, obviously doing a great deal of good."

"Thank you, my lord. I am very glad you came today. It is sometimes easier to understand the impact of charity when the recipients have names and faces and are not merely numbers on a ledger. I daresay it helped to see a woman you know in residence, did it not?"

Rochdale stifled a groan. He ought to have known that all conversational gambits would lead to this. "Yes, it did make a difference to see Jane Fletcher and her children. I was stunned to see her, in fact. I had no idea she had reached such dire straits. Thank God she found Marlowe House. Do you know anything of her life in London before she came here?"

"We don't ask questions. We assume that the situation was desperate, that is all. If you are wondering how desperate, I cannot tell you. We encourage our residents to look forward, not backward. They cannot change the past, but they can shape a new future."

"Yes, Jane told me that was the gospel preached here."

"And she told me you had offered to find her a new situation. That is very kind of you, my lord."

He did not reply. Instead, he returned his attention to the team and hoped that was the end of the topic of Jane Fletcher.

"Do you have a particular situation in mind?"

Damn. She was not going to let go of this bone so easily. "Not yet. I've only just learned of her circumstances, after all. But I will look around for something for her. Some place in the country, I should think." Jane and her children would never again live anywhere near the streets of London, if he had any say in the matter.

"On one of your own estates?"

Rochdale gave a mirthless chuckle. "I have no estates, Mrs. Marlowe. A house in London, the villa in Twickenham, and stables in Suffolk. Nothing more."

She was suspiciously quiet for a long moment, then said, "You never rebuilt the estate at Bettisfont."

He heaved a sigh. "No, I did not. But I do stable many of my racehorses and hunters there."

"Why did you not rebuild? I beg your pardon. It's really none of my business. But Jane did imply that you had loved the place."

"I did. And I spent many years paying for it. My father had mortgaged it several times over. I inherited a scorched patch of entailed earth and a mountain of debts."

"Oh, I'm so sorry. Jane hinted that things had deteriorated somewhat before the fire."

Rochdale snorted. "That is something of an understatement. That woman, my stepmother, bled him dry. He mortgaged away his future, and mine, to keep that old cow and her Friday-faced daughter in fine silks and luxurious furnishings. While the tenant farms failed, Lady Rochdale redecorated. While the Bettisfont staff was reduced to a bare minimum, her ladyship fired off her daughter in London with every luxury imaginable." The last time he'd seen his father alive, they had argued over the dowry he'd promised the wretched girl's fiancé. Guilt over that final conversation had weighed him down for years.

"Good heavens," Grace said. "Could he not have tempered her spending?"

He shook his head. "My father was a weak man where women were concerned."

He could feel her gaze hard on him again. It was easier when she knew him as nothing more than a profligate seducer. Thanks to Jane and her loose tongue, Grace was compelled to poke and prod and figure out if he was something else altogether. Rochdale had spent the last dozen years and more trying to forget what a bloody young fool he'd once been. That boy had died in the fire as surely as had his father. He hated talking about those days and was sorry Grace had learned so much about that time from Jane.

And yet, a tiny corner of his brain encouraged him to let her probe. It kept her interested, which could be a benefit to his objective.

"Is that why you've never married?" she suddenly asked.

He laughed. "Because I didn't want to be like my father? Not a chance. I have been too busy rebuilding the Rochdale fortunes at the gaming tables. Now that I have done so, I am too busy enjoying myself. A wife has never been part of my plan for the future."

"Oh? What about that squire's daughter you were courting?"

He jerked on the reins so hard that the horses rebelled and heaved against their harnesses. It took a moment to calm them and reset the pace. Damnation. "It seems Mrs. Fletcher did a great deal of gossiping about me today."

"Oh, no, you mustn't blame her. I asked how she knew you and she told me. That is all. I am afraid I asked a good many questions, so if she said more than she should have, it is my fault."

"That curious about me, are you?"

She laughed softly. "A little."

"Well, if you must know, yes, there was a certain squire's daughter. Miss Caroline Lindsay-Holmes. A fair beauty, with coloring much like yours. My youthful self was completely besotted. We had what you might call an understanding. She agreed to wait until I finished university, and then we would be married. As it happened, she much preferred me when there was a grand estate to inherit and what she believed to be a sizable fortune at my disposal. When she learned the truth after the fire, that I now had the title and little else, she quickly transferred her affections to another, more prosperous gentleman. The last I heard, she'd grown fat as a guinea hen with a brood of six or seven children at her feet. A near miss, that one."

"For you, or for her?"

He laughed. "For both of us, I daresay. Now, may we please talk of something else besides my uninteresting past?"

"If you will allow me one more question, please."

He sighed noisily. "If you must. But only one. I'd much rather talk about you."

"Jane said you were something of a scholar. That you might have gone into the church if you had the choice. Is that true?"

"Jane exaggerates. I was studious, it is true. I used to bore her and Martin to death with my books, but I was never a true scholar. And I never, *ever* had a calling for the church." He laughed. "I leave that to the likes of your late husband."

"But how did you—"

"No more questions. You requested one and I answered. If you are thinking that because I was once an idealistic young fool that I can reform my ways, you are wrong. I left those ideals behind years ago. I am what I am, and I enjoy my life. Gambling, drinking, racing, wenching. You cannot change me, Mrs. Marlowe. Now, let us talk of something else."

"I cannot help being curious."

"Just remember that cat they're always talking about."

She laughed, and he was once again charmed by the sultry sound of it. He realized that she had laughed more than once on the drive back to Portland Place. She was letting down her guard with him, maybe even beginning to trust him. Despite being forced to revisit a painful past, the day had been a success, moving him closer to his goal.

A mizzling rain began to fall as they neared Mayfair, and Rochdale stopped the team in order to raise the hood on the curricle. One more point in his favor:

The hood brought a modicum of privacy. He decided to attempt another kiss when they reached her house. They were not entirely enclosed, but were shielded enough from view that he just might be able to get away with it. If she let him.

By the time they reached Grace's house on Portland Place, it was raining in earnest. "I am afraid I have no umbrella," he said. "Let us wait here a few minutes until the rain eases up a bit. I wouldn't want you to ruin that pretty hat."

She peered around the edge of the leather hood, then quickly ducked back underneath. "Just for a moment. It is sure to let up soon." She turned on the seat so her whole body was angled toward him. With an intense look in her smoky eyes, she said, "Lord Rochdale, you must allow me to express my gratitude once again for the extraordinary generosity of your donation to Marlowe House. I cannot imagine how I can ever thank you."

He leaned in, so their bodies were touching from shoulder to knee. "I can think of one way." He dipped his head beneath the poke of her bonnet and kissed her. Before he could make much of it, she pushed him away.

"Dear heaven, stop it. Someone might see."

He took her hand and began stroking the gloved fingers. "We are completely in the shadows. No one will know."

"I will know. You kissed me once, taking me by surprise. The next time because you won the wager. There is no more reason for you to be kissing me."

"Yes, there is. I kiss you because I want to."

"But why? Why do you persist in throwing yourself in my path? We both know I am not the type of woman you prefer. Why must you pursue me like this? It is foolish."

"Is it? Is it foolish to desire a beautiful woman? Then I am a fool for you, Grace Marlowe. Yes, you are more prim than my usual fare. But you intrigue me. You fascinate me. And God help me, I could look at you all day long and never tire of the sight. I dream of seeing your hair down again like it was last night at the ball, of wrapping myself up in all its golden glory while I make love to you."

The blush he'd come to anticipate, and adore, spread across her checks. "If you think it would be a great joke to seduce the widow of Bishop Marlowe, then please allow me to disabuse you of that notion. It will never happen."

"Won't it? Whenever we kiss, there is a flare of passion that burns hot between us. We could be good together, you and me. You cannot deny you enjoyed our kisses."

"It's not the kisses. It's you. It's who you are."

"No, it's who *you* are. The great man's widow. The prim and proper Mrs. Marlowe. You can't shake that identity and what you think it means. You protest because you think you ought to, but in fact you are dying for me to kiss you again."

"No, I—"

"More than that, you are dying for me to make love to you. You want it so badly you have tied yourself up in knots over it."

She frowned. "You, sir, are every bit the cad everyone says you are."

"More so. But at least I know who I am. You're as confused as hell after a few kisses. And that's a good thing, if you ask me. It is time you shook up your life a bit. It is time you became Grace Marlowe and not the Bishop's Widow."

She glared at him, then ducked under the hood and began to step down from the curricle, making an awkward business of it as she tried to keep the rain out of her face. Rochdale quickly leapt out on his side and was there to hand her down before she had reached the second foothold. She reluctantly took his proffered hand, as the step was slippery.

"I look forward to getting to know Grace Marlowe better," he said, not letting go of her hand. "I believe you are at home to visitors tomorrow. I shall do myself the pleasure of calling on you."

"I do not suppose it would do any good to ask you not to come."

"None."

"You will plague me to death, Lord Rochdale."

"Just a little death, hopefully."

She looked confused at his words, clearly not understanding the French reference. Lord, she really had led a sheltered life. He wondered if she'd ever actually experienced *la petit mort*, then remembered who her husband had been and doubted it.

At that moment, her butler opened the front door and hurried toward her with an open umbrella. She turned away from Rochdale and followed the butler inside without a backward glance.

Chapter 9

His entrance had turned heads. Most of the ladies, and the handful of gentlemen, who crowded Grace's drawing room the next afternoon were clearly shocked at Lord Rochdale's attendance at such a proper gathering. It was Grace's afternoon "at home," and that meant she was at home to anyone who called. Anyone.

She'd been expecting him, of course, but was chagrined that he'd arrived when two of London's highest sticklers also happened to be there. Lady Troubeck looked momentarily wide-eyed, but then proceeded to ignore Rochdale entirely. Mrs. Drummond-Burrell was not so circumspect. When she suggested that he did not belong in such a respectable home, he said, "Ah, but Mrs. Marlowe and I are great friends who share an interest in charitable works. We spent the day together yesterday touring her almshouse in Chelsea. An exemplary operation. But I am sure you have taken the time to see it for yourself and know how compassionate an organization it is."

Mrs. Drummond-Burrell became so flustered that Grace had to cover her mouth so the woman would not see her smile.

"I have not had the opportunity," Mrs. Drummond-Burrell said. "I do not often get to Chelsea. But, of course, I have heard of the good work the Benevolent

Widows Fund does there. My own contributions to the Fund have surely helped in the effort."

"Indeed?" Rochdale said. "Exactly how much have you contributed?"

Mrs. Drummond-Burrell reared back in outrage. "I beg your pardon, sir, but that is no business of yours. Suffice it to say that my husband and I give generously to several charities."

"And we appreciate every shilling," Grace said, glaring at Rochdale for the benefit of the haughty woman, though she was hard pressed not to giggle. She went on to repeat what she'd been relating to several other guests, as a way of explaining Rochdale's presence in her drawing room. "Lord Rochdale has been extremely generous. He is funding a new wing to Marlowe House, which will allow us to take in twice as many families. Isn't that wonderful?"

Mrs. Drummond-Burrell blinked several times, then said in a voice dripping with cool disdain, "How very fortunate for you to have found such a magnanimous benefactor, Mrs. Marlowe. A pity the funds come from the gaming tables."

"For families in need," Grace said, "it hardly matters where the money comes from, does it? As long as it is used to save them from destitution."

"Well. You must do as you see fit. If you will excuse me, Mrs. Marlowe, I have other calls to make. Good day to you." She narrowed her eyes at Rochdale, then left.

"Well done, my dear," Rochdale said, grinning broadly. "You put that self-important harpy in her place."

Grace bit back a smile. "It is all your fault. You goaded her first. She will probably never come here again."

"No great loss. Come, my fifteen minutes are almost up. May I have a private word before I leave?"

"I cannot abandon my guests, my lord."

"Then see me to the door. I have a few matters of business to discuss with you."

They had been standing at the far end of the drawing room, and they meandered through clusters of guests toward the door while Rochdale quietly told her about setting up a special account for Marlowe House at Coutts & Company on the Strand. He gave her the name of the banker who would issue drafts to her whenever needed. When he told her how much he had deposited in the account, Grace almost stumbled, and Rochdale caught her by the elbow to steady her and then guided her out the door.

It was twice the amount they had initially discussed.

Grace was so overwhelmed that she had to fight the sting of tears building behind her eyes. She never succumbed to emotional displays in public, but the amount of his donation was staggering, and a dream come true for Marlowe House. Her lip quivered as she gazed at him, unable to speak.

With his hand still on her elbow, he led her into a small room opposite the drawing room, where tea services, urns, dishes, flatware, linens, and other such items were stored for the convenience of the servants when tea and other refreshments were laid out in the drawing room. Narrow and windowless, the room was as dark as a cave when Rochdale closed the door.

Before she could protest, he took her in his arms. He did not kiss her, but only held her in a warm, comforting embrace. She instinctively burrowed her forehead against his shoulder, as though it was the most natural thing in the world.

"There now," he said in a soft, deep crooning voice. One hand moved up and down her back, ever so gently. "No need to get all watery over a few pounds."

She lifted her head and tried to look into his eyes. "More than just a few pounds."

"Bah. It is not so great an amount. I've lost more in a single night at Wattier's."

"I trust you won it back."

He smiled. "Many times over."

"Well . . . thank you. I don't know what else to say."

"You needn't *say* anything." He tightened the embrace and pressed his hips against hers.

Grace felt his arousal and sucked in a sharp breath. She tried to wriggle out of his arms, but he would not allow it, only loosening his arms slightly. "Please, my lord. This is not right. You must leave. Now. What if someone were to see us? A servant might come in at any moment. I appreciate the generous donation. I really do. But I wish you would not come here anymore. People are beginning to talk, and you are making me . . . uncomfortable."

"And you, my dear Mrs. Marlowe, make *me* uncomfortable." Again, he pushed his hips forward so she could feel exactly how uncomfortable he was. Before she could protest, he cradled the back of her head, drew her to him, and kissed her.

There was nothing subtle in it. This was a purely carnal act, with his tongue deep in her mouth and his hips pressed against hers. It was shocking to feel the hard length of him against her belly and to know she had done that to him. The prim and proper widow had done that to the worldly, cynical rake.

A surge of pure feminine triumph fueled her reaction as she gave in to his kiss. And kissed him back. It grew wilder and more torrid, with his lips and tongue and teeth sending shafts of heat darting through her body. Every sense purred, and a turmoil of hunger, pleasure, and need possessed her. His hands cupped her bottom, and she instinctively moved against his hips. A low moan rose in her throat when she felt his hand stroke the side of her breast.

Voices outside brought her back to earth and she wrenched herself out of his arms. Lord, what had she done? What had he made her do? When she thought of how he'd just touched her, and how she had responded—dear God, she had actually pushed herself up against his erection—shame and mortification sent heat rushing into her face, her neck and shoulders, everywhere. His generosity had clouded her brain, making her forget—again!—who and what he was. This was Rochdale she was kissing in a dark room, an unscrupulous cad who enticed women to behave in the most wanton manner, not some respectable gentleman with honorable intentions.

"Go," she said. "Please go. I don't want this. Not with you. Please leave."

It was difficult to see him clearly in the dark, but she felt his finger caress her check. She shook it off, feeling as though she'd become tangled in the net of him, caught between his kindness and his immorality.

"I am leaving," he said. "But we will see each other again. And soon. You say you don't want this, this passion between us. But I do. I want it very much."

"Enough to bend me to your will."

"It was never against *your* will, Grace, and you know it. Believe me, if I wanted to take you, to hurt you, I could do it before you had a chance to fight me. But that's not what I want."

In a frustrated, almost plaintive voice, she said, "Then what *do* you want?"

"For you to want me as much as I want you. To admit that you do, and stop fighting it."

She gave a little snort. "Because that would take all the blame away from you, wouldn't it?"

"There is no blame to be assigned, Grace. The simple truth is that I want you like no other woman before. If you know anything of my history, you will understand the significance of that statement. But most other women want me before I want them. With you, it is different. But I am arrogant enough to hope that you will want me, too. And soon. I'm not giving up yet." He opened the door and walked out of the room, leaving Grace once again feeling shaken and confused.

Could she believe him? Did he really desire her that much? Heavens, how he made her head spin with such words. He had rattled her composure before, but never so much as today, both by his bald declaration of desire and by what he'd done to her in the dark of this pantry.

And worse, for what he'd made her do. For not only had she failed to rebuff him, she had been encouraged by his obvious arousal. She'd actually rubbed herself against him. Dear heaven, what was happening to her? When had it become so easy to slip into sin?

She couldn't think about such things right now. She had a drawing room full of guests who would be wondering what had become of her. Two deep breaths brought a modicum of composure.

When she stepped into the corridor, Wilhelmina was exiting the drawing room and Beatrice was coming up the stairs. Both friends stared at her oddly, and Grace realized they must have seen Rochdale come out of the same dark room she had just vacated. A rush of heat flooded her from head to toe, and she knew her face was likely as bright as ripe strawberries.

"Grace?" Wilhelmina came forward and placed a hand on her arm. "Is everything all right?"

Beatrice joined them. "That was . . ." She looked back toward the stairs, then again at Grace. "That was Lord Rochdale, was it not?"

"Yes, it was, and no, I am not at all certain that anything is right anymore. I'm so confused, I don't know what to do." She paused, took another breath, and forced the woeful note out of her voice. "Please don't go, Wilhelmina. I wish you would both stay until the other guests depart. I need your advice." She looked at Beatrice and smiled. "And besides, we must hear all about this betrothal of yours. Please, come inside."

Grace ushered her friends into the drawing room, and donned her most serene demeanor as she faced her other guests. She made it through another hour as friends and acquaintances came and went, each staying no longer than the prescribed fifteen minutes. Margaret, her stepdaughter, made one of her rare appearances, and Grace sent up a silent prayer of thanks that she had not arrived earlier when Rochdale was there. She was likely to hear about it, though, as she seemed to hear everything that happened in Society. For such a pious woman, Margaret was an inveterate gossip. Grace was probably in for another lecture on the evils of associating with libertines. Though she no doubt deserved it, she nevertheless wished Margaret would keep her opinions to herself.

Marianne and Penelope had stopped by, and Grace imposed upon them to stay as well. She needed the full contingent of Merry Widows to help her figure out what to do about Lord Rochdale.

When the last of the other guests had departed, Grace called for fresh tea and cakes, and the five friends gathered around the tea table that was set up for them. The most important news was Beatrice's betrothal to Lord Thayne, a man she loved but thought she'd lost. It was the first time any of them had had a chance to discuss it with her, for she and Thayne had disappeared shortly after the announcement at the masquerade ball.

"We had a private celebration," Beatrice said, her blue eyes twinkling. The striking redhead was positively radiant with happiness.

She told them how the intervention of her future mother-in-law, the Duchess of Doncaster, had been responsible for the betrothal. "She can be quite formidable when she wants to be, but is really a delightful woman. I am already very fond of her. And the duke."

Because of the importance of the family, the wedding would be a large and formal occasion, even though the bride was an "older" woman with two children. They were planning a September wedding at St. George's, before the parliamentary session ended and all the grand lords retreated to their country estates for the winter. Beatrice had been invited by the duchess to spend the summer months at Hadbury Park, the ducal estate in Derbyshire, which would one day be her own.

It was lovely to see Beatrice so happy. Grace was pleased that the love affairs of both Marianne and Beatrice had ended with marriage. She had never been altogether comfortable with their silly pact to seek out lovers. And yet . . .

"Enough about me," Beatrice said, reaching for an almond biscuit. "I fear I have missed something significant with you, Grace. I could hardly believe it when I saw Rochdale leaving earlier. What is going on?"

"Rochdale was here again?" Penelope grinned and fingered one of her glossy brown curls. "My, but he is becoming persistent, is he not?"

"Yes, he is," Grace said. "So much so that I am all at sixes and sevens. I don't know what to do about him."

"Rochdale is pursuing you?" Beatrice looked stunned, as well she should. They were speaking of the man who had run off with her young niece.

Grace dumped the remains of cold tea in the slop dish and poured fresh hot water into the pot. "Strange as it sounds," she said, "he appears to be. I cannot explain it. I am not a sophisticated high flyer. It makes no sense that he should want me, but he . . . he says he does."

"Good God," Beatrice said. "And we left you alone with him in Twickenham."

"That's when it began. At least that was when he . . . he kissed me the first time. But I had seen him watching me for weeks before."

"The first time?" Penelope said. "I take that to mean he has kissed you again?"

Grace nodded.

"Has he made love to you?"

"No! No, Penelope, he has not, but that's what he wants."

"And what do *you* want?" Wilhelmina asked.

"I don't know! He has me so confused." She ought to have allowed the tea to steep longer, but she felt the need for something to *do*, something that kept her eyes away from probing gazes, and so reached for her friends' empty cups.

"Grace Marlowe," Penelope said with a broad smile, "are you saying you are considering taking Rochdale as your lover?"

She filled Penelope's cup and handed it back to her. "No, not really. I could never do that. But . . ."

"You like the way he makes you feel." Wilhelmina made it a statement of fact, not a question.

Grace shook her head. "No, I don't like it at all. He makes me feel wicked. He makes me forget who I am."

Wilhelmina passed her cup, and Grace refilled it. "It is not wicked to feel physical desire, my dear," the duchess said. "It is perfectly natural."

"Yes, but it can be terrifying at first," Marianne said. "If you've never experienced real passion before, it can send you into a panic, and make you question everything you thought you understood about yourself. I know. It happened to me." She looked at Grace. "I suspect it is even more difficult for you. Considering how you disapproved of what the rest of us were doing—no, don't deny it, Grace; you know you did—I can imagine it must be terribly confusing, even frightening, to find yourself responding to Rochdale's kisses, even enjoying them."

"That is the problem, is it not?" Wilhelmina asked.

"That you liked it when he kissed you, and that made you feel wicked?"

Grace busied herself with pouring tea and merely nodded her head, too mortified to admit it aloud.

"He kissed you today, right before he left, didn't he?" Wilhelmina said.

Grace nodded again, unable to meet her friend's eyes.

"I thought as much," Wilhelmina said, "when I saw you come out of the dark room right after him. Is he forcing himself on you, Grace? Did he drag you into that room against your will?"

"No," Grace said, finally finding her voice. "It wasn't like that. He surprised me the first time, but he has never forced me. I . . . I let him kiss me. And each time, I hate myself afterward. It seems so sinful. And yet . . ."

"You enjoy it."

Grace looked at Wilhelmina and realized this woman, and all the others, had her best interests at heart. She loved them. They could be trusted. They would not laugh at her or scold her. They might not truly understand, but they would listen. And counsel her. There was no need to be circumspect with them.

"Yes, heaven help me, I enjoy it," she said, and all at once the words began to spill out of her in a rush. "While it's happening, it is quite wonderful, I admit it. It's like nothing I've ever known. My whole body tingles. I become lost in sensation. I confess that I was intrigued when I listened to all of you talk of your men and their lovemaking. I couldn't imagine it could be as good as you described, for I have only ever known . . ." She paused, unwilling to describe what had taken place in private with her late husband. She would not disparage him to anyone.

"But now I know you were right," she continued. "I felt it with Rochdale. I enjoyed it, every time, even when I pretended not to. But then I'd realize what I was doing and, worse, whom I was doing it with, and I'd fall into a muddle of guilt and shame."

"Do not be ashamed, my dear," Wilhelmina said. "You are a woman, just like the rest of us. And we have all enjoyed sexual passion with men."

"I know. And I keep telling myself that *you* aren't wicked women."

"And neither are you," Wilhelmina said.

"But *he* is wicked," Grace said. "At least, I think he is. That's another thing that has me confused. I am beginning to think he might not be entirely bad, or at least not as bad as everyone thinks he is."

"That's what Adam always tells me," Marianne said, finally getting Grace to notice her empty teacup. "I cannot believe he would keep Rochdale as a friend if the man was some kind of monster." She turned to Beatrice. "Even if he did abscond to his villa with your Emily. Remember, he did not ravish the silly girl or seduce her, though he had ample time to do so."

"I am sure you are right," Beatrice said, "though I am not yet ready to forgive him for his role in that little drama."

"And I have told you," Wilhelmina said, "that there are two sides to every story. As far as that business with Serena Underwood is concerned, none of us knows Rochdale's side of that sordid tale."

"I still say he is a rogue and a scoundrel." Penelope took a sip of tea, then looked around at each of them in turn, smiled, and said, "But I never said there was anything wrong with that, did I?"

"He has done the most extraordinary thing," Grace said, "that will interest all of you as trustees of the Benevolent Widows Fund." And she told them about his enormous donation to their charity, about his inspection of Marlowe House, and about the special account he had set up at Coutts & Company. Each of the women was amazed by the news, and delighted at what could be accomplished with Rochdale's gift.

"I can see why you begin to question your opinion of him," Beatrice said.

"But that's not the only reason," Grace said. "You see, I have learned a bit about his history, and it does not at all jibe with who he is now. There is a woman in residence at Marlowe House who recognized him yesterday. Jane Fletcher grew up on his father's estate in Suffolk. Her father was the gamekeeper. Anyway, the young man she described was studious and idealistic and honorable. She thought he might have gone into the church if he hadn't been the heir to a viscountcy."

"The church?" Penelope and Beatrice exclaimed in perfect unison.

Grace smiled. "That was exactly my reaction. Rochdale denied it, of course, but the picture painted by Jane Fletcher was of a very different sort of person than the man who told me his chief pleasures are gambling, drinking, and wenching."

Beatrice broke off a small piece of sugar from a larger lump and popped it into her tea. "Perhaps she mistook him for someone else."

"No, they knew each other well. Jane's husband had been a close boyhood friend to Rochdale. He was much affected by Jane's young son, who apparently bears a striking resemblance to her late husband. He was very kind to the boy."

"That may be," Beatrice said, her spoon clanking rhythmically as she stirred her tea, "but it still doesn't explain how a young man who once dreamed of taking orders became . . . Rochdale. Perhaps your Mrs. Fletcher's memories of a happier time have become romanticized over the years."

"Perhaps. Rochdale said she exaggerated, but he did not deny having been bookish."

Penelope giggled. "One can only imagine what sort of books interested the young Rochdale."

"I am sure there are a lot of studious young men,"

Wilhelmina said, "who come up to London and develop a taste for the wilder side of life. It is not so strange that Rochdale was once a callow youth. Most men were. Some just happen to fall more deeply into debauchery than others."

"Especially if tragedy has left them cynical." Grace passed a plate of jam tarts as she repeated Jane's tale of the declining estate and the fire, as well as Rochdale's bitter acknowledgment of his father's weakness and of Miss Lindsay-Holmes's rejection.

Wilhelmina lifted an eyebrow. "Well. That explains a lot."

"I thought so, too," Grace said. "I mean, any one of us might be similarly affected by such a series of blows, don't you think? Lord Rochdale just never allowed himself to recover. Or went about it rather badly, I should say, using every imaginable excess to dull the pain. I wonder if—"

"Don't, Grace," Wilhelmina interrupted.

"Don't what?"

"Don't start thinking you can reform him. He's not one of your destitute widows who needs your help to turn her life around."

"Oh, but I wasn't thinking—"

"Yes, you were. It is your nature, my dear, to want to help people. But Rochdale does not need your help. He is who he is because that's the way he wants to be. He's not miserable or pathetic. In fact, I should think he is thoroughly happy with his life. He may not always behave strictly according to Society's rules, but that is his choice. If you believe you have glimpsed something in him worth admiring—and it sounds as though you have—then by all means admire him. On the other hand, if you are simply attracted to him, physically, sexually, then don't make excuses for it by trying to imagine him as some sort of lost soul. He is not. And it is perfectly all right to be attracted to him."

"And you are, aren't you?" Penelope asked, her blue eyes twinkling. She was enjoying Grace's situation far too much. She was altogether too delighted that the prudish bishop's widow had been sexually aroused by a man, any man.

Grace sighed. "That's the devil of it, of course. Yes, God help me, I'm attracted to him. And you're right, Wilhelmina, about making excuses for it. I hadn't thought of it that way, but that's what I've been doing, I suppose. I've been so confused, drawn to a man so completely the opposite of everything I admire. Rochdale teased me about it, telling me I was tying myself in knots over it."

"It's time to untie them, my dear," Wilhelmina said. "Let yourself be drawn to him. Let yourself like him, even, now that you know a little more about him. Just remember what I told you before. Be careful with him. He is still a hardened rake and could break your heart."

"There is always the chance that he has softened a bit," Penelope said. "A man like that doesn't woo a woman the way he is wooing Grace. He merely crooks his finger and women follow him. But this time he is actively in pursuit. Odd, isn't it? I suppose he really likes you, Grace."

"Enough to hand over a great deal of money to our Fund," Beatrice said.

"You think that, too?" Grace asked. "Though I will accept his contribution with gratitude, I still half believe his generosity is simply a ploy to impress me. I don't understand why, but I do think that is what he is doing."

"Because he wants you, of course," Penelope said around a mouthful of jam tart. She swallowed and added, "You're a beautiful woman, Grace. Oh, and I remember how you looked at the masquerade ball. Good heavens, no wonder he is smitten. You looked positively ravishing that night."

"You certainly did," Marianne agreed, her brown eyes lit with mischief. "And I will tell you a little secret. When Adam saw Rochdale dancing with you, he joked that you must have dressed precisely to please Rochdale, with your hair down like that. He told me that Rochdale has a particular fondness for long blond hair. Said it drives him wild with desire. So, there you have it. Nothing at all mysterious about Rochdale's interest. He lusts after your hair."

The laughter of all five women, Grace included, filled the drawing room. What foolishness, she thought, that a man should be so enamored of hair.

I dream of seeing your hair down again like it was last night at the ball, of wrapping myself up in all its golden glory while I make love to you.

She gave a little shiver at the recollection of his words.

"You ladies are a bad influence on me," she said. "You make me believe my wanton reaction to Rochdale is perfectly natural, when in my heart I know it to be sinful. My stepdaughter was obliged to remind me that my behavior reflects badly on her father's memory. And she was speaking only of the fact that I had danced with Rochdale and been seen talking with him on the terrace at Doncaster House. I shudder to think how she would react if she knew all that has passed between us."

"My dear girl," Wilhelmina said, frowning, "I realize Lady Bumfries is your late husband's daughter, but I take leave to tell you that she is a pompous old cat. How dare she accuse you of dishonoring the bishop's memory? What better way to honor him than to have established the Widows Fund and built a superb halfway house with his name on it? And are you not editing his sermons?"

"Yes, though she disapproves of that project. I believe she would rather I had asked her to do it."

"Even so," Wilhelmina said, "I do not see how she

can accuse you of dishonoring his memory. Even if you were to dance naked down St. James's Street at midday, it would not negate all the good you have done as his widow. Which is surely a thousand times more valuable than anything she has done as his daughter."

Grace wanted to hug her. Wilhelmina was such a good and kind woman, and she was proud to call her friend. When the bishop was alive, he'd never have allowed Grace to associate with the duchess. He had despised women who flouted the rules of Society, as Wilhelmina certainly had done. In fact, Grace had only days before unearthed one of her husband's sermons in which he warned against allowing one's wife and daughters to mix freely with fallen women, "lest they contaminate those virtuous but fragile souls under our protection."

Perhaps she would leave that particular sermon out of the collection.

"Wilhelmina's right, as always," Penelope said. "Don't let that sour-faced baggage tell you how to live your life. You are the bishop's *widow*, not his wife. What you do now that he is dead is your own business."

"Especially what you do in private," Marianne said.

"The bishop is dead," Wilhelmina said. "Do not allow his daughter to make you believe she is speaking for him. I seriously doubt he comes to her in the night on angel's wings to tell her that you are not behaving properly as his widow. And if he did appear to her, I daresay he would tell her how proud he is of you and of all the good work you do."

Grace felt the sting of tears for the second time that day. She blinked rapidly in hopes she would not embarrass herself in front of these wonderful women who'd become such good and loyal friends to her.

Penelope stood and raised her teacup. "Here's to the liberation of Grace Marlowe. May she always be her own woman and not bound by someone else's expectations, living or dead."

They all rose and Grace's best Worcester teacups sounded their fine porcelain *ping* as they were clinked together in a toast.

Chapter 10

He drove his curricle past Marlowe House for the third time. His uncomplaining tiger would surely think he'd gone off his head. Rochdale would slow as he neared the house, then change his mind and drive past, then change his mind again and decide he really would go inside, then drive on by again instead. Feeling the perfect fool, he reached the end of the road and steered the team round once more. This time he would do it. He would stop and go inside.

Grace was not there—he knew her to be meeting with the banker at Coutts & Company—so he could not dismiss another visit to Chelsea as just one more attempt to impress her.

He'd already done that. And it had worked. His contribution to her charity had not entirely won her over, but it had altered her opinion of him, he knew, and it had given him a legitimate excuse to spend more time with her, which was critical to earning her trust. Even better, the more he was in her company, the more intrigued she became, the more she accepted her attraction to him, and the more he was able to play off that attraction in moving inexorably toward his goal.

Yesterday, in that dark little butler's pantry, Rochdale had thought for one brief moment that he was

about to win the wager. She'd been such a firebrand
of unleashed passion that he'd been very close to lifting her skirts and taking her on a countertop right
then and there. If voices outside the door had not
reminded her, and him, that it was neither the time
nor the place for such an encounter, he wondered if
she would have let him take it that far. She might
have done, but he did not believe she was ready. She
was still afraid. She became overwhelmed with her
own sexual response, probably because it was a novel
experience for her, and she was capable of letting it
lead her into new worlds of sensation. When she came
to herself, though, when she lifted herself out of the
moment, she was always startled to realize she had
gone so far. She did not need to tell him. He felt how
it frightened her. Shamed her. Confused her.

Grace had said she did not want this passion between them. She was wrong, of course. She did want
it, and he knew it. They both knew it. That was Rochdale's biggest challenge: to get her to accept that she
wanted him.

There had been considerable progress. Each time
he was with her, she let down her guard a bit more.
He no longer needed to trick or cajole her into a kiss.
She was willing, at least for a moment. And that was
a giant step toward the ultimate surrender.

God, he could hardly wait. He could not remember
the last time he'd desired a woman so completely. If
anyone had told him at the beginning of the Season
that he'd be aching to possess a starchy, tight-laced
bishop's widow, he'd have told them they were off
their feed. He could never have predicted it. While
setting out to coax a sexual response out of her, he'd
unwittingly ignited a blistering response of his own. It
was, he supposed, the potent combination of innocence and natural passion. Those few moments when
she let down her inhibitions and threw herself head-

long into a kiss, her eagerness and hunger was tempered by an artlessness so poignant it almost took his breath away.

And he had not lied when he told her he could look at her all day long and never tire of it. Grace Marlowe was flat-out beautiful. With no need of artificial enhancements or cosmetics, she was a natural beauty, polished by money and position into a high sheen of English perfection: long neck, high-boned patrician cheeks, hair as thick and shiny as a gold sovereign, and skin like a plateful of cream. She was a feast for the eyes, tempting and delectable.

Naturally, Rochdale had known his share of beauties, but Grace was different. It was that artless quality, again, that set her apart. She was no doubt aware that her looks were something above the ordinary—she surely glanced into a mirror now and then—but she did not seem overly conscious of them. She did not flaunt her beauty or use it in any way, as most women did, to gain an advantage over men. In fact, when she had dressed as Titania at the ball, she had seemed bashful about it, as though she was embarrassed to have put her best assets on display.

Yes, it was assuredly the twin virtues of guileless sexuality and unaffected beauty that had Rochdale lusting after her. She was so unlike the worldly, often jaded women he normally bedded. He suspected bedding Grace Marlowe would be an unparalleled pleasure, rare and unique.

It was almost a shame to remember that it was all done for the sake of a fine racehorse, and that he would walk away from Grace once he'd won the wager. Or soon thereafter, in any case. He might as well stick around and enjoy her for a short while before he moved on, for there was no question that having Grace for a lover was going to be damned good while it lasted.

He must remember to thank Sheane when it was over.

But Grace wasn't his problem right now. Rochdale slowed the team once again as he neared Marlowe House. He supposed he should stop being such an idiot and simply go inside. It was the right thing to do.

Before he could change his mind again, he steered the team toward the entrance and brought them to a halt. Nat, his young tiger, jumped down from the rear seat and stood ready to take the reins as Rochdale climbed down from the bench.

"Shall I walk the team, milord?"

A good question. Rochdale did not know how long he would be, especially since he was not entirely sure what he was doing here. "If I am not back in five minutes, walk them. If I'm not back in half an hour, take the seat and drive them about the area. Don't wear them out, mind you. Just keep them moving at a nice, steady pace until I return."

"Yes, milord. Take your time and don't worry none about your cattle." The boy grinned, obviously hoping not to see his employer for at least a half hour.

Rochdale looked up at the brick façade of Marlowe House and let out a breath through puffed cheeks. Now that he was here, he felt a bit stupid. He had spent two days telling himself he'd never return. Grace could do as she pleased with his money. He didn't need to witness the improvements firsthand. As for Jane Fletcher and her family, he would see that they were settled someplace safe, preferably far away from London, and him. She brought back too many memories he'd sooner forget.

He hated that starry-eyed fool he'd once been, full of high-minded ideals and pipe dreams of the future. The fire and all that followed had squashed any romantic conceits he'd still harbored. He'd been too busy climbing out of the quagmire of debt and despair his father had left behind.

It had been sheer desperation that had led him into that dingy little gaming hell on Jermyn Street, the first of many he'd haunted. From the start, he'd been a successful gambler, probably because no risk seemed too great. He'd already lost everything that was dear to him—his father, his home, the girl he loved—so that the prospect of losing everything else seemed inconsequential.

Since those days, he'd recouped the Rochdale fortunes many times over at the gaming tables and on the Exchange. He could have returned to Suffolk, rebuilt a grand country house at Bettisfont, and settled into a quiet rural life. Once upon a time, he'd wanted precisely that life, with Caroline Lindsay-Holmes at his side and a passel of their black-haired brats romping the estate. That was long ago, however, a lifetime ago, and such a sedentary existence no longer held any appeal for him.

Life was easier now. Hedonism always was, he supposed. He enjoyed his life, doing as he pleased, answerable to no one. He lived well, but never got too attached to things. Or people.

Which was why he hesitated at the humble brick portal of Marlowe House. He had no news for Jane, though his man of affairs was looking into a few possibilities. And he had no wish to reminisce about the past with her. No, it was young Toby's face he could not shake from his mind, the boy who looked so much like Rochdale's old friend. The thought of that eager lad stuck in this place with a bunch of women did not sit well with him. Martin would not have approved. In fact, he would have hated it. Perhaps Toby did, too. Rochdale feared the boy might have the same impetuous streak that had got his father into so much mischief. But getting into mischief in London was another thing entirely. It was dangerous. Toby already had some taste of life in the streets. There was no telling what sort of skills he might have picked up in St. Giles. He just might think he was clever enough to survive on his own.

That, of course, is what drew Rochdale inexorably back to Chelsea. He did not want Martin's son lost in the stews of London. He would do his best to get him away, to find Jane a position in the country, where Toby could do all the rough, dirty, noisy things that boys did. In the meantime, Rochdale meant to give him a respite from all those females.

He stepped up to the door of Marlowe House and lifted the knocker.

Grace was feeling positively buoyant after her meeting with Mr. Willets, the architect who was to design the improvements to Marlowe House. His sketches were spread out before her, covering the desk in the small office she kept there. He would provide more detailed plans soon, but the initial designs he had presented today with these drawings were everything she could have hoped for, and more.

She could never have imagined having so much money available for Marlowe House and all the services it provided. And she had wasted no time in putting the unexpected windfall of Rochdale's donation to good use.

They could now afford more than just a new south wing. They were going to add a second story to the north wing as well. Mr. Willets had been justifiably proud of the more unified design, and the way he had integrated more modern features with the original Restoration structure. But what pleased Grace even more was what all that new space represented: accommodations for a great many more residents and the expansion of other areas, like the workshops and schoolrooms.

There would now be separate schoolrooms and teachers for the younger children and the older children. Mrs. Chalk had pressed for the new schoolrooms to be used to segregate the boys from the girls, but Grace felt it more efficient to separate them by age.

It was not as though the girls here would receive lessons in deportment while the boys learned Greek and Latin. These were children who needed basic reading and writing skills, as well as simple mathematics, regardless of gender. If they learned no more than how to read, they would be in much better positions to find work as they got older. One of the guiding principles of Marlowe House was that a sound education provided one with better opportunities in life and could mean the difference between security and destitution. If the children did not have, at the very least, reading skills, they were more likely to end up in dire circumstances. Many of their mothers could not read, either, and some of them sat alongside their children in the classroom so they could learn, too. Others felt awkward doing so, especially as their children learned more quickly, as children often did. Grace hoped to introduce a special reading class for adults so that the women would feel less inadequate.

Mr. Willets had promised a final estimate of costs and a detailed schedule by the end of the week. He did, however, seem confident that all could be completed before winter.

As she gathered up the drawings and the sheets of notes on the building project, Grace felt a wave of overwhelming gratitude for Rochdale's involvement. Without him, none of it would have been possible, at least not in so short a time.

The problem, however, was that when one felt grateful to a person for doing something entirely good and worthy, one tended to overlook that much of that person's life was entirely bad. Grace tried to ignore Rochdale's reputation as a libertine and simply be thankful for all he'd done for Marlowe House. He made it difficult, though, by continuing to pursue her.

In the last week, she'd met him at every social function she attended. Every rout, every card party, every ball—Rochdale was there. He had made an appearance in her drawing room again yesterday, when she was receiving callers. This time he'd come face-to-face with Margaret, and Grace had almost lost her famous composure. Rochdale had merely smiled at Margaret—one of his teasing, devilish smiles—and she had given him the cut direct. Rochdale, as Margaret must have known, was indifferent to her insult, not caring what Margaret or anyone else thought of him, and had actually laughed about it. But Grace had been forced to listen to another of Margaret's lectures on propriety and the bishop's memory, and had come very close to telling her stepdaughter to mind her own business. She had not done so, of course, but had instead stoically listened to every scornful word.

Though he popped up everywhere, Rochdale had not kissed her again, for she had not allowed herself to be alone with him. He did, though, take every opportunity to surreptitiously touch her—a brief stroke of her arm, a quick caress of her shoulder—and each touch made her feel horribly wicked.

Because despite how wrong it was, she wanted more. God would surely punish her for such wayward desires, but she could not seem to stop them. Her friends continued their encouragement, believing she should take what Rochdale offered and enjoy it. But they did not understand. It was not as simple as that. Not for her. She could admit to feeling wicked, but to actually act on those feelings was a more serious matter.

Sometimes Grace wished she could be more like Beatrice, for example, who had entered into a love affair with Thayne without a single qualm. No, that was not true. She did have qualms, but only because of who he was—a younger man for whom her niece had set her cap—and not for what they did together. Penelope, God knew, had no reservations about taking Eustace Tolliver to her bed. Marianne had preferred an affair with Adam Cazenove before he talked her into marrying him. And Wilhelmina . . . well, there was no telling how many men she'd had in her life.

It was easier for her friends, the Merry Widows. They had not been trained by a great church leader to see the evils of physical passion. None of them became awash in self-loathing every time she longed for a man's touch, as Grace did. None of them worried about going to hell for daring to enjoy a libertine's kiss, as Grace did. None of them felt guilty for being flattered that a man like Rochdale found her attractive, as Grace did. Neither did they have to contend with a stepdaughter's Greek chorus of shame, or dreams of a saintly husband's reprimands.

They encouraged her to forget about the bishop and his daughter, and she tried to do so. She really tried. It had become easy to dismiss Margaret, whose self-righteousness had begun to pall. The bishop was more difficult to forget when a full-length portrait of him, grand and austere in his formal robes, faced her on the first landing whenever she went up or down the stairs at Portland Place. A better likeness, capturing the more gentle countenance she had known so well, hung in the drawing room.

The bishop's presence was strong in the Portland Place house, even after Grace had redecorated some of the rooms in a more feminine style. And lately, he had haunted her dreams with increased frequency, but not as Ignatius, the kindly, indulgent husband who treated her like a delicate porcelain figurine. It was Bishop Marlowe who visited her dreams, his gentle brow furrowed in disapproval as he delivered private sermons on the evils of the flesh.

No doubt the dreams were a result of editing his sermons, which she most often did in the evenings before retiring. Last night she had found one in which he wrote of the weaker sex and the fragile nature of female virtue. "The virtuous woman," he wrote, "is to be honored for the difficult burden involved in remaining chaste and modest, uncorrupted by the coarse nature of men or depraved women. Those strong, ready passions that are natural in the male are indelicate and undesirable in a female. Modesty and decency forbid them from indulging in those natural urges which, in the male, cannot be denied. The virtuous woman's rejection of such earthly desires keeps her closer to heaven."

As she read on, Grace remembered how she had always felt these pronouncements to be directed at her, as reminders that he wanted her to be a shining example of the virtuous wife, and not the naïve girl who'd come to him expecting to enjoy physical intimacy with her husband. She had a different reaction to the words now. Having friends who unashamedly enjoyed sexual intimacy gave her a different perspective. She did not believe for a moment that either Beatrice or Marianne or Penelope or even Wilhelmina was an indecent, depraved woman who would be barred from heaven. The bishop had been wrong about them.

Had he been wrong about her, too?

Grace's thoughts were interrupted by a soft knock on the door. "Come in," she called, and began tidying her desk, organizing Willets's drawings and plans into neat piles.

Jane Fletcher stepped into the room. "I hope I am not interrupting?"

"Not at all. Come in and have a seat, Jane."

She did so, then said, "I have come to thank you for sending Lord Rochdale to take Toby in hand."

"Lord Rochdale has been back?" He had not mentioned it.

"Oh, yes. He comes most every day and takes Toby off to some sporting event or other. He has even begun teaching the boy to ride." A smile lit her face, making her appear years younger. "Toby is beside himself with the pleasure of it all. Can't stop talking about his lordship and all the things they do together. It's the first sparkle I've seen in his eyes in a very long time. And I wanted to thank you for it. Lord Rochdale says it was your idea to provide Toby with more male companionship. You were right. He is surrounded by women here, with only a few younger boys to play with. Bless you for sending Lord Rochdale for him."

Grace bit her tongue. She'd been about to blurt out that she had not, in fact, sent Rochdale, but decided to allow him his little charade. So, he had not been able to resist Toby, but attributed his visits to a fictitious request from Grace. The wretched man was determined to keep his bad reputation intact. Heaven forbid that anyone should suspect he cared about a young boy, or that he had taken the boy under his wing out of kindness. The wicked Rochdale would never do anything so selfless.

Grace smiled. She knew there was good in him. No matter what anyone said, she had suspected all along that he could not be as bad as he seemed.

"I am glad to hear Toby is enjoying himself."

"He is. Thanks to you. I am no end pleased that you decided that John—Lord Rochdale, I mean—would not be a bad influence on the boy. He's a good man, and very good to Toby. Good to us all. He's trying to arrange for us to go back to Suffolk to live. Did you know? Toby has taken a liking to horses, and John thinks he would be a good stable boy at the old Bettisfont stables. He keeps all his horses there, you know, and it is where they get trained for racing."

"And Toby is to be a stable boy? How marvelous for him. But what of you and Sally? Surely you will not allow Toby to go to Bettisfont alone?"

Jane shook her head. "No, we'll go all. John—Lord Rochdale, I mean—I can't seem to get used to calling him that; it always sounds like I'm speaking of his father. Anyway, he is having our old farmhouse repaired. Imagine that. We will actually be living in our own house again, the house where I was so happy with Martin. The children have never seen it, of course, but they will love it. I'll keep a small vegetable garden and maybe some nice roses, too."

One more clue as to the true nature of Lord Rochdale. What would his gambling associates think to know that he had such a kind heart? "It sounds lovely," Grace said. "I'll miss all of you, but I am always pleased to see our families well placed. Lord Rochdale will make sure you are provided for, I am sure."

"Oh, no, we don't want to be his charity family." Jane's posture had stiffened and there was a proud angle to her lifted chin. "It's enough that he is making a home available to us. We'll pay him rent, same as anyone would. He's going to have all three of us working at Bettisfont. Seems there's a large staff at the stables, what with all the horses to look after. Dozens and dozens, I hear. I am to be a cook and Sally my helper." The challenge in her pose transformed into an almost girlish preening. She grinned and said, "Isn't that grand?"

"It is indeed. Will you like that, cooking for a group of men? I imagine the staff is all men."

"Remember, Mrs. Marlowe, that I followed the drum for a dozen years. I'm used to being around a bunch of dirty, hungry, foulmouthed brutes. I can hold my own with them, don't you worry. Though they'll watch their language around me and Sally if I have any say in the matter."

Grace congratulated Jane on her good fortune and they spoke more about Bettisfont and what the future held there. Finally, Jane rose and said she had to get back to work. "Cooking for all the folks here is good practice for me."

Grace followed her out the office door. She needed to run Alice Chalk to earth and let her know of the improvements Mr. Willets had proposed. As they walked toward the entry hall, Grace said, "Do you suppose he will ever rebuild the house?"

There was no need for Jane to ask of whom Grace spoke, or of what house. "I don't know. Someday, perhaps. When he's finished punishing God for what happened."

"Punishing God? Is that what you—"

"Mama!" The earsplitting shriek of pure delight was followed by the charge of a very dirty young boy through the front door and across the entry hall. Toby came to a skidding halt in front of his mother and lifted his face to proudly display an eye swollen shut and rimmed in a deep purple bruise.

Jane frowned. "Toby, boy, what have you done?"

"My goodness," Grace said, shocked to see how pleased with himself the child looked, though he had obviously suffered a painful injury. There was a cut above his eye and bloodstains on his shirt. "Are you all right, Toby? Does it hurt badly? We'd better take you to Mrs. Birch right away and see what she can do about it."

"Naw, it ain't nothing. I got into a fight, Mama. A real fight!"

"And he handled himself splendidly, too," Rochdale said as he walked into the hall. He removed his tall beaver hat, and a wave of blue-black hair fell rakishly over one brow. Standing beside Toby, he tickled the boy under his chin, causing him to twitch and giggle.

"You allowed this to happen, Lord Rochdale?" The goodwill she had been feeling toward him vanished at the sight of Toby's swollen eye and bloodied shirt. Grace tried to control the anger she felt for the grinning black-haired devil at the boy's side. "You allowed Toby to fight? *To get hurt?*"

"It don't hurt much, Miz Marlowe. And you should see the other feller. Whopped him good, I did." He puffed his little chest out with typical male pride.

Grace frowned at Rochdale. "What happened?"

He gazed at her intently for a moment, until she felt compelled to look away. "I took the boy to a boxing exhibition at Fives' Court."

"A mill!" Toby exclaimed. "A real one. Not one o' them street corner rough 'n' tumbles, but a real milling-match, with this raised-up platform with ropes, and rules and special gloves and everything. And science. They fought with science. Right, milord?"

Rochdale smiled. "That's right, Toby. Very scientific. Just like you learned at Gentleman Jackson's."

"There were lots of people there," Toby continued, breathlessly. "Lots and lots. Everyone cheering for one feller or t'other. We was cheering for Mr. Percy. Right, milord?"

"That's right."

"So there was this other boy. And, well, he picked a fight with me. I had to fight back, didn't I? But see, his lordship's been letting me watch him spar at Gentleman Jackson's, and I been watching real close and figured I learned a thing or two."

"That you did, Toby," Rochdale said. "Never saw better science in a lad your age."

Toby's face split with a triumphant smile and he preened like a tiny cock of the walk.

His mother scowled at him, though Grace noted a twinkle in her eye. "Are you sure you weren't the one to start the fight, my boy? So you could show off what you learned?"

Toby shrugged and grinned sheepishly. "The feller made fun o' my jacket, so what was I to do?"

"What, indeed. Well, I know what you have to do now, young man, and that's march yourself right into the infirmary and have Mrs. Birch see to that eye. *Now*. Let's go, Toby. Oh, and thank you, my lord, for getting the boy home in one piece."

"It was my pleasure. Do as your mother says, Toby. You might not be so pleased about having a face in half mourning tomorrow when it hurts like the devil and you can't see straight. Ask for a bit of raw beefsteak. That will do the trick, most likely. Off with you, now."

"Thank you, sir." The boy's one good eye gazed up at his hero with unadulterated admiration. "Milord, I mean. Thanks for taking me to the Fives' Court. And for the lemon ice before." Jane took him by the hand and tugged him to the corridor that led to the infirmary. He bounced along beside her and waved as they disappeared round the corner.

Rochdale smiled, then turned to face Grace. Who was not smiling. She glared at him. "What were you thinking," she said, "to take a young boy to a prizefight, which was no doubt packed with ruffians and cutpurses and every sort of criminal? He's just a little boy, for heaven's sake."

"An eight-year-old boy who's spent the last year in the stews of St. Giles. He is more than capable of taking care of himself. That is, if you really believe I would have deliberately put him in danger."

"You allowed him to fight."

"He was insulted by another boy. His honor required him to fight. It's what boys do."

"And what men do, when they challenge other men to duels."

Rochdale's level blue gaze did not waver. "That was years ago. Ancient history. And yes, it was always a matter of honor. But that has nothing to do with Toby."

Grace ought to have known that every ugly rumor she'd ever heard about Rochdale was true. At least he did not deny having been involved in more than one duel. But it was Toby she worried about. She hoped Rochdale was not a bad influence on the boy. "You've been taking him to boxing saloons and other such places?"

"I am merely helping to teach him to be a man. It's

what his father would have done, and his mother can't do. I'm exposing him to the sort of masculine pursuits he'll never learn here, surrounded by women. He barely remembers Martin, and has not had any man in his life since. I'm not trying to replace his father. I could never do that and would never try. But the boy needs a man to talk to, to teach him things a man needs to know. He's small for his age and will be challenged at every turn. He needs to be able to defend himself, to learn to live in the real world."

Grace's anger abated as he spoke. He was right, she supposed. Toby did need a man in his life, as Jane had said. But the sight of that small face, bloodied and bruised, had given her a scare. "I'm sorry," she said. "I am overreacting, no doubt. I just hate the idea of that child fighting. He might have been more seriously injured."

"I would not have allowed it."

"No, of course you would not." She could see that he cared too much for Toby to put him in danger. "I apologize for suggesting otherwise."

He nodded, accepting her apology. "Besides," he said, "one black eye will do him no harm. I can testify to that. The bruises are only now fading from the facer young Burnett planted on me a few weeks ago."

Grace had almost forgotten about that episode. She studied his face for signs of the bruise and saw only sharp planes picked out by the sunlight coming through the front window, offsetting deep hollows carved by shadow. And heavy-lidded blue eyes that twinkled with amusement—and something else?—as he held her gaze. Those eyes reminded her of what had happened later that same night, in Rochdale's carriage, and her cheeks flamed. She lowered her head so he would not see.

He was having none of that, however, and tilted her chin up, holding it there so she was forced to look at him again. He cupped her flushed cheek in one hand, the pad of his thumb brushing the corner of her mouth. "Yes, that was the night I first kissed you," he said in a low, thick voice. "I remember it, too."

He bent his head closer, and closer still, until their breaths mingled. Slowly, inevitably, he set his lips to hers in a kiss, excruciatingly sweet and simple. Though they were alone, Grace was aware that they stood in the entry hall of Marlowe House, where any number of people might walk by. But his kiss was subtle and tempting, and though she ought to have done so, she did not push him away. It was too delicious. Too perfect.

He did not take her into his arms, but simply kissed her, moving his lips softly over hers in the most exquisite, leisurely exploration. When she parted her lips slightly, he took her face in both hands and cradled it, then deepened the kiss. She uttered a low moan, savoring the breathtaking pleasure of his tongue caressing her own, and only then did he draw her to him. Without thought, she stepped into his embrace and became lost in his kiss.

Some minutes later, when Grace found her wits again and remembered where she was, she pulled back. "You are incorrigible, my lord. You are determined to make a public scene with me." She extricated herself from his arms and moved away, looking right and left to ensure that they were indeed alone.

Rochdale's eyelids appeared heavier and sleepier than ever. "No one saw us."

"But they might have done."

"Despite what you may think, my dear, I have no desire to embarrass you in public. I made sure no one was about. I look out for you, the same way I do for Toby. I will let neither of you come to harm."

"I have already come to harm with you. You discompose me, sir."

"I know I do. And just as it is good for Toby to

learn to fight, it is good for you to let your guard down now and then. You are too young and beautiful to live the rest of your life in the shadow of a dead husband who didn't allow you to be a real woman. And do not tell me you aren't doing that. You put entirely too much energy into polishing the old bishop's memory. You won't let him go. That's what keeps you from giving in to your desires. It will never be right with me, or any man, until you let him go."

"I cannot help it. I owe everything to him."

"But he is gone, so your debt is wiped clean."

"It is more than that, and you know it. He taught me all about living a virtuous life. It is difficult for me to . . . to allow myself to . . . to feel so wicked. So sinful."

"Grace." He reached out to stroke her cheek. "You are not wicked or sinful. You are a good person, honorable and caring. And passionate. No, don't shake your head. You *are* passionate. About widows and orphans, for example. About helping people who are less fortunate."

"That's not the kind of passion you mean."

"It is all the same," he said. "A fervor that fires the blood. I have witnessed both kinds of passion from you. You feel things deeply, whether it is compassion for a small boy with a swollen eye or passion for a man's kiss. It is who you are, Grace. A woman with a woman's feelings. With an honest response to a man's desire for you. And your own desire. It is time you lived for yourself, Grace, and stopped being the Great Man's Widow. Stop trying to remain faithful to the memory of a pompous old fool who made you believe sex was something dirty."

Grace gasped. How had he known that?

"Make your own life," he went on. "Make your own mark on the world. You can do anything, you know." He spread his arms and said, "Look what you have done here, on your own, without the bishop. Imagine what else you can do, if only you will allow yourself to *be* yourself."

"But you are not speaking of more charity work, are you? You do not kiss me to encourage good works."

"No, of course not." He flashed a grin. "Unless I am the object of those good works. Though I warn you, I am not looking to change my ways, so do not think to make a project of me. No, I kiss you because I am deeply attracted to you. You know that. I have told you that. But it's more than physical attraction. I like you, Grace. I like the woman I see beneath the public persona you have created for yourself. The passionate woman beneath the cool composure. I like everything about you."

Her cheeks flushed at his words. "I . . . I like you, too, my lord." And God help her, she did.

"John. My name is John. I have taken the liberty of using your Christian name. You must use mine. Friends should not be so formal with each other."

Friends? Were they friends? "John."

He reached out and took her hand, then kissed it in a chivalrous, almost formal way, not at all seductive or flirtatious, but as though he was honoring her, as though he truly admired her. When he looked up and smiled, she saw something more in his eye than the familiar rakish glint. Something more personal. More affectionate. How remarkable, she thought, and returned his smile. He swept her a bow, then turned and walked out the front door.

In that moment, as she stood clutching the hand he'd kissed, Grace felt as if some kind of new bond had been forged between them. She wasn't sure what it was, or how to define it—could it be called friendship when there was also desire?—but she knew she would no longer worry about his gambling and his scandalous past and his other women. None of it mattered. She thought instead of the young boy—proudly sporting a black eye—whose life had been changed forever by Rochdale's kindness. Of all that he was doing for Jane and her family. Of the extraordinary generosity he had bestowed upon Marlowe House.

This was the man she liked, the man for whom she had a powerful attraction. And, by God, she did not care what anybody thought about it.

Chapter 11

As had become their routine, Nat had taken the horses for a drive while Rochdale was at Marlowe House, and by the time he had deigned to return with his team, Rochdale had worked himself into a rare temper. The long wait had given him the opportunity to mull over what had just happened. Though he had not expected to see Grace, the encounter had worked out beautifully. He had her practically eating out of his hand. Finally—finally!—she trusted him. She *liked* him. She was right where he wanted her, a few short steps away from final surrender. And yet an unexpected stirring of guilt had come over him for what he was doing.

A flood of shame, then anger, washed over him for using her in such a selfish way, for making her believe he had no ulterior motive in pursuing her. That anger had reached a crescendo of self-flagellation by the time Nat drove his curricle into the small courtyard in front of Marlowe House.

"It's about time," he barked. "Where the devil have you been?"

The lad's face paled and his eyes grew wide with anxiety. "I'm sorry, milord, but you were gone more than a half hour, so I thought—"

"I don't want to hear your excuses. Just give me the reins, damn it all, and take your seat in back. And if you know what's good for you, you'll shut the hell up until we reach Curzon Street."

A few moments later, as he steered the team into Lower George Street, he was struck by yet another pang of guilt for speaking so sharply to Nat. The tiger had only been doing his job. It was not his fault that Rochdale was vexed with himself. He'd flip the boy a half crown when they reached the livery where his horses and carriages were kept.

That initial rush of anger ebbed somewhat as he drove, and Rochdale began to ponder these disturbing attacks of conscience that had begun to torment him of late. The business with Grace Marlowe was only a game, after all. Despite all her artlessness and enticing innocence, she was nothing more to him than a means to a prime bit of horseflesh. He would, quite naturally, be forever grateful to her for helping him acquire Albion. And that should be the end of it. He had no reason to feel guilty for seducing her into submitting to something she clearly wanted, or for pretending to redeem himself in her eyes with a fat bank draft and a few hours spent with a lonely little boy. She had done well for herself in the game, getting what she wanted from him. No woman was worth that kind of guilt.

Yet remorse gnawed at him as he drove the curricle too fast down Lower George Street, narrowly missing a head-on collision with a beer wagon, and coming so close to sideswiping a phaeton that the driver shouted obscenities and snapped his whip in Rochdale's direction. Unmoved by the danger his reckless speed was causing, Rochdale kept his thoughts on one thing only: He told himself over and over that he had nothing to feel guilty about. Grace would ultimately thank him for helping her to break loose of her tight-laced, self-indulgent propriety and to finally experience sexual pleasure. He would give that to her willingly, and she should be grateful. But . . .

His long-dormant conscience kept throwing *buts* at him. Good God, he could not remember ever suffering so much distress over a woman. But that was part of the wager's challenge, was it not? He would have to suffer in order to win. But instead of enduring the frustration of a prim woman's refusal to submit, he was enduring guilt over a good woman's inevitable surrender.

Damn, damn, damn.

When he'd stood outside Marlowe House waiting for Nat's return, the tantalizing scent of Grace's ever-present jasmine fragrance lingering on his clothes, he'd thought about what a fine woman she was and how sweet her passion was, and wondered if he should go back inside and kiss her again. Just then, a barouche had rolled by with a uniformed soldier and a flamboyantly dressed tart seated behind the driver. A heavily laden dray being unloaded at the far end of the street had slowed traffic, so Rochdale was able to watch the barouche for several minutes as it crept along at a snail's pace. The tart had her arms crossed over her chest and a scowl on her painted face. The soldier was speaking earnestly to her, but she kept shaking her head. Finally, the fellow pulled out a small box from inside his coat. Long and slim, it was obviously a jewelry case of some kind, and all at once the tart's pinched face transformed into a triumphant smile. As they had moved down the street, out of Rochdale's line of vision, he caught a glimpse of her snuggling against the young man in a manner that was almost indecent. The soldier had met her price.

Recollection of that little drama reminded Rochdale that all women had their price. Even Grace Marlowe. Her price was sitting in a vault at Coutts & Company, ready to be poured into that old brick building she loved so much. Yes, every woman had a price and Rochdale, who prided himself on his understanding of the female sex, had somehow allowed himself to forget

that nugget of wisdom where Grace Marlowe was concerned. What a fool he'd become, he thought as he
negotiated the turn onto the busy Brompton Road.
While coaxing Grace to loosen her laces, he'd been
the one to let down his guard. He'd allowed her to
get under his skin, to think he cared about her and
was not merely playacting. Bloody fool. He must be
going soft after all these years.

He maneuvered the curricle through the late afternoon traffic in Knightsbridge and toward Hyde Park
Corner, where the fashionable set was gathering for
the daily parade through the park. Soft indeed, that's
what he'd become, to have allowed himself to be manipulated again by a grasping woman. He'd set out to
trick her, and damned if she hadn't turned the tables
and tricked him, tricked him into thinking she was
different, just because she was so bloody proper and
pious, and intriguingly innocent.

In the end, she was no different from the rest, using
him, offering just enough of herself to drive him mad,
letting him inch toward a seduction just so she could
have his money for her charity. When it came right
down to it, Grace Marlowe was no different from all
the others he'd known. She was a female, was she not?

All women were users, manipulators. He'd learned
that lesson early on from his own mother, who'd abandoned him. Then again from his father's second wife,
for whom the foolish old man had beggared the estate
in order to support her expensive tastes and provide
her hatchet-faced daughter with a tempting dowry.
The former Lady Rochdale had lost no time in shed-
ding her widow's weeds for another bridal bouquet,
when barely a year after the fire she married the very
rich Lord Gillard. Rochdale often wondered if she had
not started the fire herself and allowed his father to
believe her trapped in the inferno, all because she had
taken what she could from him and there was nothing
ahead for her but years of debt and economic re-

trenching. He had suggested as much to her some years later when he'd been the worse for drink, and she had slapped him soundly for it.

Then there was Caroline, coldblooded and ruthless in her ambition, who'd broken his young heart. At least he'd been wise to female machinations by the time Serena Underwood had come into his life. He had preferred scandal and public scorn to being her scapegoat. He was a hardened realist by then, having twice been forced into duels with the husbands of women who had assured him of their spouses' indifference. In the end, all the women in his life used him in one way or another for their own gain. Even that chit Emily Thirkill had used him, talking him into taking her to the Twickenham villa for the sole purpose of exacting revenge on her mother and aunt for embarrassing her in public.

Turning into Park Place, Rochdale threaded his sleek curricle through the crowds of leisurely driven carriages and hacks on their way to Rotten Row. Fashionable women dressed in the latest designs were ready to see and be seen in the daily ritual of gathering in Hyde Park. Some of the women caught his eye, signaling various levels of interest. Others turned away.

Users, all of them. He'd learned long ago that the only way to deal with women was on his own terms, not theirs. And his terms were generally sexual. He had taken his pleasure from scores of them. If they wanted to use him for their own pleasure, then so be it, as long as he got equal satisfaction in the bargain. But he would *not* be manipulated. He would not give over control of any situation to a female. Never.

Once he had seduced Grace into becoming a real woman, he would give her a bit of pleasure in return for Albion. It was the least he could do, and God knew she needed it. He would take pleasure from her, too, of course, and he still anticipated that it would be extraordinarily fulfilling. She was so blasted desirable, with her golden beauty and her innocent passion.

Once again, Rochdale experienced the merest niggling of a doubt about his motives. He remembered her smile as he left her at Marlowe House, the almost wistful quality in it, and her hesitant admission that she liked him. He wondered if he might be wrong about this woman. Could she be the exception to the rule? But she had his bank draft, so she was really no better than the rest of them.

Or was she?

He had taken countless women to bed. He knew what they wanted. This particular seduction should be easy. She was innocent, naïve, ripe for the taking. But somehow, she had got to him, got under his skin, into his head, something. He could not explain it, but by the time he drove the curricle into the livery at the end of Curzon Street, he had come to realize that she really *was* different, that she did not deserve to be just another name on his list.

Damn, damn, damn.

If he was not careful, Grace Marlowe was going to be the ruin of him.

Things had definitely changed between them. It was almost as if they had switched roles. Rochdale had become more solicitous and circumspect, whereas Grace no longer bothered to hide their friendship.

For that is what had grown between them: friendship. He could still make her heart race with a glance from those knowing eyes. But there was more between them now. They talked. They exchanged ideas and opinions. They were comfortable together, and Grace allowed herself to enjoy his company without guilt or shame.

She grew impatient with those who scorned him, but they did not know him as she did. There were times when she longed to jump to his defense, but knew he would not thank her for it. For reasons known only to himself, Rochdale enjoyed his reputation as a scoundrel. It was not her prerogative to repair that reputation, so she let it stand. Her own might suffer by association, as Margaret was quick to point out at every opportunity, but only in the eyes of people whose judgment she no longer valued. For if they could not see beyond the lurid tales of scandal and debauchery—most of them no doubt true—to find the good and worthy man beneath, then she no longer cared what they thought.

Here's to the liberation of Grace Marlowe. May she always be her own woman and not bound by someone else's expectations, living or dead.

God bless her friends for helping her to reach the goal of that toast. She was not there yet, but there was a thrilling freedom in not caring what opinion people held of her. She still thought of the bishop, though, and what he must think if he was watching from above. She liked to believe he would applaud her for eschewing hypocrisy, which must surely be a good thing. But he had trained her to be ever alert to what people might say about her, keeping in mind his important position and how nothing must be said or done to blemish it. So, she was not entirely confident that he smiled down upon her now.

Truth be told, he would probably think her own reputation more important than that of a man like Rochdale. But in these last weeks, Grace had come to understand that both of their public personae were manufactured to achieve a desired result. They were like actors on a stage. She played the role of the Bishop's Widow just as he played the Notorious Libertine. Beneath their masks, however, were more complex personalities.

"They are just labels," Rochdale had told her, "that allow Society to catalog us more easily into predefined categories. But neither of us is that simple, that black and white. Don't allow Society's expectations to define you, Grace."

It seemed that whenever they met, he ended up saying something of the kind to her. She began to think that he was trying to undo some of the bishop's training by drilling new, more liberal litanies into her head.

And it was working.

He sat beside her on a settee in Wilhelmina's elegant drawing room. The duchess had invited a large group of friends for dinner and an informal musicale. Because all the guests were those who accepted Wilhelmina without censure, many of them friends of the late duke, Grace had no concerns that her friendship with Rochdale would be remarked upon or criticized by such open-minded company. She felt completely at ease by his side as they awaited the next performance, a duet by a harpist and pianist. As so often happened of late, they fell into comfortable conversation. They had been speaking of the new exhibition at the British Institution, a retrospective of the late Sir Joshua Reynolds that had been in large part coordinated by Adam Cazenove, one of the governors of the Institution. Adam and Marianne had joined in the discussion until they were called away by Wilhelmina to speak with another guest who fancied himself an art connoisseur.

"I was encouraged by the exhibit," Rochdale said, "to purchase a copy of the new *Memoirs of Sir Joshua Reynolds*. An interesting character, if a bit self-important. I think you might find it entertaining."

Grace was no longer surprised when he let fall these little revelations of his character. She had discovered that the studious boy from Suffolk still lurked beneath the surface. Rochdale was a great reader, though she suspected he did not allow many people to know it.

"As it happens," she said, "I was given a copy by Mr. Northcote, the publisher, though I haven't read it yet."

He lifted a black eyebrow. "You are acquainted with James Northcote?"

"Yes. He will be publishing my book on the bishop's sermons."

"Ah. And how goes the editing? Still up to your eyeballs in sanctimonious bombast?"

Grace frowned. "John."

"Sorry. Tell me what you're working on."

"A very eloquent sermon based on Genesis two, verse eighteen. 'The Lord God said, "It is not good for the man to be alone. I will make him a helper suitable to him." ' The bishop uses that passage to illustrate how a man is called to lead, whereas a woman is called to help. That is, how a man must take responsibility for his family, and a wife should be supportive of her husband."

"Subordinate to him, you mean."

"Well, yes. Someone must lead, and God has given man that role and that responsibility."

He uttered a soft but thoroughly disdainful huff. "So, a woman cannot lead? Well then, Grace, that must mean you should not be allowed to manage a large charitable fund or be responsible for the facilities at Marlowe House. And I was the one who said the old man would be proud of you. Perhaps I was wrong. Perhaps he would not be so pleased to have his 'helper' become a leader in what she does."

Grace glared at him. He was always finding fault with her late husband. "Don't be foolish. He was speaking in generalities. In a family, for instance, the husband must be the leader, for he is responsible for the protection and well-being of his wife and children. Just as the leader of a country or government, a king or prime minister, is responsible to protect its citizens."

"And what if that king is a queen? Would your bishop have not allowed Queen Elizabeth to rule?"

She heaved an exasperated sigh. Rochdale took perverse pleasure in dismantling the bishop's teachings, trying to prove them inadequate or false, even if it meant taking the woman's side in the debate. "You are being too literal."

"It should be remembered," Rochdale said, "that the Genesis passage in question was written from the perspective of the patriarchal society of the Hebrews. I daresay they would not have accepted a Queen Elizabeth to rule them. Ah, but wait. There was Miriam the Prophetess. And Zipporah, wife of Moses, who assumed the role of priest in a moment of crisis. And Deborah—judge, general, and poet—handpicked by God to deliver the nation."

She smiled. "I should know better than to engage in a discussion of theology or religious history with you." But she often did, as the bishop's sermons were a frequent topic of conversation between them. She rather enjoyed their debates, for it drew out the one-time scholar who had long ago immersed himself in the study of philosophy and religion.

"Even so," she continued, "our society is as patriarchal as that of the Hebrews. The sentiments expressed in Genesis still hold true, even with the occasional exception of a Queen Elizabeth, or a Deborah. The point is that, under most circumstances, man must accept his role as leader, and woman as his helper."

"And yet," he said, "the earlier creation story in Genesis one, verses twenty-six and twenty-seven, provides no suggestion of one being submissive to the other. 'In the image of God he created them; male and female created he them.' He tells them nothing more than to be fruitful and multiply, and to replenish the earth. That seems a more appropriate passage to me."

"But the bishop used the later passage, so it is a moot point. In any case, it is meant to be instructive, to provide guidance in living a good Christian life."

"Instructive in how to be subservient." A frown

puckered his brow. "Yes, I understand it is the way most woman live, the way they have been taught to live, even as more rational ideals and democratic principles are fomented in coffeehouses and debating societies. But I wonder how you can feel comfortable publishing such anti-female opinions under your own name. It makes you a party to subjugating your own sex. Is this reflective of how the Great Man treated his own wife?"

"Please, John, you know I dislike it when you disparage the bishop. He was a good man. He spent his entire life doing good work. Just because his political and social views were more conservative than your Whiggish opinions does not make him a bad person."

"Was he good to *you*?" He enveloped her in his shrewd blue gaze, as though he could see straight into her soul. "Did he make you happy?"

"Of course," she replied, rather too quickly. "I was blessed to know him, and honored to be his wife. He made me very happy."

His eyebrows rose sharply. "As his little helper? Can you honestly say you enjoyed being subservient to him and his work more than you enjoy managing Marlowe House and the Widows Fund all by yourself? I'll wager the old fellow would never have allowed you to be your own woman."

There it was again. The familiar litany. Grace supposed he must believe that if she truly became "her own woman," this new, liberated woman would happily fall into his bed.

"Did he even allow you to have your own opinion?" he pressed. "About anything?"

Not often, as it happened. But that was a private matter and not Rochdale's business.

He sneered at her silence. "I thought not. The truth is, he took an unfinished, biddable young girl and molded her into the perfect bishop's wife, a public paragon of his teachings. But it is not too late to smash that mold and start fresh. Fortunately, you're still a young woman and can—"

"I was one-and-thirty on my last birthday. Not so very young."

"Egad. As old a crone as that?" He gave a theatrical shudder. "I cannot imagine what attracts me to such a dried-up old stick. You are exceedingly well preserved, my dear."

She smiled. "Perhaps because I have not led a life of dissipation."

He winced. "A direct hit. Must you remind me that my craggy old phiz shows every minute of my thirty-four years? While you sit there with your fine, aristocratic, ageless beauty."

She chuckled softly and said, "I am neither fine nor aristocratic. Did you know that? Unlike yourself, I come from very humble stock."

"Do you?"

"Yes. My mother was a farmer's daughter, my father a country vicar in Devon whose own father had been a mine foreman who made enough money from a rich lode to send his son to school. Papa read for the church and started his career at the bottom, as a minor curate."

"I daresay your mother was a beauty, then, even if not a highborn one. But to return to my point, I only meant that you are still young enough to—"

"I know what you meant. There is no need to repeat it. I understand your point, John, I really do. You must not feel obliged on my account to drum it home so loudly and so often. Now, hush. The musicians are ready to begin."

As she listened to the music, or tried to listen, Rochdale's words rang in her ears, drowning out everything else. He was the only person who ever dared to criticize the bishop in her presence. Grace would continue to defend her husband and his teachings. She owed him that much. But more and more often she found herself wondering if he had indeed manipulated her, as a naïve young girl with a malleable mind, into becoming his own creation. It was certainly true that he had taught her how to behave properly, in public and in private. Even in the bedroom. Had he erased everything that had been the lively young Grace Newbury to create the coolly reserved Mrs. Grace Marlowe?

No, he had not. She smiled to herself as she realized there was still an eager young girl buried under eleven years of a closely guarded marriage and three years of immaculate widowhood. No wonder she and Rochdale were such good friends. They were much alike. Each of them had lost their young selves and become something quite different. Perhaps they could each help the other unlock that youthful idealism that had been hidden away for so long.

Or was it too late?

After the musicians had played and a young soprano had sung two beautiful airs, tea and brandy were served as the guests mingled in the drawing room or on the terrace. Rochdale led Grace outside into Wilhelmina's lovely formal garden, beyond the lights of the house and a few paper lanterns hung in the trees. She knew what he wanted, and she wanted it, too. He had not kissed her since that day at Marlowe House, though they had seen each other several times. This was their first opportunity to be alone, and Wilhelmina's guests were not the sort to judge or gossip. Or to spy.

Grace allowed him to lead her into a far corner of the garden, where he stopped and leaned back against a large tree. Moonlight fell through the leaves and across the harsh planes of his face. Dear heaven, did his eyes have to be so blue? Blue as the sea. Blue she could drown in. Die in.

He took her hands and gently pulled her toward him. "I want to kiss you, Grace."

"I know."

"Will you let me?"

"No."

His eyes widened and he looked completely startled. "Why not? It's been so long, and I am hungry for you. Why can't I kiss you?"

She grinned. "Because *I* am going to kiss *you*."

"Are you?" He smiled and her knees grew weak. This was not his wicked smile, his scoundrel's smile. This was a real smile that lit his eyes and put creases in their corners, a smile that softened the hard-edged arrogance of him. A smile that made her want to love him, just a little.

"Yes, I am."

"Well, then, what are you waiting for?"

She put her arms around his neck and he slid his arms around her waist. He did not pull her close, though, but waited for her to make the next move. She smiled; then she placed a hand on the back of his head, pulled him down to her, and kissed him.

Remembering all that she liked most about his kisses, she tried to give him the same pleasure. She first moved her lips softly over his, nipping and tasting. She kissed his upper lip, the corners of his mouth, and finally took his lower lip between hers and sucked gently. He groaned into her mouth and, just as he had done more than once, she took advantage of his parted lips and slid her tongue inside. His tongue met hers hungrily, circling and thrusting together in a mutual dance of pure pleasure.

The kiss became a battle for control then, with first Rochdale and then Grace taking the lead with lips and tongue and teeth. And hands. She explored his back and shoulders and buttocks, and did not flinch when he palmed her breast.

They kissed and kissed for what seemed hours but was more likely only a few minutes. When they pulled apart at the sound of nearby voices, both were breathless, panting.

He put his mouth next to her ear. "Thank you, Grace. That was the best kiss anyone ever gave me."

She laughed aloud. Lord, he was a heady potion. But then, he'd had a lot of practice. Still, to know that he wanted her, as a woman, as a lover, continued to be a revelation she had never expected in her life.

She knew what the next step would be. Was she ready to take it?

That night, her dreams were full of Rochdale. First they were standing and kissing, fully clothed. Then, in the illogical way of dreams, she was suddenly naked in his arms—naked!—as they lay together on her bed. He smiled at her as he pulled her hair over one shoulder and combed his fingers slowly through it, over her shoulder and breast. He buried his face in it, smelling it, rubbing his cheek against it, taking thick handfuls of it and breathing it in. And then he was kissing her neck. He kissed her everywhere, in places she had only heard about from the Merry Widows, finally taking her breast into his mouth and sucking. She arched up off the bed, wanting more of his mouth, wanting to crawl right inside it, and she ran her fingers through his black hair. And then her arms were wrapped around his bare back—dear God, he was naked, too— as he pushed himself inside her. Again, and again, and again. It was not quickly done, as it had been with the bishop, but slow and deep and unlike anything she'd ever known.

And she cried out his name. "John. John. John!"

Chapter 12

"Do you understand what I mean, Marianne? You told me you had been afraid at first."

"I would say I was anxious rather than frightened," Marianne replied. "And more than a little shocked."

Grace and Marianne strolled arm in arm on a path that led toward the Horse Guards Parade, taking advantage of the sunny weather to enjoy a walk through the parkland. They had just visited an exhibition of paintings at the Great Room in Spring Gardens, where the Society of Painters in Oil and Watercolors displayed their works. Marianne had a passion for watercolor paintings, with a fine collection in her home on Bruton Street, and had been a regular patron of the Society for several years. She had been vocal today in her disappointment that the Society's members, who'd originally banded together to support the efforts of watercolorists only, had last year decided to include oil paintings in their exhibitions.

"There are simply not enough of us," she had said, "with an interest in the watercolor medium. Most people prefer the more polished finish of oils. The Society was forced to either introduce oil pictures into their exhibitions or disband entirely, which they actually did for a brief time last year. It is not the same, though. I miss the old Bond Street exhibitions with rooms filled to bursting with delicate watercolor pictures and nothing else."

She had bought two pictures today, both landscapes.

As much as Grace enjoyed looking at the paintings and listening to her friend's insights on style and technique, that was not the reason for accepting Marianne's invitation to join her. After the tryst in Wilhelmina's garden with Rochdale, not to mention the embarrassingly vivid dream that followed, Grace knew she was heading down a path that would inevitably lead her to Rochdale's bed. And the idea both tantalized her and scared her. She had needed someone to talk to, someone who would understand the inner turmoil brought on by the wanton behavior that was so out of character for her.

"I want to confess something to you," Marianne said, "because I believe it will help you to understand the cause of my anxiety. When Penelope first spoke of her love affairs, I was stunned. I had no idea such things happened in the bedroom."

Grace's eyebrows shot up to her hairline. "Truly? I assumed that you and David . . . that you had . . . I mean, the way you embraced Penelope's pact and so enthusiastically went in search of a lover, I assumed it was because . . ."

"It was because I was curious. As good a marriage as I had with David, I had never experienced anything like what Penelope described. When Beatrice implied that her marriage to Somerfield had been equally passionate, I realized I had missed something fundamental, and I found that I wanted to experience it. I now understand that there was indeed a missing element in my marriage with David, that our marital relations were . . . well, to be perfectly candid, they were almost chaste. There was love between us, to be sure, but no physical passion. With Adam, I have both. It is a more complete relationship, and I have never been happier."

Grace fell silent as she pondered her friend's words. It sounded right, that a marriage should include both love and passion, that a man and wife should share . . . everything. And yet, the bishop had taught her differently.

The Palladian grandeur of the Horse Guards and the Treasury loomed to her left, and the gardens of Carlton House spread out on her right, but Grace paid them no mind as she contemplated, yet again, all the bishop had said about wifely behavior. Would he scorn Marianne for being physically fulfilled in her marriage?

"But to return to your question," Marianne said, interrupting Grace's thoughts, "yes, it was a bit scary at first to feel so many new sensations running through my body. To feel that I had no control over my own reactions, as if my body had a mind of its own, if you take my meaning."

"Yes! That is exactly how I feel with John. With Lord Rochdale. It is so confusing to me! I've never felt anything like it before, and yet I . . . I enjoyed it, even though I know it is wrong to allow myself to do so."

"What are you talking about? How is it wrong?"

"I know it to be sinful to give in to that kind of passion. It is an unforgivable weakness that I should be able to control. But this time, I can't. And worse, I find that I don't care. I am willing to sin."

Marianne stopped walking and turned to face Grace, her head tilted to one side. "Is that what . . . Forgive me, Grace, but is that what the bishop told you? That it is sinful to experience physical passion?"

Grace nodded, suddenly embarrassed by the conversation.

"Even in private with him," Marianne said, "it was wrong to respond to . . . to physical intimacy?"

Grace nodded again. "A virtuous woman does not give in to base reactions, does not allow herself to experience lascivious feelings of any kind," she said in a voice barely above a whisper, quoting the bishop's words to her on their wedding night.

Marianne's face crumpled into a mask of dismay and she reached for Grace's hand. "Oh, my dear. I am so sorry. If he were still alive, I would keep my opinions to myself, though I would wish to throttle his holy neck. But since he is gone, I take leave to tell you that he was wrong. I daresay he was a pious man, a godly man. But he was *wrong*, Grace. Very wrong. There is nothing sinful in what a man and woman do together. Not if they care for each other. It is joyful and natural and good. And it is *shared*, something experienced *together*. It is not right for the man alone to take his pleasure while the woman suppresses hers. That is not fair to either of you. Oh, Grace, no wonder you are so confused!"

Marianne pulled Grace to her side so that they stood shoulder to shoulder, their hands still clasped. Grace's lip quivered slightly and she blinked furiously to hold back tears that threatened to overcome her. Heavens, she had become so emotional lately. She lowered her face so that her bonnet's brim would hide her discomposure. She remembered her younger self, so eager to share the marital bed with her fine new husband, and having him mortify her so thoroughly. She'd spent a decade and more trying to make up for that shameful blunder, ultimately establishing herself as a model of female virtue.

Until she'd met Rochdale.

"I have been thinking . . ." She paused to control her voice, which had come out reed-thin and tremulous. She took a few breaths before continuing. "I have been wondering if . . . if he might have been . . . mistaken. I think of you and Beatrice and Penelope, and I cannot believe he would have considered any of you sinful. He would have disapproved of Wilhelmina, of course, but not of the rest of you. And yet you—"

"We do things he considered sinful."

"Yes."

Marianne clicked her tongue disapprovingly. "Oh, Grace, I am trying hard not to say something hateful about a man of the church. I consider myself a good Christian. I go to church every Sunday. I do charitable work. I am kind to children and animals. I don't lie, cheat, or steal. I believe I am a good person. And I will *not* be thought sinful simply because I take pleasure in the man I love."

She was right, of course. None of her friends were sinful. Which could only mean one thing.

"He was wrong, wasn't he? The bishop was wrong."

"Yes, Grace, he was wrong."

Her mind drifted back to those first few days of her marriage, when she had been made to feel so depraved, when she had exhibited passions she now suspected had been perfectly natural. Grace wanted to hate him for it, for doing that to her. But she could not. Her husband had not been mean-spirited or malicious. He had been a gentle man. He simply believed what he preached, truly believed it, and lived his life according to those beliefs.

"You do see that, don't you, Grace? You see how wrong he was?"

"Yes. Yes, I do." She could no longer hold back the tears that fell down her cheeks. "The bishop, may God rest his soul, had believed he was right, but he had been wrong. About you. About me."

"Promise me you will not forget that."

Such a momentous epiphany would be hard to forget: that just because the bishop had believed her natural passions had been a sign of weakness, of sinfulness, did not make it true. His interpretation of Scripture made him believe that women were weak, that their inherent weakness was symbolized by the betrayal of Eve, who did not have the fortitude to resist the devil. It had been his fervent belief, but only that. A belief, and not fact. Grace wished she had been stronger as a girl, less vulnerable to the bishop's declarations. She had known, deep in her heart, that she was not wicked. Yet she had allowed this great, eloquent man to make her feel as if she were.

How sad that he could not have accepted her as she was, without trying to shape her into something she was never meant to be.

"I promise I will not forget," she said. Marianne still held her hand and Grace gave it a grateful squeeze. "Even when I am with Rochdale and he is making me feel weak with desire, I will try to remember that the bishop was wrong about me, that I am not sinful or wicked, that it is perfectly natural to feel that way."

Marianne beamed a smile. "Good for you, Grace. Oh, good for you! It pains me to think you have believed yourself to be sinful and wicked. Thank God you are still young enough to right that wrong."

Grace gave a watery chuckle. "That's what Rochdale always tells me, that I am young enough to start fresh, to change my life. That I need to stop being the Bishop's Widow and just be plain Grace Marlowe."

"He's right."

"I think he must be. And you, too. All of you. I must try to put eleven years of the bishop's instructions in perspective and learn to make my own decisions, based on my own conscience."

"Brava, Grace. I cannot tell you how pleased I am to hear you say that. And God bless Rochdale for encouraging you to find your own way."

Grace sometimes wondered if all his encouragement to find her own identity was nothing more than a ploy to get her into his bed. For the Bishop's Widow would be highly unlikely to capitulate, whereas Grace Marlowe just might surrender.

"So, Rochdale has become your friend, it seems,"

Marianne said. "And now you think to become lovers?"

"It is what he has always wanted. At least, that is what I have assumed. Why else would he pursue me?"

"And you? Is it what you want?"

Grace thought again of her dream, of being naked in his arms while he made love to her. "I do want it. Oh, Marianne, I think about it all the time. But is he the right man? Should I wait for someone more respectable?"

Marianne laughed. "Someone more respectable is unlikely to make you feel the way you do. His roguishness is part of his charm, I daresay."

"But all those rumors and scandalous tales. The duels. The gambling. That business with Serena Underwood. I realize there is more to him than that. I have seen his kindness and compassion, his generosity, his intellect. I know he is not all bad. Still, it concerns me. The women, especially. Did you worry about that with Adam?"

"I certainly did," Marianne said, smiling broadly. "For one thing, I worried that I would not measure up to all those other women. Like you, I was basically inexperienced, even though I'd been married. We are different, you and I, from Beatrice and Penelope, who knew what to expect, knew what to do." She chuckled. "But there is an advantage, as it happens, to having a worldly rake as a lover. *He* will know *exactly* what to do, and will be happy to teach you. You must trust me on this, Grace. The benefits of his rakish history will outweigh the drawbacks. As for all the other things, the unsavory rumors and such, you must decide how important they are to you, because I am fairly certain most of the stories are true."

Grace sighed. "I suspected as much."

"I think you must listen to Wilhelmina's wise counsel on this matter. If you decide to take Rochdale as your lover, take care to guard your heart. He may provide you with unparalleled pleasure, but remember his history with women. He never stays with one for very long, and he can be callous in ending things."

"Wilhelmina says that is because he dislikes, or distrusts, women. I wonder if that is true? He says . . . he says he likes me."

"Just be careful, Grace. Since I have not heard you hint that you are in love with him, I will trust in your strength of character to endure whatever happens."

Was she in love with him? There were moments when she thought she might be, but perhaps it was simple lust and nothing more.

"I appreciate your confidence in me, Marianne. And I am very grateful for your frank advice. I have been confused and confounded such as I have never been in my life. I'm still not sure I'm ready to take a lover, Rochdale or anyone else. In the end, I might find it is simply a step I am not willing to take. Propriety was bred in me from the cradle, you know, well before I met the bishop, and is bone-deep at this stage of my life. But whatever happens, you have helped to make it a less tumultuous decision, to see that I must not give so much weight to certain things the bishop taught me. I will follow my instincts—my own instincts, not his—and do what seems right."

Marianne reached out and hugged her. Their bonnet brims knocked together, causing them both to laugh. "I am so proud of you, Grace. You have come such a long way toward achieving that toast of Penelope's."

Thanks to Rochdale, who, by making her feel like a woman for the first time in her life, caused her to question things she'd long taken for granted.

The two women resumed their walk, skirting the Parade grounds where a group of soldiers marched in tight formation. Grace linked her arm with Marianne's, grateful to have a good friend willing to tell her the truth, no matter how uncomfortable. What might her marriage to the bishop have been like if she had had such a friend to advise her?

"I am taking one more bold step," she said, "toward that liberation Penelope toasted. I am going to the opera tonight. With Rochdale."

Marianne's eyes widened. "You are ready to announce your connection to him publicly?"

Grace shrugged. "We have been seen to dance together at balls and talk together at parties. It should be no surprise to see us together at the opera."

"Except that he will be seen as your escort. You will arrive with him and leave with him, not meet him casually as you would at a party. People might talk."

"They might. Margaret will likely be on my doorstep tomorrow morning. But even if Rochdale and I never become lovers, he is my friend and I am not ashamed of that. And I like to think my reputation is solid enough to withstand being seen with him in public."

Marianne arched an eyebrow. "Perhaps *his* reputation will be improved by his association with *you.*"

Grace laughed. "He would not like that. He has often told me not to try to reform him. He enjoys being a notorious scoundrel."

"Yet, he has reformed you," Marianne said, a twinkle lighting her dark eyes. "Who knows? You may become the merriest of the Merry Widows. I never dreamed to see you, the most tightly laced of us all, loosen your stays a bit, to allow yourself a little freedom, but I am so glad you have done so."

And so was Grace.

At least a dozen pairs of opera glasses were turned upon Rochdale's box at Covent Garden. Others stared without the benefit of magnification. Yet Grace sat beside him, cool and composed, seemingly unaffected by the stir she had caused by arriving with him.

"You are handling this very well, my dear," he said.

She turned to him and smiled. "Perhaps they are simply admiring my dress."

He grinned. "Yes, I daresay that must be it. How foolish of me to have thought otherwise. You look stunning tonight. The dress is splendid. Just the right touch of bold color, yet demure and modest in style, befitting a respectable lady. It suits the occasion perfectly. And suits you."

The dress was virginal white, in a soft, swishy fabric with a polished sheen. The low-cut bodice was filled in with transparent white silk edged with lace high on the neck. One had to look closely, which he, of course, had done, to glimpse the dim shadow of cleavage beneath the silk tucker. To the casual or distant observer, she appeared very properly covered to the throat. The edge of the square-necked bodice as well as the hem was edged with a wide band richly embroidered in bright colors. Over the dress, Grace wore a claret-colored cloak with a high standing collar, trimmed with the same bold embroidery as the dress. It was a costume of understated elegance, much like Grace herself. He had been proud to arrive with her tonight. A few high sticklers may have glared at her in disapproval for having such a blackguard on her arm, but many more gentlemen gazed at him with envy for the beautiful woman on *his* arm.

"I confess," she said, "that I did actually spend a great deal of time selecting just the right dress. It is something of a special occasion, you see. It is the first time I have been escorted to the theater by a man who was not my husband."

"And not anything *like* your sainted husband, either. I am honored that you accepted my invitation, my dear. I thought it might be a bit of a trial for you, knowing that we would draw attention. It is not often that a respectable lady shares my box. In fact, this may be the first time."

"And since I have never been escorted by an infamous libertine, I daresay we have struck a balance of sorts."

"People will think that either you have become fast," he said, "or that I have reformed."

"Let us confound them all by being precisely who we are."

"The Bishop's Widow and the Libertine."

Grace chuckled softly. "It sounds like the title of a farce."

"In which the beautiful and virtuous young widow is seduced by the evil libertine—"

"—who immediately abandons her, having achieved his objective to prove that no woman, no matter how virtuous, is immune to his charms."

"But being made of sterner stuff than he, she laughs in the face of Society—"

"—pleased to be forced out of her widow's weeds at last—"

"—because black never did flatter her—"

"—and she runs off to Paris to have his child—"

"—which she supports by opening an exclusive brothel—"

"—which our libertine crosses the Channel to visit, having heard of the extraordinary, um . . ."

"—*talents* of its employees."

"But it is the lovely proprietress who catches his eye, though he does not recognize her."

"Because she wears a wig and affects a French accent."

"But no matter how hard he tries, she will not succumb to him because she wants him to suffer for having abandoned her."

"Finally, though, she is no match for his irresistible charm and gives in—"

"At which point he reveals that he knew all along it was her. They fall into each other's arms, declaring their eternal love—"

"—and live happily ever after." Rochdale grinned.

"Not a bad effort, my dear. Perhaps we should write it down and sell it to Sheridan for Drury Lane."

Grace laughed, that rich, deep-throated laugh that always took him by surprise. It was a sound so lush and sultry it made his spine tingle, made him want to put his ear to her belly—preferably her naked belly—and feel its soft, low vibration against his cheek.

He noticed more heads turning at the sound of her laughter. So did she, for she quickly brought it under control and hid her mouth behind her fan. He could see that she was still smiling, though.

She turned her profile to him as she watched the audience members take their seats in the boxes and the gallery above, and the rowdy set milling around in the pit. She had pulled her hair in what appeared on first glance to be a simple, thick chignon anchored high on the back of her head. But it was really quite an intricate arrangement of twists and coiled plaits and gold combs. Like everything else about Grace Marlowe, it was more complicated than it looked.

Since that day at Marlowe House when he'd become so torn between guilt and anger at feeling guilty, Rochdale had stopped trying to fit her into the mold of other women, stopped trying to convince himself she was no different from all the rest. In fact, he had stopped thinking at all and simply followed her lead into an easy friendship.

There was nothing easy about it, though. Or about her. He watched her and knew she was going to be trouble—his beautiful golden-haired Grace with the perfect patrician profile and the almost bawdy laugh. Trouble, because she was becoming more to him than merely the means to win a wager. Trouble, because at times like this the enchantment he felt for her was entirely real, and not pretense for the sake of adding Albion to his stables. Trouble, most of all, because the lust he quite naturally felt for her was becoming all mixed up with something else, something he did not care to analyze or name, but which threatened to scare the life out of him.

"Oh dear," she said, peering through her opera glasses to a box on the opposite side of the stage. "We seem to have lost our cachet. All eyes are now on the Duke of Cumberland and a very ornately dressed young woman at his side." She dropped the glasses and turned to look at Rochdale. "We are not much of a sensation after all. How very lowering."

He laughed, then raised her gloved hand to his lips. "Ah, Grace. You never cease to delight me."

She shot him a quizzical glance. "Do you really like me, then? I mean, really and truly?"

He raised his eyebrows. "Of course I do."

"Even though I'm a priggish bishop's widow?"

He laughed. "Despite that. Actually, I like you because you realize—and deep down you always have—that you're more than that. That you can *be* more than that."

She retrieved her hand and returned her gaze to the boxes opposite, which were now almost completely filled. "Someone suggested to me once," she said, "that you don't like women."

"An odd thing to say, given my history."

"The implication was that you liked to . . . to take your pleasure from women, but that you didn't actually like them. As people, I mean."

What a provokingly astute analysis of his character. He wondered which of her friends was responsible for the critique. "To be honest, there have not been many women I've actually admired and respected."

That admission surprised her, or perhaps it was disappointment in her eyes when she turned to look at him. "Why? I can't believe there are really so few of us to admire. What about your mother?"

He snorted. "My mother was the first to disillusion me. She ran off with another man when I was a young boy and I never saw her again."

A chagrined expression crossed her face. "Oh, I'm terribly sorry. I had heard about that but had forgotten. It must have been difficult for you after she left."

"My father told me she had died. I suppose to him she had."

Her face screwed up into a grimace. "How awful! What a monstrous thing for him to have done. But I'm sure she wanted to see you, if only your father had allowed it. She must have loved you and missed you dreadfully."

"In point of fact, she didn't much care for me. She's the one who asked my father to tell me she was dead. She didn't want me looking for her. I didn't learn any of this until she actually did die and my father remarried."

"Oh, John, how singularly cruel. But you must not judge all women by her unnatural treatment of you."

"I don't." His mother had been merely the first of many women to reveal their true colors to him. There had been countless others since. "I've met precious few women to admire in my life, fewer still whom I truly like. You are one of them, Grace. At the top of that short list, in fact."

Her cheeks colored at his words. Rochdale watched the pink blush suffuse her face and neck. He'd grown fond of her blushes, anticipating them, often encouraging them. Like everything about Grace, it was a refined sort of blush, a lovely shade of rose pink and not the furious blotchy red that he'd sometimes seen in other fair-skinned women. He was quite sure he could make her entire body blush pink like that, and could hardly wait to see it.

"Thank you," she said with her eyes on the hands in her lap. "That is very kind of you to say. And I assure you, the admiration is returned."

Ah, poor woman. She was doomed to disappointment.

The evening passed quickly in her company. Grace

sincerely enjoyed the opera, *La Dama Soldata*, and he enjoyed watching her. During the first interval, several curiosity seekers visited the box, as well as a few friends. Lord Sheane stepped in with his latest bit of muslin, clearly nervous that Rochdale had made such obvious progress with Grace. But Rochdale did not allow the man and his ladybird beyond the threshold. It was one thing for Grace to be seen in Rochdale's company, quite another for her to be forced into the company of a Cyprian. Her indomitable reputation could only bear so much.

Cazenove and Marianne stopped by the box as well. While the women talked, Cazenove pulled Rochdale aside and quizzed him about Grace.

"What are you? Her father?" Rochdale asked. "Do you want to know if my intentions are honorable?"

"Something like that."

"Look at her. She's a beautiful woman. That should tell you all you need to know about my intentions."

"The thing is," Cazenove said, "the woman is a close friend to my wife. If you hurt Mrs. Marlowe, I shall feel obliged to rip your heart out with a rusty blade on behalf of Marianne. Do I make myself clear?"

Rochdale's eyes widened. "Good God, man, there is no need for such melodrama. I am not planning to hurt her."

Cazenove continued to glare at him. There was a time when he would not have dreamed of questioning Rochdale's actions, or any other man's, where women were concerned. He would not dare, since his own activities did not often bear scrutiny. Only see what marriage had done to the poor fellow, making him an instrument of his wife's whims and fancies.

"It's that damned pact, isn't it?" Cazenove said, lowering his voice. "The one with the other widows, the one about finding the best lovers. I wish to hell I'd never mentioned it to you."

"As I recall, you were foxed at the time."

"What are you up to, Rochdale? Are you hoping that by seducing the most prudish of the widows that they will elect you as the best lover?"

Rochdale grinned. "An intriguing possibility. Do you suppose they will award some sort of prize? But no, my interest in Mrs. Marlowe has nothing to do with that bloody widows' pact. And I repeat: I have no intention of hurting her."

"I daresay you never set out to deliberately hurt a woman," Cazenove said. "But it happens. All too frequently. I just wish I understood your interest in Mrs. Marlowe. Only a few months ago you declared your aversion to 'ladies who do good works' and this lady in particular. What changed?"

"Perhaps I got a better look at her."

Cazenove lifted an interested eyebrow. "At the masquerade ball, when all that golden hair was flowing down her back? Ha! I ought to have known you could not resist that hair. I told Marianne as much. You'd seduce the Dog-Faced Girl if she had long blond hair to wrap yourself up in. Just be careful with Mrs. Marlowe, Rochdale. She is not your usual hardened sophisticate. Don't break her heart."

During the second interval, Rochdale received a similar warning from the dowager Duchess of Hertford. While Grace chatted with Lord Ingleby, the duchess's escort and current lover, Wilhelmina took Rochdale aside and said, "Take her to bed if you must, and treat her well, for she needs it. But do not, by God, trifle with her heart. Or you'll have me to reckon with."

He hoped Grace's heart was not involved, for he was going through with the seduction of her regardless. He had to, else he'd lose his best horse to Sheane. But he did not believe she was in love with him, or in any danger of falling in love. He was more inclined to believe it was curiosity that drove her. He had awakened passion in her, and once she became accustomed to the idea, she wanted to see how far she could take it. Building a friendship made it easier for her to justify using him as her tutor in the amorous arts. Grace was the type of woman who would need to admire and respect the man who was finally allowed to take her to bed, even if she had to manufacture that respect built on little more than a large bank draft for her charity.

Rochdale sensed she was almost ready for her first lesson. And he had a plan ready to set in action.

Later, when his carriage slowed to a stop in front of her Portland Place home, Rochdale pulled Grace into his arms for a brief kiss. She responded with an eagerness that told him she was ready to take the next step. In fact, he was certain she would surrender to him tonight if he asked. But he would not. Not tonight. He wanted her to endure a bit of frustrated sexual desire, so that when he finally did suggest that he take her to bed, she would want it so badly she could not refuse.

And so he kissed her again, more deeply, as his hands roamed over her hips and thighs and up to the bit of soft flesh above the stiff bones of her corset, protected by a mere wisp of gauzy silk. She moved into his touch and moaned into his mouth.

Finally, he pulled away. "I must not keep you out here," he said between ragged breaths. "Your neighbors will talk." God, he was panting for her. It happened every time. He'd set out as the seducer and end up as the seduced.

"Perhaps you . . ." But she shook her head and did not finish her thought. Had she been going to invite him inside? He was far enough gone to want it, but had just enough resolve to stick to his plan.

"I would happily stay here in this carriage with you for hours," he said, "but that would be too selfish, even for me. I'd be even happier to follow you inside, but that would be the worst kind of selfishness. Just because I don't care what people say about me does not mean I should play as fast and loose with your reputation. If I were to go inside with you, I daresay there is at least one neighbor who would make note of what time I entered and precisely what time I left."

"Yes, you are probably right."

He could not suppress a smile at her words, a veiled admission that she might indeed have invited him inside. Into her bed. It took a supreme effort of will not to drag her into his arms again and woo her into taking him upstairs.

"May I see you tomorrow?" he asked instead. "I'd like to take you to a horse race."

Grace offered a wary smile. "Oh! I've never been to a horse race."

"Then it is high time you went, don't you think? My best horse is racing. I'd be very pleased if you were there to watch the race with me."

Her smile broadened into a radiance so bright it shot like a bolt of lightning straight through his chest. "Oh, yes, John! I should love it more than anything. Will there be wagering?"

"Of course."

"Then, since it is your best horse, perhaps I should place a bet on him."

"Her. She's a chestnut mare named Serenity. And she is a winner, so your bet will not be too risky. The odds will be in her favor."

"A horse race and gambling. What a bad influence you are, sir."

More than she knew. "I shall come by to collect you at eight. Rather early, I fear."

"Eight o'clock? I did not realize horse races were held at such an early hour."

"They aren't. But it is a bit of a drive. I want to be sure to have time to check on Serenity, to speak with the rider, to inspect the field, and so on. It requires that I arrive well before the race. I hope you do not mind."

"Not at all. I look forward to it."

At Rochdale's signal, Nat, in full footman's livery tonight, leapt down from his perch in the back, opened the carriage door, and pulled down the step. Rochdale stepped out and handed Grace down. He walked by her side to the door, careful not to take her arm or otherwise touch her. The nearby streetlamp put them too much on display. And he really did care about her reputation. He had not lied about that.

When she reached the door, it was opened by a stern-faced butler. She thanked him for waiting up and then sent him away, promising to lock the door herself. The fellow gave Rochdale a challenging look, then did as he was asked, leaving Grace and Rochdale alone in the doorway. Was she going to invite him inside after all?

She turned to him and said, "Will you tell me something truthfully?"

"Anything."

"Why are you doing this?"

"Doing what?"

"Pursuing me. Am I some sort of challenge for you? A novelty? You've never been with a respectable woman before? A good woman?"

He winced. What could he say that was in any way related to the truth? It was true that wanting her in order to win a bet had changed to simply wanting her. But it was also true that there would never have been a pursuit without that damned wager.

"Oh, but of course there was Serena Underwood, wasn't there?" Her words were laced with the merest hint of sarcasm. "She was respectable. *Was.*"

Was she afraid he would treat her the way he'd treated Serena? The situations were not remotely alike, and neither were the women. "Many women are respectable," he said. "Very few are truly good."

She lifted an eyebrow. "There is more to that story than any of us know, isn't there? Serena was not entirely without blame, was she?"

Poor Grace. She was trying so hard to make him out to be a better man than he was, so that he might seem worthy of her. "I regret the scandal," he said, "for Serena's sake. And that is all I have to say on the matter."

"You did tell me once that you were a man of discretion. Now I know it to be true. I am proud to call you friend, Lord Rochdale."

Dear God, she was killing him. He bowed to her. "You honor me, madam."

Grace put her hand on his sleeve, in full view of any neighbor who happened to be spying. "Thank you for the lovely evening. I have enjoyed our time together. I wish you were not so determined to have people think badly of you. If only they knew how generous you have been to Marlowe House."

"Is that why you condescend to be seen with me, to allow me to kiss you? As some kind of reward for my bank draft?"

She blushed. Again. Prettily. "No, of course not. Your donation has nothing to do with it. That would be cruel and dishonest. I enjoy being with you, that is all. You make me feel . . . special."

Her hand still rested on his sleeve and Rochdale covered it with his own. "You *are* special. And very beautiful. Has no one ever told you that?"

"The bishop did. He was very taken with my looks. But in many ways he was distant, as though he was afraid if he touched me I'd shatter like a Meissen figurine. You tell me I'm beautiful, but you also talk to me. You treat me like . . . an equal. With the bishop, I was always his precious helpmate. He never really talked to me the way you do. I thank you for that, and I look forward to tomorrow's race."

Trouble and more trouble.

On the long, meandering drive to Curzon Street, Rochdale began to have second thoughts about what he'd planned for tomorrow. She refused to be cruel or dishonest with him, and yet he was about to do something thoroughly selfish and deceitful—and ultimately cruel, if she ever learned the truth. He anticipated a full-fledged seduction, and he was certain she would surrender to it. Because he made her feel special.

Yet she made him feel like the world's worst cad.

What the devil was he going to do about Grace Marlowe?

Chapter 13

It was not until they stopped to change horses for the third time that Grace began to get suspicious.

Rochdale had come by her house at the appointed early hour in a plain black traveling chariot. The absence of the Rochdale crest on the door was obviously a matter of discretion, as was the fact that he had not brought a curricle or other open carriage in which they would be easily seen. Another demonstration of his concern for her reputation was his request that she change her bonnet.

"As delightful as that little confection is," he said, "I would recommend that you wear a bonnet that includes a veil. The race is likely to draw a motley crowd, including a few Corinthians from town who might recognize you. I fear I have been having second thoughts about taking you with me, worrying that you might become the object of gossip. However, I do not want to deprive you of seeing your first horse race; therefore I believe it is best that we take care that you are not recognized as Mrs. Marlowe."

With some reluctance, Grace exchanged her brand-new cottage bonnet, with the sweet little bunch of cornflowers that exactly matched her pelisse, for a Victoria hat with a short veil that could be rolled back over the upturned brim. It was not as stylish as the cottage bonnet, but it would serve the purpose. Roch-

dale declared it perfection as he handed her into the
carriage.

Grace found herself rather charmed that this man,
who cared nothing for his own good name, was so
solicitous of hers.

He told her it was a long drive to the racecourse,
and she should tell her butler not to wait up for her
as it might be late when they returned. She wondered
how they could possibly spend such a long time at a
horse race. Did he have something else planned that
had nothing to do with horses?

The carriage was plush and elegant inside, with
walls and seat cushions of tufted velvet, and polished
brass fittings throughout. There were woolen lap robes
tucked into deep pockets beneath the front window
and footrests that pulled out from under the seat.
Grace settled in comfortably for the journey and soon
forgot any anxieties about what Rochdale might have
in mind for her. He kept to his side of the seat, showing no inclination to take her in his arms. She was not
sure whether she was relieved or disappointed. Instead, they fell into easy conversation about horses
and races and stables and other equine matters. Rochdale obviously had more than the average understanding of horses, explaining the features that made certain
horses faster than others, about breeding and training,
about the proper riders. When Grace expressed her
admiration for the depth of his knowledge, he merely
laughed and said, "Recollect that I am a gambler. I
have been betting on the ponies for many years, and
one takes note of these things if one wants to win.
Some years ago I decided I wanted to go after the
purse as well, so I started my own stable of racehorses.
I've had several winners, but none as promising as
Serenity."

"I look forward to meeting her."

"She's an Irish lass and very sweet-tempered. You
will like her, I think."

Their conversation meandered from topic to topic as the drive took them farther into the countryside. Grace could not remember ever having such a comfortable talk with a gentleman. She was generally on her guard in mixed company, reticent to speak too openly or to say much at all beyond the prescribed trivialities of small talk. It was different with Rochdale, each of them expressing opinions openly, without the polite niceties that controlled most conversations with men of the *ton*. They spoke of Marlowe House and the Fletcher family, of opera and the latest novels, of recent bills in Parliament and the latest news from the war. She was surprised to learn that Rochdale, who gave the impression of a man interested in his own pleasure and little else, was well versed in political issues, and took his seat in Lords when a particular vote was important to him. And he seemed surprised that she kept up to date with current events, obviously assuming she would be more interested in the latest fashions than the latest battle in Portugal.

"I read the newspapers," she said, "just like you, and subscribe to several magazines as well. I enjoy following news of Bonaparte and the war and political debate."

"Let me guess: All that newspaper reading is something you are enjoying as a widow that you were never allowed to do as a wife."

Grace offered a sheepish grin. "How did you know?"

"I have often heard men say that they do not allow their wives to read the newspapers. They think it might offend their delicate sensibilities or some such nonsense. Seems damned foolish to me. If a woman wants to know about something badly enough, she will find it out eventually, so why stop her? You did mention that the old man treated you like a porcelain doll, so I assume he also protected you against the horrors you might stumble upon in the *Times* or the *Morning Chronicle*."

"Definitely not the *Morning Chronicle*," she said, wagging a finger at him. "Too Whiggish for Bishop Marlowe, let alone his wife. But you're right. Like many men, he did not think women should trouble their minds with men's business. In fact, I found a sermon of his among his papers in which he specifically warns men against allowing their wives too much freedom in their reading material. Newspapers and novels were to be avoided at all costs."

Rochdale arched an eyebrow. "And yet now you enjoy them both, do you not?"

Grace shrugged. "My first little act of independence as a widow."

"But not your last. Here you are on your way to a horse race."

"Where I hope to place a bet. See how wicked I have become under your influence? The bishop would be aghast at my imprudent behavior."

"And the day is still young." He shot her a roguish look that made her smile. "Tell me, Grace, how did you meet the bishop? I assume through your father, since he is a man of the church, and yet you said he was a simple country vicar."

"He was, but he had ambitions. When he heard that Bishop Marlowe was coming to Exeter Cathedral, he packed us all up and made the twenty-mile journey so he could meet the great man he'd heard so much about." Grace chuckled as she remembered that day. "We had not been away from home much, my brother and sister and I, and so staying in a coaching inn not far from Cathedral Commons seemed very grand indeed. Mama was less sanguine about it, however, and brought her own sheets."

Rochdale laughed. "A practical woman, your mama."

"Which made her a perfect vicar's wife."

"And so you met Bishop Marlowe in Exeter?"

"Papa was introduced to the bishop, and was asked, along with other local clergy, to officiate at a service with him. It was quite an honor. Afterward, he trotted all of us out to be properly introduced."

"And you caught the bishop's eye."

"Yes, I suppose so."

"I daresay he was smitten by your beauty. How old were you?"

"Eighteen. I felt very gauche and awkward at first, but also very flattered that he should deign to notice me."

"Any man with breath still in him would notice, my dear. So, did he lay his heart at your young feet?"

"Oh, no, nothing like that. It was all very formally done. My parents said I had to marry him because he promised to give Papa a post as a rural dean."

"They sold you to him."

Grace shot him a perturbed look. "No, it wasn't as bad as that. It was simply an arranged marriage like any other. As it happened, I was very fortunate in my parents' choice of husband for me." Her poor sister had not fared nearly as well with her ne'er-do-well husband, who didn't even try to make a go of their farm.

"It sounds to me as if your parents got more out of the bargain than you did, saddled with a man more than twice your age. I hope they appreciated your sacrifice."

"It was no sacrifice, I assure you. I went from a small, crowded vicarage to the very grand official residence of the Bishop of London, and later our private residence on Portland Place, which he very kindly left me in his will. I have led a life of wealth and comfort such as I had never imagined. It has not been a sacrifice."

But it had been exceedingly uncomfortable at first.

Grace had been self-conscious about her humble background when the bishop brought her to his official residence in London at the Old Deanery, which was large and ornate and bustling with servants in elegant livery, and minions in more somber black, ready to do the bishop's bidding. She'd felt so out of place and horribly unprepared. Her husband understood, however, and taught her everything—how to behave, how to dress, how to speak, what to say to whom. Even how to behave with him in private. Everything. And Grace had been a fast learner. She'd become the perfect Bishop's Wife.

And until recently, the perfect Bishop's Widow.

"Are your parents still alive," Rochdale asked, "reaping the benefits of your marriage?"

"Yes, they are alive and well in Devon. My sister and brother are still in Devon as well."

"Do you ever see them?"

"Not often. None of them ever comes to London, and I seldom have time for a visit to Devon. But we are great letter writers, the Newbury family is. I receive long letters from at least one of them every week, relating all the country news, and I write to them weekly about the news in town."

More often than not, the letters from Devon contained veiled requests for money, especially from her sister, Felicity, who had seven children and figured since Grace had none—a barb she never ceased to fling—she should help to support her nieces and nephews. Her brother, Thomas, also needed assistance from time and time, and even her mother had hinted now and then that a contribution to her father's deanery would be welcome. Grace had come to think of the Newbury family as her second charity.

"I do not know," Rochdale said, "how you manage to accomplish so much with your time, my dear. Your charity fund and all its balls, the management of Marlowe House, all that letter writing. It boggles the mind.

Ah, here is the Red Lion." He signaled to the postilions to pull into the inn yard. "We'll change horses here and stay for a quick luncheon. You must be as famished as I am."

As he led her into the inn, Grace realized they were changing horses for the third time and had been traveling for almost four hours. He'd kept her so engaged in conversation that she had lost all track of time. Where was this horse race that it took so long to get there? Anxiety danced down her spine as she wondered what Rochdale was up to.

He procured a private parlor for them and ordered food and drink. Tea for her, porter for him. She walked to the window and looked out to see where they were. She had barely noticed the landscape as they drove. The inn was situated on rising ground above a wharf that jutted out into a river. The remains of an old castle could be seen on a hill in the near distance. "Where are we?" she asked.

"Hockerill. Just at the border of Essex and Hertfordshire."

"Are we near the racecourse?"

He shook his head. "Not yet. We still have a bit of a drive."

She stared at him for a moment, and saw something flicker in his eyes that unsettled her. Was it guilt? Shame?

"John, where exactly are we going?"

He could no longer meet her eyes and dropped his gaze, making a show of brushing a piece of nonexistent lint from his sleeve. "To a racecourse a bit north of here."

"How far north?"

He shrugged. "A ways."

"John. Look at me."

He did. His brow was furrowed and this time there was no mistaking the look of guilt in his eyes.

"Tell me where we are going."

He sighed, but kept his eyes squarely on hers. "Newmarket."

"Good God." She ought to have guessed it. Newmarket was, as she understood it, where a great many important races were run. It was also at least sixty miles from London. "We cannot possibly reach Newmarket in time for a race today."

He looked at her for a long moment, then said, "No, we can't. The race is tomorrow morning."

Dear God, he meant for them to stay together, overnight, in Newmarket. To share a bed. To make love.

She had expected something like this, had been prepared for it. But now that she was actually faced with it, with the possibility of doing with Rochdale in life what she had done with him in her dreams, the enormity of what that meant to her was quite simply overwhelming. She felt the blood drain from her face and a twinge of dizziness made her lift a hand to her head.

Rochdale was at her side in an instant, hand on her elbow, leading her to a chair.

"I'm sorry," he said after she was seated. He pulled a chair close to hers and sat down, taking her hand in his. "It was wicked of me to trick you like that."

"Trick me?" She felt dazed and stupid.

"Into spending the night with me. I had hoped you wanted it as much as I do. And I thought it might be easier for you if we were away from London. I'm sorry if I misjudged your interest in me, Grace. If I have made a horrible blunder, tell me so, and we shall return to London at once."

"But . . . but your race is in the morning. Unless that was also a ruse?"

"No, there really is a race tomorrow."

"And you must be there."

"I am willing to miss it if you wish to return to London."

Grace turned away from him, unable to look any

longer into those seductive blue eyes while she decided what to do. In truth, she had already accepted the idea that they would become lovers eventually. She had been half ready to take him to her bed the night before, and he knew it. That was why he had felt bold enough to take her on this absurd journey, because he knew she *wanted* him to make love to her. If she backed down now, not only would she feel cowardly in the extreme, but she would force him to miss the race in which his favorite horse was running. He would resent her on both counts. And she would feel like a fool.

But she did not want to back down. She wanted to share his bed. She wanted to be a Merry Widow like her friends, to experience all the intimacies they talked about. She wanted to *live*.

Wanting it was one thing; doing it was more difficult that she'd expected. The significance of what she was about to do weighed heavily upon her. She had convinced herself, with Marianne's help, that physical passion was not always sinful, but those doubts still lingered along the edges of her mind. To take this next step with Rochdale would be a defining moment. A life-changing moment. She would no longer be the prudish, naïve widow. She would be . . . a woman fulfilled.

Grace felt as though she were about to leap from a bell tower, to dive headlong into . . . what? Deliverance? Renewal? Destiny? Sin? With so many questions and doubts still swirling in her head, she was not certain she was ready to take that leap, but by God she was going to try.

She turned back to face Rochdale, looked him squarely in the eye, and said, "I will go to Newmarket with you, John."

He did not smile triumphantly, as she expected. His only reaction was to blink. His brow still wore a troubled frown as he gazed at her for a long, silent moment. Finally, he said, "Are you sure? I do not want you to feel forced into doing something you don't feel right about. If you have any doubts at all, we will return to London."

"I am consumed with doubt," she said, offering a shy smile. "But it is what I want. With you and no one else. I trust you, John."

He closed his eyes for a moment, and when he opened them again, Grace noted a glint of something that might have been gratitude. Perhaps he was thankful not to have to miss the horse race tomorrow after all. He lifted the hand he still held and kissed it. "You honor me, Grace. I am not worthy."

His expression all at once transformed into one of absolute delight. He gave her one of those magnificent smiles she'd come to anticipate, teeth flashing, eyes crinkling with merriment. Not one of his slow, seductive smiles, but a full-out smile of pure joy. It transformed him utterly—from hard-edged, slightly dissipated cynic into a carefree, handsome, and thoroughly engaging man. It was a smile that shot straight through to her heart.

"Even so," he said, "I am truly and completely thrilled that you are willing to go to Newmarket with me." He pulled her to her feet and took her in his arms. "Grace, my dear girl, you never fail to surprise and enchant me. We will be so good together, I promise. I will show you pleasures you never dreamed existed."

She had no doubt of it as he kissed her with such passion that her toes curled up inside her slippers. His mouth had traveled down her jaw and throat when the parlor door opened and the landlord's wife entered, followed by a young man bearing a tray laden with covered dishes. Rochdale and Grace leapt apart, laughing sheepishly as the woman glared at them with disapproval.

As they shared a meal of cold veal pie, sliced ham,

excellent cheese, and grainy brown bread, they talked of everything except what was surely on both their minds. Finally, Grace interrupted a discourse on the history of horse racing at Newmarket to say: "Oh dear, I feel so stupid. How do we do this, John? Do we take a room pretending to be a married couple? Do we use false names? And I have no maid with me. Will that seem odd? And, oh my goodness, what about my people at home? Spurling will worry himself to death when I do not return home tonight. What should I—"

"Hush, my dear." He grinned as he covered her hand with his. "Leave everything to me. I will send a messenger to your home telling them you were the victim of a carriage accident, that you suffered a bad sprain of the ankle and are resting at an inn for a day in order to recuperate."

"Oh. That sounds reasonable. Perhaps I should write the note myself to be delivered to Spurling."

"An excellent idea. As for Newmarket, the rooms are already reserved in my name. Two bedchambers. Just in case you change your mind."

She felt color rise in her cheeks. "I won't change my mind." In for a penny, in for a pound.

It was high summer, when the days were long and the twilight seemed to go on forever. There were several hours of light left when they arrived in Newmarket.

There had been less conversation between them since leaving Hockerill. Once his intentions had been laid bare, and she had accepted them, the tension between them fairly crackled in the small carriage. He kept to his side of the bench, afraid to touch her for fear he'd lay her down and ravish her on the spot.

The long silences gave him time to consider his actions—never a healthy thing to do. His conscience, which had grown overactive of late, was plaguing him with guilt over what he was about to do to this women. He wanted to make love to her—he wanted it badly, desperately—but he felt damnably guilty for bringing her to the point of wanting it, too. He was pleased to have coaxed the passionate woman from deep inside the prim and proper widow. It would have been a bloody shame and a waste for such a magnificent woman to allow her passions to dry up, which is precisely what he believed would have happened to Grace if she had continued down her self-imposed path of tenacious virtue and propriety.

And yet, she *was* virtuous and good and decent. That very goodness defined her. She'd probably never done an unkind thing in her life, never spoken a cruel word, never behaved in a hurtful manner toward anyone. She was a woman of honor and compassion and dignity. She deserved better than him. She certainly deserved better treatment than to be the means of winning a bet.

Never in all his life had Rochdale felt so torn up inside over a woman—pulled in one direction by a deep and potent desire, pulled in the other direction by an almost overwhelming guilt.

I trust you, John.

Her words rang loudly in his head like a punishment. He thought of all the women in his life who'd manipulated him, or tried to, in one way or another, and how he despised them for it. Yet he had just as despicably manipulated this good woman into trusting him. What a monstrous irony. All for the sake of a wager.

But he would take Grace to bed tonight, and he would likely find intense pleasure in it. Afterward, though, he suspected he might crumble into a thousand pieces of guilt and shame. For he would have sacrificed the virtue of the only good woman he had ever known, just to win a horse. Surely he was the worst cad that ever walked the earth.

To delay the inevitable, he took advantage of the light to visit the stable where Serenity was being kept. Before leaving the carriage, he asked Grace to lower her veil. He didn't expect to see anyone she might know in the stables, but he was determined to protect her reputation. It was the least he could do. She pulled the thin blue silk down over the brim of her bonnet, tucked it under her chin, and tied it at the back of her neck. It was an effective disguise. Her features were blurred behind the blue veil, and not a hint of blond hair was visible. No one would recognize her.

He took her arm and led her into the stable yard. Rochdale allowed the sights and smells he loved so much to wash over him, taking him away, for the moment, from guilt and shame. The air was pungent with the odors of alfalfa and hay and horse. They walked down the long aisles strewn with straw and lined with stalls. One horse whinnied. Another struck his hoof against the stall wall. They found Serenity in the second aisle. Samuel Trask, one of Rochdale's senior grooms, sat on a low stool outside the stall, polishing a harness. When he saw them approach, he jumped to his feet.

"Evenin', milord." He touched the brim of his cap and dipped his head. He looked at Grace and did the same. Rochdale decided not to introduce her. It would be assumed that she was his doxy, and would therefore be more or less ignored.

"How's our girl, Sam?"

"Sound as a brass bell, milord. She'll be in fine form for tomorrow's run."

Rochdale opened the stall door and stepped inside. Reaching into his coat pocket, he pulled out a scrap of linen, unfolded it, and retrieved a slice of apple he had saved from Hockerill. Serenity nipped it from his hand and chewed it. When she was finished, he stroked her elegant neck and whispered soft endearments in her ear. She nuzzled his face, and rested her head on his shoulder while he gently scratched her between the ears.

That sent her into a trance of sheer pleasure—the girl was so easily pleased—and he motioned for Grace to come inside the stall. Continuing to scratch, he spoke to Grace in a very soft, even voice. "You are not afraid of horses, are you?"

"Not at all. I grew up in the country, remember?"

"Good. Come in and meet my favorite girl. Sam, do you have anything to give her?"

"Some alfalfa buds, milord."

Sam retrieved a handful from a small bag and Rochdale indicated that Grace should take them. She did, and approached the horse quietly with her hand extended. Serenity fell out of her blissful state to take the treat. Grace came closer and allowed the horse to sniff her and nuzzle her. When Serenity went for her bonnet, Grace laughed and held it on tight while she stroked the horse's long, glossy neck.

With the lift of an eyebrow, Rochdale sent Sam away, allowing a private moment with his two favorite girls. "Serenity, meet Grace. She is a very nice person and I can tell she likes you already."

"You're a beauty," Grace said as she continued to stroke the mare's neck. "And you know it, don't you?"

"That she does. And she knows she's better than the rest and will win me a great purse tomorrow, won't you, my girl?"

They spent a few more minutes with Serenity, and then returned to the carriage that would take them to the inn.

"I can see why you love her," Grace said. "She is a splendid animal."

So splendid that Rochdale was willing to debauch this fine woman in order to keep her in his stable. "She is my most winning horse. She's won several cups here at Newmarket, as well as the king's plate at

Nottingham and several large purses. Tomorrow's race is not one of the eight established races here at Newmarket, but is something of an informal affair with a private purse. I just wanted to give her a practice run before the Goodwood."

"I look forward to seeing her run."

She gave him a shy look that hinted there were other things she was looking forward to as well.

They reached the King's Head and left the postilions to look after the chariot and the team. Rochdale retrieved a small case from the boot, which he carried inside the inn. The landlord knew him well and had been paid generously to usher them quickly and discreetly to their rooms: two bedchambers separated by a small private parlor. By prior arrangement, a cold supper awaited them along with a decanter of the landlord's best claret. Another sovereign was slipped into the innkeeper's hand as he left them, further insurance that their privacy would be respected.

They retired to their separate rooms to wash off the dirt from the road. Rochdale did not miss Grace's look of relief that she would have a moment alone before facing what was to come. He flung his hat upon the bed and removed his coat, then used the water and basin to clean up. He took the time to shave, as his beard was rough by this time of night, and he did not want to abrade Grace's delicate skin.

He did his best to push all guilt aside. Seeing Serenity reminded him how important it was that he win the wager. It was more than winning Albion from Sheane; the thought of losing Serenity was too painful to contemplate.

When Grace joined him in the parlor, she had removed her bonnet and pelisse. Her dress was plain white muslin with some sort of fancy work at the hem and along the edge of the bodice. The sleeves were short, leaving her slender, pale arms deliciously bare. Her hair was twisted into a simple chignon at the back of her neck. Rochdale remembered how it had looked at the masquerade ball, hanging loose down her back, and he became aroused at the thought of seeing it again.

With some effort, he held arousal in check while they dined. Grace ate little, and he could see that she was nervous. He encouraged her to drink the wine. When her glass was empty, he refilled it. She quickly swallowed down the second glass, hiccupped, and grinned sheepishly.

"Dutch courage," she said.

Another wave of guilt swept over him at the simple words. It was another kind of courage entirely that had brought her here tonight. He would probably never understand how big a step this truly was for her, never understand what she was giving up of herself to be with him. But it was a great deal—he knew that much.

He kept their conversation light and tried to amuse her. She seemed to relax a bit, but anxiety was still apparent in the way she sat and played with her food. The laughter he coaxed from her was not the deep, sultry resonance he loved—it was tentative and brittle.

Finally, Rochdale excused himself and went into his bedchamber, where he opened the small valise he'd brought. He retrieved two flimsy garments and returned to the parlor.

"Since I did not give you fair warning of my plans," he said, "I took the liberty of bringing these along for you. I wasn't sure what else you might want. We can visit the shops tomorrow if you like."

He held out the two garments, a pink silk nightgown and matching wrapper. He had spent a great deal of time choosing just the right nightgown for her. It was not too risqué, nor was it too spinsterish. It was pretty and elegant and seemed the sort of thing Grace would wear.

"Oh. How . . . how lovely, John. I hadn't realized . . .

I had thought . . . Oh dear, I am feeling rather flustered, I fear. You must forgive me, but I do not know what happens." Her skin flushed pink from her face to her throat and all down her arms.

"It shall happen in whatever way makes you comfortable, my dear. We can both retire to your bedchamber and undress each other, forgoing the nightgown entirely, or I can wait to join you after you have put it on. It is up to you."

"I believe I would prefer to undress myself, if you do not mind. This is all so new to me, and I am nervous enough without having you undress me. I fear I might swoon and miss the whole thing."

Rochdale smiled. Her candid admission was rather sweet. "We shall go slowly, then. Go change into the nightgown. I will join you when you are ready. Do you need help with your stays?"

"No!" Her eyes grew wide with apprehension. "No, thank you. I can manage."

He went into his own bedchamber and changed into a heavy brocade dressing gown. He cinched it tight at the waist, but wore nothing under it. Never had he prepared to make love to a woman with such misgivings. This poor, nervous woman trusted him to teach her the secrets of lovemaking, for he had no doubt the bishop hadn't done so. He desired her more than any woman in his life, but as the moment of surrender neared, he found that desire tempered by feelings of deceit and unspeakable guilt. But, dear God, how he wanted her.

When he stepped back into the parlor, Grace was just opening her bedchamber door. He almost groaned aloud at the sight of her. The fine pink silk of the wrapper, bound tightly at her waist, clung to every soft curve. The light from a branch of candles somewhere in the room behind her limned her golden hair and the lustrous silk so that she seemed to glow, like a vision of an angel. She stood just inside the doorway, straight and tall and proud, so that her breasts strained against the silk, the peaks of her nipples clearly outlined. Her hair was still up, though one long tendril had fallen loose at her neck. She looked so good he wanted to devour her in small bites.

"I'm ready," she said in a surprisingly steady voice. She appeared more resolute than nervous now. Perhaps the gown gave her renewed courage. No, it was not courage. The look in her eye was pure feminine pride. She knew she was beautiful; she wanted him to look at her.

And he did. Then, he walked straight to her and took her in his arms, kicking out one bare foot to close the door. He simply held her, savoring the warmth of her skin beneath the thin silk. "My God, Grace. You take my breath away. You are so beautiful."

"So are you, John."

"But you, my dear, are beautiful inside and out." He bent and kissed her. The silk wrapper was slick and smooth beneath his roaming hands, and highly erotic. He touched every part of her as he plundered her mouth, gripping her soft buttocks and pressing her hips against his erection. She moaned softly when his lips left hers and trailed kisses around to her jaw and throat and neck. His hands crept up her nape and into her hair.

"Take it down, Grace. I want to see it down."

While he continued to kiss her neck and ears, her hands worked at the back of her head. He heard the *ping* of pins hitting the floor, and all at once the heavy golden mass fell over his hands. He pulled away, turned her around so that her back was to him, lifted the thick hair, and buried his face in it. Good God, it was glorious. Then he pulled her back against him and ran his hands over her breasts, keeping his nose pressed against her sweet-smelling hair. She shivered at his touch, but allowed him to explore.

Reaching down, he loosened the tie at her waist.

He turned her around to face him again and slid his hands under the wrapper, then pushed it over her shoulders and down her arms until it slithered to the floor. There was now only one thin layer between his hands and her skin.

He took her again in an urgent kiss, hot and greedy, sliding his tongue in and out in an imitation of what was to come. He left her lips again and nibbled his way to her earlobe, down her throat, to the tender curve where her shoulder met the elegant white column of her neck.

As he did so, her breath came in shallow pants and the occasional "Oh." He pushed the strap of the nightgown down over one shoulder, kissing as he went. Down and down until one pale, perfect breast was uncovered. He touched it lightly, and Grace gave a little squeal of alarm.

Rochdale pulled back and was jolted at the sight of her: hair loose and disheveled, skin flushed, one breast exposed, lips parted, eyes wide. This was Grace Marlowe, the fine upstanding woman who devoted her life to good works. Good, decent, respectable Grace Marlowe. He had brought her to this.

Suddenly all the guilt and shame he'd been feeling coalesced at the sight of her in such confused disarray. He had set out to have her, but at that moment, the thought of taking her seemed wrong, a violation of something good and pure.

He couldn't do it.

He had wanted this, exactly this: to see the Bishop's Widow's modesty and dignity annihilated. But now it seemed a hateful, childish thing to have planned, and he could no longer bear to look.

He couldn't do it.

Grace looked at him in confusion. "What's wrong?"

Rochdale shook his head. He reached out and pushed up the strap of the nightgown so she was decently covered. "I'm sorry, Grace. So sorry."

She looked panicked. "Was it something I did? I don't know how to do this. You know that. Have I done it wrong? Tell me, John!"

He cupped her cheek lightly, then stepped back and away from her. "You have done nothing wrong, my dear. I am the one to blame. You are too good for the likes of me, Grace. I had no business taking it this far with you. It was wrong, very wrong. You're honorable and decent, and I am neither of those things. I cannot drag you down to my level. I thought I could, but I cannot. I do not want to be the ruin of a good woman. I care for you too much to do that to you. I'm sorry, Grace. Truly sorry."

He turned away from her look of wide-eyed disbelief, and left the room, closing the door behind him. When he reached his bedchamber, he sank into a chair, propped his elbows on his knees, and dropped his face into his hands.

Damn, damn, damn.

What a fool he'd been. He hadn't believed it could happen, hadn't realized it *had* happened. Rochdale, the debauched, unscrupulous libertine, had somehow become the noble ass Grace had wanted him to be. He had just done something entirely selfless for the first time in more than a dozen years.

Why, then, did it make him feel so damned bad?

Chapter 14

How dared he!

Grace stood alone in the room, dressed in the beautiful nightgown he'd bought her and staring at the closed door in utter disbelief. She crossed her arms over her chest and shivered. Not from the cold, but from pure white-hot anger.

How dare he bring her all the way to Newmarket, have her put on a thin nightgown that left little to the imagination, kiss her until she was senseless, and—my God!—touch her bare breast . . . and then leave. What was wrong with him, that he would make such an about-face?

Or, what was wrong with *her*?

No, this was not her fault. It was not. She had done nothing wrong. Rochdale had done this *to* her, leaving her alone and aroused and confused. He must have known what it had taken for her to put on the nightgown, to stand before him practically naked. He must have known how she would be affected by the sight of him clad in nothing more than a dressing gown—she was sure he wore nothing underneath—exposing a vee of bare throat and chest dusted with dark hair. He must have known how he made her feel when he touched her.

Yet, he'd bolted. Damn him!

Grace had decided to allow him to take her to bed. It was a huge decision, enormous and life-altering, but, by God, she had made it and was prepared to see it through. She had been willing to have Rochdale make love to her. More than willing, she had wanted it. Truly wanted it. She wanted to know what it would be like to experience the physical passion the Merry Widows so often discussed, and Rochdale was the one man she trusted to teach her. Because he liked her and respected her, and knew how momentous a step it was for her to take.

She could not help being nervous about it. She'd never seen a man's bare chest before. She'd never allowed a man to see, much less touch, her naked breast. Naturally it made her nervous.

Was that what had turned him away? That little squeak of surprise she'd uttered when he touched her breast? Surely he understood the shock—and thrilling pleasure—she'd felt. But perhaps he'd misunderstood her shock for fear, and decided she was not ready for such intimacy. Or decided he had no interest in tutoring such a skittish novice.

In the end, he did not find her desirable enough to make love to her, though that is surely what he had intended. But no, she had felt his desire. Besides the obvious sign, which he had made certain to press against her, there had been an urgency, almost like a hunger, in the way he had kissed and touched her. If nothing else, he desired her hair. Grace had almost swooned at the tender way he had handled it, as though it were precious gold. He'd made her feel beautiful, desirable, and she was more than ready to do as she'd done in her dream, to lie naked with him on the bed.

But he had denied her that pleasure.

Though Grace had all but discarded her Bishop's Widow mantle, perhaps Rochdale was unable to get beyond that image of her. Perhaps he had discovered that he could not, after all, abide physical intimacy with such a paragon.

She was tired of being the Bishop's Widow, thanks in large part to Rochdale's encouragement to craft her own, separate identity. He had taught her to want more from life, and God knew she did. He'd taught her what desire truly was. Not the sinful urges the bishop had insisted she suppress. But honest, natural desire for a man. He had taught her this, and she wanted more. She wanted passion and love and . . . sex. Dear heaven, she ached with wanting it, the way a drunkard craves another bottle.

Damn Rochdale for making her want all that but refusing to give it to her. Damn him for taking her body to such heights but not finishing the job. Damn him for being a coward!

He was not going to get away with it. Grace was no longer the passive, reserved, quiet little mouse she'd once been. He had wanted her to be strong and independent, to be "her own woman" and she was. She certainly felt like a new woman. The old Grace would never have dared to come to Newmarket with the infamous Lord Rochdale. Yes, she had changed. But, by God, he had not yet seen the full force of the new Grace Marlowe.

The door to his bedchamber opened with a loud crash as she slammed it against the wall. Rochdale looked up to find Grace standing in the middle of the room in the pink nightgown, hands on hips, outrage and fury oozing from every fine pore.

"What a coward you are." She almost spat the words at him.

He shook his head. "No, Grace, it is not cowardice. I am simply trying to do something good for once in my life." And the sight of her was making it very difficult to maintain those good intentions.

"And it is good to leave me alone and wanting?"

"I'm sorry, Grace. That was unforgivable."

"Yes, it was. And cowardly. You are afraid to seduce me. Afraid of the ghost of Bishop Marlowe."

"No, Grace, that is not—"

"But I will no longer be a martyr to that ghost. You taught me that. I am not the Bishop's Widow, standing here in a nightgown. I am just plain Grace Marlowe, an ordinary woman with ordinary needs. You brought me here to seduce me, and I am ready and willing for you to do so. You set out to make me want you, and by heaven, you did. And now you decide to leave me unsatisfied. How dare you be so cruel?"

Every word was like a knife being plunged into his gut. "You are right. I did set out to make you want me. You were a challenge I could not resist."

"I knew that. I have always known that. But I needed your challenge. I needed to stop being so closed up and untouchable. You helped me see that I could be something more. You made me feel like a woman, a desirable woman, for the first time in my life. I have come alive since knowing you. I even dream of making love to you. But out of some sort of twisted honor, you refuse to fulfill my dreams."

The blade sank deeper, slicing his insides to shreds. But he cared about her too much to be the instrument of her ruin.

Appealing to her better nature, he quoted Proverbs: "'Beware of false prophets which come to you in sheep's clothing but inwardly they are ravening wolves.'"

"But you never wore sheep's clothing, John. You never pretended to be other than a wolf. And even though I have seen more good in you than you allow others to see, I have always been aware of the ravening wolf. I know you for both the good and the bad in you, and I want all of it. I want all of you." She slipped the nightgown from her shoulders and let it slither to the floor. "And I want you to have all of me."

His eyes widened, he sucked in a sharp breath, and his erection throbbed. She stood before him, naked and unashamed, wearing nothing on her perfect white skin but the light from a single candle on a nearby table. Dear God, she was gorgeous. Tall and slender, she was not voluptuous, but elegantly proportioned with graceful curves. Her breasts were not large, but firm and lovely with dark nipples standing at attention. Her waist was small, her belly not quite flat but softly rounded, her hips wide but not too wide, and her legs long and shapely. At the juncture of her legs was a thick tuft of golden curls.

And every bare inch of perfect flesh was flushed pink, just as he'd expected.

Rochdale rose and walked to her. "My dear Grace, you are making it very, very difficult for me to behave honorably." He reached out to the long, glorious hair he had waited so long to see like this, hanging thick and loose over her shoulders. He lifted it and let it spill over his fingers like water. There was so much of it. So much of her. Good intentions be damned, there was no way in hell he could resist her now.

"The honorable thing to do," she said, "would be to finish what you started."

To his surprise, she reached for the belt of his dressing gown and untied it. Her eyes widened when it fell open to reveal his nakedness and a rampant erection. Undaunted, she pushed the heavy brocade over his shoulders. He shrugged it off and let it fall to the floor.

He took her hands and held her away from him as they both studied each other's bodies. Her flush deepened as she looked at him, and he smiled.

"You've never been naked with a man before, have you?"

She shook her head, her gaze still sweeping over his

body. "You are . . . very nicely made, John. Quite . . . magnificent, in fact."

"The only word I have to describe you, my dear, is perfection. I feel honored to be allowed to look upon you. To be the first to do so."

"I want to touch you, John. To feel your skin against mine."

"I am your servant, ma'am." And he took her into his arms and kissed her.

The kiss became wild and unbridled as they explored each other's bodies. She gave a plaintive moan as his hand caressed a breast, his fingers fondling a nipple. Her knees seemed to buckle slightly, and he scooped her up into his arms and carried her to the bed.

They quickly became a tangle of arms and legs as they kissed and kissed and kissed. Grace was awash in sensations she'd never imagined. Even her vivid dreams had been nothing like this. Rochdale's chest and legs and arms were covered in black hair, and she loved the feel of it against her smooth skin. In fact, her skin had become so sensitive that every touch, every stroke, every rub, every lick of his tongue sent her into new raptures.

The whole experience was indescribable. Unexpected, and yet everything she'd expected.

Rochdale crawled on top of her, and Grace thought they were about to finish, but he did not enter her yet. He took first one breast into his mouth and suckled, then the other. She writhed beneath him, beneath the unimaginable bliss of his lips and tongue. Without conscious thought, she arched up into his mouth, into pleasure, wanting all of it, and more.

While his tongue painted wet circles around her nipple, his hand roamed lower, stroking her stomach and hips and thighs. His fingers trailed along her inner thigh and she instinctively parted her legs. His hand then crept up her thigh and into the soft curls that hid her sex. She cried out when he parted her and inserted a finger inside. Grace spent the merest instant in embarrassment over the dampness he found there, but she immediately lost all inhibitions as he slid the finger in and out, sending her into an oblivion of sensation. She almost leapt off the bed when his damp finger began to stroke the tiny nub above her sex. Lord, it was so sensitive it was near impossible to bear his touch, as if this intimate caress was never meant to be, was too wicked to be allowed. And yet she pressed up against him, wanting more.

Rochdale's mouth left her breast and returned to her mouth, taking her in a kiss that ravished her senses. He pressed his lips against her ear and whispered, "Is it good, Grace?"

"Yes. Oh, yes."

"And I am on fire for you. You are wild and wonderful, Grace. Hot and slick and ready to be loved. Do you want more?"

"Yes."

"Everything?"

"Yes!"

"Then let me give it to you."

He trailed his hot tongue down her throat and between her breasts, licking the underside of each, down her ribs and abdomen and her belly, and finally to the very edge of that most private part of her, where his fingers had been before. *Dear God, this, of all things, must be truly sinful.* It could not be right or normal. Could it? "W-what are you doing?"

He lifted his head and said, "You want it all, don't you, Grace? Relax your legs for me. Open up for me. Let me pleasure you."

And, God help her, she welcomed him. She shuddered as the velvety tip of his tongue began to stroke her sex and the sensitive nub above it. It was sinful and wicked . . . and wonderful. She had never felt

anything like this before. It confused and compelled
her. She writhed against his mouth, lifting her hips off
the bed. She reached and reached . . . not knowing
for what . . . but there was something . . . something
more. She pushed and arched, rocking her hips. She
could not be still, and he grabbed her buttocks, lifting
her, holding her in his grip, forcing her to accept the
pleasure of his tongue. Her muscles strained and
clenched tightly, and she moaned in agony, unable to
bear it much longer. Finally, when she thought she
might die—of what? pleasure? pain?- -her sex con-
tracted into a single, massive convulsion that tore
through her like an explosion, sending her arching off
the bed and shouting his name.

Before she could begin to wonder what in heaven
had happened, Rochdale moved up her body, spread
her legs wide with his knees, and pushed himself deep
inside her. He held himself still for a moment and let
out a long sigh. This, at least, should have been familiar, but there was nothing in her experience that re-
sembled what she felt now, stretched and filled by
Rochdale. Grace sensed an odd little pulsing in her
sex, an aftermath of the explosion, and each pulse
seemed to tighten her inner muscles around him.

"Dear God, Grace. You are killing me."

For a moment, she thought that somehow she was
hurting him, but he began to move in her and it felt
so good she wondered who was killing whom. He
moved very slowly at first, lifting himself off her and
pulling almost all the way out, then plunging deep
inside again. He bent down and kissed her tenderly
while he moved in her, taking her hands and holding
them next to her shoulders, linking his fingers with
hers. He thrust into her again and again, and Grace
marveled that this act of intimacy, which had lasted
for only brief seconds with her husband, could provide
such prolonged pleasure.

If this was wicked, she no longer wished to be good.

Before her mind was lost again to all rational thought, she reflected for an instant on the bishop, and hated him a little for denying her this. And pitied him, too, for denying himself.

Rochdale increased the tempo of their rhythm, groaning as he buried his face in her hair. She pushed harder against him. Pleasure grew with each thrust. Grew and grew until it became almost painful to endure, almost unbearable. And just like the first time, the coiled knot of tension exploded, and she soared to some new and dazzling place, a pocket of pure, brilliant sensation that closed around her, and she cried out at the force of the flight. Then she slowly, tremulously settled back to earth. And there was no pain at all. Only peace and overwhelming joy.

Rochdale's release came close on the heels of hers. He continued to pump into her, faster and faster. And then, with a ragged groan, he pulled out, spilling his seed on her stomach. When she realized why, tears built up behind her eyes. He was protecting her. Again. He would not want a babe to be the result of this night. She'd been too emotional, too lost to all sense to even think of such a circumstance. Wilhelmina had warned her to take precautions, reminded her that the absence of pregnancy during her marriage might have been the bishop's fault and not hers. But none of those warnings had entered Grace's mind. Thank heaven Rochdale had had the presence of mind that she'd lacked.

He collapsed on her, panting and damp with sweat. "My sweet Grace," he said breathlessly. "That was . . . amazing."

"Yes. Amazing."

After a moment, he rolled off her and fell onto his back. He took her hand as they lay side by side. "You survived?"

"Barely."

He laughed, and she could feel the mattress shake with it. "Was it . . . was it what you expected?"

Grace shook her head. "No. I had no idea. . . ." Nothing she had heard from her friends or dreamed about, nothing from her relations with her husband, had prepared her for what had just taken place. Especially those two explosions of sensation that she still did not entirely understand.

"But it was good?"

She turned her head to look at him. "Very, very good. And to think, you almost denied me all that pleasure, you wretch."

"I was trying to be noble, but you did not play fair. Offering your naked self to me like that. What's a poor fellow to do?"

"I am glad we did it, John. I am glad we made love."

"I am, too." He leaned over and kissed her briefly, then rose from the bed.

She watched him walk naked across the room. Everything she'd dreamed of was there, on full and uninhibited display. The lithe animal grace of his body. The masculine solidity. No wonder so many women found him irresistible.

He dropped a cloth into a basin of water and, with his back to her, proceeded to wash himself. He rinsed out the cloth and brought it to her, turning away to give her some privacy while she cleaned off the evidence of their lovemaking.

When she was finished, Rochdale returned the cloth to the basin, snuffed out the lone candle, and crawled into bed. He pulled the covers over them, and gathered her close to his side. She wriggled against him, loving the sensation of being skin to skin. Grace had never imagined that nakedness could feel so . . . nice. Not at all wicked, as she had imagined it would, but instead most pleasant. She loved the soft sheets against her heated flesh. She loved the weight of her hair on her bare back. She even loved the cool air of the room on her shoulders and upper arms. Every inch of her seemed to have come alive to new, simple, pleasurable sensations. Not the least of which was the warm contact with the man beside her.

She wrapped an arm around his waist and flung a leg over his. She'd never felt more cozy and comfortable in her life.

He placed a hand in her hair and ran his fingers lazily through it. "Grace, are you sure you do not mind that I have made you a partner in debauchery? I am still riddled with guilt over it, you know."

"If that was debauchery, then I gladly give in to it. You need not feel guilty. I got naked first, after all."

He chuckled. "So you did."

"You are just feeling unsettled because I am not your usual type of woman. Just because I am a respectable widow does not mean you have done anything wrong in making love to me. It only means that you are irresistible to women of all stripes."

"Am I?" He flashed an intimate smile. "Well, none of this would have happened if *you* had not been so damned irresistible." His hand crept down and stroked her buttocks. "The thing is, Grace, your respectability is very much on my mind. Whatever happens between us after tonight, I will not have your name in any way sullied. We shall be discreet here in Newmarket. Most people will think you are my latest bit of muslin, so long as you keep your veil down. Do you have a middle name?"

"Yes. It's Marie."

"If anyone insists on knowing your name, I shall introduce you as Marie."

"I feel like a new person. I might as well have a new name."

"It's been a long day," he said, rolling onto his side and turning her around so that her back was against his chest. He tucked her tight to him and put an arm around her, one hand on her breast. Grace had never slept in a man's arms before. She expected she would be too keyed up to sleep, but she felt deliciously languorous. And so snug and warm with Rochdale wrapped around her.

"Let's get some sleep," he said.

As it happened, desire kept them busy much of the night, and they did not get very much sleep at all.

After a quick visit to the stables to check on Serenity, Rochdale took Grace to the High Street shops so he could buy her a fresh dress and whatever undergarments she needed. He'd expected her to object, to complain that it was improper to accept any more such intimate gifts from him. Instead, she entered into the expedition with glee, pretending to be Marie, his doxy.

Her style was not the least doxylike, however, nor did her taste run to the inexpensive. He didn't care how much she spent. After a night with her in his arms, he was ready to buy her the moon if she wanted it.

This new love-struck attitude amused him. He had spent a lifetime honing a fine cynical edge that Grace had effectively dulled in a single night.

She chose an elegant dress of striped muslin and a green spencer jacket trimmed with gold braid, both ready-made and each a near-perfect fit needing no alterations. The blue-veiled bonnet looked wrong with the new costume, so Rochdale insisted on a new hat as well. The milliner, who knew a good mark when she saw one, was very accommodating about adding a veil to a shallow-brimmed chip straw bonnet. At first she attached a short veil that hung loose over Grace's face, but "Marie" insisted on a longer piece of gossamer silk that she could wrap under her chin and tie in the back. It was not the current fashion, but Grace had such natural flair that it looked stylish on her.

Rochdale walked with her back to the King's Head so she could change into the new clothes. He helped her to undress, and soon they were naked on the bed together. They made love again, though she must have been sore from the three times last night and the slow, lazy coupling that morning.

Now that he'd had her, he couldn't seem to get enough of her. No doubt the novelty would soon wear off, but for now he was obsessed with her. And more than a little besotted.

Grace had always been beautiful, but she had blossomed overnight into a radiant creature full of merriment. She smiled constantly. Her gray eyes never stopped twinkling. And she laughed often. That rich, throaty laugh added to the notion that she was his doxy. It was a laugh straight out of the bedroom.

Their first lovemaking had been new and shocking to her, but every one since then had seen her uninhibited, experimental, and even playful. She was open to anything, and he had taught her how to please him as well as herself. He had never been with a woman who was so thoroughly honest in her sexuality, without pretense or artifice, frank in her pleasure, open to providing pleasure to him. It was refreshing to be with someone who was not practiced or jaded, someone who genuinely enjoyed being with him.

Rochdale was accustomed to women who were thrilled by his dangerous, wicked reputation, and used him for adventure. It was different with Grace. She wanted him not for the thrill of the forbidden, but for . . . him. She wanted *him*. The realization threatened to suck the air clean out of his lungs.

"We'd better hurry if we are to place your bet," he said, lacing up her stays. "We have already missed the first race."

She looked over her shoulder. "Oh, no, tell me we haven't missed Serenity's run."

"Not a chance. I would not have allowed you to distract me if she were running next."

"Ah, but you are so easily distracted, my lord."

She grinned flirtatiously, and bounced about the room like a giddy schoolgirl as she dressed. Her high spirits were infectious, and the two of them left the inn grinning like a couple of fools.

He took her to one of the betting posts, where she placed a small wager on Serenity to win. Since the odds were in Serenity's favor, Grace would recoup very little from her wager, but the very act of placing the bet excited her.

"The only other wager I've ever made in my life," she said, "was the one with you about the line from Proverbs."

"And look where that wager got you."

She smiled and wiggled her eyebrows up and down suggestively. "Yes, look where it got me. In Newmarket with a dashing gamester."

They were jostled and nudged by men eager to place bets. Rochdale kept Grace close at his side as he steered them through the crowd, and she kept her head bowed, as he'd requested. Several gentlemen of his acquaintance approached Rochdale outside the betting post, consulting him on the upcoming races, asking his opinion on various horses, and so on. Grace remained silent by his side. Some gentlemen ignored her completely; others eyed her with interest. Rochdale did not encourage any of them to ask about her or speak to her, and fortunately, they did not.

He'd hired a viewing box from which to watch the race. It was one of the royal boxes, not in use during a privately funded race, set well above the course and away from the prying eyes of nosy Corinthians. It was large enough to hold a sizable party, but Rochdale had reserved the entire box for just the two of them.

It was ornately decorated in red and gold, but Grace expressed surprise at the shabbiness of the furnishings.

"This doesn't look worthy of royalty to me," she said.

"The crown is responsible for maintenance of the boxes," he told her, "though it cannot be high among their priorities at the moment."

Since no one could see into the box—unless he was riding past on horseback, in which case he would have other things on his mind and in his sights—Grace removed her veil so she could get a better look at the action.

She peppered Rochdale with questions about the track, the rules, the colors—Rochdale's riders always wore black and red—and the horses. She was fascinated by the judge's box, a large open-air structure on wheels that was moved from one winning post to another. Their viewing box was adjacent to the current winning post, so they would have a good view of the end of the race.

The courses were short today, only a mile and a half, so there were several races. Grace was overwhelmed by the noise of the first race: the pounding of dozens of hooves on the dirt track, the shouts of the jockeys, the louder shouts from the spectators. As they passed beneath their window, the horses sounded like a thundering herd about to careen smack into the box, and Grace grabbed on to Rochdale as though in fear for her life. By the second time around, she had become accustomed to the din and was sitting on the edge of her chair, caught up in the race, leaning forward to glimpse the winner's colors displayed by the judges.

By the time Serenity's race began, Grace had left her chair altogether and was standing at the window. Rochdale watched his prize mare closely, making sure that O'Malley, the little jockey from Kildare, was not running her too hard or too close. But his attention was drawn to Grace, who was so overcome with excitement when Serenity took the lead that she bounced all over and shouted along with the rowdy crowd in the grandstands below, pumping her hand in the air. The finish looked like it would be close, but at the last instant O'Malley whipped the mare into a final sprint, and she crossed the line in the lead by half a length or more.

When the judges waved the red-and-black flag to indicate Rochdale's victory, Grace shrieked and threw her arms around him while still jumping up and down. She rained kisses on his face, laughing joyously, and he lifted her off the ground and swung her around and around.

Rochdale had been watching horse races for most of his life, but he'd never enjoyed a finish more than at that moment. He'd become so involved in the details of breeding and training, and even the complexities of odds and betting, that he'd lost some of the pure enjoyment of the sport. He found it again that day, by watching Grace.

"Oh, John, that was the most exciting thing ever! How stupid that I never thought to go to a horse race before. I can't remember when I've had so much fun. And I won my bet!"

"We must return to a betting post to collect your vast winnings, my dear. And I should go congratulate Serenity and O'Malley."

But she would not let go of him, keeping her arms tight around his neck. "I've had the most wonderful time, John. Thank you for bringing me here with you." And she kissed him, sweetly and briefly, without passion.

His heart did a little dance in his chest as he looked into her bright eyes. In that instant, he knew he was falling in love with her, with this new Grace—passionate and radiant with happiness. No, she was not new. She was renewed. The fire and passion had always been there. They just needed letting out. He kissed her back with equal tenderness, and the look in her eyes afterward knocked the breath clear out of him.

They left the box arm in arm, and several men shouted out bawdy remarks he wished Grace did not have to hear. But she pressed herself closer against him and laughed. The sultry sound brought more whistles and hoots, which made her laugh more. He wondered if she had ever laughed so much as she had in the last two days.

They made their way to a secondary track, where O'Malley was walking Serenity to cool her down. Rochdale put an arm around her slick, warm neck and blew into her nostrils. "You're a fine lady," he crooned softly, so that only she could hear. "The finest there ever was. Thank you for this victory, and all the others as well. You make me so proud. I fear there will never be another like you, my girl. Unless we find a fine Arab worthy to cover you someday. But not for a few years yet. For now, you just keep running like the wind, my fine Irish darling."

He rested his cheek affectionately against her neck and gave her a quick scratch between the ears. He stood back and beamed at her like a proud father. Serenity responded by playfully knocking his hat off. When he bent to pick it up, she nudged his bottom. Grace laughed delightedly and stroked the mare's neck, congratulating her on the win, and for treating her owner like the rogue he was.

As they walked away, Grace said, "Oh, I do like her, John. She has a charming, mischievous personality. Just like her owner."

"I love her madly," Rochdale said. "She is the best horse I ever had."

"And you run her next at Goodwood later in the month?"

"Yes. She goes back to Bettisfont until then."

"I should like to see her run at Goodwood," Grace said. "Perhaps you will invite me."

Rochdale looked at her and grinned. "What a brazen hussy you have become."

She laughed. "I know. Isn't it wonderful?"

"Come along, my little doxy. We must collect your winnings."

They strolled arm in arm to the nearest betting post, waited for the rush of bettors for the next race to disperse, then cashed in her wager. It was only a matter of a few pounds, but Grace giggled with glee at having won at all.

As they turned to leave, Rochdale saw a familiar round figure approaching. Damnation, it was Lord Sheane, with that same ladybird on his arm he'd had with him at the opera. Rochdale quickly glanced at Grace to ensure her veil was in place.

He put his arm around her. "Turn your face into my shoulder," he whispered. "A London acquaintance is coming near and will no doubt speak to me. He knows you, for I have seen him at your charity balls, and he tried to insinuate himself into our box at the opera. He is just the sort of fellow who will spread tales if he recognizes you. Take care, my dear. Here he comes." He tightened his arm around her and turned her so her face was hidden against his shoulder.

"Rochdale! Well met, old man." Sheane was dressed as usual, in a gaudy waistcoat that served to accentuate his girth. The buxom young redhead on his arm was no less gaudy, with too much jewelry dripping from her neck and too many plumes on her bonnet.

"Sheane." Rochdale nodded an acknowledgment.

"I just saw that mare of yours take the last race," Sheane said. "A fine horse. It would be a shame to lose her, would it not?"

"She ran a good race. But if you will excuse us, I have business to attend to."

"And, if I may be so bold to observe, you also have

bigger fish to fry than this bit of muslin clinging to you like lint on velvet. One large Christian fish in particular. Goodwood is less than a month away. Time is running short. Of course, the more you dawdle here, the better it is for me, is it not? My stable awaits its newest occupant."

"Good day to you, Sheane." Rochdale moved away quickly before the wretched fellow could say more.

"What was that all about?" Grace asked when he finally released his death grip on her. "What did he mean about a large Christian fish?"

Rochdale waved away her question with a flick of his fingers. "Nothing to concern you, my dear. It has to do with horse breeding. Euphemisms for certain intimate animal behaviors you would not care to know about, I assure you. Now, let us go see about that purse Serenity just won for me."

It was surely one of the happiest days of her life. The skies were blue, the sun was bright, and all was right with the world. With her world, anyway. Grace had become a Merry Widow at last, probably the merriest widow of them all. She was so pleased with herself that her cheeks hurt from smiling. She was ready to burst with joy.

All because she had allowed Rochdale to become her lover.

Being with him had changed her even more completely than she had expected. Awakening the passions in her body seemed to have stirred every sense into new life. Everything was more vivid, in the way a shortsighted person might feel when putting on spectacles for the first time. Colors were brighter, sounds clearer, flowers more fragrant, food more flavorful. And she felt as though she wore a new skin. She was sensitive to everything that touched it, aware of the textures of every fabric, aware even of the air upon it. And she relished every new sensation. It seemed she had been slumbering through all of her life, and only now had come awake.

Newmarket, as it happened, was a grand place to be when one's physical being was awakened. There was so much to stimulate the senses. The crowds of people, the horses, the turf, the heath. And Rochdale. Nothing brought her senses to life as he did.

Grace stood to the side as he spoke with a gentleman outside the Jockey Club about the purse Serenity had won. Her eyes greedily drank in the sight of him. She could no longer look at him without picturing the body beneath the finely tailored coat and tight-fitting pantaloons. She was acutely aware now of how tight they really were, aware of every muscle and contour. He was as beautiful an animal as Serenity. Each movement sleek and powerful, sinuous and graceful. She could not take her eyes off him, and was glad the veil shielded her face. If anyone were to see it, they would know she was as smitten as a schoolgirl.

Her feelings for Rochdale were too jumbled up to express. They had spoken of everything together, but not about this, about how they felt. Grace's emotions were so intense, so singular, it had to be love. Or was it simply the rush of her first real sexual encounter— the novelty of pure carnal lust? She thought it was more than that, but was not inclined to examine her feelings more closely, especially since Rochdale had spoken no words of love to her. He would not, of course. This sort of thing was routine for him. If she were to lay bare her confused heart to him, he would no doubt think her naïve and foolish. So she said nothing. But her heart was full and her spirit sang.

They remained at the racecourse for several hours, taking in a few more races, with Grace placing more bets and winning. They visited the stables again, where Rochdale discussed with Samuel Trask plans for returning Serenity to Bettisfont. When they finally made the walk back to the King's Head, fatigue was causing

Grace to flag. Considering how little sleep she'd had the night before, it was no wonder.

"I have only just realized," she said as they approached the inn, "that we are staying a second night here. I mean, of course we are, but how strange that I have not been thinking of going back home."

"I had hoped for another night with you," he said. "One night was not enough."

She smiled at him. "No, it was not." How many nights would be enough? How long would this hunger for him last? "Besides, I would not have missed today for all the world. It was such fun, John."

"I'm glad you enjoyed it. But we still have the night. There is yet more to be enjoyed."

And so there was. After a brief supper, they fell into bed together again, neither of them willing to waste a single moment.

Rochdale knew exactly how to give a woman pleasure while taking his own. He moved her expertly into positions she'd never imagined. The fact of all that knowledge and how he had achieved it ought to have been off-putting. But she found she was glad for his vast experience, for she was certainly benefiting from it. She laughed aloud as she suddenly realized why rakes were so popular with women. Of course they were! And hadn't Marianne told her of the benefits of having a rake for a lover? Grace also found that his history with women in some odd way allowed her to trust him. It was purely a physical trust and not emotional—she was not ready to tread those dangerous waters yet—and it allowed her to open herself completely to him. There was no part of her, inside or out, that she did not want him to touch. She wanted him everywhere on her and in her. If he could have crawled inside her skin, she would have allowed it.

Tonight, he rolled beneath her and had her straddle him. He lifted her hips and eased her down onto his erection. "Your turn, Grace. Ride me."

She had never imagined a woman could have control like this, but he encouraged it, and so she took charge. Placing her hands on his shoulders, she pulled up and then slid down his erection, repeating the movement again and again in a slow gliding motion. She looked down at him as she moved, a man in the throes of agony or ecstasy or both. His head was thrown back, his neck arched, but his heavy-lidded eyes remained open, barely, as he watched her.

"Yes, yes, that's it," he said, his hips moving up to meet hers. "Ride me, Grace. Ride me hard."

And she did. Finding just the right angle to produce just the right friction, she rode him with increasing dominance, taking all she wanted and more. Finally, her release was so explosive, so thoroughly shattering, that she could do nothing but collapse upon his chest, breathless.

He pushed up hard into her once, twice, then quickly rolled her under him and pulled out, releasing onto the sheet.

They lay side by side for several minutes, neither of them willing or able to stir. She had watched him in passion. Now it was pure pleasure to study him in repose, to take in every detail of his body. It was an extravagance that she indulged with wonder, like a child who had been presented with a grand new toy, or a new pony.

Finally, he rose, as he always did, and saw to cleaning them both. After the first time, when he'd given her privacy to clean herself, she had ever since allowed him to minister to her. She enjoyed his gentleness and his care.

When he came back to bed and gathered her into his arms, neither of them seemed ready to sleep. She lay on her side and watched him, studying his face, admiring every beautiful part of it. "Some say you have bedroom eyes, but I never knew what it meant. Now I do."

"Bedroom eyes?"

"Yes. They have a look about them—smug, self-satisfied, lethargic—as if you had just risen from a woman's bed."

"Do they look that way now?"

She smiled. "Yes, they do."

"Good. Because that is exactly how I feel. Smug, for being the only man to have discovered the secret passions of Grace Marlowe. Self-satisfied for having enjoyed an extraordinary bout of lovemaking with her. And lethargic because she has taken from me all I can give and I am spent."

"You must carry that feeling with you all the time. Or have you learned to mimic it?"

"All I need do is think of a moment like this, and my eyes grow heavy with desire. But what about you? I may have bedroom eyes, but you have a bedroom laugh."

"A what?"

"When you laugh, it is husky and intimate, as if you've just had a good loving."

She laughed.

"You see? That's exactly the sound. Every man who hears that laugh imagines hearing it in bed. I certainly did the first time I heard it."

"What a pair we are, then, to always be making people think of beds."

They continued in lazy conversation while his hands gently stroked her hip, and hers traveled over his chest. They talked of Serenity and wagers and why he liked to gamble. And of the Fletcher family, who would be relocating to Bettisfont next week.

All at once, triggered by thoughts of his generosity, a wayward thought entered Grace's mind. "You never made Serena Underwood pregnant, did you?"

He raised his eyebrows. "What makes you think that? We were lovers."

"But you are more careful than that. Look how much effort you made to ensure no one recognized me today. And . . . and how you take care not to . . . to finish inside me. I think you are far too protective of women to have made her pregnant and abandoned her."

"I protect myself, Grace, make no mistake. I want no accidental babe trapping me into marriage."

"And yet Serena had a child."

"So I have been told."

"It was not your child, was it?"

He allowed a long silence to fall between them, and she wondered if she had been wrong.

"No," he said at last. "It was not my child. I doubt she knew whose it was. But do not absolve me of all blame. I did seduce her. And had I been a gentleman, I would have married her, regardless of the child's paternity. Instead, I walked away, leaving her alone and helpless."

"But it's not the entirely hateful tale that you allow to be spread. You could have let it be known that it was not your child. Instead, you allow people to think the worst of you."

"Better the worst of me than the worst of her. I had no desire to reveal her true nature to all and sundry. So I allowed her to use me as an excuse for her predicament. It did her some good and me no harm. I was already labeled a scoundrel by then."

"But it is only a label, as you have said so often to me. A label just like mine of the Bishop's Widow. They don't define us. You aren't entirely bad and I'm not entirely good."

His hand moved up to cup her breast. "Oh, but you are, Grace. You are very, very good."

He kissed her, and within a moment passion flared to life again. They made love slowly and easily at first, then more frantically, finally collapsing into an exhausted, tangled, satisfied heap. Rochdale fell asleep at once. Grace lay awake a bit longer, thinking of the return to London tomorrow and what would happen.

Here at Newmarket, with Rochdale, she had become a new woman. No, she had become herself. Completely without inhibition, she did and said what she pleased. She opened herself to him as she had with no other person, not even her friends, certainly not her husband. Back in London she would have to don her cloak of respectability. She could not completely abandon her old life and all the work she did. But inside she now knew who Grace Marlowe really was. And maybe now and then, perhaps with Rochdale, she would allow the real Grace to be revealed again.

Chapter 15

"At Newmarket, I became a new kind of fool, Cazenove. I went soft. I lost my head." And something else besides. In fact, Rochdale figured he'd lost a great deal, when it came right down to it, and wondered if what he had gained in return was worth it. But then he'd think of Grace in his arms, and nothing else seemed to matter much.

"It serves you right." Adam Cazenove scowled at him from across the thick plank table blackened with age. "It was a despicable wager, even for you."

Rochdale had returned from Newmarket with his head full of Grace Marlowe. At times he would simply sink into vivid recollections of each sexual encounter— a rather significant number of them, considering they had spent only two nights together. He became aroused just thinking of her dropping that nightgown and daring him to make love to her. He'd just as often recall her radiant face, glowing with sexual fulfillment or the thrill of her first horse race, and his heart would melt a little.

At other times, little panicky moments came over him, when he felt trapped. It made no sense, but he could hardly breathe from the sensation that he was pinned like a dead butterfly on a specimen board. Pinned down. Tied up. Trapped. But no one constrained him and nothing held him back. Except

Grace. She held him with her beauty, her passion, her new and radiant happiness, her strength, her courage.

She confounded him. He had felt so off balance since returning to London yesterday that he'd sought out Cazenove, hoping for some masculine commiseration and good sense. Sitting in their favorite old-fashioned coffeehouse, the Raven on Fetter Lane, away from the prying eyes and ears of Mayfair or St. James's Street, Rochdale had confessed all to his friend. And had been roundly rebuked.

"If you have fallen in love with the woman," Cazenove said, "then I say it is what you deserve for allowing Sheane to drag you into such a damned fool wager. You deserve the pain and heartache and general feeling of having entered Bedlam that comes when a woman takes possession of your heart. It's an unsettling business, but you will survive. I did, and have never been more content in my life."

A roar of laughter from a group of men seated near the huge open fireplace rose above the general din. The squealing giggle of a serving girl followed, and Rochdale looked over just in time to see a bewigged old fellow pinching her bottom. The pink-cheeked girl in a huge mob cap wagged her finger at him and appeared to scold him, though her face was wreathed in a broad grin. The old man and his companions, all dressed in the style of twenty or more years ago, could be found in that same spot by the fire almost every day. Sometimes they drank the splendid coffee served there, and other times partook of a bowl of rum punch. A large blue-and-white bowl on their table, plus the bawdy behavior, indicated that this was one of their punch days.

Rochdale wondered if he and Cazenove would still be holding down their regular table in another thirty years, reminiscing of the old days and flirting with the serving girls.

Alfred, the head waiter and another permanent fixture of the Raven, approached with a tray. He placed a pottery cup in front of each of them, then poured steaming dark coffee from a tall white pot. Leaving the pot on the table, along with a bowl of coarse sugar chunks, a creamer, and two spoons, he tucked the tray under his arm and disappeared without a word.

Rochdale took a sip of the rich brew, found it to be too hot, and set it down to cool. "This thing with Grace," he said, getting back to the business at hand, "it isn't like you and Marianne. You knew her for years."

"Yes, but falling in love with her took me completely by surprise." Cazenove dropped a lump of sugar into his coffee and stirred. "Just as it has with you."

"I don't know if it's love. It's definitely obsession. I can't get the blasted woman out of my mind. If you can believe it, I can't seem to work up interest in any other women. To be honest, I haven't been with another woman since I began my pursuit of Grace. She's had me entranced for weeks. And now . . . now I fear she has spoiled me for anyone else."

Cazenove's eyebrows shot up and he flashed a wicked grin. "The devil you say! She was that good?"

"That's not what I meant, though she was . . . well, that is none of your damned business. But, unlike most other women I've been involved with, she is not a conniving bitch. She's . . . a good woman, a decent woman. Genuine, truehearted, unjaded. Artless as a newborn colt. It's been a long time since I've known such a woman. If ever."

"Because you deliberately avoid decent woman. But they are out there, my friend. Marianne is such a woman."

"Don't point fingers, Cazenove. Up until a few months ago, you followed the same path as me. A parade of willing women in your bed. Demireps and doxies, titled women with loose morals, anyone available for a quick shag or two and nothing more. Neither of us sought out decent women."

In fact, Rochdale had convinced himself years ago that women like Grace, or Cazenove's Marianne, truly good and worthy women who were not scheming or manipulative or grasping, did not exist. Those who pretended to be good and decent were the worst, hiding their plots and machinations behind masks of propriety, and he did indeed avoid such women. Instead, he sought out willing widows and unscrupulous wives and the occasional highborn young slut, like Serena Underwood.

Cazenove took a long sip of coffee and said, "Yes, I would have to say that, over the years, we both have played the licentious rake to perfection. I am not sorry that my rakish days are over. I have no desire to be with any woman other than Marianne. Did you ever know old Lord Monksilver?"

"Can't say as I did."

"A jolly old sort who'd cut quite a dash in his youth. I met him when I was just out of university, a young pup ready to hump anything in skirts. I've never forgotten what he said to me. He told me I could have sex with a different woman every night for years on end, but then one day the right woman would come along, and I would never want another woman in my bed again." Cazenove chuckled. "The old fellow was right. Maybe Grace Marlowe is that woman for you."

"I honestly do not know if she is, but I will tell you something, Cazenove. I'm tired of being a so-called libertine. Do you know that most of the women I've been with felt anonymous to me? They meant nothing to me. They could have been nameless and faceless, as long as their bodies were desirable. In bed, one was much the same as the next. Between you and me, I find I am tired of that anonymity. The encounters gave me no more than a moment's physical release, and left me empty. I came home hating the smell of perfume and powder on my skin and in my hair."

"And this is only since Grace Marlowe has come into your life?"

"No, I have been getting tired of the game for a while now. Grace has just made me realize how tired." He took a drink of coffee as he pondered how much she had brought into focus for him. "I just don't relish any more of those anonymous encounters. Oh, I still feel the urge. Hell, even that buxom serving maid over there tents my breeches and makes me want to mount her. But it is almost like a reflex, animalistic and base. It's nothing like what I felt with Grace. Somehow she made sex into something new for me. Something . . . important. Even reverent. Damn it all, I'm not making any sense."

"You're making perfect sense. You've just discovered how love changes everything, even sex. Especially sex. It will never be the same for you, my friend. You had better marry her."

Rochdale snorted. "She'd never have me. And I don't think she wants that from me. She is still starry-eyed from newly discovered lust—she obviously never had more than a quick poke and a grunt from the old bishop—but I don't believe it goes any further than that. There was an unspoken acknowledgment between us that Newmarket and anything beyond is only what it is . . . a discreet affair and nothing more."

"Will she allow it to continue here in London?"

"I assume so. She made it sound as if she wanted to be with me again. We made plans to go to Drury Lane next week, so I am hoping we will resume our affair that evening."

Cazenove lifted an eyebrow. "And if not? If she decides it's too risky to see you in town, or has second thoughts about an affair at all?"

"Then I fear I am destined for a monastic existence, at least for a while."

"And what of the wager? What if she finds out you made love to her only to win a horse?"

"She won't find out because I will not win."

"But you *did* win."

"As far as Sheane is concerned, I did not win. I am going to tell him tomorrow that I concede defeat."

Cazenove almost dropped his cup and had to steady it with both hands. "And you will lose Serenity?"

Rochdale shrugged. "That is the price I must pay for having involved Grace in this damnable business. Even if she never learns of the wager, I find the idea that she gave herself to me in exchange for a horse to be intolerable. So there will be no exchange."

Cazenove smiled. "And this is precisely why a woman like Grace Marlowe is drawn to you. Deep down, my friend, you're a good man."

Rochdale winced. "Don't go spreading any rumors. I've got a reputation to protect."

Grace paced anxiously in the rose garden behind Marlowe House, the gravel crunching loudly beneath her half boots. Today was the last gathering of the trustees of the Benevolent Widows Fund before some of them left town for one of the spas or country estates. They met here as a group regularly while they were all in town, going over the lists of residents and reviewing any progress made in finding permanent situations for them, and generally inspecting all the workings of the house. Each of them visited on their own more frequently, but they gathered together at least once a month in their formal capacity as the board of trustees.

Grace, however, did not have board business on her mind. She was fairly bursting to tell them her news, but she wanted all of them to be present, and Penelope had yet to arrive.

"Is something troubling you, Grace?" Beatrice, seated on one of the stone benches that lined the gravel paths, looked at her with concern. "You seem very . . . anxious. Is everything all right?"

"Oh, yes. Everything is fine." She suppressed a giggle. The old Grace Marlowe never giggled. The new one found herself giggling at the oddest moments. "More than fine. I will tell you all about it when—"

"Here at last!" Penelope's breathless voice rose above them as she came dashing down the path from the herb garden. When she reached the arched entrance to the rose garden, thick with the blush pink blooms of a Chinese trailing rose, she paused and fanned herself with a gloved hand. "I am sorry to be late. Eustace dropped by with this cunning little floral offering." She gestured to a pretty cluster of red rosebuds pinned to her bonnet. "Aren't they sweet? And I had to thank him properly, didn't I, before I could dash away."

"Red roses." Marianne was seated on another bench, across from Beatrice. "A sign of love?"

Penelope went to sit beside her and made a great show of arranging her skirts. At last she looked up with an uncharacteristically demure expression. "Yes, as a matter of fact, Eustace has declared his love for me."

Marianne flung an arm around Penelope's shoulder and squeezed. "Oh, Penelope, how marvelous! I knew that man was besotted. And I think you must be in love with him, too. You haven't shown the least interest in any other gentleman since Eustace Tolliver came into your life."

Penelope smiled. "Yes, I will admit that I love the sentimental fool."

"Are you going to put the poor fellow out of his misery," Beatrice said, "and marry him?"

Penelope shrugged. "I haven't decided. I have been enjoying life as a Merry Widow. I don't know if I'm ready to give up my independence again."

"You will find that you can be just as merry as a

wife," Beatrice said, grinning, "as I am sure Marianne will agree."

"Even more so," Marianne said, a wistful look in her eye.

"I hope you will agree to marry him," Grace said. "He looks at you with such longing that I fear you will break his heart if you do not."

"We shall see," Penelope said. "It is rather delicious to have a man so infatuated with me. I do not wish to give in to him too soon. I'd much rather enjoy being wooed for a bit longer."

"Don't be too long about it," Wilhelmina said, bending over a bush of white roses. "He might get tired of waiting. And speaking of Merry Widows"— she straightened and turned to face the group—"I believe Grace has something to tell us."

"Oh my goodness," Penelope said, leaning forward and cocking her head to one side as she studied Grace. "You have that glow about you. Doesn't she, ladies? Just look at her. Grace Marlowe, you sly cat, you have done it, haven't you?"

Grace laughed, then remembered what Rochdale had told her about her laughter, and her cheeks flamed. "Yes, I have. I am now, really and truly, a Merry Widow. Rochdale and I have become lovers."

"How wonderful!"

"I can't believe it!"

"My, oh my."

"With Rochdale?"

"I am so pleased for you, Grace."

"You really are glowing."

"Are you as happy as you look?"

"Are you in love with him?"

"He is said to be one of the best lovers in London."

"Tell us everything."

Swearing them all to secrecy, she told them about Newmarket and Rochdale. Grace owed them the truth, since that had been part of their Merry Widows pact. She was not as comfortable as Penelope or Beatrice in relating the intimate details of their lovemaking, but she did want these women, her dearest friends, to know how she had been changed by it.

"You were right, of course," she said, "all of you, about the importance of physical pleasure in one's life. I just hadn't known what I was missing."

"The old bishop never made your eyes shine like they do now, did he?" Penelope asked.

"No, I am afraid he never did. I do not believe he thought of marital relations as pleasure, but more as coarse urges that men had to give in to from time to time. I am sorry he felt that way, but that's who he was and he could not have changed. I think, now, that I was not the right wife for him. I had those urges from the start, you see, but he would not let me express them. I feel so much more alive and complete now that I have given in to them. I am not the woman he thought I was, a prim paragon of virtue. And I no longer wish to tie myself to his memory as the Bishop's Widow. I need to make my own way in life, as Grace Newbury Marlowe."

"Thank heaven you have finally come to that understanding," Marianne said, reaching out and taking Grace's hand. "It is a life-changing epiphany, is it not? I went through the same thing with David's memory, so tenaciously bound to my identity as his wife and his widow that I couldn't imagine giving that up. I almost lost Adam over it. I am so pleased that you have decided to get beyond the bishop's memory."

"Toward that end," Grace said, "I have decided not to continue with the work I have done in editing his sermons. I am not the right person for the job. Not only is my heart no longer in the work, but I find I can't accept some of what he wrote, especially about the role of women and their inherent weaknesses."

She now understood that her husband had seen women as either black or white, madonnas or whores.

Grace knew in her heart that she was neither of those, and never had been. And neither were any of these women who offered her so much love and support. She could not, therefore, in good conscience put her name on a book of sermons she no longer believed in.

"I applaud you, my girl," Wilhelmina said. "I had not wanted to disparage your late husband, but I never did like the idea of you burying yourself in his hidebound attitudes by editing those sermons. Put them in a drawer and move on to something more interesting."

"Actually," Grace said, "I have decided to bundle them up and take them to Margaret. She has always disapproved of my editing them. I shall turn the project over to her."

"An excellent idea," Beatrice said. "I have always thought she was even more tied to the bishop's memory than you were. More the Bishop's Daughter than the wife of Sir Leonard Bumfries."

"Surely the most henpecked husband in all of London," Penelope added.

"I believe it is only fitting," Wilhelmina said, "that Lady Bumfries edit her father's sermons. It is wise of you, Grace, to allow her to do it. Perhaps it will keep her too busy to be vexed about you and Rochdale."

Grace hoped Margaret would never learn of the extent of her relationship with Rochdale. The Merry Widows would not betray her secret. And though Rochdale hadn't specifically promised he would not tell anyone, she did not believe he would spread tales about her. She had discovered a core of honor in him that she trusted would oblige him to protect her.

Later that afternoon, when she accompanied boxes of the bishop's papers brought to Margaret and Sir Leonard's house on Henrietta Street, her stepdaughter's manner dripped with icy disdain. Margaret said only that she was glad Grace had dropped the project, then ushered her into the morning room on the ground floor while the boxes were carried upstairs to the library.

Margaret did not sit or give any indication that Grace was welcome to stay. Instead, she stood before the fireplace, as stiff as a poker, hands clasped tightly at her waist.

"If you had not brought the bishop's papers," she said in a voice that bristled like a cat's fur, "I should have come to collect them. After the spectacle you have made of yourself with that . . . that scoundrel, you are no longer fit even to handle them, much less edit them."

A tremor of anxiety danced down Grace's spine. Margaret could not possibly know about Newmarket. At least Grace prayed she did not. "I have told you, Margaret, that Lord Rochdale is a major patron, the most significant patron, of Marlowe House and the Benevolent Widows Fund. I have not—"

"I shudder to think what you have given him in return."

"Margaret! What a hateful thing to say."

"I am only grateful that you have turned over Father's papers voluntarily and not forced me into public battle with you over them. Because there is no way in heaven I would have allowed your name to sully the work of such a great and pious man. Not after what I have heard."

Grace had to wonder again if Margaret knew about Newmarket. But she simply couldn't believe it. Her own household staff did not know where she'd been. It was unlikely she had been recognized there. The veils had been effective masks, and the only people to see her without a veil were the dressmaker and milliner, who believed her to be "Marie."

Grace was greatly tempted to simply turn and walk away, tired of Margaret's self-righteousness. But curiosity compelled her to discover what Margaret knew, or thought she knew. "I have no idea what you are talking about that could be so shocking. Unless you believe sharing Lord Rochdale's box at the opera somehow puts me beyond the pale."

Margaret uttered a contemptuous huff. "To be seen on that man's arm in public is bad enough. I cannot believe you have so little concern for your name and position. But when you become the object of a wager between two lecherous scoundrels, it is simply too much."

A wager? Dear God, had she become fodder for the betting books at White's and other gentlemen's clubs? How mortifying. Heat rose in her cheeks at the very idea. It was common knowledge that wagers were often logged in the betting books regarding the outcome of various courtships: Mr. Smith will marry Miss Jones before Michaelmas, or Miss Jones will reject a proposal of marriage from Mr. Smith. Surely they were not wagering that Rochdale would marry her. From what she had learned about odds, such a wager would be far too risky.

"I know of no wager," she said, "but I cannot be held responsible for the thoughtless cruelty of certain gentlemen, no doubt in their cups, who make game of respectable women in the betting books by wagering on the outcome of courtships and weddings."

"From what I hear, it had nothing to do with a respectable courtship. On the contrary, it was something much more . . . unsavory."

The merest flush of alarm prickled Grace's skin. "Either tell me your gossip or don't. I have no patience for your innuendos."

Margaret's face pinched up into an angry scowl. "I do *not* gossip. You cannot imagine I would take pleasure in spreading tales about my father's wife. But I cannot help it if I happen to hear things. And what I heard shocked me to the core."

Grace glared at her, not willing to give her the satisfaction of asking what she'd heard. She knew Margaret would tell her anyway. It was what she was dying to do.

"Mrs. Randall heard it from Lady Handley, who heard it from her husband, who heard it from Sir Giles Clitheroe, who was there when the wager was made. Apparently Lord Sheane bet Lord Rochdale that he could not seduce a certain woman. Speculation is that the woman is you."

The words stung her like the barbs they were meant to be. There was a moment of almost physical pain, a sharp twitch across her chest and throat, and then a flush down her arms and legs that felt like a fever.

"Given the amount of time Lord Rochdale has been spending with you," Margaret continued, "the speculation seems logical, don't you think? And that large donation to your charity . . . it is suspicious, you have to agree." A glint of triumph shone in her eyes.

Grace was finding it difficult to breathe, but she managed to say, "That is quite enough, Margaret."

"What a fool you have made of yourself. I should have thought you had more strength of character than to be susceptible to a bit of flattery from a horrid man like that. You know what he did to Serena Underwood last year. He is a blackguard and a cad, and yet you let him . . . Dear God in heaven, have you no shame? If not for yourself, at least for staining the memory of the great man whose name you still bear? Don't you realize how much your behavior reflects on him, on all of us? Selfish, foolish woman!"

Grace had to leave. She could not listen to any more of this. A hint of dizziness put her off balance—dear God, don't let her swoon!—but she called upon every reserve of calm within her. She tried to collect herself, tried to put on that cloak of cool reserve she wore so well. But she could not do it. She was too disjointed, frazzled, shattered in too many pieces. She was uncollectible.

After a deep breath, she was able to slowly turn and make her way out of the room.

"You will go straight to hell for this!" Margaret called out from behind her. "Straight to hell! Harlot! Wanton! Whore!"

Margaret's taunts filled the air as Grace stumbled out the front door. A footman guided her into the carriage and shot her a concerned look as he closed the door. She fell heavily against the squabs, limp as a rag doll, and utterly dumbfounded.

It had all been for a wager. He had never cared for her in the least, never truly desired her.

Margaret was right. She had made a fool of herself, had fallen right into Rochdale's trap, lured by his seductive charm and his pretense of friendship. How he must have laughed at her, the prim, inexperienced widow who knew nothing of physical passion. And what an easy mark she had been, ready to break free, ready to experience all that her friends had described.

She groaned aloud and clutched her chest as she recalled Newmarket and how happy she had been there. He had become much more than a friend to her. She had fallen in love with him. She loved him. And there had been moments when she thought he loved her a little, too. But all that gentleness and compassion, all that understanding and consideration, had been nothing more than an act to get her into bed.

Because she was a challenge worthy of a wager. A woman immune to seduction. A woman so prudish and proper that Lord Sheane thought she could never be seduced.

And yet, somehow Rochdale had believed he could do it. And he was right. All the times when he had been encouraging her to find her own way, to make her own identity, had been a part of the seduction. All the times he allowed her to see a hint of something good in him had been a part of the seduction. The donation to Marlowe House, the display of compassion for Toby Fletcher, had all been a part of the seduction. By heaven, the man was skilled. A master of the game. He had known exactly how to play her, to make her want him.

Even that scene in Newmarket the first night, when he said he couldn't go through with it and left her, even that had been a part of the plan. And Grace had done precisely what he'd expected. She had stripped bare and invited him to make love to her. What a brilliant move on his part. He could claim that it was Grace who had done the seducing. Oh, what a devil he was!

And what had he won? No, what had she won for him? What was the challenge worth?

Suddenly she remembered the brief conversation between Rochdale and Lord Sheane at Newmarket.

A fine horse, Lord Sheane had said. *It would be a shame to lose her, would it not?*

So Rochdale had been arrogant enough to offer Serenity as his stake in the wager. He must have been damned sure of himself, for that horse meant the world to him and Grace knew he would never do anything to lose it.

He cared more for the horse than he did for her. He had never cared for her at all. She ought to have known such a man could never have a genuine interest in her, a woman so opposite him in every way. Despite what he had so often said, he had not, after all, wanted her for herself, for Grace Marlowe, that new woman he had coaxed out of her with his charm and his kisses and his false friendship, but had in fact wanted the Bishop's Widow. The tight-laced, virtuous, oh-so-proper widow of the famous man. *She* was the challenge.

By the time the carriage arrived at Portland Place, Grace was stricken with despair. Ignoring the butler's indication of a tray of receiving cards and a maid's offer to have tea prepared, she climbed the stairs to her suite of rooms, went into the bedchamber, and locked the door. She carefully removed her bonnet and pelisse and put them away so that Kitty would not fuss at her, then flung herself facedown on the bed and wept.

Grace did not leave her bedchamber the rest of that day or the next. She accepted meals brought to her on trays, but found she could eat very little. Most of her time was spent in bed, sleeping a little, crying a lot, and generally feeling sorry for herself.

She had never felt so betrayed, so abominably used. The love she had begun to feel for Rochdale in Newmarket, that affection she hadn't been ready to name, had developed into a full-blown romantic passion. And because he hadn't cared for her at all, she decided her heart had been irrevocably broken. She wallowed in the pain of it.

She came to realize, while lying in bed and staring at the underside of the canopy, that she ought never to have tried to be something she was not. She was the wife and widow of Bishop Marlowe and always would be. It was something to be proud of, not to be discarded. It had been a terrible mistake to sacrifice that comfortable, important identity for something new and mad and thoroughly improper.

Between bouts of self-pity and tears, Grace considered how to put her life back together. She could not undo what had taken place between her and Rochdale. But she could go on as though it had never happened. She would became the most proper Christian woman who ever lived, and her reputation would be salvaged.

Just as she became convinced she could do it, she fell into despair again at the thought that her good name could never be rehabilitated. She was lost. She was miserable. She was heartbroken.

And the cycle of hope and hopelessness continued. By the morning of her second full day in bed, Grace had become tired of despair, tired of tears, tired of self-pity. Overnight, despondency had turned to anger. She bounded out of bed and pulled the curtains back from the windows to relieve the gloom. By God, she would not let him do this to her. She refused to be turned into some sort of pathetic, woeful creature. Grace Marlowe had never given in to weakness in her life, and she would not start now.

She rang for her maid and began pulling clothes out of the press, muttering to herself, chastising herself aloud. She would not allow that scoundrel Rochdale to turn her into a wounded weakling, not after she had made so many positive changes in her life. He had endlessly provoked her and challenged her until she discovered the real woman beneath the public persona of respectable widow and do-gooder. And damned if she didn't like this new woman better than her former self.

How dare Rochdale give her a new outlook on life and then negate it all by using her as the means to win a bet. How dare he treat her with such insolent disregard. How dare he manipulate her.

He would not get away with it. For Grace Marlowe, strong and independent and proud, was not going to let him off the hook.

The door opened and Kitty walked in, looking wary. "Are you feeling better today, ma'am?"

"Much. Send up hot water, if you please. I need to wash. And a pot of tea as well. And bread and jam. Perhaps some eggs. A bit of ham, if there is some. Then come and help me dress. The new sprigged muslin and the pink sarsnet spencer with the Maltese buttons."

"You are going out, ma'am?"

"Indeed I am. I have to see a man about a horse."

Chapter 16

"What is it, Parker?"

Rochdale's butler looked uncharacteristically flustered as he stood in the door of the breakfast room.

"A lady to see you, my lord."

"A lady?" Surely not. Ladies did not come to a gentleman's house in the bold light of morning, if at all. And if she did, chances were she was no lady.

"A Mrs. Marlowe, my lord. I have put her in the drawing room."

Good God, Grace was here? Was she mad? Someone might have seen her. Rochdale rose so quickly he almost knocked his chair over. She had been adamant about maintaining discretion here in London, even more so than in Newmarket, for she was well known in town and could hardly run around in a disguise in order to be with him. Perhaps she had grown too impatient for their evening at the theater tomorrow and her famous decorum had deserted her. But it was sheer madness to come to his town house at this hour when all the world might see her.

He, too, had been waiting, rather impatiently, for tomorrow night, and had made enormous efforts not to seek her out and carry her into some dark corner and have his way with her. He wanted her badly, desperately. But not here in this house. Not in this den of iniquity, where so many of his worst debaucheries had taken place. The thought of Grace even stepping foot on the same carpet where other, less respectable feet had trod—where various couples had rolled and frolicked with abandon when his gambling parties had disintegrated into orgies—made him feel ill.

He hurried to the drawing room but came to a halt when he reached the door. Grace stood in the middle of the room, looking as stiff and grave as a statue. All of the cheerful brightness that had shone from her eyes in Newmarket and on the drive back to town was gone. Instead her eyes were as hard and cold as chips of gray agate. Her eyebrows knit together in a frown so tightly that they formed deep furrows above the bridge of her nose.

Something was wrong. A knot of anxiety began to twist in his gut.

He ignored it and walked into the room, hands outstretched to take hers. "My dear Grace, I am delighted to see you." And he was. It had only been a few days, but it felt like forever.

She did not take his hands, but kept hers tightly clenched at her sides. "You bloody bastard."

He gave a start and took a step backward; it was such a shock to hear the words from her lips. Despite the naked passion they'd shared, she was still a proper lady who never used profanity.

The knot in his belly tightened.

"Perhaps you had better sit down," he said, indicating a nearby settee. "You are upset."

"I am beyond upset."

She made no move to be seated, so he simply stood before her, hands behind his back, waiting to hear what heinous thing she had learned about him. The choices were legion, though there was one particularly loathsome act he hoped she had not discovered.

"A rumor has been passed along to me," she said in a voice as brittle and sharp as a sliver of broken glass. "A particularly unpleasant rumor, related to me by a member of my own family."

Oh, God. Please let it not be what he suspected. Please let it be something else. He did not speak, but lifted his eyebrows in a reluctant invitation for her to continue.

"I want to know if it is true."

He maintained his silence but kept his gaze steady on hers, even as the knot grew thicker and more twisted in his gut.

"Did you make a wager with Lord Sheane that you could seduce me?"

Rochdale closed his eyes as the pain in his belly—or was it his heart?—became a punishment. Hell and damnation. How was he to face her? How was he to open his eyes and look into hers? What could he possibly say to make it any less hurtful? Of all the women he'd ever known, she was the one, the only one, he never wanted to hurt. He had not felt that way about her at first, of course, when this wretched business had begun. He hadn't cared about her at all then, because she was just a woman like all the others. Or so he had believed. But she was not like anyone else and did not deserve what he had done to her. And it was too late to do anything about it.

He blew out a breath and opened his eyes. There was only one answer he could give her. "Yes."

Her face collapsed into a mask of pure misery; then she covered her mouth and turned away, as if she might become sick. He moved closer, but she waved him off with her other hand.

"Oh, Grace, my dear Grace, I cannot tell you how sorry I am. Yes, it started out as a wager, but it became something else entirely. At Newmarket—"

She whirled around, and rather than the anguish he'd expected, her eyes blazed and her face was pink with fury. "How *could* you? How could you be so vile? Oh, but of course. You are the notorious Lord

Rochdale, the famous debaucher of women, the callous rake, the unscrupulous libertine. Why should I have ever expected otherwise from you? Oh, you are heartless, my lord. I was a decent, respectable woman before you entered my life. But you were so smooth, so charming, a practiced seducer who knew exactly know to manipulate the prudish widow into your bed. No wonder you were so quick to accept Lord Sheane's wager. You knew how to break me, you knew where I was vulnerable, and you poured your poisonous charm in all the right places to ensure my capitulation."

Rochdale wanted to explain that the wager didn't matter now, that he had come to care for her, but she was riding her fury and did not allow him to interrupt.

"The bishop warned me. 'You are a beautiful woman,' he said, 'and men will covet you. Unscrupulous men who will flatter and beguile and try to coerce you into wicked behavior. But you must stand firm against them, for your very soul is at stake.' And he was right. You have robbed me of my soul, my dignity, all for the sake of a horse. A horse! How could I have been so stupid to allow you to make me distrust *everything* the bishop taught me when he was obviously right on at least one count."

"Grace, I—"

"Oh, yes, you were ruthless in your quest to make me forget who I was, to reject my principles and come down to your level. You made me believe you cared. You made me believe you wanted what was best for me. Most of all, you made me trust you. And all along you were making a joke of me."

"No, I—"

"But I will not be your victim, John. You have taken me on a mad run, and in the running I nearly lost myself. But I will not let you destroy me. I am better than that. I am better than *you*."

Lord, he wanted to find a dark hole and crawl inside. She made him feel lower than a toad under a harrow. "Yes, you are, Grace. You are a hundred thousand times better than me. You are better than any woman I have ever known. I have hurt you, badly, but I never wanted to destroy you."

"You never think about who you might destroy with your callousness. You never think about anyone but yourself. You don't care how your actions might hurt someone, as long as you get what you want. You make a great show of not caring what people think of you, because you are a coward. If you dared to care, you might, heaven forbid, experience a moment or two of regret or sorrow. Instead, you care for nothing and no one and are therefore safe from pain."

"I never cared before, but I care about you."

She rolled her eyes. "Oh, stop. Don't try to make an even bigger fool of me. Excuses and apologies will not make a difference. I want nothing more from you, Lord Rochdale. Ever again."

She spun on her heel to walk away, then stopped and faced him once more. "No, there *is* something I want from you. I want you to stay away from me, to stay out of my life. And if you dare to besmirch my name in public in any way, I swear I will have your head on a platter."

With that, she swept out of the room in a flurry of muslin skirts, and was gone.

Rochdale stood frozen, stunned by her assessment of him. After a moment, he walked to the window and watched her enter the carriage that stood waiting at his door, then stared after it as it drove off. He continued to gaze, almost desperately, at what was likely his last glimpse of the woman he'd grown to love. Even though he could not see her, he could not tear his eyes from the carriage, knowing she was inside. It drove down Curzon Street, past the Mayfair Chapel, and turned left onto Queen Street and out of sight.

When he was able to stir himself from the window, Rochdale walked back into the room and collapsed into a wing chair. Damnation. Who would have thought the prim and polite Bishop's Widow could be such a firebrand? She was so beautiful in her glorious, blistering passion that he fell even more in love with her. Which only made the pain in his belly worse. Everything she'd said was true, of course, and he did not think he'd ever been more ashamed in all his life. He deserved her scorn and hatred.

She had been so righteous in her outrage, armed with every sling and arrow she could conjure up, that he was never given the chance to tell her he had conceded the wager. But in the end, what did it matter? The damage to her was already done, regardless of the wager's outcome.

For a moment, Rochdale considered going after her and making her listen to him, until she understood that he was truly sorry and that he loved her. But no, she had asked him to stay away and he would honor that request. It was the least he could do for her. A man like him could only ever bring scandal and shame to a woman like Grace. And so he would give her up just as he'd given up Serenity.

He supposed it was never too late in life to learn a lesson. The gambler for whom no risk was too great had just discovered that he did, after all, have something in life left to lose.

Grace took no joy in having railed at Rochdale. She had so hoped he would deny the rumor, and then she would have flown straight into his arms. But when he'd baldly admitted it was true, she could not hold back her anger. Now that she knew, really knew, what sort of man he was, it was easy to put him out of her life. No, not easy, but sensible. Even though she had changed as a result of what had happened—she would never again be the docile, uncompromising prig she'd once been—there was still a core of steady common sense at the heart of her, and she knew she had to move on.

In the days that followed, she found some satisfaction in the fact that no public scandal had attached itself to her. The rumors Margaret had heard had not spread, or if they had, Grace was unaware of them. Friends and acquaintances treated her normally, without a hint that they suspected she had, for two extraordinary days, behaved with wanton abandon with the most notorious rake in London. It became easy to fall back into the role of the Bishop's Widow, but no one would ever know the heartache she felt over the loss of the man she'd believed Rochdale to be, the fantasy she had fallen in love with. She suspected she might never find another man who could or would show her the pleasure she'd experienced with Rochdale. Sometimes she wished she'd not had those two days with him, for she would always know now what her life was missing. But most of the time she silently thanked him for giving her that amazing, wonderful experience, and for teaching her that she was not wicked for enjoying it.

She ran into Wilhelmina on Conduit Street not long after the confrontation with Rochdale. Over tea and cakes in an elegant little pastry shop, Grace told her everything that had happened.

"What a horrid thing to have done," Wilhelmina said. "It is to be expected, I suppose, from a man who has always enjoyed being a cad. But in the end, you may have gained more than you lost, my dear."

"What do you mean?"

"Consider all that you have learned from the experience. You are stronger. More confident. More sure of who you are and what you want out of life. And you have finally shaken off the mantle of the Bishop's Widow."

"Oh yes. Margaret has made sure of that. But you are right, I have learned a lot. But at what price?"

Her face must have given her away, for Wilhelmina said, "You fell in love with him after all, did you not?"

Grace felt her cheeks flush. "Despite your good advice, I fear that I did."

"My poor girl. But you must not suffer alone. All your friends are here to help you through this rough patch. And you will get through it. I promise you."

"Thank you, sir! I promise to take extra-special good care of it." Young Toby Fletcher grinned from ear to ear as he proudly held on to the brand-new currycomb Rochdale had just given him.

"Mr. Trask and the other boys will show you how to use it properly," Rochdale said, "but it is yours alone and not one of the ordinary stable brushes. That's why it has your initials on it."

"Cripes, they will be jealous, I bet."

"Very likely," Rochdale said, tousling the boy's blond hair. "But try not to lord it over them too much. You will want to make friends with them, not make them think you are better than they are."

"And you are not better," Jane Fletcher said. "You have a lot to learn and all the other boys will know more than you. You will need to pay close attention and be friendly if you want to learn how to be a good stable boy."

"Maybe I can let them use it sometimes," Toby said, his brow puckered and serious, "if they're careful."

"An excellent notion," Rochdale said. "Now, put it in a safe place so you do not lose it during the journey."

"Yes, sir! I mean, my lord." With a quick grin, Toby scrambled up into the waiting carriage.

"Thank you for the cookery book, my lord," Sally

Fletcher said in a bashful voice, without looking at him.

"You are very welcome, Sally. I hope you will find it useful."

"She will, my lord," her mother said, putting an arm around the girl's thin shoulders. "And so will I, if she will let me have a look from time to time. Up you go, now." She held Sally's hand as she climbed into the carriage.

When both children were inside, Jane turned to Rochdale and said, "I do not know how to thank you, my lord. For everything."

"It was my pleasure, Jane. You belong at Bettisfont, not here in London."

"I cannot imagine what we would have done without you. I suppose Mrs. Marlowe and Mrs. Chalk and the others would have come up with something eventually. But it would not have been the same as going back home. I cannot wait to see it again."

"I am told everything is in good repair, and I've had a few new pieces of furniture brought in for you and the children. I hope it will suit you."

"It is home. Of course it will suit us. And John, Lord Rochdale, I hope we will see you at Bettisfont one day soon."

"Very likely you will. Now, let's not keep the horses waiting any longer."

He handed her into the big traveling carriage with the Rochdale crest blazoned on the door, said final farewells to them all, then stepped away as the coachman steered the team out of the Marlowe House courtyard and onto George Street.

It had cost him very little in time or money to help this one family, and it gave him a warm feeling to have done something good for someone without any ulterior motives. This satisfied feeling must be what drove Grace to do so much good work.

He considered that he might be able to help other

families at Marlowe House. But that would mean coming into occasional contact with Grace, and she did not want that. Instead, he would continue to funnel money into the Coutts & Company account so there would always be funds at her disposal. He supposed he was trying to assuage his guilt with money. But no amount of money could ever make up for the wrong he had done Grace.

Later that night he was sitting alone in one of the out-of-the-way taverns he liked to frequent, far from the Mayfair crowd, sipping a second pint of ale, and thinking about Grace. He was always thinking about her. His mind could not let go of the images of her long legs entwined with his, of her satiny skin beneath his hands and mouth, of the warm, tight passage he had worked, of her uninhibited and glorious climaxes. The sweetest part of it all was that he had been the first and only man to see her like that. Her husband never had. She had told Rochdale that she and Marlowe had never removed their nightclothes when he came to her. Grace had been practically a virgin. She had certainly never before experienced sexual fulfillment. He had given her that. And quite a bit more. He had been pleased and proud to be her first true lover. And he couldn't help but wonder if, now that she'd had a taste of it, she would seek out another man to pleasure her. She was young and beautiful and desirable. Some other man would surely have her eventually.

The thought of Grace in another man's arms turned his stomach. He could not bear to think of it.

Perhaps he could get Grace Marlowe out of his head if he had sex with another woman. Any woman. The buxom barmaid bending over him would do. She was certainly willing. But as she began to fondle him, he felt oddly detached. He knew where this was headed. Five minutes in the stables or against the kitchen garden wall. He'd done it enough times to know the routine. He'd button his breeches, flip her a coin, and never see her again. He wouldn't even know her name.

He pushed her away and said, "Not tonight, sweetheart."

She looked angry, disappointed, but he did not care. He produced a few coins for the ale and left.

What was wrong with him? He was not prepared to give up women altogether just because he'd driven one special woman away. He certainly was not going to save himself in hopes of her return. But at the moment, tonight, when the rift with Grace was still a fresh wound, he could not stomach the usual routine of anonymous sex with whores or indifferent sex with *ton* trollops. That life held no satisfaction for him anymore.

Instead, he took a hackney to St. James's Street and alighted in front of White's. If he could not escape his troubles by wenching, perhaps a good game with high stakes would distract him. He entered the card room and saw Cazenove in conversation with Aldershot and Dewesbury. He caught his friend's eye, and Cazenove soon made his way to Rochdale's side.

"Egad, man, you look dreadful," Cazenove said.

"A life of dissipation will do that to a person."

Cazenove flagged down a waiter and ordered two brandies, then led Rochdale to a small alcove, where a pair of worn and comfortable leather armchairs had just been vacated by two gentlemen who were now joining one of the games.

"What has happened?" Cazenove asked once they had taken seats. "You really do look bad, you know."

"You needn't remind me. The fact is, I feel as bad as I probably look. Grace found out about the wager."

"Good Lord. How?"

"I don't know how. She only mentioned hearing the rumor from one of her relatives."

Cazenove winced. "Dear God. She must have been furious."

Rochdale told him everything that Grace had said to him, every barb and arrow that had so neatly pierced him.

"When I publicly humiliated Serena Underwood," he said, "I felt not a twinge of guilt or shame."

"Because she wanted to trap you into marriage to give your name to another man's babe."

"Even so, I was the cause of her public ruin, and I didn't much care. I never lost a moment's sleep over it. But this time . . . Well, if I had a heart, it would be broken. I cannot forgive myself for hurting Grace. She doesn't want to see me, so I have been thinking of leaving town. She lives here all year long, like you do, so I believe I will have to leave London permanently."

"Where will you go?"

"I have thought about returning to Bettisfont and putting it to rights. Maybe I can find an architect to design a new home, and I could live there and tend to my stables."

"You astonish me, Rochdale. I thought you never meant to go back to Bettisfont."

An image of the barmaid he'd rejected earlier flashed through Rochdale's mind, and he realized that was not the only part of his life he was now prepared to reject. "I am through with this life. It is time to go home."

And never to see Grace again.

Wilhelmina had advised Grace to attend as many *ton* events as she could manage, that it was important to be seen in public, enjoying herself, behaving as though nothing had happened. For there were surely more people than Margaret Bumfries who had heard the rumors of Rochdale's wager. If Grace behaved normally, Wilhelmina had said, her reputation was formidable enough to negate any gossip. And so that is what she had done. The Season was waning, with many people already gone for the summer, but there were always social events to attend at any time of the year.

A week after the confrontation with Rochdale, Grace accepted an invitation to a card party at Lord and Lady Raymond's grand town house on Park Lane. There were several rooms set up with card tables, and several other rooms where various refreshments were served. After a long game of whist, partnered by old Lord Hextable, who was deaf as a post and shouted commentary to every play, Grace made her way to one of the tearooms, eager to escape the old man. It was called a tearoom, though every sort of beverage was served. Most people seemed to be drinking wine or sherry, but Grace ordered tea and made her way to a small table in the corner. After the noisy card room, she relished a few quiet moments alone. Once she'd had a restorative cup of bohea, she would return to one of the card rooms and be sociable again.

"Well, if it ain't my benefactress."

Grace looked up from stirring her tea to find Lord Sheane, obviously foxed or nearly so, hovering over her table. He was the very last person she wanted to see. She made an effort to compose herself, for she was of half a mind to box the scoundrel's ears.

"I do not mean to be rude," she said, "but I would prefer to be alone, Lord Sheane. I have no wish to speak to a man who would make me the object of a scandalous wager." She returned her attention to stirring her tea.

The man ignored her dismissal and sat down opposite her. "Ah, but you must allow me to thank you, Mrs. Marlowe. I *knew* your defenses were too solid to be breached. A capital woman, you are. Old Marlowe would be proud. Easiest win I ever had. And what a prize! I'm sure to win the Goodwood Cup with Serenity. The finest jewel in the crown of my stables. Exceptional horse, Serenity."

She did not understand. "You won Lord Rochdale's mare?"

"Yes. Did you not know Rochdale had staked Serenity against your virtue? Ha! I knew he could not win. And now that sleek little mare is housed in the stall next to Albion, the gelding Rochdale hoped to win off me. Ha! The fool. Easiest win ever, I tell you. Saw the mare race in Newmarket last week. Prettiest finish you ever saw. Caught Rochdale there with one of his doxies. Now that I think on it, he must have already given up on you. Two days later, he delivered the mare to my stables, saying I'd won. Knew I would, of course. Couldn't break you, could he?"

Grace stopped listening as he went on in a slightly slurred monologue about how his instincts about her had been right, how she was the most stiff-rumped woman in town, and on and on. While he disparaged her to her face, Grace sat dumbstruck. No wonder she had heard no gossip about being Rochdale's lover. He had conceded the wager, telling Lord Sheane he had not seduced her. And he had sacrificed his favorite horse in the bargain.

Dear heaven, he had done that for her.

Grace had seen how much that horse meant to him. She could not believe he had given her up. Could it possibly mean that he cared for her, after all, more than the horse? She almost groaned aloud. Oh, the dear man. The very, very dear man.

While Lord Sheane prattled and chuckled over his good fortune, Grace realized that she had wronged Rochdale by accusing him of not caring for anything or anyone. He *did* care. Enough to pretend he had not won the wager, enough to allow her reputation to remain unsullied, enough to lose his best horse to the cretin who sat opposite her. And he had already done so before she had confronted him. If she understood Lord Sheane correctly, Rochdale had come to him the day after their return from Newmarket. Two days before she had stormed into his house and said hateful things to him.

How could she not love a man who would do something so selfless? Of course, she could not entirely forgive him for accepting Lord Sheane's odious wager in the first place. But in the balance, Rochdale had done more good than bad in this silly business, and Grace had come out the biggest winner of all. Not only had he taught her all the pleasures of the bedroom, but he had also realized how badly she needed to step out of her role as the Bishop's Widow and become . . . her own woman. He had helped her to become that new woman, and she would be forever grateful to him for it.

More than that, as her head swam with images and recollections of every aspect of Rochdale, Grace realized that she loved him desperately and wanted to spend the rest of her life with him. For no other man would ever know her, the true Grace Marlowe, as well as he did. And, God help her, she wanted to wake up in his arms every morning of her life.

But would he have her? Did he want her?

Grace had not considered marrying again, had not wanted it. Like her friends, she was fond of the independence widowhood brought her, the sheer joyous freedom of being in no one's power but her own. Yet here she was, contemplating marriage, if he'd have her, to a man who would bring her a new and perhaps more uncomfortable identity than she'd known as the Bishop's Widow. To willingly allow this reckless, unscrupulous, dangerous man to have power over her—over her fortune, over her future, over her body—would have been unthinkable mere weeks ago. Yet she thought of it now with a yearning suddenly so consuming that it made her dizzy. Could she truly spend a lifetime with such a shameless, foolhardy man? Was she really ready to give up her neat, organized, highly civilized way of life and let this audacious adventurer wreak havoc with it?

God help her, she was. And she would, if she could convince him. And all at once, a plan took shape in her head. A plan rather stunning in its symmetry. And as daring as anything she'd ever done in her life. But the new Grace Marlowe was ready to be a little foolhardy herself.

"Lord Sheane?" She interrupted his triumphant chortling over his victory, and he raised his thick eyebrows in question. "You are obviously a man who enjoys a good wager."

He beamed. "Indeed I do. Can't resist a bet. Never could."

"I should like to offer a wager to you."

The man's eyes bulged like two boiled eggs. "A wager? With *you*?"

"If you please."

"But I did not think you approved of such things. The good Christian widow and all that."

"Nevertheless, I wish to propose a wager. But it must be between you and me only, with no one else to know about it. I will have your word on that before anything else."

"Yes, yes, I promise. Just between you and me. Won't tell a soul."

"All right, then. Here is what I propose. I will bet you that I can get Lord Rochdale to marry me."

"Marry you?"

"Please, my lord, keep your voice down. I do not wish for *this* wager to become public. If I can get Lord Rochdale to marry me, I want the horse, Serenity."

Lord Sheane threw his head back and laughed. "You cunning little vixen. You wanted him to seduce you, but wouldn't uncross your legs without marriage banns. And now you think you can get him to accept a leg shackle just to get you in his bed? Ha! Another easy win. Rochdale will never marry. Not you or any woman. It is not in his nature. And even if it was, he prefers his high flyers, not a prudish do-gooder. But you think you can get him to the altar, do you?"

"That is the wager I am offering."

He cocked an eyebrow. "An intriguing wager, to be sure. But only if the stakes are more interesting than a horse."

"What do you propose?"

"Perhaps you have heard that I am an amateur painter."

"No, I had not heard."

"Well, I am. It is one of my greatest pleasures. If I win the wager, I want you to pose for me."

"With pleasure." She held out her hand. "We have ourselves a wager. Let us shake hands on it."

"I should first, I think, make it clear exactly what sort of paintings we are talking about. I paint nudes, Mrs. Marlowe. In various provocative poses."

Grace's cheeks flamed. Dear God, he wanted her to pose for him in the nude? To bare her body to this disgusting man? How could he even ask such a thing of her? But she wanted to win Serenity for Rochdale. And she was determined to convince Rochdale to marry her.

"All right," she said. "I stake a pose for one painting against Serenity that I can get Lord Rochdale to agree to marry me. An announcement of our betrothal in the papers will be proof of my success. Are we agreed?"

Lord Sheane sneered, but took the hand she held out and shook it. "We are agreed. Very sure of yourself, ain't you?"

"Very hopeful, my lord."

Chapter 17

"Lord Rochdale."

He gave a start at the familiar voice as he walked down Bond Street toward Gentleman Jackson's and looked up to find Grace's face peeking out from the window of her carriage. The coachman held the horses dancing in place and a liveried footman stood stiff and straight on the rear platform. Grace's gloved hand rested on the window edge. Her eyes were hidden in the shadow of her bonnet's deep poke, so he could not read her face. Pleased to see her, but more than a little wary, he approached the carriage.

"Mrs. Marlowe," he said, taking his cue from her formal use of his title. He touched the brim of his hat and dipped his head in greeting. When he looked up, he was awarded with a better view of her, and a rush of excitement flowed through his blood at the sight of a sort of half smile. He'd expected, if anything, a cool, expressionless face, or even a scowl. But perhaps it was merely a public show of politeness meant for any passersby who might see her, and not directed specifically at him.

A thousand explanations flew through his head at this unexpected encounter. Not so many days ago, she had never wanted to set eyes upon him again, and he had done his best to stay out of her orbit. Yet here she was, initiating an indiscreet conversation in the middle of Bond Street, where genteel ladies seldom ventured alone, and where the only women ever seen to hail a gentleman from a carriage were Cyprians and demireps.

"I wonder, my lord, if I could prevail upon you to call on me later this afternoon?"

His heart lurched in his chest. She wanted to see him again? She wanted him actually to come to her house? His complete astonishment tied his tongue in knots and precluded an immediate response. He felt stupidly dumbstruck for an instant and could only stare.

"I have something I need to speak with you about," she continued.

Mentally shaking himself out of the idiotic stupor, he found his voice and said, "I would be pleased to call upon you, ma'am. But I confess I am surprised at the invitation. I was under the impression you never again wanted me to darken your doorstep."

"I was precipitous in my anger, my lord. As it happens, there is some unfinished business between us that I should like to clear up. I shall be at home at four o'clock. Would it be convenient for you to drop by at that time?"

Perhaps she wanted to peel another layer of flesh off his hide. Perhaps she'd thought of ten more reasons why he was a scoundrel and wanted to fling them in his face. He did not care. She had invited him for what he assumed would be a private visit, and that was all that mattered. He had been given a brief reprieve and he was going to make the best of it.

Putting every ounce of humility he could muster into his voice, he said, "I would be honored, ma'am."

"Excellent. Until four o'clock, then." Giving nothing away in her face, no hint as to whether it was to be a reconciliation or another confrontation, she disappeared back inside the carriage, gave a signal to the driver, and was gone.

Rochdale stood there for a moment, in the middle of Bond Street, astounded at what had just taken place. Could she possibly want him back in her life after all? Was it even imaginable that she might actually forgive him? He pushed aside all other less agreeable reasons for the invitation and allowed his hopes to take flight. Regardless of her motives, he'd been given another chance with her, and by God, he was not going to bungle it this time. He would swallow every vestige of foolish pride that had kept him so guarded for so long. He would lay his pitiful heart and his soiled life at her feet, and beg her to let him love her.

"Ye gonna stand there in th' middle o' th' bloody street all day, ye beef-witted cawker, or ye gonna move your bloomin' arse?"

The angry bellow was followed by laughter from passersby, and Rochdale dragged his head out of the clouds to find a heavily laden dray bearing down upon him. He quickly stepped out of the street and onto the pavement, waving an apology at the driver.

"Damned fool," the man muttered as he drove past.

The fellow's assessment was bang on the mark. Rochdale had been a damned fool for too long. Full of pride, cynical suspicions, and, yes, cowardice. Grace had been right about that. Believing that all women were like the few bad apples he'd encountered early in life, he'd been afraid to trust any woman. Afraid of being hurt or disappointed again. So he'd become a cold, heartless pleasure seeker who let no one woman worm her way into his heart or his life.

Until Grace. Putting all his armor aside, he was willing to bare his soul to her. If she threw it on the ground and trampled it into dust, so be it. At least he had to try. This might be the one chance he had at true happiness. The kind his friend Cazenove had with Marianne. He was ready, for once in his life, to risk pain and humiliation in the faint hope that she might be willing to be a part of his life. For, all things considered, his life would be forever empty without her in it.

Instead of going in to spar with Gentleman Jackson, as planned, Rochdale turned and walked in the opposite direction, where a particularly exclusive jeweler had his premises.

Rochdale spent the rest of the day in preparation for his visit to Portland Place. He shaved and splashed his face with bay rum. He dressed with care in a bottle green top coat, gold-striped waistcoat with stand-up collar, fitted pantaloons, and high Hessian boots with leather tassels, polished to a high gleam. And he practiced a dozen different speeches.

Filled with a mixture of excitement and anxiety, he arrived at Grace's door at the stroke of four o'clock. A footman took his hat, gloves, and walking stick, and Spurling, the stone-faced butler, led him upstairs to the drawing room. He opened the double doors and Rochdale saw Grace rise from a chair. She was dressed simply but with her usual elegant flair, in a dress of printed muslin with long full sleeves tied in bows at the wrists. The low neckline had been left bare, with no shirt or tucker of lace to hide her bosom. His heart flipped over at the sight of her. And she was smiling! He could no longer quell the hope that cavorted in his breast. Rochdale almost rushed to her side, but the punctilious butler would not allow him to pass.

"Lord Rochdale," he announced, as though she couldn't see for herself who it was. Only when she had given a slight nod did the stiff fellow move aside and let him walk into the room.

"Thank you, Spurling," Grace said, walking around Rochdale to the door behind him. "That will be all."

He watched, mesmerized, as she closed the door, locked it, and removed the key.

"There," she said. "Now we shall not be disturbed."

Feeling strangely off balance, Rochdale held out the

flower he had brought her. One perfect red rose, its thorny stem wrapped in white ribbon and lace. "For you, my dearest love."

Her eyes widened along with her smile, and she took the rose from him and brought it to her nose. She closed her eyes and inhaled its heady fragrance. When she opened her eyes and looked at him, he saw what he'd never expected to see again: the brilliant, slightly glassy gaze of pure happiness. "Oh, John."

Without warning, she threw herself upon him, wrapping her arms around his neck and raining kisses on his face. He laughed giddily and enclosed her in a tight embrace. "Grace, my love, what is this?" She continued to kiss him, on the cheeks and nose and eyes, on temple and jaw and ear. "Dare I hope that this affectionate display means you forgive me?"

The kisses ceased and she looked him square in the eye. "No, I do not forgive you. It was a most ungentlemanly wager. But I do love you. Madly. Utterly. Deeply. I am consumed with love for you."

Her words momentarily robbed him of breath, and he crushed her in his arms, burying his nose in her golden hair. His heart soared. He did not deserve this joy, but he was determined to hold on to it and never let go. Rochdale knew what it must have cost this proud, dignified woman to so boldly confess her love, without knowing whether it was returned. When at last his throat opened up and allowed him to speak, he said into her ear: "And I love you, Grace. More than life."

She gazed at him, eyes brilliant with contained emotion. "More than Serenity."

"You know about that?"

"You gave her up for me."

"Yes."

"Because you love me?"

"Yes. And because I had done you enough harm. I could not go to Sheane and tell him I had made love to you. To provide him with an image of you naked in my arms seemed obscene."

An odd expression flickered in her eyes, then disappeared when she smiled again. "I am sorry about Serenity. I know what she meant to you."

"You mean more to me than any horse, Grace. More than any human."

"I said hateful things to you."

"No more than I deserved. And nothing that wasn't true."

"I accused you of not caring for anyone but yourself. But that is untrue, and I have always known it to be untrue."

"I care about you."

"I know. You cared enough to push me into taking more from life. You cared enough to help me discover the importance of finding my true self. You cared enough to show me how to take pleasure in my body without feeling wicked. I do not wish to be estranged from you over that wager, John. I hate that you did it, but I am ready to put it behind us. I want you in my life. And in my bed."

"Ah, Grace." He put his lips to hers and kissed her, very tenderly, letting his mouth speak his love.

Within a moment, the kiss had grown wild and lush and urgent. His hands roamed over her hips and buttocks, up her corseted waist to cup her tightly bound breasts. Slowly he inched her backward toward a sofa. When it caught her behind the knees, he took advantage and eased her down, twisting her until she was prone beneath him.

"I want you, Grace. Right now. Right here."

"Yes." She was panting hard, each breath causing her bosom to strain against the edge of her bodice.

"You did lock the door, as I recall."

She grinned. "I wanted to be prepared. Just in case. And I see that you are prepared as well." She placed

her hand over the swollen length tenting his pantaloons.

"Dear God, woman. You will have me embarrassing
myself like a schoolboy."

"Make love to me, John. Now. Please."

"With pleasure, madam."

She helped him to wriggle out of his coat and waistcoat, which were flung willy-nilly across the room;
then she went to work on his neckcloth and loosened
his shirt. Her hands explored his bare chest while he
eased a sleeve over her shoulder, exposing more of
one breast. He managed to free it partially from the
stiff whalebone stays and kissed every liberated inch
of skin.

His tongue found the depths of her cleavage while
he pushed up her skirts and began to stroke her leg.
His hand made its way up the silk of her stocking and
above her garter to the bare skin of her thigh. She
called out and he took her cry into his mouth, hoping
the servants would not come running to her rescue, thinking she was being murdered. He stroked her soft thigh,
then inched up to the damp curls of her sex, and plea-
sured her with his fingers.

She writhed beneath him and said, "I want you inside me, John. Please!"

He bunched her skirts up around her waist and un-
buttoned the fall of his pantaloons. A quick adjust-
ment to his smallclothes, and his erection sprang free.
She helped him pull the pantaloons down over his
buttocks, then took his erection in her hand and
guided him inside her. He reached underneath her and
lifted her bottom so he could plunge deeper inside.
She wrapped her legs around him and pushed up hard
against him with each stroke, meeting him movement
for movement. Her breath came in short gasps and she
whispered his name over and over until she convulsed
beneath him.

Her climax pushed him near the edge and he pulled back with a groan. But she held him tight and said, "Please, stay. Don't leave me this time. I love you, John. I love you."

It was too late in any case, for he could hold back no longer and pushed deep into her once more as release overtook him.

He collapsed upon her and tried to catch his breath. He had seldom allowed himself to come inside a woman, or used French letters if he did. He had no wish to be trapped by an accidental babe into a life he did not want, and he took care that it never happened.

Strangely, as he lay panting on Grace, he didn't feel trapped at all. He felt . . . free.

After a moment, fearing he was crushing her with his weight, Rochdale sat up, tucked his pantaloons up over his bare ass, and gathered Grace close beside him, each of them in a languorous and, if anyone were to see them, rather shocking sprawl.

He wrapped an arm around her shoulder and dipped his hand downward to stroke the soft skin of her bosom. "We may have made a baby, Grace."

She lifted her head from his shoulder to look at him. "I do not know if I can conceive, but if I did, I don't mind."

She did not care if she became pregnant? Grace Marlowe was not the sort of woman to have a child out of wedlock. It could only mean one thing.

"My love, are you saying—"

"I . . . I am not sure being your lover is enough. I want more."

"Grace—"

"I know I am not the sort of woman you prefer. I'm not sophisticated and clever and experienced—"

"Have I ever complained?"

"Well, no, but—"

"And I never will. I love you just as you are. It is your innocence, your lack of experience, that utterly charms me. If you were a jaded sophisticate, I would never have fallen in love with you."

She placed a hand on his cheek. "And I love every part of you, John, the rakish scoundrel, the reckless gambler, the well-read scholar, and the compassionate man."

He took the hand and kissed it. "So you say, Grace, but I am not the man you want me to be. Everything you've ever heard about me is true, and more. I have never cared about being respectable or following rules, about being a 'gentleman.' I've done as I pleased with whom I pleased and hurt a lot of people along the way. Everything you accused me of was true. I do not have a charitable bone in my body. I did it all for you, to win the wager. I'm a gambler, not a philanthropist. I prefer horses over impoverished orphans and cockfights over the opera. I've never given a damn what people think of me. But I care about you, and I would be ashamed to offer up my ruined and scandalous life to you. You deserve better, Grace. You deserve the best."

"You are the best."

"No, I—"

"You are the best for *me.* You taught me how to be my own woman and not live in the shadow of my late husband's memory. You taught me about passion and how not to be afraid of it. You taught me how to have fun and enjoy life instead of constantly being on guard, worried what others may think of me. You taught me how to live. How could any man measure up to that? You *are* the best, John. For me."

"Does that mean you would have me, Grace? Would you marry me if I asked?"

"Are you asking?"

He took both her hands and pulled her to her feet. He wanted to do this properly. This was an important moment for him, not a moment to be in disarray, so he tucked in his shirttails, buttoned the fall of his pantaloons, retrieved his waistcoat and top coat, and made quick work of his neckcloth. Watching him, Grace shook out her skirts and straightened her bodice. They had each regained some semblance of order when he took her hands again and kissed each one in turn.

"My dearest Grace," he said, clasping her hands against his chest, "you are the finest woman I have ever known, and I love you with all my heart. Will you do me the very great honor of being my wife?"

Her eyes grew watery for a moment, but then she threw her arms around him and said, "Yes, yes, yes!"

He picked her up and swung her around and around, and she laughed, that voluptuous laugh that conjured up all the wicked things he wanted to do with her. And now they would have a lifetime to be wicked together.

He brought her back to earth, set her feet on the Turkish carpet, and kissed the end of her aristocratic nose. He reached into his coat and brought out a small shagreen box, which he held out to her. "For you, my dearest Grace: a symbol of my commitment to you, a pledge to love you forever."

She took the box and opened it, then smiled up at him with pure feminine delight. "Oh, John, it's beautiful. How did you know that emeralds are my favorite gemstones?"

He took her hand and slid the ring on her fourth finger. The large table-cut emerald was surrounded by small diamonds and set in gold. "It was a lucky guess. The color suits you."

She held her hand this way and that, studying the ring from every angle, then looked up at him with a smile so dazzling he had to blink. "Thank you, John. I love it. You could not have chosen a better emblem of our love. Heavens, my friends will be jealous when they see this!"

They laughed together and kissed again. And again.

"I can hardly believe this is happening," Rochdale said when they had both resumed their places on the sofa, her head on his shoulder. "Can you imagine a more unlikely match? The Bishop's Widow and the Libertine?"

"But remember, they lived happily ever after."

"Ah, yes. They did indeed. How prescient we were. Still, it is rather astonishing that we found each other and fell in love. I daresay the *ton* will be shocked."

"Yes, and please may we shock them a little more with a very short engagement?"

"Wicked woman. Impatient to have me in your bed again, are you?"

"Of course I am. And to wake up beside you every morning. Oh, John. I am so happy. Can we announce our betrothal right away? Tomorrow?"

"Egad, woman, you *are* impatient."

"I am. But I am also thinking that there might still be rumors buzzing about the wager. If my stepdaughter heard them, others must have as well."

"Your stepdaughter? Lady Bumfries?"

"Yes, she is the one who told me about the wager."

"Dear God. That must have been awkward."

Grace snorted. "Much worse than awkward, I assure you. But that is water under the bridge. I was just thinking that if we were to marry soon, the rumors would have no teeth."

"I will procure us a special license as soon as I can. I am not acquainted with any bishops to smooth the way. I would ask to use your contacts in the church, but that might be awkward. The normal channels will have to do. Cazenove said it took him almost a week of haunting Doctors' Commons to get a license. I will begin my own haunt tomorrow."

"And will you also put an announcement in the papers tomorrow as well?"

"It is important to you to make this formal and respectable, is it not? All right, then. I will place the announcements tomorrow."

"Thank you, John."

"Anything for you, my love. My future Lady Rochdale. Ha. You will lend more credit to the title than the other two ladies I have known who held it."

"I hope I will. Because I am more honored than you will ever know to have been offered the opportunity to be your viscountess."

The honor, in point of fact, was all his.

Two days later, Grace clipped the betrothal announcement out of the *Morning Post* and folded it inside a letter. She sealed it and wrote Lord Sheane's direction on the outside.

It had been a risky wager. She had *hoped* Rochdale wanted to marry her, but she had not known for sure if he would. She did not need the odious Lord Sheane to tell her that Rochdale was too much of a libertine ever to marry. From the beginning, she had guessed him to be one of those lifelong pleasure seekers who never marry. She'd imagined that he would live out his days like the infamous Old Q, the Duke of Queensbury, a bachelor roué to the end. But at Newmarket, she could have sworn there was something more than lust between them. She had trusted in her intuition that he cared for her. Thank God she had been right. Otherwise, she might be sitting naked right now in front of Lord Sheane while he painted her picture. And heaven only knew how many people would have seen that picture. She would have been forced to sell the Portland Place house and retire to the country.

But she had trusted herself to be persuasive, and trusted Rochdale to do the right thing. Everything had worked out perfectly. She was in love, was now to be Lady Rochdale, and had never been happier in her life. She had most definitely become a new woman this Season. No longer the Bishop's Widow, she was to be the Libertine's Wife.

Grace sat at her writing desk, threw back her head, and laughed for pure joy.

Chapter 18

The newspaper announcements caused quite a stir. At the end of any Season, there were many betrothals and weddings, but none took the *ton* by storm quite like the betrothal of Rochdale and Grace Marlowe. The shocking news had become the juiciest topic among the gossips and scandalmongers. Rochdale could not enter a room, a shop, a tavern, or a club without being subjected to bawdy innuendo, backslapping, and endless rounds of toasts. He was teased, taunted, ridiculed, and congratulated.

It was deuced embarrassing.

"You are a man transformed," Cazenove told him when he heard the news. "The last time we met, you had that pathetic hangdog look about you. Now, I could swear you've grown younger. You look . . . happy. Sadly, that is not a word I would ever have associated with you, my friend. I am glad things worked out so well." He chuckled. "This has been quite a Season for us, has it not? We both found love where it was least expected."

Cazenove was right. He did feel younger. He hadn't smiled so much since he was a boy in Suffolk. He supposed he must look as calf-eyed as Cazenove had looked when he'd fallen in love with the widow of his oldest friend. Rochdale ought to have been mortified, but it was too late in life to start worrying about what people thought of him.

Rochdale decided to buy Grace a horse as a wedding present. It would be a fine thing to ride in the park alongside her in the early hours of the morning, when few were about and they could let their mounts run fast and free. She'd told him she liked to ride but hadn't done much riding since leaving Devon. No doubt the bishop had disapproved of women on horseback. But Rochdale could picture her in a smart habit with a feather in her hat, riding like the wind, and was determined she should have a proper mount.

He was leaning against a broad pillar, watching a sweet, high-headed little bay mare being put through her paces in the ring at Tattersalls, when he overheard a snippet of conversation behind him that caught his attention. He rolled his eyes as he heard his name mentioned and the words "leg shackle," followed by loud hoots and guffaws. It really was getting tiresome, this interest in his private life. He kept himself hidden behind the pillar so that he would not be seen and be forced to join in a conversation in which he was the central joke. Couldn't a man be allowed to love a woman in peace without all the world making sport of him?

". . . wager with Sheane."

Rochdale's ears perked up. Damnation. He'd hoped rumors of that confounded wager had dried up.

". . . a woman like that making a wager with an unsavory bastard like Sheane."

"God only knows what stakes she offered."

"They would have to have been . . . interesting for Sheane to agree to them."

Ribald laughter filled the air. Rochdale ignored the mare and concentrated on the conversation. Something was wrong here. It did not seem they were talking about *his* wager. Had there been another?

"Since he lost, we'll probably never know."

"Wonder what she won?"

"Knowing the Widow Marlowe, she likely got a fat bank draft for her bloody charity. That's all she ever cares about, according to my wife."

"You're right—she probably landed a large donation, and brought Rochdale to his knees in the bargain."

More raucous laughter.

"Got to admire the woman's pluck, to wager she could get Rochdale to marry her."

What?

"Thought he'd have been a tough nut to crack."

"She must have thrown a bit of his own back at him, seduced him into marrying her."

"A churchwoman, at that."

"Churchwoman or Cyprian, they all get their way in the end."

The men wandered off and Rochdale heard no more. But he'd heard enough. Grace had made some kind of wager with Sheane that she could get Rochdale to marry her. And, of course, she had won.

Anger began to fizz in his stomach.

No wonder she had invited him to her home and had thrown herself at him. No wonder she had hinted so broadly that she wanted more than a love affair. But why? Why would she make such a wager? And with Sheane, of all people. And what *had* she won? Yet another wing to Marlowe House? A second story? A third?

Hell and damnation. She'd played him for a fool. He wasn't sure why, or what she had gained from it, but that whole scene in her drawing room began to make more sense. She wanted him to marry her to stave off rumor over his wager. And with some incentive or other from Sheane, she wanted the betrothal and wedding to take place right away. No doubt Sheane had given her a time limit, just as he had done with Rochdale. And she'd needed that announcement in the papers as proof that she'd won.

All at once he remembered how she'd insisted he not pull out during sex, so that there would be the risk of a child to further bind him to her.

Red-hot anger rushed through him, flooding his veins. Damn her to hell. Rochdale had thought she was different. But she was a user, just like all the others, manipulating him for her own ends. Just like every other woman he'd known. And he had been too blinded by love to see it.

His vision had cleared now. He saw her for what she was. And he wasn't sure he wanted what he saw. The woman he'd thought was so pure-hearted and good had made a fool of him. She had made him wallow in guilt, had made him grovel for forgiveness, had made him love her. All to save her reputation and to win something from Sheane.

In the end, she was no better than he was. But it was not too late to put an end to this game before he was hopelessly trapped.

It was too early in the day for champagne, but Grace did not care and neither did her friends. There were two betrothals to celebrate: Penelope's to Eustace Tolliver and Grace's to Rochdale.

The Merry Widows were gathered once again in Grace's drawing room, their favorite meeting place. A footman had uncorked two bottles of French champagne and poured it into fluted glasses with delicate air-twist stems. A maid placed trays of sweetmeats and pastries on nearby tables, but no one seemed interested in food. The mood was as bubbly as the wine, with everyone laughing and talking at once.

Wilhelmina rose to her feet and held up her glass, calling for silence. All eyes turned to her and waited.

"At the beginning of this Season," she said, "this group made a pact to become Merry Widows, to seek out lovers and enjoy the pleasures of the bedroom again. But that is not what the pact was really about. It was about taking life by the horns and living it to the fullest. You have all done that, and found love and happiness along the way. With one of you already happily married"—she nodded to Marianne—"and three of you soon to be wed, I believe it is time to offer a toast to the Merry Wives. May love and laughter and happiness rule your days, and may you continue to live full and rich lives with the men you love."

They all stood and raised their glasses.

"To the Merry Wives," Wilhelmina said, "and one last Merry Widow. To us."

They clinked their glasses together and repeated, "To us."

More laughter and talk filled the room as the afternoon grew into twilight and the champagne bottles emptied. Wedding plans and summer holidays dominated the conversation. Grace had no plans to speak of. "I cannot leave London for the time being," she said. "There is so much work yet to be done at Marlowe House, and I feel obliged to stay on. You can't imagine what this additional money means for the future. When we began the Season, I never dreamed such a windfall would come our way. We can now accomplish so much more than—"

"Yes, your goddamned widows and orphans are all you care about," a male voice said. "How fortunate that yet another 'windfall' has come your way."

Grace's mouth dropped open at the sight of Rochdale standing in the drawing room doorway, fury blazing in his eyes. All conversation ceased as everyone stared at him in puzzlement.

"I am sorry, madam," the butler said, looking chagrined as he rushed up behind Rochdale. "I could not stop him. He dashed right past me before I could announce him."

"That is all right, Spurling." Grace kept her eyes

warily on Rochdale. "His lordship is welcome at any time and need not be announced."

"I am about to wear out my welcome, madam," Rochdale said, "for I will not be returning."

What was he talking about? And why must he say such things in front of her friends? She grew so warm she knew she must be red from head to toe.

"What do you mean you will not be returning?" she asked. "You know you may always—"

"I am through with your games, madam. I have learned of your little wager with Sheane. Ah, yes, you may well blush, my dear. You almost caught me. You almost had me convinced that you were different. But you are not and I ought to have known better. It was a near thing, was it not? But we have both learned, before it was too late, how despicable the other is. We can walk away unscathed, more or less."

"But, John—"

"You really had me fooled, you know. I thought you were so damned good. So sweet and innocent. But you manipulated me like a marionette, dancing on your strings. All to save your face and to win some new 'windfall' from Sheane."

"No, John, you have it wrong—"

"Thank God I found out just what sort of person you really are before you closed the final shackle on my leg. There will be no marriage, my dear. People may call me a jilt, but I've been called worse. And I won't bow to public pressure to marry a woman who has manipulated me so thoroughly. Good day to you. I will not darken your door again."

He turned to leave, but stopped and said, "If there is a babe, at least I know it is mine this time. Contact my man of affairs and I will have him send you another bank draft."

With that he was gone.

Grace was so astounded, so mortified, so heartbroken that she could barely breathe, much less move.

How could he say such hateful things to her? And in front of her friends? Why wouldn't he let her explain? How could he break their betrothal when they loved each other?

Oh God oh God oh God. What was she going to do?

In the awkward silence of the room, her choked sob rang out like a clarion. Her friends grabbed each of her elbows as her knees gave way beneath her and she cried out in misery.

"My lord?"

Rochdale turned to the butler who had rushed to follow him out the front door. "What?"

"May I recommend that you leave by way of the mews?"

Rochdale glared at the man. He'd just ended his betrothal with a woman he'd thought was something special, and this pompous retainer was worried about which direction he would take?

"I will leave by whichever route I like, Spurling. If you are worried that I will be seen leaving your precious Mrs. Marlowe's residence, it is too late to worry about that. And I don't give a rat's ass who sees me."

"My lord, please." A plaintive note tinged his voice and a hint of what might have been despair flickered in his eyes. "Please go through the mews. Madam's section is clearly marked. I suggest you take a look inside."

"What the devil are you talking about, Spurling? I don't have the time or inclination to visit Madam's mews."

"Forgive my boldness, my lord, but if you look in on the mews, I believe you will understand what a big mistake you are making. Please do not make me say any more. It is not my place to have said this much. But I cannot bear to see Madam so miserable."

His curiosity piqued, Rochdale heaved a sigh and

agreed to go round to the mews. The butler thanked him profusely and went back inside.

He left his own carriage waiting in front while he walked to the corner and turned into the mews. He walked the length of the horse stalls and carriage houses until he found the one marked "Marlowe." He walked inside and saw Grace's town carriage and tack on one side. Several stalls on the opposite side held the carriage horses. But there were five horses, not four. He slowly walked past each until he came to the last stall.

Good God. It was Serenity. She saw him and whinnied. He reached out to stoke her beautiful neck, so pleased to see her again. But what was she doing here? And all at once, he began to realize what mistake Spurling had been talking about.

"Can I 'elps yer, guv'ner?"

Rochdalc turned to find a groom he hadn't noticed before, sitting on a stool near the carriage, polishing the brass fittings.

"Loverly, ain't she?" He nodded toward Serenity.

"Yes, she is. How does she come to be here?"

"Can't say as I know, 'xactly. Per'aps Madam bought her, though she never said so. The mare, she were brought over yesterday by one o' Lord Sheane's grooms. Said summink about winnin' 'er in a wager, though Madam don't gamble. An' this one's a bit of an 'ighflier, I'm thinkin'. Not your av'rage 'ack."

No, Serenity was not your average hack. And Rochdale was not your average fool. He was the greatest fool that ever lived.

The sight that met him when he returned to Grace's drawing room, courtesy of Spurling, broke his heart. She was on the sofa between Wilhelmina and Marianne, curled up into a tight ball, her face buried in Wilhelmina's lap. Her shoulders shook as she cried softly. Wilhelmina stroked her hair and Marianne held one of her hands. The other two women had pulled their chairs close to the couch and were bent over Grace, so that she was cocooned by her friends.

His cruelty had been unspeakable. To have reduced that good woman to this . . . it was beyond brutal. He ought to be flayed alive for doing this to her. What he ought to do was leave. He had caused her enough grief. But he loved her.

He stepped into the room. Wilhelmina noticed him first, and she practically snarled at him. But he moved closer, undeterred by the anger in her eyes. Marianne saw him and sucked in a sharp breath. She opened her mouth to speak, but he held up a hand to stop her. He wanted to talk to Grace and no one else. The others could ring a peal over his head later. Grace was his concern now.

He walked around the chairs where Penelope and Beatrice sat, and sank down on his haunches in front of Grace. Both women behind him began to speak, but Wilhelmina signaled for quiet. He ignored them all.

"Grace? My love?"

Her head jerked up from Wilhelmina's lap, and she gave a little gasp. Rochdale almost groaned aloud at the sight of her ravaged face. Her eyes were puffy and red, her skin pale, her cheeks wet with tears. This woman who prided herself on her cool composure in any situation had fallen apart. He had done this to her.

She shifted her weight and sat up to face him. Swiping an unsteady hand across her cheeks, she stared at him, desperation in her eyes, but said nothing.

"I have been to the mews," he said softly. "And now I understand. I don't suppose you are willing to forgive me for that unholy outburst. In fact, you'd probably be wise to send me packing, after what I've done. But please don't. I don't deserve any consideration from you, God knows, but please hear me out."

He reached out and took her trembling hand in his.

He was encouraged that she allowed it, and hope flared in his wretched heart.

"I love you, Grace. I love you wildly and beyond thought or reason. And the force of that love scares me, for I have not allowed myself to feel this way for anyone in a very long time, and I haven't learned quite yet how to accept it unquestioningly, this love I feel for you. You called me a coward once, and you were so right. I never wanted to feel pain or disappointment or betrayal, so I closed myself off to all feeling. I was afraid of being hurt.

"When I heard by chance about your wager with Sheane to get me to marry you, I felt betrayed. I lashed out because I wanted to place all the hurt on you, coward that I am. I wanted to hate you so I wouldn't feel the pain of loving you. But I didn't know then what the wager had been about. I didn't know it was to win back Serenity. That's why you made the wager, is it not? To win her back for me?"

She nodded her head, and wiped away tears.

"Oh, Grace. What a wonderfully bold and foolish thing to do." He kissed her hand and then, because it still trembled, he covered it with both his hands, and held it like a tiny wounded bird.

"And how typically thoughtful and generous and selfless of you. How could I have thought otherwise, my darling girl? I do love you. And I know you love me, so I hope you will forgive me for being such an idiot. You told me once that you loved all of me, the good and the bad. I hope that includes the stupid as well. Because not only do we love each other, Grace, but we need each other. Without you, my life is aimless and empty. Without me, your life is hopelessly earthbound. But together, we can fly. You were only just beginning to spread your new wings. Come fly with me, my love. Let us jump off the edge of the unknown together. Let us be wild, unprincipled adventurers together, and make love every night until we can barely move. Will you do that with me, Grace? Will you marry me after all?''

She shakily reached out to him, and Rochdale leaned forward and lifted her to her feet and into his arms. He had not noticed that the other women had moved. All four of them now stood to the side, and out of the corner of his eye he saw each of them wiping away tears.

"Yes," Grace whispered against his shoulder. "Yes, I'll still marry you." She lifted her head, wiped a hand across her face, and said, "But don't you dare scare me like that again. We have to trust each other, John. Completely."

"You are right, my love. But this business of loving and trusting is new to me. I helped you to understand passion. You must help me to understand trust. And courage. Your courage is breathtaking. And I am still bound in cowardice. Only see what I did tonight."

"It took a great deal of courage to say all you have said in front of my friends."

"They had witnessed my cruelty. They may as well witness my apology and declaration of love. They will hold me to it, I suspect."

"Indeed, we will, my lord," Wilhelmina said.

Rochdale looked over Grace's shoulder and smiled at the duchess. "You have devoted and loyal friends, my love."

"The very best friends in the world." She kept her arms around his neck, holding him close as though afraid to let go. He was content to oblige. "I am surprised they did not pull you limb from limb when you returned."

"So am I." He looked again over her shoulder at each of them and mouthed a silent, "Thank you."

"Now," he said, "perhaps we can forget all this unpleasantness and move on. You spent the first part of your life with the bishop being good. Spend the rest of your life with me, Grace, being bad."

And there, in front of all the Merry Widows, Grace and Rochdale kissed each other with a passion so deep and so hot, their entwined hearts soaring so high with love and desire, they almost forgot the other four women were in the room.

Until the sound of applause and laughter brought them back to earth.

JUST ONE OF THOSE FLINGS

Candice Hern

*The Merry Widows are thought to be the finest
ladies of society... though secretly their thoughts
are quite unrefined.*

Beatrice, Lady Somerfield, is too busy chaperoning her
headstrong niece and overseeing her own young
daughters to find time to take a lover—until one night at
a ball when a masked stranger makes her realize the
delights she's been missing. He is Gabriel, the Marquess
of Thayne, just returned from India, the catch of the
Season—and the one man half the debutantes of
London (including Beatrice's niece!) want for a husband.

But Thayne is thoroughly captivated by Beatrice, and
their attraction leads to several mutually satisfying
encounters. As he searches for a bride among the
Season's young ladies, he finds himself increasingly
drawn to sensual Lady Somerfield, and suspects his
mistress might make the perfect wife. But will Beatrice's
deepening feelings for Thayne be enough to overcome
her vow never to marry again, and the scandal once
their relationship is revealed?

**Available wherever books are sold or at
penguin.com**

IN THE THRILL OF THE NIGHT

Candice Hern

Assured of both money and position, none of the five
respectable ladies who form the Merry Widows need
ever marry again, so they make a daring pact—each will
consider taking a lover for the pure pleasure of it.

Marianne Nesbitt adored her late husband David,
but the racy reminiscences of the Merry Widows make
her wonder if she missed something special.
Might she find it now through a love affair? Uncertain
how to go about it, she asks Adam Cazenove,
an old friend and notorious rake, to tutor her in the
arts of seduction—a brazen request that turns Adam's
world upside down.

**Available wherever books are sold or at
penguin.com**